Praise for *MetalMagic: Talisman*

"Derek Donais is a fresh, new voice in fantasy fiction. The twists and turns in *Talisman* are unexpected and delightfully satisfying. His sense of story is sound. This tale does not disappoint."
BILLIE MILHOLLAND, Author, *Women of the Apocalypse*, Saint Albert, Alberta

"Derek Donais has taken the classic hero's myth and reinvented it to great success, to the point where I wasn't able at any point to say 'I see where this comes from'…. It feels fresh and new. Each character is uniquely drawn and textured, and their various storylines are so well told that I never felt like I had to slog through chapters just to get back to the storyline that I was interested in."
STEVEN HANULIK, High River, Alberta

"This was an outstanding first book for a new voice in fantasy fiction. I highly recommend reading this book and watching Derek Donais over the coming years. I am hoping for many more novels from this writer."
TOD LANGLEY, author, *The Erinia Saga*, Lafayette, Indiana

"Truly a great start to what I hope will be a long fantasy series. As a fan of another Canadian author in Kay and others like Goodkind, this was exactly what I was looking for. Great characters, a great story and truly left me wanting more."
ROB LACHAMBRE, Toronto, Ontario

"I loved it! It really is a terrific story, amazingly well written, and full of twists, turns and excitement. I couldn't put it down! Great job!"
JO-ANNE SIEPPERT, Author, *Nytstars*, Calgary, Alberta

"I loved this story. The characters are people you care about; the story was well written and moved at a really great pace. I myself have already recommended it to my friends and family who enjoy fantasy. If you like fantasy, give this one a try. Looking forward to the next in the series!"

Susan A. Hudson, Calgary, Alberta

"I was utterly blown away by this novel. I hate to compare, but it is reminiscent of David Eddings in its delicate handling of characters. If you like fantasy, buy it. You will not regret it."

June Harle, Lethbridge, Alberta

For all those who still believe.

Published by Trail Quest Books
8 Hillview Drive
Strathmore, Alberta, T1P 1S6
Phone: (403) 983 • 5341
E-mail: dragonwind2000@hotmail.com
Website: www.derekdonais.com

First Paperback Edition – June 2012
17 16 15 14 13 12 — 1 2 3 4 5 6 7 8 9

Library and Archives Canada Cataloguing in Publication

Donais, Derek 1972–
    Revelation / Derek Donais.

(MetalMagic ; bk. 2)
Issued also in electronic formats.
ISBN: 978 – 0 – 9869212 – 4 – 7

    I. Title. II. Series: Donais, Derek, 1972 – . MetalMagic ; bk. 2.

PS8607.0626R48 2012   jc813'.6   C2012 – 903991 – 8

TECHNICAL CREDITS:
EDITING: Tracy Blaine, *Creating Context, Inc.*, Calgary, AB
COVER ILLUSTRATION: David Willicome, <david-willicome.daportfolio.com>, Calgary, AB
MAP: Rob Antonishen, <www.cartocopia.com>, St. Catharines, ON
DESIGN & PRODUCTION: Jeremy Drought, *Last Impression Publishing Service*, Calgary, AB
Printed in Canada by *Houghton Boston Printers & Lithographers*, Saskatoon, SK

MetalMagic

Revelation

Derek Donais

TRAIL QUEST BOOKS
Strathmore, Alberta

The Six Realms of EVARLUND

ISLE of ICE

DRISIA

JAMNAR

CARATHON

Colm

Nesmara

Eidara

Aesin

Dyda

Svarda

Jynne

Thulse

Marthuin River

Dal Farrow

Nether Haddie's

Nesmene

Ansalar

Carter Hold

Aendaras

Ensin Llaws

Ensin Tower

Tlygan River

Ghulflane

Agdala

Corche

Teta

Taldor

The BARRENS

The Barrens

Vetalas

VETIA

PARCEA

ISLANDS of
the SYLVARII

N

• Contents •

• Prologue •

ELLSON'S PULSE RACED AS HE HURRIED ON. With each beat, his thundering heart threatened to burst free of his chest. White robes trailing out behind, he passed a pair of senior *Valir*. Their lips drew to thin lines. The apprehension he felt only intensified under their weighty stares. Ellson attempted to straighten, but that simply made him stumble. The wizards' disapproving eyes glared from above scowls, chasing after him. *No matter*, he reassured himself. The information he carried was worth any damage done to the reputation of a fledgling *Valir*.

Ellson barely managed to come to a stop before the doors to the grand hall. Both armoured guards eyed him with obvious distaste, their foreheads creased.

"I must speak with *Valir* Vallanor and the rest of the council," Ellson panted. "Immediately!"

The guard on the right cocked an eyebrow. He looked Ellson up and down, then inhaled as if about to undertake a monumentally undesirable task. "Wait here." He disappeared into the antechamber.

The apprentice nodded and offered a weak smile to the remaining soldier. The guard did not acknowledge it, pointedly staring straight ahead.

Without the rush of air that accompanied his lengthy sprint, Ellson began to perspire more freely. He wiped absently at his dripping brow and its screen of lank brown hair, peering down at the parchment clutched in his other hand.

He started at the beckoning of the guard who had gone to announce him, then entered the antechamber.

"Be quick about it," the guard's voice grated behind him. "They've got more important things to do than listen to a pimpled little sot like you."

Ellson quickened his step, the cool of the air in the chamber a welcome caress across his reddened face. He scurried to the center of the rectangular room, to stand before the council seat, aware of numerous eyes following his every move.

"I hear you've something to tell us, young man," said Cabral Vallanor, High *Valir*. He shifted slightly, eyes questioning. The midnight-hued, flowing robes and golden trinkets adorning his fingers and neck presented a striking contrast to Ellson's plain apprentice vestments and noticeable lack of jewelry. Cabral's chiselled features were set and sombre, but at least he didn't look too impatient. Yet. Ellson knew from others' accounts that he was not a man to displease.

"Y-yes, High One. I've discovered some startling information." Ellson's bowl-cut hair bounced with the enthusiasm of his nodding.

"I believe we've already established that," Cabral's face darkened. "Please, enlighten us."

Ellson twitched. "I c-came across some old d-documents in one of the rooms below the library, High One. Much older than anything I've read or heard of before."

Cabral raised an eyebrow and his dark eyes grew more intense, though his voice became softer. "Go on, young man, and be at ease." He made a sweeping gesture to emphasize his next words. "You're among brothers and sisters." The barest whispers of movement sounded from those gathered about the seat. Ellson shivered, though his body was still far from cold.

"I...I think I've come across something that contradicts points of the official histories—it is a recounting of the story of Ravien Alluminara, but what I've read so far.... There are discrepancies." Ellson's tone grew anxious and his words tumbled out.

For the briefest of instances, Cabral's eyes darted to another's close by, and he leaned forward, nodding. "I see. Continue."

Somewhat emboldened with Cabral's interest, Ellson went on, "If what I read is true, then we need to begin researching the rest of the documents." His expression turned sheepish as Cabral gave him a scrutinizing look. "I have had time to go through only the initial sections but I've seen enough to know it is definitely a departure from the known accounts." After another encouraging nod and the faintest of smiles from the High *Valir*, Ellson added, "We could be on the verge of the most important historical find in over a thousand years, High One! Though, it may mean that we must reconsider the past, especially the official recorded founding of our order." He licked his lips. "I believe that this discovery marks a great opportunity for all of us; a time to revisit our oaths and the calling we've received. Truth be praised!"

"I must know: have you mentioned your findings to anyone else?" Not taking his eyes from the young man, Cabral raised a finger in a brief, beckoning gesture.

"No, High One. I felt that you should be the first informed. I have not spoken to another of this discovery, though it has truly been a burden!"

"Ah. That is good," Cabral replied, settling back into his chair. "It would not do for us to act too hastily, without proper and thorough investigation. Ours is a grave responsibility, young man."

Ellson gave a start as a dark figure materialized beside him. The man was tall and outfitted in layered leather armour, secured atop garments of similar deep greens and blacks. A dark mask and hood revealed only his piercing blue eyes.

"Tell me, young man, have you been to the Hall of Winds before?"

Ellson's attention snapped back to Cabral as he tore his wide-eyed stare from the dark-clad warrior with a blink and a shake of his head. "N-no, High One, I have not."

"Then I will have Aras, here, escort you. I'd like you to make a report to the council chair in Eidara, personally. *Valir* Cronvell should be in the tower at the moment. He can guide you through the operating of the Hall and its communication links. Just be sure to show Aras where you found the documents before heading up, will you?"

"At once, High One!" Ellson beamed. He spun and hurried to exit the chamber.

Cabral flashed a dark, slit-eyed look at Aras. The other responded with a slight, terse nod, then turned to follow the young apprentice.

◆ ◆ ◆

Aras stormed into the narrow room, yanking the veil from his stubbled face and throwing back his hood. "It's like sending a lion in to snatch a hare." He slammed the heavy door behind him and paced about, scrubbing the scalp beneath his short black hair in agitation.

"Take care, Aras. Such hubris often leads to trouble." Malhaena smirked, dark eyes flashing as she stood to lean on the desk. Her outfit was similar in colour to Aras's, but the leathers fit her frame much more snugly. They also sported numerous fastenings that secured wicked-looking throwing knives.

Short black hair, glossy and cut to her jaw line, framed a face that was at once attractive yet devoid of warmth; it could have been sculpted from ice. "Besides, what point is there in grumbling about it? The pay is the same, either way." She, too, had lowered her shroud and hood.

"An executioner is paid nearly as well," Aras rounded on Malhaena, "but would you wish to do that work?" There was little room within the small, dimly lit chamber but Malhaena did not back off.

"Hardly. We aren't nearly as limited in carrying out our duties, and you know it. We are free to conduct our business, without heed for borders or the status of our prey."

"If I wanted to slaughter helpless people by the score, I'd have taken up the headsman's axe."

"So, what's this about then? Pride?"

Aras crossed his arms and scowled at her. "I make it a point to go after only the hardest of marks. I find out all there is to know about them, then strike when the time is right. And I give them every opportunity to defend themselves."

"So it's a game. A stupid one: allowing a mark the chance to fight back."

"It's about *honour*, Malhaena! I had reservations when we opted to accept this contract from the *Valir*. I am Jade Talon, not some drunken street thug!"

"All right, calm yourself, Aras! No need to become angry. Besides, what's done is done. And, more importantly, you have a new assignment."

"Who am I to target next? A dairy maid?"

"A farmer. Or, the son of a farmer. And his companion."

A black look clouded his features and he opened his mouth to speak. He abruptly closed it again and his expression softened. "The boy? The one from Ergothan we've heard about?" Aras's face brightened.

"Yes, I think it's him. Why should this please you? From what I've gathered, if he's seen sixteen summers, I'll be the next High *Valir*."

"You're not treacherous enough for that," Aras shot back. "Stick to killing for hire. There's less politics involved." Aras couldn't help but think about the prospect of bringing in the young man. It was rumoured that he was *An'Valir*, preposterous as that sounded. Still, if it were true, he would be a worthy opponent. If the boy truly was able to use magic without the aid of *metanduil*, a feat no other mage could boast, he would be formidable. Aras's eyes shone with a predatory gleam.

Malhaena appraised him, her brow peaked. "Don't tarry, Aras. The Talons have a name to uphold."

"Yes. And you will remain in Neval Ketarra to watch over underlings and attendants?" Aras sneered, stirred from his contemplation of a glorious hunt.

"Until further notice, yes." Malhaena shrugged. "I can be patient."

"Now, it's my turn to caution you, Malhaena: don't become too complacent. It will dull your skills."

"Not to worry, Aras. I have enough competition from within our ranks to keep me sharp."

Aras moved to open the door. "Just be careful not to get cut."

Malhaena waited until he was gone. "I don't intend to, dear Aras." She smiled wolfishly, absently tracing the dark green, tattooed slash across the bridge of her nose and cheek with a long-nailed finger. "Not in the least."

◆ ◆ ◆

Engram cursed. This was always the worst part of the journey. Nothing serious had yet transpired during their many passages through these steep-walled, narrow canyons that descended onto the eastern flats of The Barrens. It was no assurance that something dire never would.

This time, it didn't feel right.

"What's eating you?" asked Durneth. They had ridden together in escort of the *metanduil* ore caravans for several years. He was a decent fellow, really. He simply had little patience for anything other than dicing for money or chasing after tavern maids. As it had been nearly a week since he played a round of dice with anyone other than fellow mercenaries with little coin, none of whom was female, he was especially cranky.

"Nothing. I'll just be glad when we're clear of these infernal rocks." A crisp, late-autumn breeze blew through the pass and past them, tossing about the grey-streaked shock of hair flowing from his top knot.

"Bah. You Parceans worry too much—you all wear your hair cinched too tight. It's not like we're transporting gold, Mate."

Engram shifted in his saddle to glare at Durneth. "To many, it's worth more. Far more."

"Maybe when it's worked into something so the *Valir* can use it to do their magic. Right now, it's just a bunch more rock. Just like the blasted rock we're heading through. So get used to it."

"Right. Thanks for the advice."

"Hey, do you think the new hand will play again tonight?" Durneth's narrow face brightened at the idea of throwing the bones, his gap-toothed grin spreading wide in anticipation.

"Why?"

"I think he was holding out. I heard the others say he's got a purse full of coppers. Maybe even a few crowns." Durneth was near to drooling and his dark eyes glinted.

Engram chuckled. "If he's not too put off by you licking your chops, maybe. When he gets back from scouting with Jergant, you can ask him."

It was Durneth's turn to laugh. His mirth cut short as an arrow sprouted from his throat. Gurgling and reaching for the shaft, he fell from his saddle.

Engram reined in his mount, the animal rearing and wheeling in response, as he scanned the cliff tops for the source of the attack.

"To arms! Bandits! Arm yourselves!" Engram cried.

Short songs of steel rang out as the mercenary company drew their blades and collapsed their formation inward, protecting the wagons.

Silhouettes appeared above the cliff walls, too many to count in haste. The air filled with the whistling of swift arrows as curved, horn bows released their deadly missiles.

Shouts of pain rose up and more men toppled to the ground. Some writhed in agony but most lay still.

A few of his company broke ranks and fled but it was hopeless. Soon, they too lay unmoving in the short grass as arrows brought them down.

Engram and the few remaining survivors dropped their swords, raising their hands in surrender.

The wagon drivers also yielded, dropping from their seats to cower by the wheels of their carts. Engram didn't blame them. He felt like finding a hole to crawl into, himself.

A knot of scimitar-bearing figures approached from the canyon trail beyond, moving with a subtle, yet menacing grace. They wore grey and brown leather armour, some splinted with rings or bands of iron, and pointed metal caps. From beneath these, straight, dark hair flowed, some of it braided. The faces of their attackers were similarly dark in complexion and, to a man, they sported thin-lined moustaches that ran in straight lines and curved downward to their chins.

Engram knew them from appearance alone: Jhud'Hai.

"True One help us," he murmured.

Two horses brought up the rear of the group. Jergant was slung across his mount's back, numerous arrows protruding from his torso. Brandal, the new recruit, remained in his saddle, head lowered. Engram thought it curious that the attackers would not only leave him mounted, but with his reins in hand. He didn't have much time to think on it, as one of their captors stepped forward, head held high.

"Dismount and kneel in a line, here," he ordered.

Engram was unfamiliar with the Jhud'Haian accent, but he could make out the words clearly enough. He and the others did as they were told. Small, sharp rocks bit into his knees, but he paid little heed to the discomfort.

"Are they all accounted for?" asked the figure that had ordered them from their mounts.

"I...I think so." Engram looked up, confused. Brandal had replied. Engram's expression turned to dismay.

"You had best be certain, boy," the Jhud'Hai warrior growled. "Or do you need to take a closer look? Your newfound coin will be of little use down there with the others."

Brandal raised his head, trying hard to avoid eye contact with Engram. "Yes, that's the rest of them. None are missing." He briefly glanced at Engram, then quickly down once more.

"Yes—keep your head down, you worthless cur," Engram seethed. "Your eyes can find kinship with the dirt!" he spat.

The Jhud'Hai warrior's eyes passed over Engram. "At least one of the sword-hands has fire in his belly. It's a pity your spirit is wasted." He nodded to a pair among his war party. "Burn the bodies. The mistress wants as little evidence left as possible."

As he spoke, he peered upward to a lone, dark figure on the ridge, palely illuminated by the last rays of Evarlund's sun. The cloaked and hooded observer turned and disappeared from view.

• 1 •

A King's Plight

ALDRAIN'S BOOTED FOOT SCRAPED ON the rough stones of the dungeon floor. The hushed coughing of other prisoners echoed. Only these sounds interrupted the slow, incessant sound of dripping water within the prison catacombs.

As the King of Carathon, he was afforded his own personal corner of this forsaken place. Not a common thief or bandit, Aldrain Draegondor warranted special treatment and his own cell. And both had been provided.

His head lolled, his filthy blonde hair covering his face, filling his nostrils with the sour taint of sweat. Iron Shackles bound both wrists, connected via thick, rusted chains to a pulley system that held his arms tightly stretched from either side atop wooden stocks. Stone channels fastened upon the blocks surrounded each arm, carrying a chill through to his core. The cruel mechanism was built at just the right height to prevent him from settling into either a proper standing or kneeling position. He was forced to bend uncomfortably or hang by his shoulders while trying to prop his body up.

The voices kept him company throughout his torment.

Indeed, the dead king and queen, along with a host of others, frequented Aldrain's cell. *At least you've someone to talk to,* Aldrain chortled.

"Come, Father. Speak with me. Mother?" He gave another, bitter chuckle.

Only the fading echo of his faltering laughter and the dripping answered. *Well enough,* he reasoned. *I have time to wait.*

He was not surprised to find that Aldradein Draegondor had joined him some moments later.

"Greetings, Father," Aldrain croaked. "I trust I'm not keeping you from anything too important."

"Aldrain, why do you mock me?"

"Think nothing of it, Sire. My apologies." Aldrain bowed his head, which brought a hiss of pain as his stiff neck objected. Lank blonde hair obscured his vision but he hardly noticed.

"Ever do you test me, my son. You must be vigilant: the time approaches."

"The hunt…yes. I've been practicing, Father. I'll take a prize stag that will make you proud."

"No. This is by far the most important hunt you will ever face. But you do not seek an animal. Treachery is afoot. You must avenge me."

Aldrain closed his eyes. His thoughts seemed to scatter before he could make sense of them. What was his father talking about? It was a simple outing to the preserves, like any other, was it not? Nothing he couldn't handle.

"I am counting on you. Aldrain. You know what must be done."

The knowledge skirted the edge of his consciousness, dancing just out of reach. Yes, it was important. More important than anything else. Why couldn't he remember, then?

"The time is coming…they are coming. You must be ready."

Who was his father talking about?

"Think!" Aldrain rasped out loud. "Father, I can't remember…just tell me what I must do."

He peered about. His father had left. Aldrain laughed: a haunted, maddened cackling.

Closing his eyes again, Aldrain lowered his head, concentrating as well as could be managed. Several figures floated within the fog of his mind, coming and going in turn. One was a dark-haired youth, not quite yet a man. He seemed friendly enough, but there was something different about him, a sense of something more than his appearance suggested. Next was the shimmering form of an older man. He wore a dignified expression to match his garb. Flowing white hair with some remaining strips of grey framed a regal face, one drawn into a pensive frown. A *Valir*? He couldn't put a name to either of them, though he surely knew they should have been familiar enough. Was it one of these two his father was talking about?

Then, he saw the one. He was certain. This one's name he would never forget, although the reasons didn't register automatically. "Pacek. Count Rondul Pacek." Aldrain seethed, the words coming through clenched teeth. A flood of images and memories assaulted him and he reeled as if struck.

Pacek is to blame for this. For everything. Isn't he? Perhaps he wasn't the only one behind each of the events that had occurred—the death of Aldrain's parents, the destruction of the royal palace and the killings of Sonja and Ordren, among other, equally terrible crimes—but he was instrumental in all of it. That was enough.

The door to Aldrain's cell swung open to the grinding objection of rusty hinges.

"I was on my way here and heard you calling. I trust everything is all right?"

Aldrain fumed and looked upon the smug, chubby face of Rondul Pacek. The king's hands clenched to fists and his feet moved as he struggled futilely against his bonds.

"I'm glad to see you're getting some exercise," Pacek mocked, "because you'll need to keep up your strength for tomorrow's...ceremony."

Aldrain's eyes bored into Pacek through the veiling strands of sweat-slicked hair. "I will see you dead. One way or another." His voice grated.

"Your Majesty," the rotund man approached, leaning his bulk to whisper into the king's ear. "By tomorrow evening, you will either be dead yourself or you'll beg me for it."

◆ ◆ ◆

The huddled knots of refugees became more frequent now that Jaren and Iselle neared Eidara. It was not a mass evacuation, but more than a few citizens were obviously leaving the city.

Jaren's quarterstaff tapped on the hardpan clay of the road with every other step. He frowned and glanced at Iselle as a family passed by, keeping to the far side of the road, trudging through the thick layer of yellow and brown fallen leaves. Heads down, the father and mother shepherded their children past as quickly as they could, their bundled possessions jouncing and clanging along in their haste to be somewhere else.

Iselle merely shrugged. "Not a good sign," she said.

"I wonder why so many are leaving?"

"Taxes?" Iselle offered lightly.

"Iselle, this is not the time," Jaren chastised. "I'm being serious."

"So, be serious. I like to be positive, not gloomy like you."

Jaren exhaled. "Fine. But that still doesn't answer the question. What's making them leave the city?"

"Want me to find out?"

Jaren's eyebrows shot up. "I don't know if you've noticed, but they don't seem very willing to chat."

"My dearest Jaren," Iselle chimed, "when will you learn?"

Jaren studied his friend as they continued. Nothing seemed to bother her for long. Nothing that she would admit, anyway. Her dark brown hair tossed lightly in the chill breeze, a reflection of her normally carefree spirit. A trace of a smile touched her full lips, reflecting some mischievous thought or other that also brought a sparkle to her azure eyes. That look had usually accompanied a good measure of trouble back home in Dal Farrow.

But home seemed a long way off and a long time ago.

"You're scowling again," she observed.

"It must be the company I keep." He ran a hand across his brow, brushing at the stray brown hair that blew across his face.

"Well, if you'd prefer to travel alone, that can be arranged." She feigned a bow, sweeping her dark cloak back in a conciliatory gesture.

"Hmm. Let's see, no one to ridicule me, point out my mistakes and, generally, tell me that I'm doing everything the hard way. Who would want a peaceful life like that?"

"Exactly." Iselle laughed. "I knew you'd come to your senses."

Jaren's dark brown eyes took on a mischievous glint of their own. He winked. "I always do."

"How many times have I told you to stop doing that?" Iselle grumbled, her smile forgotten. "Further reminders of Turan, I do not need." She stooped to pick up a rock and hurled it into the brush along the roadside.

"But you two had so much in common." Jaren smiled. "I only did it in case you were missing him."

"If I see him again," Iselle vowed, "he'll be missing something. A lot of somethings."

"All right, I'm sorry I teased you. Forgive me?"

"Hardly." She closed her eyes and pursed her lips, drawing a deep, calming breath. "I can't believe the sneaky little lout fooled me so easily. He seemed really sincere, even sweet. If only I had been smarter. I might have been able to save some of Aldrain's men from being captured at Caren Hold. Maybe even Aldrain."

"Iselle, his task was to deceive everyone. He was a skilled thief, among other things. He first had to trick the king and his men, which was no small feat. You weren't the only one. Don't let it bother you."

"Yes, I suppose you're right." Her thin smile had returned. "Oh, look—now we can find out what's going on."

Jaren followed her line of sight. Another family approached, huddled and apprehensive as the rest.

"And how do you plan to do that?"

She flashed a playful grin. "Just watch me. And don't say anything. At all."

Jaren opened his mouth to object, but her raised finger cut him off.

Iselle turned toward the family, her attention trained on a young man near their age.

Jaren shook his head and smiled.

◆ ◆ ◆

As Jaren and Iselle continued on their way, the family—now with a love-struck young man in tow—slowly diminished and then disappeared in the distance behind them, lost within the dun, autumn landscape and skeletal trees. Jaren was sure he could still feel the poor fellow's longing gaze.

"You must have a headache after that." Jaren said.

"Why, what do you mean?"

"You batted your eyes so much you could have been blinking to rid the burn of searweed. It causes headaches, too."

Iselle laughed. "It's a girl thing. We can do it on demand. Something else you'd learn if you ever paid attention."

"I'd rather not."

"Live in ignorance, if you must," Iselle countered, "at least I got the information we needed."

Jaren nodded, conceding the victory. "So the one who's on the throne, this Machim, he's King Aldrain's cousin?"

"Apparently. I...I remember Aldrain talking about him some time back."

"Yes, I think you're right."

Iselle stared at him blankly.

"As usual," he amended, none too enthusiastically.

"Thank you." Her mischievous smile returned. "A woman likes to know she's appreciated."

"Okay, then. Let me appreciate your part of the plan for getting us inside Eidara without being recognized. The watch will no doubt be alerted to keep an eye on the gates for anyone matching our descriptions."

"All in good time, Jaren."

"Meaning you haven't a clue, yet."

"Don't be silly," Iselle said. "I'm just not ready to share it with you."

"All right. While you're thinking up your strategies, don't forget that we not only have to get into Eidara, but into the dungeon to free Aldrain. And get out again." Jaren tried to huddle further into his cloak to ward off the chill of the rising wind.

"Jaren, your cup is always half empty, did you know that?"

• 2 •

Of Meetings

MORGAINE KNEW IMMEDIATELY THAT SOMETHING was wrong, even before she saw the blasted doorway and charred slashes that marked the front of her family's home. It was utterly silent. There was no sound of livestock and even the creatures of the surrounding wood had ceased their routine chatter.

Several chickens lay scorched and smoking before the railed stoop and soot-covered, broken pottery lay scattered about the few short steps to the porch and across the landing. By the acrid stench that wafted past, the chickens weren't the only things fire had claimed.

She paused, listening intently, peering through the yawning entry and into the gloom beyond. Only her long, silver-streaked chestnut hair moved, stirred by the afternoon breeze.

"Who's there?" Morgaine demanded, as she perceived a whisper of sound from within: a soft shoe scuffing the hard wood of the floor?

No answer came.

"I'll warn you, do not trifle with me!" She took a step forward, planting her feet, feeling the magic respond to her summons. Whoever had done this was still here, waiting inside. "Show yourself!"

A figure half-materialized within the shadows of the house to stand at the blackened sill.

"If you don't tend to affairs befitting your station, bad things can happen. Will you peasants never learn?" The figure, clearly female, added an audible *tisk-tisk* at the end.

Morgaine struggled to maintain her calm. *Joselle.* She could not see the other girl fully, but there was no mistaking that voice. It was cruel and full of self-righteousness.

"What are you doing here? What have you *done*?"

"I thought I'd pay a visit to your dear parents, Morgaine." A twinkle of white teeth showed. "They were worried sick about you, leaving like you did and sending no word. Really, I think their grief would have overtaken them, eventually." She took a step forward and Morgaine observed her more closely.

Her scarlet, hooded robes—much like those of her adopted Mother in the magic, the Warwitch—stood in stark contrast to the pale cast of her skin, her red hair laced with streaks of *metanduil*—like Morgaine's. These features were part of the price of their transformations.

"If you've harmed them—"

"*You* caused their deaths, *farm girl*. If you'd known your place, you and your bothersome brother, all of this could have been avoided. Both of you caused this. I stayed to deliver a message."

Morgaine's hands shot forward of their own accord, white fire lancing out toward Joselle.

The other stepped back, countering with a warding gesture. She snarled and bared her teeth.

The tongues of flame spread across the spherical, blue shield that sprang forth to protect Joselle and deflected into the farmhouse. The white, blazing streams of fire seared black furrows into the wood of the building. Glowing embers flew into the air.

A wicked grin settled on Joselle's lips. "Pity you betrayed the Mother, dear Morgaine. Despite coming from peasant stock, you've developed some skill." The grin turned into a bitter frown. "Our Mother welcomes you back, if you will but take her hand."

"She is *not* my mother. And she has given too much already," Morgaine hissed. She circled, poised to defend against Joselle's magic. Morgaine was all too aware of the paleness of her own raised arms, shot through with veins of silver. *Metanduil.* Her gift from the Witch. She and Joselle had been altered, changed into unnatural creations by their new *Mother*, who through an earlier process, had undergone a similar transformation herself.

"We thought you might say that," Joselle crowed. "It is the reason this… lesson…had to be given. You have loved ones and friends who still live. Must they be destroyed because of your ingratitude? You are a peasant. Remember your place—accept what you are given!"

"This is madness!" Morgaine cried. "Look at us—look at yourself—we've become monsters, Joselle! Did you really want this?"

"Monsters? You are confused, *sister*. We are like gods, now. We have power beyond any other in the six realms. Who wouldn't want that?"

"It's not power, it's a curse. And I don't want it. Do you really think your new *Mother* cares for you? She cares only for the power you add to hers. You are a tool, nothing more. Don't be a fool, Joselle!"

"You are the fool, *farm girl!*" This time it was Joselle's turn to lash out. She released a crackling spear of lightning. The strike glanced off Morgaine's shield and tore into the earth, melting the dirt and stone into a glassy rent. "I have delivered our Mother's message. Now, I will tell her your reply."

Joselle summoned, weaving her arms in circles. Her form began to dissipate. "I expect you'll need more lessons. I will gladly provide them. Just remember, dear *sister*, that the ties to your old life make you weak. Others will suffer because of you. You have nothing the Mother or I cannot take away." Joselle's words died to echoes as the last of her substance melted into nothingness.

The white fire that Morgaine threw at her in response sliced harmlessly through the swirling mists that had spirited Joselle away. Her summoned attack continued on into the farmhouse once again. This time, though, Morgaine did not end her summoning. She fed her anger, fear and frustration into the magic, into an inferno of rage and destruction, until all that remained of her home was a ruined mound of ashes.

◆ ◆ ◆

"What were you saying about half-empty cups?" Jaren whispered to Iselle as they approached the rough-looking band.

"Well, it was probably your ill thinking that drew them to us!" she scolded in reply. "Just make sure to do something about it."

Jaren's forehead furrowed, his grip tightening on his staff. He had not needed to use the magic, other than to practice, since his confrontation with the Warwitch. The battle had gone remarkably well, considering he only survived because of some last-minute, desperate guesses, his sister's help, and a good deal of the True One's grace. He still was not convinced he wanted to summon, but at least the knowledge that his human nature had compelled him—that it was not some dark call of the magic—helped Jaren come to terms with using it. There was also the fact of necessity. Jaren and Iselle had talked at length about it. Even if he ignored his calling, others would be sure to take advantage of that decision and attempt either to destroy him or to control him. Neither outcome was overly appealing.

He tried to center himself, but the magic hesitated to respond while he was moving. Once they were a few dozen paces from the leader, he stopped, and his concentration came more easily. Iselle kept abreast of him.

The copper-skinned man who faced them was clothed in well-used leather armour and leaned casually on a thick quarterstaff about the same size as Jaren's. His long, dark hair was pulled into a top knot and he sported a thin-lined moustache and beard, typical of southerners. His companions sported a motley collection of mismatched, apparently cast-off equipment. They looked a truly ragtag group.

Brigands, Jaren thought.

"Greetings, young travellers," the man said, his voice thick with a Parcean accent. "You look to be heading into the city, no?"

"We have business in Eidara," Iselle responded, head high. "Not that it's any concern of yours."

This elicited a chuckle from the man. "Well, as it so happens, the king's men are rather indisposed at the moment, so we've decided to help out by adding our own little contribution to the protection of wayfarers."

Iselle and Jaren shared sidelong, apprehensive glances.

"What does that have to do with us?" Iselle questioned. "We were doing just fine until we came across you lot."

"Directly to the point, eh? Well, that's an admirable quality, young lass. I am Jentan, newly appointed...Marshall of Highways." He glanced around at his comrades, who murmured in amusement. His eyes returned to Jaren and Iselle. "These are my...associates."

"Self-appointed, no doubt." Iselle huffed.

Jaren settled himself. *She aims to start something, so I had better be able to finish it.*

"You know, young lady, once in a while someone comes along to make us truly appreciate the work we do. Now if you don't mind, the toll for safe passage, please?"

"How much?" Iselle asked.

"We offer a means-based fee service. Whatever coin you have, you give us!" Jentan and his men laughed menacingly.

"How about we pay you in leather goods? Like the sole of my boot to your—"

"Take them!" Jentan cut Iselle off, tamping an end of his quarterstaff on the ground in emphasis while offering a smug grin.

The several bandits who rushed forward all crashed heavily into an invisible barrier. One of them hit it so hard he collapsed to the ground and flopped about, hands clasping his nose, blood leaking between the fingers. The other two just stepped back, rubbing their heads and exchanging confused looks.

Jentan's face blackened as his eyes bored into Jaren's. "We've a summoner here—use the bolt!"

Jaren heard the order, but it did not faze him. He knew nothing could penetrate his shield; it had withstood the Witch, Morgaine and Joselle, combined. What could a group of lowly highwaymen possibly have that would defeat such magic?

Then, a white flash enveloped his vision and all thoughts ceased.

◆ ◆ ◆

Jaren opened his eyes to find Iselle scowling at him. Their wrists and ankles were bound securely with heavy ropes and they were propped against a broad, gnarled tree.

"You can't stop a bunch of worthless bandits? What kind of *Valir* are you, anyway?"

"I'm *An'Valir*, Iselle, and I really don't have much of an idea about anything that comes with it. I'm learning as I go."

"You always were a bit slow with your lessons," she chided. "I suppose I'll have to get us out of this?"

"Let's just wait and see. What happened? Where are we?"

"They hit you in the back of the head with a padded crossbow bolt. They've taken us deeper into the woods to their camp. And there are a few more of them."

"They shouldn't have been able to get through my barrier," Jaren said.

"Well, they did."

"Why didn't they just rob us and leave us on the road, I wonder?"

"I heard them say they wanted to ransom you to the *Valir's* Guild. Just what we need," Iselle moaned.

One of the bandits appeared before them, startling the two. Jaren wondered at how he was able to move silently across the carpet of fallen leaves and dry twigs. He should have made some sound.

"You've quite the talent, young master," he said. He knelt before them, a bemused light in his striking blue eyes. His hair was shaved closely about his skull, his features angular and strong, and the growth dusting his face suggested he had gone at least a day without using a razor. "A *Valir* who needs no *metanduil* to summon. A rare gift, indeed." Perceiving their anxious reactions, he shook his head to allay their fears. "Don't worry, I'm not going to tell anyone."

"There's nothing to tell," Iselle offered. "He must have lost his talisman in the struggle. It happens a lot." She shook her head in admonishment, eying Jaren. "I've offered to put a string on it, so he can fasten it to his sleeve, but he's not fond of the idea."

Jaren frowned at her. "I'm sure it will turn up."

The bandit's eyebrows peaked in amusement. He pursed his lips, as if wanting to say more, then simply added, "We'll talk later. I hope you don't mind travelling at night."

Iselle waited for several minutes after he had left before speaking. "What was that about?"

"Never mind. How did he know I don't use *metanduil*?"

"They searched us when we were taken."

"But he's the only one who put the facts together?"

Iselle shrugged. "I guess just because he's a brigand, doesn't mean he's a mindless dolt like the rest. He's probably one of the leaders."

"And what did he mean about travelling at night? I thought you said we were already at their camp."

"Like I know how many little hidey-holes they keep. Just you worry about getting ready to summon, and I'll make a plan."

Jaren attempted to center once more, but found he could not. He scowled and tried again. Still, nothing happened.

Iselle must have noticed his worried look. "What's wrong?" she said.

"I don't know. I can hardly feel the magic. It's just like before, when I had those magic-metal irons on."

She studied him more closely. "Is that a collar?"

Jaren craned his head down to get a glimpse of whatever it was she had seen, but it was no use. He reached up and touched a cool band of metal encircling his neck. "I can't see it, but it must be *metanduil*. It's made to block summoning."

She squinted. "Yeah, it's *metanduil*, all right. Hang on and I'll see if I can get undone enough to take it off." She exhaled wearily. "Jaren Haldannon, I don't know what would become of you without me."

Jaren decided it was neither the time nor place to give her the answer that first came to mind. He offered a knowing smile but held his tongue.

• 3 •

Taking Leave

"IT'S NOT A USUAL TASK FOR US," Malhaena offered, ignoring Cabral's frown, her back stiffening. "We are hunters of people, not places."

"Your clan was hired to execute the will of this council. That should be sufficient motivation, I believe." Cabral leaned back to look down his nose at the assassin. "Unless you wish to terminate the agreement? I know of several other bands, your rivals most likely, who would jump at this chance."

Malhaena inhaled deeply, then pursed her lips and bowed her head. "As you wish, *Valir* Vallanor. The Jade Talons are at your disposal."

"A wise decision." Cabral turned to the other black-hooded *Valir* seated at the great, polished table, the two highest-ranking council members in Neval Ketarra apart from him. "I told you she was wise beyond her years…and her station." He focused again on Malhaena. "You will lead the search. I have a crude map, but that can't be helped—it's a millennium old. Take what supplies and others of your clan as are required. It is of the utmost urgency that we find this location quickly."

"Very well." She leaned forward, bracing her leather-clad arms on the table's edge. "However, this will more than double our price. We were not expecting the costs to provision such a journey."

"Your fees are of no consequence," Cabral offered a wan smile and dismissive wave. "All that matters is the end result."

"Agreed. Have you arranged for transportation, or will that also be left to me?"

"Your passage to the mainland has been arranged. You will acquire the necessary supplies when you reach port in Thurssen. From there I thought it best to leave matters in your hands, although I'll be sending one of our own from the city along with you."

Malhaena planted her hands on her hips. "That will not do. A mage will only slow us down."

"I'm afraid this is not negotiable. There will be magic involved in accessing the location. For that, you'll need one of mine. I can offer a bonus, mind you."

The assassin paused, then gave a shrug. "Fine, we'll depart at once. But he looks after himself. I may have agreed to this journey, but I'm no nurse maid." Malhaena threw the *Valir* another curt nod and turned to leave.

"One moment more, my dear," Cabral called. "Have you heard from Aras? It has been some time since we last received word of his progress."

"No, and I wasn't expecting it. If Aras hasn't contacted you, be assured that it's by design. He's one of the best."

"Oh. I was led to believe he *was* the best."

Malhaena flashed a cool smile. "The best in the field up to now, perhaps. In any event, you will hear from me once we've determined our route on the mainland."

"Of course," Cabral said. "And remember, an expedient result to this mission is imperative."

The only response was the heavy thud of the door swinging closed behind Malhaena.

Cabral turned to his fellows. "Her spirit will serve us well."

"But can we trust them? Assassins are little more than talented thieves." It was Delaine, a fair-haired, stern woman from Drisia. The severe look on her face matched her concerned tone.

"She would not dare to cross us," Cabral replied. "Besides, I've contacted the heads of the rival assassin clans. If the Jades decide not to honour our contract, arrangements have been made."

"As usual, Cabral, you've left nothing to chance," Delaine's slight smile appeared to pain her.

Zhevram stroked a steel-grey beard as he spoke. "What's to be done when we find it?"

"We shall make our decision once we have the information," said Cabral.

"But why was it abandoned in the first place? Surely there must have been a reason," Delaine pressed.

"I expect we'll know that once the search is over."

"And the boy?" questioned Zhevram.

Cabral's peers exchanged anxious looks.

"For Aras's sake, I expect to hear of him soon enough."

◆ ◆ ◆

The hiss of the wind whistling through naked tree limbs continued all night, interrupted only by the occasional snap from the embers of dying campfires, the snoring of their captors, and the lonely calls of nocturnal animals. Despite the quiet, Jaren still could not sleep. A twig or stick beneath him seemed determined to bore a hole through his lower back and, try as he had, eluded all attempts to clear it from his tiny patch of forest floor.

"Will you stop that and go to sleep?" Iselle grumbled.

"I'm trying to, but I can't get comfortable."

"Maybe you should go to the leaders' tent and ask for a canopied bed and feather pillow."

"Very funny."

"No, actually it's very annoying. Sort yourself out, already." Iselle rolled onto her side, facing away from her friend.

Jaren stopped rustling around and stared up at the clear, starry sky. He wondered if his sister was peering at the same stars tonight—and if she still remembered him. At the onset of his encounter with the Witch, Morgaine had not recognized him. His big sister, always there to take care of him—to the point of bossing him around—forgot who he was. Worse yet, she attacked him. She stood with the Warwitch against her own brother. Jaren thanked the True One that Morgaine finally came to her senses and turned on the Witch and Joselle. It was a fortunate turn of events. If she had not intervened.... Still, Morgaine disappeared afterward, and Jaren had not heard from or seen her since.

"I hope I'm not disturbing your rest," said a low, firm voice.

Jaren started, but the voice was familiar: the bandit from earlier in the day.

Jaren pushed himself to a seated position. "I wasn't sleeping." He prodded Iselle. "Neither is she."

Iselle growled in irritation but turned and sat up, hugging her knees. "Are we leaving?" She glanced around briefly.

"Yes," the outlaw replied.

"But no one else is up."

The man smiled. "Quickly now, and please don't make too much noise."

"But—" Iselle started again.

The bandit levelled a pointed glare at her. "Or, I could leave you here to your fate with them."

Jaren began to gather up what few of their belongings had not been taken and Iselle, scowling, soon did the same.

Once they were ready, the two huddled close to their brigand guide.

"Just follow me," he said, "and you'll be fine. Take these in case we're discovered. We may need to fight our way out." Reaching behind into the shadows, he produced Jaren's quarterstaff and Iselle's long hunting knife.

"Where are you taking us?" Iselle asked.

"We'll find out soon enough," Jaren said when no reply came.

"Please, both of you be silent. I'll explain as soon as we're clear." The outlaw peered from one to the other. "And try not to trip on anything." He looked straight at Jaren.

Iselle did not miss the slight. "He seems to have a good read on people."

"Just you never mind," Jaren shot back. "Don't you do any *gathering* while we're in the camp, even though there's likely to be lots of shiny things."

"I'll be too busy making sure you don't stumble and wake everyone."

"If you two are finished?" The man's eyebrows peaked.

They nodded as one and followed their mysterious new friend as he spun about and padded off.

◆ ◆ ◆

It was a short passage through the camp as the bandits were not an overly large group. The outlaw picked his way easily, making no discernible sound, at least none that Jaren could make out. They stole past several sprawled, snoring forms and navigated around a number of dark trees, tall sentinels that observed in silence as they passed like creatures of the wood.

After the lights of the camp disappeared behind them, their guide turned and spoke, still in hushed tones.

He smiled warmly. "Well, now. That was simple enough. I believe an introduction is in order." He made a bow and a flourish. "I am Kalon Eversmere, at your service."

"I'm Jaren Haldannon, and this is my friend, Iselle Breit."

"Greetings, Iselle and Jaren."

"Okay, now that we're all friends, why did you help us?" Iselle asked.

Jaren rolled his eyes. "She means to say, '*Thank you, though we're not sure why you helped us?*'" After a pause, he added, "Aren't you an outlaw like them?"

Iselle shook her head at Jaren. "Same question, more words."

Jaren ignored her.

"I'm a greycloak, an agent of the king," Kalon replied. "I was sent here to keep an eye out for a young man and woman making their way down from the north. By your appearance, you fit the description. Though, with so few people coming *this* way these days, I didn't have many travelers to pick from."

"Aldrain sent you?" Jaren wondered aloud. "How is he? We've heard disturbing news."

Iselle kicked his ankle, attempting to be discreet about it. "How do we know Aldrain sent you?"

"You'll just have to trust me for now. Unless you'd like to take your chances on your own? Or, I could take you back to the camp."

"No, that's fine," Iselle said, "just be careful. I'm not easily fooled."

Kalon chuckled and Jaren rolled his eyes once again.

"No, I can see that," Kalon offered. "What are your plans now that you are here?"

"We need to get to Aldrain and help him," said Jaren.

Kalon stared blankly.

Iselle's eyes narrowed, "You do know what Jaren can do, don't you?"

"King Aldrain informed us that Jaren has a great deal of potential, but he was rather short on details. There have been rumors, but not much else."

"I'm—"

"—a very talented *Valir*. Still a little clueless, but promising," Iselle cut Jaren off. She emphasized the word *clueless* heavily.

Kalon observed Jaren's disapproving look, the amused expression returning to his own features. "It's unusual for someone so young to be…so gifted. You must be special, as Aldrain believes." He bowed and made a conciliatory gesture. "Forgive me, I must have simply missed seeing your talisman when you were searched. If you don't mind, what sort of *metanduil* token do you use?"

Iselle's face tightened. "He's very protective of it. Very secretive—hid the thing in his breeches so it wasn't lost again. That's why it was missed. I haven't even gotten a good look at it."

Jaren said, "Actually, I use magic to keep it hidden. It's just a small nugget, that's all."

Iselle nodded. "Right, it's almost like he doesn't use anything!" She laughed and her voice cracked.

Jaren joined in, but his laughter sounded equally forced.

Kalon smiled knowingly. "Very well, young ones. I appreciate your honesty."

"Ah...*ahem.*" Iselle inhaled after trailing her laughter to a stop. "All right, I guess we can trust you, Kalon. At least you're not another avatar or something." Her mouth clicked shut as the final, unwitting words tumbled out. Her face paled in shock.

This time, it was Jaren's turn to kick Iselle. His was even less discreet.

"Another what?" Kalon looked puzzled. He shook his head after a pause, perhaps concluding he had not heard what he first thought. "But...pay me no mind. If you wish to help free the king, then we'd best get moving. It's not going to be easy."

Jaren knew the greycloak was speaking for the two of them, rather than for himself. Jaren eyed Iselle again, but she just shrugged him off and turned to follow Kalon.

• 4 •

Friends and Foes

THOUGH THE BANDIT CAMP WAS SOON FAR BEHIND, Kalon led them stealthily on, advising the two youths that other outlaw groups patrolled the lands about Eidara with near freedom due to the troubles within the capital.

Kalon moved with a cat's grace and an utter absence of sound. Jaren was painfully aware of his own noisy footfalls. Each one seemed to shout his presence out to the world and he grimaced as he plodded on. At least Iselle had not given him a hard time about it. She must have either resigned herself to his commotion, or she was pointedly ignoring him after her unfortunate slip about the avatar.

Jaren smirked, wondering how long such good fortune might last. *That's Iselle for you.* She threw enough sour looks and elbows at Jaren over what he said, but when she made a mistake she acted as if it was nothing. Jaren huffed in frustration.

His thoughts turned briefly to Ver, the guardian avatar sent to protect them during their past adventure. He arrived mysteriously and disappeared in the same way, after helping Jaren to reach the stronghold of the Warwitch. He looked skyward and wondered if the avatar would cross his path again sometime.

Scattered patches of stars shone between the bare branches where they could be observed through the broken cloud cover; in the crisp fall air the celestial bodies twinkled brightly for a brief time before disappearing once again. Jaren shivered, clutching his cloak more tightly about him as the breeze picked up. Every breath turned to vapour.

Kalon halted ahead, a hand raised in warning. The two of them stopped and crouched, waiting for the greycloak's signal.

Off to the side, a blurred movement caught Jaren's attention. He peered toward it. Had there been something familiar about the vaguely-glimpsed shape? Jaren shivered as he recalled their encounters with the beings called blacktongues—agents of the Deceiver, his dark champions. They were deadly foes and Jaren hoped they were not about to meet another. As competent as

Kalon had proven so far, Jaren did not know if he could stand against one of those unnatural creatures. Only Ver had managed such a feat. And the avatar had done it twice.

Kalon drew a compact, hand-held crossbow from beneath his cloak, cocked it, and loaded a bolt. He took aim in the direction of the last movement.

The slightest whisper of leaves, now from behind, drew Kalon's attention and he pivoted to face the sound.

Another twinge of recognition tugged at Jaren's thoughts.

"Wait," he said in a hoarse whisper. "Don't shoot."

"Do you know who it is that tracks us?" Kalon countered.

"I think so," Jaren said.

"I need more certainty than that, Jaren. We are in dangerous country." As if to emphasize his words, Kalon adjusted his aim to a new angle.

"Please, just hold off a moment," Jaren pleaded.

"In a moment we could all be dead."

"No, wait," Iselle added. "I think I know what Jaren's talking about." She turned to Jaren. "Do you think it's him?"

"I can't be certain, but there's something about the way it moves."

"If you two don't let me in on whoever—or whatever—you are talking about, I have no choice but to shoot."

"Please, wait a moment more," Jaren pressed.

A knot of brush and dry grass parted nearby. Immediately, Kalon's crossbow swung to target the movement. Jaren lunged forward, blocking the shot.

The greycloak moved to regain a clear line of sight. "Don't be a fool—"

An enormous shadow materialized before them, powerfully muscled and sleek. It bounded forward, bowling Jaren over to land on his chest, its great, clawed limbs pinning him to the ground, his staff clattering from his grasp. The dark form's yawning maw spread wide to reveal a broad, lolling tongue and wicked-looking teeth.

Kalon took aim again, but this time Iselle leaped between him and the target.

"Dagger!" Iselle exclaimed, rushing to embrace the huge dog. She looked at Kalon. "Don't worry, Dagger will be a great help. He's a good dog, and very strong. He must have tracked us all the way from Aendaras, where we had to leave him."

"Gah!" Kalon shoved the weapon and bolt back beneath his cloak, then crossed his arms in frustration. "I would appreciate more warning the next time you receive company," he grumbled. After a moment the warrior continued, "The city is not far now, and dawn is still some time off. We might as well stop for some rest."

◆ ◆ ◆

"The *Valir* acted as your father's right and left hands," Pacek mocked, glancing coolly at the black-cloaked *Valir* who had accompanied him. "Until they were his undoing. You see, you must keep these…conjurors…in check. They are useful, but only to a point. They must be controlled." He regarded the king again. "Now, you too will be a victim of the magic-metal. Until it destroys you." He laughed as the *Valir* fastened wooden forms over the channels that held the king's arms.

"My own *Valir* tells me that you won't die right away. It will be a slow, gradual process. One that will remind you of your failure and the destruction of your entire house." He laughed coldly. "I may even release you into the city for a time, to beg for food or shelter from the people you betrayed. From those who you forsook to follow a hapless farm boy and his wretched sister. They're the same, you know. The same as the *Valir* who destroyed your family's reign. It was all arranged, and you were led to the end like one of your own game flushed into the open," he snarled. "Pathetic."

Two soldiers shuffled into the cell, awkwardly sharing the heavy burden of a steaming cauldron between them. A thick liquid sloshed about within.

"Ah! I see the treatment has arrived." Pacek nodded in approval, his double chin outlined starkly in shadow.

Aldrain fought to keep his vision clear, but the vapours from the cauldron set immediately before him didn't help. He recognized the contents. *Metanduil.* In molten form. An horrific thought began to take shape in the recesses of his mind. Aldrain looked in alarm at the wooden forms built over the stone channels that now enclosed both limbs to his shoulders.

The count must have read his darkening face. "You begin to understand your doom? Good. That means it is all the more satisfying. You see, the properties of the *metanduil* will keep you alive for a time, at least that's what I'm told. But your imprisoned limbs will be unable to manage the most basic of tasks. Like feeding yourself, or brushing away the flies that come out in the heat of the day. Pity it's autumn and there aren't more about. But, what's a person to do?"

Aldrain shifted in his restraints, vainly struggling against the chains and forms that held him fast. Moulds. They were going to pour the *metanduil* into the forms that covered his arms. He threw back his head and howled in rage and despair.

Pacek laughed in glee, his pudgy body shaking with the movement. "Excellent! This is most entertaining, Your Majesty!" He briefly mocked a deep bow, then straightened. "Begin!"

The midnight-clad *Valir* approached, a funnel clutched in his leather-gauntleted hands. He placed it into an opening in the mould on Aldrain's right arm.

"Do not do this," Aldrain did not beg, but neither was it a commanding voice in his present state. "You will pay, Pacek. I promise you that."

The *Valir* turned to regard Pacek.

"I'm afraid your days of issuing orders and decreeing sentences are at an end, Your Majesty." The count nodded impatiently to the summoner, scowling. "I said begin, you fool."

The mage lowered his head and closed his eyes. The cauldron rose from the floor and hovered in place above the funnel. It tilted slowly until the molten *metanduil* poured down in a thick stream.

Aldrain inhaled sharply and clenched his teeth as the searing liquid poured over the flesh of his arm. He thrashed his head and legs about mindlessly. All coherent thought vanished, replaced by maddened images and blinding explosions of colour. He lost track of time, drifting in and out of consciousness, awakening to fits of screaming or to shuddering in silent delirium.

Sometime later, he realized they had moved to his left arm and begun the process anew, but the burning agony that scoured him in relentless waves soon washed away this moment of awareness.

The last image he remembered with any clarity was that of Pacek's face, up close. The count was saying something, laughing. Aldrain couldn't make sense of it through the pain. That seemed to displease Pacek, who grabbed a handful of Aldrain's hair and shook his head violently back and forth, before finally striking him and then leaving in a bluster, followed by the others. Aldrain felt none of the count's assault. He was aware only of the pain devouring him.

The king's eyes rolled and his head fell forward.

"*Son. My son.*"

Aldrain looked up, his neck trembling.

"*They are coming, my son.*"

"Who, Father?"

"*The boy. And the girl, his meddling friend.*"

Aldrain's brow furrowed as he tried to remember.

"*They are responsible. For all of this.*"

"They...what?"

"*Because of them, our family has fallen. Draegondor has fallen because of this peasant boy and his sister. The boy turned the wrath of the Witch upon you, and his friend let them in—she and that street thief. The boy and his friend return.*"

"But, they didn't—"

"*Listen to me!*" Aldradein scolded. "*You do not yet understand. But you will. They are coming to you. They will tell you they are trying to help. Allow them to do so. But, be wary. They are not as they seem.*"

"Father, I don't...that doesn't make sense."

"*All will be revealed in time.*" He caressed Aldrain's cheek. "*My son. Look what you have become. At what you have allowed to happen to yourself and to the lands of your birthright.*" He sighed. "*You must believe me and do as I say.*"

"Yes, Father," Aldrain cast his gaze on the floor. "It will be done as you ask."

"*Good. Be vigilant. Our family name must be avenged. House Draegondor will rule again.*"

· 5 ·

An Unexpected Visit

JAREN STARTED AWAKE TO A SENSATION OF DANGER. Something nearby threatened. He tried to force away the clinging fog of slumber.

"I was wondering when you would wake," an eerily familiar voice purred.

The Warwitch! He would never forget that voice. It was burned into the foundations of his mind. But how was she here? Jaren scrambled to a sitting position, scattering dirt and leaves into the remains of the fire.

"Please, don't be alarmed," Rhianain said. "I have come only to bring you a gift."

She sat on a large boulder not ten feet from Jaren, the cowl of her crimson robe drawn back to fully show her face. It was drawn and haggard, a far cry from her appearance at their first meeting. The *metanduil* worked into her features shone dully in the early morning light.

"I've seen your gifts," Jaren replied, "and I want nothing from you."

"Still holding to misguided beliefs, are we?" The Witch shrugged. "I must apologize: I left our last meeting on bad terms, and without a proper farewell."

Jaren looked down at Iselle and Dagger in dismay. He could understand that Iselle still slept, but where was Kalon? If he were on watch, then he should have been alerted by the Witch's presence. And what about Dagger? He should have awakened at Jaren's stirring and given some warning. Something was wrong. Calming himself, Jaren tried to center. Instead, a cold realization struck. They had not been able to remove the collar yet. *I can't summon!* Jaren's inner voice wailed. *What if she knows?*

"Be at ease, boy," the witch soothed. "I did not come here to renew our conflict. As I said, I have something for you. And, I think, once you've seen it and had a chance to ponder the implications, you will come to understand that I am not your enemy."

"You kidnapped my sister, turned her into…into something unnatural—some abomination of magic, like you—and used her against me in battle." He cocked his head to the side. "I may not be a scribe, but I'm not the village idiot, either. By my reckoning, all of that makes us enemies."

Rhianain sighed and shook her head. "Granted, there have been some… undesirable and unfortunate actions that we'd both like to take back. But whether naturally derived or wrought with the knowledge I've gained, we have been given great blessings by the True One."

Jaren opened his mouth to protest again, but the witch raised a conciliatory hand.

"I do not expect you to come to the realization lightly. I am prepared to wait, this time. Please, forgive my previous…haste…and consider this." She produced a small, leather-bound tome from the folds of her cloak. "This is the journal of Ravien Alluminara. Have you heard of her?"

Jaren nodded, eyes narrowing in suspicion. "Not much, though."

"I thought not. You will learn more through her writing. The book is enchanted, mind you, and you must read it as written, from front to back. It was created that way to prevent anyone from simply scanning segments and, therefore, getting only part of the message she wanted to communicate."

"Why are you giving me this?"

"Because you need to read it. You need to know how you've been fooled— how we've all been fooled—by a thousand-year deception. The *Valir* are behind it, as you'll see. I need you, and you need me, to right this terrible wrong." Rhianain nodded, placing the journal on the stone before her.

The Witch stood and straightened, her face tightening in concentration. Jaren could sense magic coalescing, energy drawing to her, and mist formed in the air surrounding her. He shrank back, wary of her intent.

"Farewell, Jaren Haldannon. We will talk again, soon."

"Wait!" he called to her ephemeral form as it began to dissipate. "Where's Morgaine? How can I reach her?"

His words echoed through the small clearing.

Jaren stepped forward and picked up the book. The dark leather of the cover was scored and pitted in several places. It looked as if it had survived much. If it truly was a thousand years old, it must have done so. Glancing down at his slumbering companions, he shrugged and tossed some kindling into the tiny fire's embers.

Hunching closer to the glow for a better look at the tome, Jaren tried to quiet his racing thoughts as he studied it. He didn't know if he could bring himself to open the thing. Was it some sort of trap? Considering where it had come from, what else could it be?

"I feel as though my head remembers more than a few pitchers of mead and the ruckus of a tavern rather than a few hours' watch," Kalon said as he entered the clearing. He eyed Jaren, "How long have you been awake?"

"An hour or so," he replied, looking up from the journal. "I...I couldn't sleep."

"Well, it's time to rouse your friend." Kalon began gathering his belongings.

Dagger raised his head and wagged his tail. The great dog eased to his feet and then trotted off, sniffing out the perimeter of the campsite. He didn't even pause at the boulder upon which the Warwitch had sat.

Jaren hefted the journal, its weight reassuring him that his encounter with Rhianain hadn't been imagined or dreamt.

He noticed that Iselle was staring at him from her bedroll, her sapphire eyes peering out from between puffy lids.

"You could have at least gotten breakfast ready if you were up first," she complained. "Why does my head hurt?"

Jaren shrugged and tried to hide a grin.

"Don't you smile at my expense, Jaren Haldannon, or you'll be sorry." She stumbled to her feet and shambled to the edge of the clearing, where Dagger joined her, nuzzling a hand. "We're going to the stream. I want to wash the cotton out of my mouth. We'll be back shortly." She turned to glare at Jaren and Kalon, in turn. "You boys would do well to have something ready to eat when we get back. You wouldn't want me grumpy all day, would you?"

Jaren rolled his eyes at her retreating figure.

Kalon shook his head. "She's a ray of Sholara's light in the morning," the greycloak muttered.

"Just thank the True One she didn't wake up in a *bad* mood," Jaren said with a wry smile.

◆ ◆ ◆

"I don't smell any cooking," Iselle declared upon her return some minutes later.

"We don't have time to prepare a feast, girl. We're to be on the move shortly."

Iselle sniffed. "I suppose you'll just have to get up earlier next time."

Jaren chuckled and looked over at Kalon. The man wore a blank expression.

They ate a meal of thinly sliced, fried meat and potatoes, which Jaren hastily cooked. Afterward Kalon fixed them with a measured gaze.

"I need to know how well you can handle yourselves in a fight, in case it comes to that. Tell me, young lady, how are you with that knife of yours?"

"I can handle myself well enough."

"Take a fighting stance, then," Kalon instructed.

Iselle stood, unsheathing her knife and dropping into a crouch.

"Hmm. Not too bad, but hold the knife in front of you, blade forward, and keep your free hand behind it." As he spoke he moved to her. "May I?" In response to her curt nod, he adjusted her positioning to mirror his advice. "Like that. You can use the knife to block, or strike, and your trailing hand to capture."

Iselle tried to perform a few moves under Kalon's guidance and Jaren watched with a slight grin.

"Definitely needs some work," Kalon observed, "but a marked improvement."

Iselle huffed and scowled at Jaren's obvious amusement.

"And now for you." Kalon fixed his eyes on Jaren.

Jaren gathered his staff and took up a fighting posture.

"I'm pleasantly surprised," Kalon offered dryly, bringing a smile to Jaren's face, "I thought you would be worse. But I suppose it's manageable."

Jaren's smile disappeared. Iselle chuckled lightly. She sat near the fire, elbows on knees, her chin resting on her hands.

"Well, I really haven't used it to fight," Jaren admitted sheepishly. "I've only competed during the Highsun and Midwinter festivals back home. It's not really combat, just sparring."

"You don't say?" mocked Kalon. He put up a hand, "Actually, it's not so awful. Even competitions like that can help with your reflexes, strength and general familiarity with the weapon." As with Iselle, the warrior adjusted Jaren's stance and then guided him through a few basic attack and defense moves. "Well then," Kalon said, "that's not looking *too* shabby. We can try to get some of the farm work out of your techniques later."

"What he's saying, Jaren, is you're not threshing grain!" Iselle crowed.

Jaren's forehead wrinkled as he scowled at her.

"Pay her no mind," Kalon said. Turning toward Iselle he added, "She's equally unskilled."

It didn't help Jaren to feel any more comfortable, but at least it stopped Iselle from heckling.

"I need to scout out a bit before we leave," Kalon announced with a nod. "You should practice on your own a bit—both of you. Be ready to leave when I return, or you'll learn what grumpy really means." He stole quietly from the campsite and disappeared into the woods with a last, pointed look at Iselle.

"I think he's warming up to you," Jaren said with a snicker.

"Never you mind," Iselle replied, though her sly grin spoiled the severity of her tone.

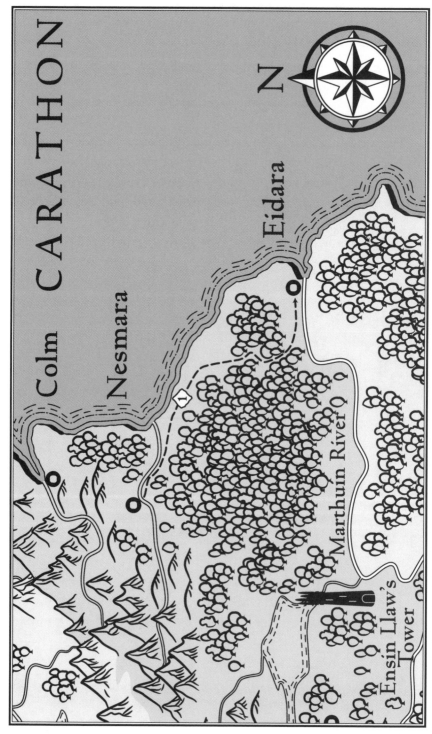

1. Jaren and Iselle journey to Eidara in hopes of rescuing King Aldrain.

• 6 •

Comings and Goings

AS THE OUTER GATES OF EIDARA NEARED, Kalon gathered the two friends close and offered some advice.

"Stay near me at all times. The city has become a dangerous place, and you may be in great jeopardy if we are separated. Let me do any talking. If, for some reason, we do lose track of one another, head immediately to the Gilded Rose Inn. That's where we're going. It's at the northern end of the commons, not far from the entrance to the city proper. Tell them Kalon sent you, and wait for me there." He eyed them in turn, first Jaren then Iselle. "Understood?"

Jaren nodded, as did Iselle, though she bristled under Kalon's gaze.

"Good. Let's see if we can get through the morning without any mishaps."

Iselle rolled her eyes, though she did not try to distance herself from Kalon. If anything, she moved even closer.

The trio, trailed by Dagger, passed without incident through the gates. Kalon and his young companions garnered little interest from the guards other than cursory glances. Yet another mercenary heading inside to find work, Jaren supposed they were thinking. Such business was plentiful of late, according to Kalon, and who were the guards to care if this one brought along his children? Apparently, they were not of a mind to bother with such questions.

The small group soon melted into the crowds that had gathered in the marketplace, blending into the greater commotion of the awakened city. Even with the increasing exodus of citizens, the streets were crowded with colourful people and filled with a wide variety of sights and sounds. Though it was not their first trip to a large center, Jaren and Iselle were still unaccustomed to seeing so many brought together in one place. Ten seasons of celebrations might pass in Dal Farrow and they would encounter only a fraction as many people.

If you did not look too deeply into anyone's eyes, Jaren supposed, you might believe circumstances were no different than usual, that no troubles plagued Carathon. But when you peered more closely, too many eyes were wary and apprehensive. Too many conveyed suspicion and mistrust between vendors and customers, neighbors and passersby. And entirely too many were predatory, sharply focused and hunting for easy prey. For all of the bustling activity, there was a feeling of building tension, a sense of disquiet that intensified the normal clamour.

Eidara was the center of a gathering storm.

As dire as Kalon's warning was and despite their surroundings, at times the youths found themselves straggling behind their escort, distracted by this display or that intriguing scent, a street performer here or a town crier there. Either a nudge from Dagger's nose or their own sense of vulnerability brought them aware and they soon enough caught up with Kalon. The atmosphere of mistrust and simmering unrest was simply too palpable to ignore for long.

For his part, Kalon navigated the crowds easily and, though he appeared no more than a simple weapon-for-hire, no one got in his way. Perhaps it was the steely set to his ice-blue eyes, or some other quality that Jaren could not quite put a name to, but the man moved virtually unhindered through the mobs. Whatever the reason for his ease of passage, Jaren and Iselle had to hurry to keep up with the greycloak.

Long after the colourful scenes and clamorous noises of Eidara had transformed into a wearying, extended performance that dizzied their senses, Jaren and Iselle followed Kalon up the few steps to the entrance of the Gilded Rose. It was a multi-storied building in a decent state of repair, at least compared to a good number of others they had passed on the way.

Kalon entered the place without hesitation. After gaining the innkeeper's attention, he flashed a curious gesture that earned a slight nod in return from the slim, balding fellow. Kalon then led them through a doorway and into a private room off the back of the common area, closing the stout door behind them.

The chamber was relatively spacious and featured a low table surrounded by a chesterfield and several comfortable, padded chairs. In the corner was a stone-lined fireplace, though only embers stirred within it. One lone, dust-covered window looked out from the room, but Kalon quickly drew the deep maroon curtains across it, darkening the interior. Small streams of light escaped from behind them, streaking the wall and floor.

He took a seat on one of the chairs. "I hope you're not too tired from the walk. We are safe enough in here to discuss our plans."

"I thought we already had a plan," Iselle said bluntly.

"Perhaps the beginnings of a plan," Kalon corrected, "but *going in and getting Aldrain*, as I've heard you suggest, doesn't make for a proper strategy."

"Sometimes too many details just confuse things," she countered.

"And too few will land you in irons right beside the king."

She thought on that for a moment. "Well, if you really are a greycloak, then just put on your uniform and we can walk in. Pretend we're your prisoners or something."

Kalon laughed, a hearty and genuine sound. "My, my. That's precious. For starters, young one, the greycloaks are a rather loose bunch, and we don't have *uniforms*. That would pretty much render our existence useless, as we are a unit of stealth and covert operations. Uniforms don't lend themselves well to being invisible, which we need to be at times."

"Don't you have badges or something that you use to identify yourselves? Belt buckles?"

Kalon laughed again. "If we had any trinkets like that and were captured, discovering our allegiance would be a very simple matter. No, we use hand gestures and such. A sort of sign-language."

Jaren spoke, "Like you did with the innkeeper?"

The man nodded, apparently impressed. "You noticed that, did you?"

Iselle grunted, "A wave is a wave, if you ask me. Anyway, since you don't think much of *our* plan, what's *yours*?"

"Well, I do like your idea of pretending to be prisoners," Kalon admitted, "but I will have to check the situation out before we just venture onto the royal grounds. In this state of affairs, things change very quickly in Eidara. Someone else might decide to take you for themselves, in order to gain status. I'll need to be a little more certain of the circumstances before we can try that approach."

"So we just wait here while you go see if the plan is workable?" Iselle said.

"Unless you'd like to go sightseeing in the meantime, "Kalon replied.

"I think I like this room just fine," Jaren said.

"Fine. But can we at least eat while we wait?" Iselle demanded.

Kalon's smile returned. "Of course," he said. "I'll have Brom send something in for lunch." He rose to exit the room. "I should be no more than a few hours. Try not to be too sick of each other by then," his voice trailed off. As he left, Kalon directed one last sympathetic glance at Jaren. Iselle did not appear amused.

◆ ◆ ◆

From his vantage point outside the manor that now served as Eidara's royal grounds, Aras Endemol observed people as they passed without really registering their presence. Guards, messengers, servants and a noble here and there hurried into or out of the estate. Aras gave them barely a thought. He was not altogether ignorant of the bustle; no one in his line of work survived long without paying sufficient heed to his or her surroundings. All the same, his attention was focused more on the boy and his companion.

Right now, Aras was at war with his own thoughts. It was beyond his understanding why he had not simply killed the girl and taken the boy back to Neval Ketarra, instead of participating in this absurd ruse. The boy was completely vulnerable with the collar Aras's colleagues had fastened about his neck. The girl would have been little more than an afterthought.

So why are you still here?

Perhaps it was for just that very reason—the boy was helpless and a sure capture—that he hesitated.

His distaste for the *Valir* contract had grown steadily since the Jade Talons took the job. After dispatching the young apprentice back in Neval Ketarra, his patience for their tasks had nearly reached its limit. There was no sport in it. No honour.

Aras allowed himself a quiet chuckle. *Before, that wouldn't have mattered to you, would it?* But things had changed. The struggles of a starving street urchin were long behind him. It had taken time and great sacrifice, but Aras Endemol had risen through the ranks steadily to become the professional killer he now was. He had gone from being a lowly, street-corner pickpocket to one of the most feared assassins in the six realms.

Now you can't bring yourself to seize a boy and kill a girl.

It was not good for business, Aras knew. Then again, when you were the best, you could afford to bend the rules. There would always be a need for his services. Even if an employer tried to hire a lesser in his stead, he would be called upon to finish the job when the others proved inadequate. So what if he took his time doing it?

But that was not the whole of it. There was something about the boy, some quality that stood out. Aras had heard rumours of him. Things seemed to happen where the boy was concerned. Extraordinary things.

Aras wondered if the destruction of the original royal palace here in Eidara had something to do with the youth. Jaren had apparently been nowhere near but, soon afterward, the newly crowned king of Carathon crossed paths with him. Then things became very interesting, as far as his sources suggested.

What harm could there be in learning more about him? It would make the inevitable end that much more enjoyable. Of course, that was it; that was the reason he had postponed acting on the contract. *Wasn't it?* Jaren would be a much more satisfying conquest if he had the chance to fight back. The fact that he was supposedly *An'Valir* was just that much more enticing, despite his and the girl's denials. None had existed for a thousand years.

It followed that no one had faced such a challenge in that time. It was too exceptional an opportunity to rush through just for the sake of fulfilling the provisions of a contract he reviled more with each subsequent task. No, this was an opportunity to savour, to relish. No matter what anyone else thought, he would do just that.

That's why you're taking your time, Aras reassured himself.

But what about Malhaena? She would no doubt be using the delay as leverage. She was more than dangerous. She was calculating. Aras had never been much for the political side of things. There were too many intangibles. Too many things did not rely on your strength, stamina or wits. Malhaena could keep the political capital she won. He did not need it. As long as he was the best, *she* needed *him*. How long would it be until she decided to find out if he really was that good? How long until she challenged him? It was something that he had to consider. Politics aside, she was a very capable assassin in her own right. *As capable as you?* He chuckled darkly once again.

Such was the nature of the business. You could not remain the alpha wolf forever. Sooner or later, someone would come along who was just that tiny bit stronger, that small margin smarter. Or more cunning. Malhaena was devious, all right. The other two qualities, Aras believed, he still possessed in greater measure over her.

Aras shifted slightly, careful to make as little sound as possible. Among its several useful abilities, his *metanduil*-threaded cloak helped him merge with the shadows, or blend into his background, whichever the circumstances required, but it did not do much to dampen noise. He glanced upward, gauging the time from Sholara's position in the late-afternoon sky.

He hoped the youths did not lose patience and try to investigate matters for themselves. Aras wasn't worried about the boy so much. It was the girl who might attempt it. And she could probably get him to follow along. Realizing that he had allowed a smirk to form, Aras wiped it away and intensified his gaze at the estate across the way.

At last he saw the soldier he had come to find. The assassin paused for the briefest of moments to ensure that his cloak had completely transformed his appearance into that of Kalon, the unfortunate greycloak whose identity he'd assumed. *Time to resume the charade.*

At the very least, he loved a challenge.

· 7 ·

Questions of Trust

CURIOSITY HAD FINALLY PREVAILED OVER CAUTION and Jaren found himself turning the pages of Ravien's journal whenever he found a spare moment. He had heard little of her apart from Llaw's brief account months back, so he read carefully, not wanting to miss any important information. Since reading was not an easy task for him to begin with, he made sure to go slowly.

It took some time to settle into the process, as he was still wary of the witch's intentions and that anxiety made a difficult task all the more demanding. Nothing that the Warwitch did, in Jaren's experience, had indicated a kind or compassionate nature. He was certain that her stated intention to help Jaren had more to do with helping herself. Rhianain had suggested they would both benefit from Jaren's exploration of the book, but he was not naïve enough to believe she valued his wellbeing over her own ambitions.

He promised himself he would be careful.

The first entries had provided little more than background information about Ravien and her era, which he supposed was useful enough. It was helpful, but did not contain any startling revelations about the magic or his role in things. Perhaps those would come later.

Ravien Alluminara was from one of the islands to the south of Evarlund. She had joined the *Valir* in her late teens, leaving her home to study with the masters because she, like Morgaine, had shown a great deal of potential. Apparently, Ravien's people—the Sylvarii—had migrated to their islands millennia ago. All Jaren knew about their home were snippets of legends that occasionally circulated, usually mentioned by travellers passing through Dal Farrow. Jaren's father, Jens, had scoffed at the stories and dismissed them as so much nonsense. Since leaving his home, however, Jaren had seen the stuff of dismissed lore come to life—a fact that went a long way to tempering his natural doubts.

There was one passage that Jaren found particularly interesting:

I leave for the halls of the Valir soon, to learn from and practice under the leaders of the mainland summoners. This journey is one that tears at my heart. I only hope that the knowledge I gain can help my people recover what was taken from us. The mainlanders have sent warm invitations and encouraging advice, and I know it both pains and shames the elders, adding insult to the considerable weight of injury that we have suffered at their careless hands. Our history demands that I proceed with caution. The hope is that we can begin to bridge the gap that has developed between my people and the magic. This gulf has widened, becoming ever greater in recent years. If I can do this, if I can begin to bring healing and a sense of direction back to our people, then my studies will not have been in vain. May Vraellon see it done.

"Finally, some news," Iselle moaned wearily as a series of knocks sounded on the door. "Maybe now I'll have a chance to *talk* to someone else, instead of just watching your lips move, as entertaining as that is."

Jaren sighed, setting down the journal and rising from his chair. "Do you want another match?"

She glanced at the squat table where a checkered game board sat. It currently hosted twice as many upright black figures as white. "I couldn't bear to beat you at pieces yet again. That's even worse than boring. It's cruel." Her attention turned to the door again. "Why would Kalon knock?"

Jaren paused halfway there. "Maybe he's sent someone else to give us word?"

"I suppose," Iselle considered. "Well, don't just stand there, answer it!"

Jaren frowned at her but continued to the door and pulled it open. His eyes went wide in shock.

"Greetings, lad," a strong, deep voice announced. "I trust you've kept yourself well since we parted ways?"

From where he sat curled by the fireplace, Dagger raised his head and offered a single bark. The apparent greeting complete, he lowered his head to his paws once more and closed his eyes.

The older gentleman waited just without, an amused, though expectant expression on his face. He leaned slightly on the dark-stained staff gripped in his left hand. Kind eyes shone beneath bushy grey eyebrows, though most of his long hair and beard had lost that darker hue and showed mostly white.

"*Valir* Llaw!" Jaren blurted. "How did you find us?"

"I could tell you from out here," the mage replied, "but wouldn't you rather take a seat to hear it?"

Jaren shook himself from his stupor. "I'm sorry, *Valir* Llaw, I just didn't expect to find you on the other side of the door. Please, come in."

Once they were seated and Llaw had looked them over approvingly for a moment, he produced a thick, curved pipe from his robes, lit it with a snap of his finger, and began. "It is good to see both of you again. Where to begin? After you went off to rescue your sister from the Witch and I recovered from our ordeal with Andraste, I made my way back to Aendaras from Ghalib. There, I received a message from the *Valir* council requesting me to locate you once again and assist further in your development. Once I heard that you'd prevailed in your struggle against Rhianain—and you simply must tell me how that encounter transpired—I decided to come to Eidara. I suspected you'd want to help King Aldrain as your next order of business."

Llaw put the pipe to his lips and drew on it, then sent a few smoke rings floating lightly into the air above their heads. "I made sure to have some of the locals watch over the entrances to the city with instructions to notify me at once if someone matching your description arrived. There aren't so many people coming to Eidara as going these days, which probably helped. It's just as well we're here rather than in the barrens, as we'd originally planned; there are some decidedly nasty rumors issuing from the west these days. Anyway, I've found you at last. Here I am, at your service."

Jaren pursed his lips. "Do you know what's happened to Aldrain? Does it have something to do with that count? What was his name?"

"Pacek," Llaw said.

"Yes, him," Jaren grimaced. "What's he done?"

"And why didn't you help Aldrain?" Iselle demanded.

"Iselle!" Jaren flashed her an irritated look.

"No, it's a good question, really," Llaw responded. "But I'm afraid you may not like the answer. You see, the council suggested that I not intervene. In any case, I hadn't enough people here to do anything about the count. Before now, that is." Llaw's eyes struck a new sparkle. To Jaren, it appeared much the same as the look Iselle got when she was considering mischief of one sort or another.

"But doesn't the council still want you to stay out of it?" Jaren asked.

"Why would they not want you to help Aldrain?" Iselle added.

"As I said, I took it as a suggestion. Probably because they didn't want it to interfere with my task of finding you, Jaren. Since that business is wrapped up, we can lend a hand."

"We're already doing something," Jaren said. "Well, sort of."

"Oh? So soon?" Llaw said, thick eyebrows raised. "What are your plans?"

"It's not our plan," Iselle scoffed. "We're here with one of Aldrain's greycloaks. Right now, he's scouting the royal grounds to see what he can find out."

"Well, then, I suppose we'll just have to wait and see what he comes back with," Llaw said.

Iselle coughed, glancing up at the thickening cloud of bluish pipe smoke hovering above her, then back at Llaw, with a questioning look.

"Forgive my indulgence, dear girl," Llaw dipped his head in acknowledgement and replaced it within his robes after tapping the contents onto the floor. He regarded Jaren. "In the meantime, my boy, why don't you humour a poor old soul and tell me about your encounter with the Witch?"

The *Valir's* mention of age rang true; he did appear older than when they had first met back at his tower several months ago. Jaren had believed it was simply a consequence of being attacked by several of the Witch's minions—the latest instance having given him the limp he still sported—and that the mage would have recovered by now. It seemed not to be the case. Along with the whitening of Llaw's hair, new lines of worry crisscrossed his aged face.

"It all happened so quickly," Jaren began, his eyes becoming distant for a moment. "It was not at all as I'd planned, even though I had decided exactly what I would do. I honestly didn't think I was going to make it out of there alive. I meant not to." Jaren's hand moved absently to his thigh, as one moves to clutch a nagging injury. "For a while afterward, I had a limp, too, though it doesn't bother me now."

Llaw gave a chuckle. "Just wait until you get to be as old as me, my boy," he grimaced. "Your body will remember many of the bumps and bruises you thought you'd long since left behind. You must have done a good many things right, or we wouldn't be having this conversation."

"In the end, it came down to the *three selves* you told me about. That knowledge eventually sparked my understanding of what I had to do to protect myself, and what was required to defeat the Witch."

"I see," nodded Llaw. His hand went to the folds of his robe, apparently of its own accord, to the place where his pipe was stored. One look at a frowning Iselle, however, and he settled for smoothing the fabric while giving her a wan smile.

"I could see the Witch, not as a person normally appears, but as she was with the magic. Her form was blurred, out of time, it seemed. I kept wondering what that meant until I thought back to my own trials with the magic. I could only summon when I was completely focused on the result I was after, when all three of my *selves* were linked to a common purpose. I thought that if the witch was not completely centered—if she had been able to force the magic through the process she'd undergone—I could try to get to her by using that inner division. Luckily, I was right."

"I'm sure fortune played a role, but it wasn't the only reason," Llaw commented. "You did well to mind the ramblings of an old fool and then puzzle things out for yourself, even though I'm sure you thought me entirely bothersome at times."

"Even annoying?" Iselle teased.

Llaw's eyebrows went up at that, but he smiled warmly despite the slight. "Indeed, young lady. But necessary intrusions it seems they were, and fortunately, they offered a measure of useful material in spite of the fact I had little idea of what we were dealing with."

Jaren shot Iselle an irritated look. "I have to admit, *Valir* Llaw, you weren't my favourite person through much of the journey. Especially the prodding and poking with the magic. I really didn't like that." He shrugged. "But it turned out that I needed to go through it to get a better insight into the way the magic worked. And the way it didn't."

"Which reminds me, young man, what sort of band is that you've got about your neck? To me it looks like *metanduil*. Is it?"

"We can't get it off," Iselle blurted, before Jaren could open his mouth in reply.

"And I can't summon with it on," he admitted after a sidelong, frowning glance at his friend.

"Perhaps I can help with that," Ensin Llaw suggested. "Come, let's have a look."

Llaw leaned in and examined the collar, pushing Jaren's chin up to get a better view, then twisting his head to the side to see it at another angle. "Ah, yes," he mumbled. A hand disappeared into his robes once again, not near the concealed pipe, though, a fact that he emphasized with a placating nod to Iselle. He produced a slight, peculiar-looking *metanduil* rod about the size of an infant's finger. Placing it against the band at Jaren's neck, he uttered a few more mumbles, incomprehensible this time, and then gave a triumphant, "Ha!" as a faint click sounded. The collar opened and Llaw removed it promptly.

Jaren breathed a sigh of relief.

Iselle, however, peered at Llaw through narrowed eyes. "Why do you have the key to a lock like that?"

"Oh. It was among the equipment the council provided with my assignment. I would suppose most of the senior people involved in looking for Jaren were given keys of this sort." He stopped, a concerned expression darkening his features as if he were considering something for the first time. He shrugged off the thought, apparently dismissing the issue. "Perhaps it was supplied to ensure that you weren't held like a captive in case someone more…zealous… came across you first."

Iselle did not look very convinced. "What were you supposed to do when you found Jaren?"

"The details were rather vague, but they want you brought in to be studied. To see what makes you special. That will be valuable information— and not only for the council. In fact, for you, it could be vital." He noted the deepening lines of disapproval creasing Iselle's youthful face. "Not to worry, my young friends, as long as I'm involved, nothing will happen to Jaren that I don't approve of. You have my word."

Jaren nodded. He could trust Ensin Llaw. He very likely would not be alive now had it not been for the man's earlier mentoring. Tossing a glance at Iselle, though, he doubted that she shared the sentiment.

• 8 •

Heading In

WHILE THE CHILL OF THE SEASON gathered in the lowlands as fall drew on, in the mountains the icy grip of winter had already taken hold. The dry, frigid air stung exposed skin and burned throats. A steady gale whipped away the vapour of their breaths and drove tiny shards of ice into the company like thousands of glass splinters.

Malhaena cursed as she tramped through the knee-deep snowdrifts, though the grey skies responded with their typical, indifferent silence.

"Tell the tracker to come to me," she called, uncertain whether or not the cold ice and stone of the mountain had simply devoured her words.

Soon enough though, a figure ahead wound its way back through the line of her companions, steadily becoming more discernible through the crystalline veil stirred by the cutting wind.

"Yes, my lady?" the Drisian offered through his ice-encrusted scarf as he fell in beside her, forced to labour along outside of the packed snow of their path.

"How long before we reach the Forge?" Her lips felt frost-thickened, and she had to carefully annunciate her words to properly voice them.

"A few hours, maybe more if the weather worsens. We should be there by nightfall at the latest, either way."

"We had better. I've lost enough people to this accursed country already."

"Yes, my lady."

Malhaena scoffed. "Well, back to your scouting, then. And pray you aren't wrong. I'm not feeling overly generous at the moment."

"Of course, my lady. May you walk in the Truth." With that, he scurried forward, weaving ahead through the others to resume his place on point.

Malhaena scowled at his back. The True One would have nothing to do with the success or failure of her expedition.

As distasteful as the present situation was, a fruitful search would result in a good deal of prestige for the Jade Talons. It was not every day that one uncovered a citadel lost to the centuries. Perhaps there would be artifacts, as well. Judging by the significance of the site, Malhaena would be surprised not to find some manner of ancient, magical tools. And if they weren't readily usable or identifiable by the Talons, the *Valir* would no doubt pay handsomely for them.

As they should, for sending me to this forsaken wasteland in the first place.

Her mind strayed to Aras. The prestige gained on this discovery might be needed to allay the *Valir's* disappointment in his apparent lack of results. It was disconcerting. Aras did not seem to be his old self lately. His grumblings at their duties on behalf of the *Valir* were...uncharacteristic.

As good as he was, perhaps he had become more of a liability than an asset. It was something she definitely needed to consider. That and the question of who would take his esteemed place as lead assassin for the Talons. Two candidates came to mind immediately, Sithas and Galda, but Malhaena was uncertain whether either would suffice. That was one of the reasons she brought them along.

Sithas was the more skilled of the two and by far the more cold-blooded. He was ruthless and did not share the same disdain for tasks that Aras had recently expressed. On the one hand, Sithas's ambition would prove a definite danger to Malhaena. On the other, she could count on him to be predictable. Sithas always did whatever benefited him most. It was a given. As cunning as he could be, it was his regularity that offered a counterbalance.

Galda was strong, both physically and mentally. However, he was less a thinker and invariably decided on the direct approach. It was nearly absurd that he had become an assassin at all, opting to use a great axe as his weapon of choice. Still, he was so large that it could be hidden easily enough until it came time to hew his target like he was felling a tree. The bonus was that Galda was loyal, also an uncommon trait among assassins. He was particularly smitten with Malhaena, so she need not worry where his allegiance lay. She doubted there was room in his mind for more than one central, driving thought anyway. That too, was the disadvantage. Any foe Galda faced could immediately begin devising plans to counter a direct assault. It was not entirely a credit to him that sheer strength of arms and will had seen him survive so far.

Malhaena hunkered down within the thick folds of her robes in a vain attempt to ward off the encroaching chill. Perhaps, she thought, it was time to seek elsewhere for Aras's successor. Bringing in an outside rival would not only mean that the individual would be starting from scratch within the Talons and have no pre-existing ties to anyone in the organization, but it would weaken the other clan.

"We've reached the Forge, Malhaena," Galda's low voice rumbled sometime later.

Malhaena grumbled to herself, cursing the frigid weather and the dulling effect it had on one's sense of mind. She realized the band had stopped ahead, where Galda was huddled with several others. He looked like a full-grown tree surrounded by saplings. She half-saw, half-felt Sithas's presence off to the side in the deepening shadows. She could hear the crunching of snow as the remainder of the group filed up behind her.

Malhaena nodded to Galda, smiling, though the gesture was not borne of any kindness she held for the giant assassin.

◆ ◆ ◆

"I've found us a way in—" Kalon announced as he burst through the door, then gathered himself on seeing Ensin Llaw. The shift in his posture was instant. Though he always carried himself with a dangerous edge, now Kalon's posture warned of deadly violence.

Jaren sprang from his chair. "It's all right, Kalon," he said. "This is Ensin Llaw, a friend of ours."

Though he relaxed his stance perceptibly, the greycloak remained stone-faced. His eyes strayed to Jaren's neck. "This may complicate things," he said simply. *No collar.*

"Not to worry, my good man," Llaw rose to greet the other. "I am used to undertakings of this kind. In fact, I've been on a few merry adventures with these two already."

"You're *Valir*," Kalon stated flatly.

"Yes, but I must admit, for some time I was removed from the grand scheme of things." Nodding to Jaren and Iselle, he continued, "It wasn't until these young ones arrived on my doorstep that I took up a more active role again."

"One of your obvious status must surely have received a summons to Neval Ketarra?"

Llaw chuckled. "Hardly. No, my talents were directed to the care of this young man, seeing as I had experience with him already." Llaw's lips became pinched. "The two of them have related how you came to meet. King Aldrain was right to have placed such trust in you."

The *Valir's* eyes sought his—pointedly—Kalon thought.

"What's the plan, then?" Iselle asked. At her question, each man broke from his silent inspection of the other.

"I arranged for the two of you to be my prisoners, as Iselle suggested, and to be let in through a side door. Though that arrangement was made based on three people. Adding a fourth—and a *Valir*, no less—will very likely mean coming up with a new plan."

Kalon's tone did not disguise his displeasure.

"If it was only you that needed entry," Llaw said, "would the arrangement hold?"

"Very likely, yes," Kalon shrugged, "but I have no magic of use in freeing the king. From what I've gathered, magic will be necessary. A good deal of it. Going in by myself would accomplish little."

Jaren spoke, "A few months ago at his tower, Llaw cloaked us with invisibility so we could escape the forces of the Witch."

Kalon cocked his head and regarded the *Valir* with an apparent new respect.

Llaw smiled at Jaren and Iselle. "Well, my young friends, are you ready for another disappearing act?"

◆ ◆ ◆

Fragments of rock and ice pelted Malhaena as the boulder slammed into the cliff wall not ten paces away. Cursing, she remained in her crouch, daggers in hand. What good they would do against their current foes, she didn't know, but she felt better wielding them.

"Keep going," she hissed over her shoulder, willing the others to move faster in their retreat.

A flash and resounding roar from ahead signalled that the *Valir* yet lived. Malhaena cursed again. She wished he *was* dead for bringing such destruction down on them. In fact, if he somehow managed to escape his fate and rejoin the group, she vowed to kill him.

But first, she had to survive.

A high-pitched whistle and a sense of danger reached her, and she instinctively dropped to the rough stone beneath her feet.

A dark blur sailed past, mere hand spans above her prone form, followed by another explosion of rock and ice. It was accompanied by the screams of several men unlucky enough to be caught by the hurled stone.

Malhaena sheathed her daggers and, on all fours, scrabbled backwards through the rubble and fallen men. At least their pursuers had given up following and were content merely to lob boulders at the fleeing party. It would have been much more comforting had they not been able to loft the great rocks so far or accurately. But one could not ask for everything.

Once she cleared the debris field, Malhaena resumed her crouch and, keeping an eye to the danger, continued her retreat. She could sense that several of the group were still on their feet behind her. She no longer had to encourage them to hurry, either.

Minutes stretched on without any further assaults from above, and she began to relax more with each cramped stride. A moment later she turned and made her withdrawal more dignified.

Several forms became visible in the darkness ahead. She could tell at once that Galda was among them. That, or they huddled around a large statue. As she approached, Sithas emerged from the shadows as well. Other than the three of them, a full third of the apprentice Talons and mercenaries had not made it to safety.

"Settle in for the night," she instructed. "Sithas, keep the first watch."

No sooner had the words left her lips than he melted away once more.

"Malhaena, what devilry was that?" Galda wondered, eyes wide in alarm.

He was not afraid, she knew, but at the same time he did have a superstitious side.

"Sentinels of some sort, I expect. Made to guard the entrance to the passages beneath the Forge."

"Do you think the *Valir* is dead?"

"I caught one last glimpse of his summoning just before the final boulder hit," she began, with no hint of sympathy. "If he hasn't caught up with us by now, though, I'm certain he's lost. Just as well. Idiocy of that nature is inexcusable."

"We had orders to go inside once we found the gateway," the giant man shrugged.

"If I reached into a hole without first checking to see if a wolverine lived inside, I'd deserve what I got as well," Malhaena frowned. "He knew those statues posed a danger, but he went ahead without conferring with us. At least now we know what we deal with. Now we can make proper plans to find our way in and fulfill the rest of the mission."

The clicking of rocks up the canyon brought her about in a flash to face the darkness. "Sithas!" Malhaena called harshly. He must have been on the other side of their encampment not to intercept this newcomer.

She scanned the blackness. Then, perceiving movement, she let fly several throwing knives in a blur of limbs and steel. A muffled cry sounded and after that, a thump.

Less than a moment passed before Sithas's voice called out, "It's the *Valir.* Apparently he wasn't dead, after all." His voice carried no more sympathy than had Malhaena's. "He is now."

Malhaena wore an approving expression.

Her hand moved to the *metanduil* disc suspended by a length of leather cord about her neck. The warming metal indicated that her presence was requested. Privately.

"Get rid of him," she ordered the apprentices. "Wait for me here—I'll be back shortly." She raised her voice. "And Sithas, please, no more unexpected company." With that, she disappeared into the shadowed reaches of the canyon.

• 9 •

Deceptions and Guises

JOSELLE QUICKENED HER PACE AS SHE PASSED row upon row of dun-coloured, canvas-and-hide tents. Rancid smoke curled from holes in the tent-peaks, the result of the Jhud'Haian practice of using dung as fuel. The smell here was no better than the stables she had just left. *No wonder these Jhud'Hai are feared warriors, when their stench is enough to drive an enemy away!* Joselle wondered if a little summoning might ease her discomfort, so she focused on clear, scent-free air and drew on the magic. Almost immediately, the putrid aroma of the nomads and their filth left her nostrils. She smiled in triumph.

Rhianain had noticed and complimented Joselle on the rapid development of her skills. Her transformation at the Mother's hands was a gift, indeed, whether the wretch Morgaine would admit it or not. One day soon, Joselle would make her. She would enjoy doing so; Morgaine, not nearly so much.

She smiled wickedly, a pale-skinned silhouette of death traversing the camp.

The Mother should just allow me to kill Morgaine and be done with her. Surely, Joselle and the Mother were more than a match for Morgaine's cursed younger brother, *An'Valir* or not. There was no need to attempt the forced reconcile of her errant sister in the magic in order to face Jaren, united again. *Perhaps I'm up to the challenge myself.* The thought of seeing Morgaine's face should she learn of Jaren's death was compelling. After all, her reaction at the news of her parents' demise had been a delight.

Joselle approached the Mother's tent and, frowning, eyed the two hulking Jhud'Haian guards stationed to either side of the entrance. They wore the typical pointed iron caps and fur-lined, animal skin clothing of their people. Though the Jhud'Haian wastelands regularly suffered chilling temperatures at night, it was a mystery to Joselle how these people could wear such clothing during their hot, dry days. Even here, further east and in the autumn, such nonsensical dress was dumbfounding. The guards paid her critical stares little mind, for the expression was as common as her coming and going. She assumed her usual look of haughty indifference and, sweeping back the skin draped across the opening, stepped inside.

"Ah, my daughter," Rhianain greeted with a wan smile. "I expected you earlier." The Warwitch gestured to a smaller chair near to hers. "Sit and tell me of your visit."

"Yes, Mother," Joselle nodded in compliance as she tried not to bristle at the criticism.

Rhianain's tent was spacious. Spread about the center of the floor were a number of thick, animal-fur rugs, on top of which were her throne, another several chairs and a rectangular, gilded table. A red and black, scroll-worked wooden screen at the back of the tent hid most of a great, canopied bed.

Joselle kept the subservient set to her features in place, fighting down a twinge of jealousy as she surveyed the relatively opulent quarters. *The Mother shares everything with you, especially the most important gift of all: the magic.*

"I went to the home of the Haldannons as you requested, Mother. As you predicted, Morgaine came to me there."

"And what of her response? Does she still spurn us?"

Joselle glared down at the carpet beneath her feet, her face flushed. "Yes, Mother. She did not accept your offer of forgiveness." Her eyes lifted to meet Rhianain's. "She does not know her place!"

"It is as I thought, though troubling. Such ingratitude for what I have provided.... Still, we can use this to our advantage, daughter." Rhianain smiled, as warm an expression as she could manage with *metanduil* fused into half the flesh of her face. "Do not trouble yourself over it, child. She will either accept the truth of it and join us, or be destroyed. Much like her dear brother."

Joselle's eyes found the Mother's. "You have given him the journal, then?"

"Yes, dear one. From it, he will learn of the deception perpetrated by the *Valir* for so many years. And, predictable as he has shown himself to be, he will confront them." Again, the Warwitch smiled, this time making no attempt to soften the look. "And we will be there to pick up the pieces that remain."

"What if Morgaine does not come to help him?"

"Then we will deal with her separately. But, like her brother, the girl is predictable. Human frailty is what links them. Their ideals and commitment to each other make them weak. We will use it to destroy them."

Joselle nodded obediently, still fuming over the thought of her once-sister.

Rhianain, apparently sensing her disquiet, placed a hand over Joselle's. "All in due time, my daughter. You will have your opportunity."

"But, wouldn't it be better to take care of her first? She could fail you again at a critical time."

"I have faith in you, dear one. You will be more than a match for her if that time comes—should she stand with her brother or face us on her own. Until the truth is known, however, we've much to do." Rhianain tapped Joselle's hand lightly, then clasped it. "These smelly Jhud'Hai need better equipment, wouldn't you say?"

Joselle laughed along though she could not banish the frustrating image of Morgaine entirely from her mind.

✦ ✦ ✦

Aras—again disguised as Kalon—approached the guard casually, as arranged. Barely acknowledging his presence, the other man stepped aside. As he passed, Aras pressed several crowns into the fellow's palm with a quick sleight of hand. Just as quickly, he was inside the entrance, his eyes adjusting immediately to the dimness. He stepped to the side, propping the door open with his foot for the prearranged five-count: just long enough for the *Valir* and the youths to slip in behind him, but hopefully not so long as to alarm the guard.

After the door swung to once more, Aras heard the hushed confirmation of the others' presence. He made his way deeper into the palace, using the mental map he had made from a copy of sketches also procured from the door guard. There were few about in the halls this mid-morning; the occasional maid or butler crossed Aras's path but paid him little mind. During the reign of Machim Aesirian, puppet of Count Rondul Pacek, the count's estate had become the *de facto* palace grounds, at least temporarily. His servants were well versed in the realities of working for one such as him, Aras had gleaned from his investigation. That meant the help steered clear of anything or anyone not directly related to their tasks—it was safer that way.

As Aras descended the staircase to the basement level, he felt the rise in humidity carried on the dank air. The plush carpeting of the main floor had alternated with checkered tiles or hardwood and now switched to rougher flagstone. Tapestries hung at intervals to ward off the chill. *Good,* Aras thought, *they will help to deaden the noise the others are making*. Not that they were careless or overly loud, but one trained as Aras could hear them plainly. If it served to do nothing more than soothe his own annoyance, so much the better.

Glancing about to ensure the corridors were empty, Aras slipped into a side chamber. It was a small room filled with crates and barrels. A sour smell assaulted his nostrils and became stronger as he eased the door closed.

Three figures materialized before him, seemingly painted into place before his eyes, their appearance vivid in contrast to the drab interior of the room.

"Well done, my good fellow," Llaw acknowledged in hushed tones. "How far to the dungeon holding Aldrain?"

Aras appeared unmoved by the older man's praise. "Just down the corridor, through the doors, and at the end of the cell wing. I'll have to scout out the location of the hidden passage you mentioned. Are you sure it exists?"

"Aldrain told me of it when we first met at my tower. He said the count had used it to bring mercenaries into the inner city against him. I have no reason to doubt Aldrain's recollection."

"Very well," Aras acknowledged. His eyes took in all three companions. "While you attend to the king, I'll find the passage. Remain there unless forced to do otherwise. Either way, I'll find you and we'll make our way out." He nodded, and was gone.

"All right, young ones, are you ready?" Llaw asked.

"Just a moment, *Valir* Llaw," Iselle said. "Don't you think that Kalon would know where the secret passages are? You know—if he's one of Aldrain's men?"

"I suppose it's possible. But he said he's been posted out of the city looking for you for some time."

"But wouldn't he pretend to be working for Count Pacek? He should have been inside the palace at least a few times before now, and known in general of the hidden ways. He is a spy of sorts, isn't he?"

"Iselle, you're over-thinking this," Jaren observed.

"I just don't like the feeling I have," she shook her head. "It feels…it feels like the last time I was tricked into believing someone."

"If he isn't who he says he is," Llaw added, "Aldrain will be able to tell us. He won't fool his own master."

"I guess." Iselle grimaced. "I still don't like it though."

"Well, if we're wrong, you can say *I told you so*," Jaren chuckled.

"That's little comfort, knowing what happened before. It's not a game, Jaren."

"Wow. That coming from you, I may start to worry." He gave Iselle a playful shove.

"Do not fret, young ones," Llaw promised, "I'll be watching him, too. If he is not what he appears, we shall discover the truth of it."

Iselle huffed, pushing Jaren back. "Well, let's go then."

Llaw peered out of the chamber, then signalled that the way was clear.

The *Valir* picked his way forward; Jaren and Iselle followed closely behind.

They reached the stout cellblock door: a great, steel-reinforced wooden portal with a square cut into the upper third, the latter secured with thick metal bars. Again, Llaw verified that no one occupied the corridor beyond, then grasped the latch. It was fortunate that the passage was empty, as the door produced a high-pitched squeal as it swung open. The group froze for a moment, ears straining for any sign that they had been discovered. Hearing nothing, they proceeded into the hallway.

Several sputtering oil lamps, located at intervals along the corridor, were the only source of light. They cast the scene in dim, orange hues. Their footfalls echoed faintly along the rough stone of the dungeon floor until the trio reached the passageway's termination. A final, stout door, a miniature version of the first, stood closed before them.

Llaw regarded them sombrely. In a hushed voice, he called softly through the barred opening to the darkness within.

There was no reply.

"King Aldrain, can you hear me?"

Again, only silence answered.

• 10 •

Feats of Desperation

LLAW LIFTED THE BAR AND PUSHED the cell door open. A ribbon of pale light from the corridor swept into the room, falling upon the head and shoulders of a man. His head drooped forward and his blonde hair hung in dirty tangles, veiling his features.

For a moment, the three would-be rescuers simply stared. Then he stirred.

"Who's there?" croaked a weak voice. "Come to finish me off, Pacek? Or do you wish for more of your sport?" Unsteadily, the head rose to reveal a gaunt, lined face, covered in grime. Deep blue eyes regarded them without the glimmer of recognition.

"King Aldrain," the *Valir* said, "it's me, Ensin Llaw. I've come with Jaren and Iselle. We're here to help."

The man's expression changed first to puzzlement, then suspicion. "How do I know this is no figment of my imagination? Another trial of Pacek's, perhaps." He uttered a hollow laugh without mirth. His head dropped forward once more.

Llaw and the youths stepped forward, and for the first time, they regarded the full measure of Aldrain's condition. They gasped as one. Iselle rushed to Aldrain's side, embracing him.

"What have they done to you?" she lamented. "I'm sorry, King Aldrain… I'm sorry I wasn't more alert. If only I could have seen that Turan was lying the whole time… I could have—I'm so sorry!"

Jaren put his hands on her shoulders in a vain attempt to comfort her. He looked aside at Llaw. "How do we help him out of *this*?"

The *Valir* had come forward, too, and began to study the blocks of cool metal that encased Aldrain's arms. He shook his head in disbelief, muttering to himself. "*Metanduil*…but he survived? True One's grace…"

"*Valir* Llaw," Jaren said again. "What are we going to do?"

Llaw returned a hopeless stare. "I have absolutely no idea. I've never seen anything like this. I'm not sure there is anything we *can* do for him."

Hearing this, Iselle hugged the king more tightly, moaning in her grief.

"No," Jaren declared. "I won't let this be the end for him. I have to do something."

Llaw made a hopeless gesture toward the block nearest him. "What could you do, Jaren? Where would you begin?"

"No offense, *Valir* Llaw, but I've done a good deal of self-teaching in your absence. I think...if I take a good look something will come to mind. There is magic at work here. I can do something. I *will*." He patted his friend's shoulder. "Iselle, you have to let go of Aldrain for a moment. Please."

Though Iselle hesitated, she withdrew several paces from the stricken king, arms crossed against some apparent chill only she perceived.

Jaren took Iselle's place before Aldrain. Placing a hand on both of the other's shoulders, he began to center himself. The magic washed over him like a cool wave, a welcome sensation after its recent obstruction. The sensation turned to one of warmth, like the comforting embrace experienced as one succumbs to a pleasant sleep, only Jaren's senses were awakened.

His vision switched to the now-familiar silver hues of the magic-enhanced sight, and the cell became clearly defined in its peculiar cast. Even upon closing his eyes, Jaren still perceived everything around him in perfect detail. Concentrating further, he reached down into the source of the energy, and sent it into Aldrain, seeking, searching.

Were he not enveloped within the folds of the magic's serenity, he would have cried out at what he found. Jaren witnessed unbelievable pain and suffering, anguish and despair. Though the process was some time past, the raw agony that emanated from Aldrain's imprisoned limbs remained, nearly unbearable. Almost as devastating, Jaren found that Aldrain had all but given up hope. Finally left alone and without the need or distraction of decision-making, the king had succumbed to a mind-numbing depression. He had lost everything over the past several months: his family, home, and best friend. Now, the entire kingdom was lost to him and a shroud of black despair engulfed the king.

Hold on, King Aldrain. Jaren willed his thoughts to touch the stricken man. *I will help you. I know you are suffering, but I'll find a way to get you out of this."*

Who visits me now? Aldrain's mind wondered. *Father, is that you again?*

No, King Aldrain. It's Jaren Haldannon. I've come to help you.

Jaren...the farm boy? I believed you lost to the Witch.

I prevailed, King Aldrain. Now I'm here with Iselle and Valir Llaw to aid you.

It's too late for that, Jaren. It would be better for you to leave this place. It is cursed, as I am now.

I won't give up on you, King Aldrain. You must not give up hope!

The king's shoulders shook with silent laughter. *Hope? What hope is left me? The True One has abandoned Carathon. You would be wise to do the same. All is lost….*

Jaren left the king to his despair for the moment, fearing nothing that he could say would change the other's mind. The only way to bring him back, it seemed, was to show him that help had arrived.

He felt resistance to his seeking. Aldrain's mind warded itself from his touch, the dark hopelessness pushing Jaren away. It was to be expected, he reasoned, after the ordeals the king had experienced. Still, Jaren sought deeper, searching for the magic that was the sole reason Aldrain yet lived. He could sense it was here, somewhere, but it hid from him, as if crafted to elude such efforts.

Finally, Jaren succeeded in locating the twisting bands of magic that pulsed through Aldrain's *metanduil*-encased limbs. They entwined about his very bones, securing the sustaining energy to him. Jaren seized hold of the magic strands, and pulled ever so slightly. Instantly, he felt Aldrain's body tense, and the king's spine arched in agony. He threw back his head and wailed in anguish.

Jaren released the coils and studied them anew, searching for a way to undo their hold without doing further harm.

If such a thing was possible.

"Someone comes," Llaw announced, glancing at Jaren and then Iselle. "Can he hear us when he's summoning?"

"I think so," Iselle said, "but I doubt he'll answer. He has to focus on being centered, whatever that means."

"Well then, my dear, we'll have to keep whoever this is occupied until Jaren is finished."

Iselle nodded grimly. "Let's just hope he doesn't take his time as usual." She drew forth a short bow and nocked an arrow.

A clamour grew down the passageway. Shouts of alarm rose, and the sound of running, booted feet carried to them. The glow of torches appeared in the far doorway, dancing along the walls and casting maddened shadows about the tiny cell.

Silhouetted shapes rushed toward them down the narrow cell corridor.

Llaw erected a curved, blue shield of energy before them. A series of short bursts erupted across the barrier. Iselle saw that they were crossbow bolts as they fell harmlessly to the floor, their tips melted or bent from the impact.

She raised her bow and fired, hoping that her arrow would find its way through the shield. The resulting yelp of pain reassured her. She readied another and took aim at the dark figures that were nearly upon them.

Llaw moved the barrier to block the doorway, sealing their attackers outside.

Iselle released another arrow and another cry resulted. More men gathered before the barrier, those with the thickest and strongest armour pushing to the fore.

Iselle's third and fourth arrows splintered and fell away harmlessly from links of mail or plates of steel. Soldiers continued to arrive, bolstering the ranks of the assailants. Iselle peered back at Jaren. He was still fully engrossed with the king.

Hurry up, Jaren, or we'll never get out of here!

◆ ◆ ◆

Jaren cursed silently, the resulting break in concentration reverberating through his grip on the magic.

It seemed there was no way to remove the metal. The king was doomed.

Even worse, Jaren was well aware of the growing danger. He had no fear that Llaw and Iselle could hold out against common soldiers, but surely Pacek had *Valir* in his service. Their presence might tip the balance.

Jaren willed himself once more to concentrate on his link to Aldrain. *Valir* had done this to Aldrain through magic. They had imprisoned him with *metanduil*—a process meant not only to torture the king but to keep him alive throughout. That meant the magic-metal was a part of him now. *Like the Warwitch…and Morgaine.* Jaren shuddered. It was the only thing that seemed to make sense, the only option that presented itself.

And time was running out.

Once more, he reached forth with his own magic, taking a firm hold of King Aldrain's ethereal bonds. Again, he felt the king tensing, bracing himself for more excruciating pain. But instead of attempting to separate Aldrain from the flows, he worked to combine them more closely, to heal and mend. Jaren was not at all sure of the result, but he felt there was no other choice.

He directed the healing energies into the stricken king, sensing the other's relief, feeling him finally drop his guard against Jaren's efforts. Aldrain relaxed, likely comforted for the first time in a long while.

Jaren continued to feed streams of magic into Aldrain's limbs. Magic to unite, to strengthen. Magic to revitalize and liberate. The blocks of *metanduil* began to glow. Softly though at first, the bluish illumination grew in intensity until he could sense that the soldiers gathered about the entrance had to shield their eyes from its brilliance.

Aldrain fell forward, his limbs freed from their entrapment but still glowing dimly with magical essence. As the light slowly faded, his arms appeared as they had been. Except they looked to be formed entirely of *metanduil*.

"Iselle, help me with the king," Jaren called.

She shook her head, clearing the wonder from her eyes. "What did you do?"

"The only thing I could do. There's no time now. Just help me get him up and *Valir* Llaw can lead us out of here."

"Well done, my lad! I just wish I could have had a better look."

"I'll tell you all about it later."

Iselle stowed her short bow and attended to the half-conscious king. She and Jaren each lowered themselves and hoisted an arm across their shoulders. Aldrain's legs wobbled, but he assisted them as best he could in his exhausted, delirious state.

"We're ready," Jaren said.

"I'll get our welcoming committee to move for us," the other replied. The *Valir* then gestured toward the floor beneath the soldiers. It instantly burst into flames. The men began to panic, jumping about at first, then turning to sprint back down the corridor in retreat, boots and various other pieces of clothing scorched and smoking. One or two were still alight, and they beat frantically at themselves while attempting to keep up with their fleeing comrades.

Llaw led the way with his barrier. Jaren and Iselle struggled after, supporting the king.

They reached the entrance to the cellblock. Jaren had just passed through when a crossbow bolt buried itself into the frame beside him with a loud *thunk*.

"*Valir* Llaw!" Jaren called out. "Magic bolts!" He could not renew his grip on the magic to aid the *Valir* without stopping to put the king down. And they could not stop.

Instantly, another shield appeared just behind Llaw's first. "Keep going, Jaren. I have it," Llaw's voice was calm, measured.

A series of bolts lanced toward them only to be thwarted in their paths by the newest barrier. The missiles burst into a number of tiny, white explosions.

The knot of soldiers, having regained their wits and renewed the attack, gave ground as Jaren's trio advanced. From behind them came a sudden flash, and Llaw's shield shivered with the impact of a bolt of red fire.

"*Valir!*" Jaren yelled.

"I am aware of that, thank-you," Llaw replied. "My shields will hold for now. But we must find Kalon." His forehead creased as he focused past the milling warriors.

Several flashes appeared behind the soldiers and in return a series of explosions hammered Llaw's barrier.

A magical barrier identical to Llaw's flared up opposite his. After a few steps, the shields met and their progress halted. Multicoloured sparks flew from the point of contact between the round, ethereal walls and an electric crackling sounded, one that seemed to penetrate the very stone of the passage walls. It was unnerving, making all who heard it cringe.

Llaw cast his gaze about as if searching for options, offering a scowl that deepened by the second. "Where is that greycloak, by the Truth?"

His attention drew elsewhere and his eyes narrowed. "Jaren, be alert."

Jaren had already observed the focus of the *Valir*'s attention. He considered how to deal with the thin shaft of light that pressed down onto Llaw's spheres, pushing them inward. The stalactite of energy forced downward slowly.

"What's that, now?" Iselle demanded.

"They are trying to destroy the barriers!" Llaw growled.

"Can they do that?" Iselle gasped.

"They've received more help!" The *Valir* called back. "Jaren, don't let that flow reach the floor!"

In response, Jaren tried to connect with the magic once more, to send it against the probing finger of energy. It was impossible to re-establish his center with the king's weight still bearing down on his shoulders but, since they had stopped moving, letting Aldrain down did not matter. He and Iselle lowered the limp form. Jaren's magic flared to life and he felt the contact between the intruding magic and his own as he sent it outward. He sensed more than heard the crackling and snapping of energy as the two sources opposed one another.

"I hate to point out the obvious," Iselle moaned, "but we seem to be trapped. Didn't any of this occur to you or Kalon when you made the plans?"

"We didn't count on being so long with the king," Llaw replied. "No one could have foreseen his condition. We need to adjust."

"Well, we're doing a great job of it so far."

The electric squelching grew louder and more invasive, unnerving even Jaren and Llaw to the point that their concentration broke for an instant. Jaren felt his defense give way and the ethereal finger pressed down further.

"Can they cut you off?" Iselle asked again, her voice edged with panic.

"If they receive enough help, yes. And that's entirely possible with the time we've spent here already!"

A shout of pain rang out from the ranks of the enemy; the probing energy dissipated and the white shield barring their way vanished. Several other shrieks and yelps followed and the soldiers began to waver, unsure which way to face: the group they were struggling against or the unknown assault from behind them.

Llaw threw his right hand forward, fist clenched, and the knot of soldiers fell back as if swept by a great current. Only Jaren saw the flow of energy rushing outward like the ripples of a stone cast into a pond.

"I think Kalon has found us," Llaw shouted. "Follow me quickly!"

Jaren and Iselle rushed after him as best they could, the king's feet half-dragging, half-stumbling in an attempt to assist them. *At least Aldrain is gaining back some of his sense,* Jaren thought. *Hopefully he recovers soon!* Jaren was also aware that the *Valir* kept his shield intact while on the run. At a more opportune time, he would have to ask Llaw how he managed it.

"What kept you?" Kalon hissed as they drew up, his hands flashing for the briefest of instants as he sheathed his blades.

Jaren blinked and wondered if the warrior had been standing empty-handed all along. The still forms littering the ground at his feet dispelled the idea. A handful among them wore *Valir's* robes as dark red as the life blood that seeped from them. *He's as fast as Ver was,* Jaren thought in awe.

"It was rather complicated," Llaw responded. "Have you found the passage?"

Kalon was already moving. "This way!" he called back over his shoulder.

"Kalon..." Aldrain mumbled, staring at the retreating figure. Seeing the loyal greycloak seemed to provide a measure of strength to the king and he stumbled forward without support.

Jaren and Iselle followed closely behind, just in case Aldrain faltered.

Kalon stopped at a passage intersection, allowing the others to gain some ground, then darted off to the left swiftly once more. "Just down here," came the echo of his voice.

Part of the wall beside them burst into angry splinters of stone, showering the group with fragments of rock and mortar.

The king lurched to a stop and turned, throwing up his arms to shield his face. Jaren and Iselle crouched low and whirled about. Llaw wheeled and began chanting in low tones, his arms moving as he summoned.

Aldrain's reaction saved his life. Another bolt of red energy slammed into his raised arms, dispersing harmlessly on contact. The king stumbled backward, reacting instinctively at first. His limbs appeared simply to absorb the energy. He turned his palms inward, staring wide-eyed at them, as if noticing their appearance for the first time.

Fire energy burst from the passage the group had just fled, silhouetting a group of cloaked figures on their heels.

The lance of orange light broke Aldrain's reverie. He took a tentative step forward and raised his left arm, palm outward. The searing bolt curved into his hand, flared brightly, then dissipated. A tiny glint of determination kindled in Aldrain's eyes, the first real emotion Jaren had seen in him since their arrival.

· 11 ·

From Flight to Fighting

"J AREN. ISELLE. GET BEHIND ME. Follow Kalon. Llaw—keep them safe. I'll be right behind you." Though ragged, his voice had regained a good measure of its habitual iron. He shuffled slowly backward, arms held at the ready.

Jaren and Iselle did as he asked, mouths agape. Llaw moved to head down the passage after Kalon, though he was clearly astounded as well.

They proceeded as quickly as they could, though the trio were careful not to let Aldrain get too far behind. He was still bone-weary and exhausted, no matter the new ability he had discovered. Should he fall, Jaren and the others wanted to be close enough to support him once again. Now and then, explosions of light and colour erupted behind them, but no magic was able to penetrate Aldrain's surprising defense.

A shadow separated from the wall ahead, startling them, but it was Kalon. "I didn't realize you'd come for the scenic tour," he grumbled.

"We can't go too fast, or King Aldrain won't be able to keep up," Jaren replied. "Besides, I don't think anything will get by him, now."

Kalon's expression turned from annoyance to puzzlement. Then he shrugged. "This is the entrance to the hidden tunnel. Quickly now, get—"

A crossbow bolt from further down the passage struck Kalon on the shoulder. While it glanced off his armour, it had force enough to half-spin the greycloak about.

Immediately, Jaren shot his hand in the direction of both the warrior and the darkness beyond.

Kalon had just managed to crouch and slide over to the wall when another bolt shattered into blue sparks against Jaren's shield. It would have struck Kalon's upper body. Several others smashed into the barrier in quick succession, all destined for the same area.

Kalon, eyes shining fiercely, turned his head to nod at Jaren. "Inside now, quickly. We can lock the door from the inside—and even knowing generally where we've gone, they'll not have the skill to find it so soon, much less open it again."

"Maybe they'll think we just disappeared," Iselle said.

"If we're lucky, perhaps." Kalon did not sound convinced.

Aldrain was the last to enter, backing into the narrow corridor. He continued a few paces, then sank to his knees against the wall, head in his hands.

Kalon pressed a series of points on the wall and the sound of grating stone filled their ears. It continued to reverberate for a moment, then stopped abruptly with a crash and a series of metallic-sounding clicks.

The greycloak moved to Aldrain, placing a hand on his king's shoulder. "Your Majesty, we can rest for only a moment. I'll scout on ahead and wait for you." He turned to the others. "Don't be overlong." As he turned to head off, his eyes fell on Jaren once more.

Kalon's look was surprising, seeing as Jaren had just saved the man's life. Even with the briefest of glimpses through Llaw's dim, summoned lighting, Jaren could make it out. He was angry.

"*Valir* Llaw," Aldrain began in a determined tone as he rose to his feet more steadily than before. "Following our escape, what does your plan entail?"

"We arranged to have you delivered from the city to a safehold nearby. We thought it best to leave the remainder of the designs to you. I'm sure you'll want to rally as many of those still loyal to your side as possible. Hopefully, we can help with that."

"Agreed," the king nodded. "Kalon and others will still have connections to the greycloak network, so sending word should not be too difficult. Unless, of course, Pacek has purged them all from his service." Aldrain sighed wearily, though to Jaren he looked to be continuing his physical recovery. "A long delay will surely allow the traitor to bolster his position. I fear a drawn out and costly campaign would push the kingdom over the brink. Even now, it will take much to undo the harm that has befallen us."

"We may only offer our best efforts, though that is often little comfort in troubled times," Llaw said. "Perhaps the True One will provide assistance."

"Do not speak of the True One's blessings. None have come for some time. None will come now. We must depend on ourselves in this."

Jaren blinked, and looked sidelong at Iselle. She too, appeared surprised at the king's words.

"The True One sent Ver to help us and to protect me," Jaren said. "Please, King Aldrain, do not give up hope."

"No young one, I do not give up hope for Carathon. Yet I will not wait for aid that may or may not arrive. I am glad that the True One sees fit to watch over you but I despair that those same eyes overlook the Carathonai. And their king." He nodded gravely. "We should go."

Llaw's enchanted illumination, though pale, lit the passage ahead for a surprising distance. As they made their way, rough stone walls and an uneven dirt floor slid past, all revealed dimly amid dancing shadows. After some moments, the figure of Kalon appeared in the distance, hurrying toward them.

"Your Majesty," he called in a hoarse whisper as he drew near, "there is a large company of men approaching from the tunnel exit. They will be upon us in moments."

"How many?" Llaw asked. "Do they have *Valir* with them?"

"At least two dozen, perhaps more. I do not know about *Valir*. I did not see any, but I only glimpsed them before I had to fall back."

The king's jaw clenched. "*Valir* Llaw, can you cloak us with your summoned invisibility?"

"I'm not sure there's enough time, but I'll try."

"Kalon, go on ahead and signal us when the company is here—"

A shout from the distance reached the group. Jaren thought he could just make out a pinpoint of yellow light far down the corridor.

Aldrain closed his eyes and exhaled deeply, chin lifted. In a blur, he struck out an arm with a howl of rage, slamming his fist into the rough-hewn wall. Instead of injuring his fist, though, the blow carried on several inches into the solid rock, the impact sending stone fragments flying. The king gasped in disbelief, his anger fading. He retracted his fist, first examining it before looking at the small crater he'd punched into the wall.

"Get behind us," Aldrain ordered, his wits apparently recovered. He nodded to Jaren, Iselle and Llaw. "Protect yourselves first, then worry about the enemy if you must. Kalon and I will try to hold them off. Perhaps we'll finally have some good fortune and be able to force our way through."

The torchlight ahead brightened as the source drew nearer, then it stopped its advance.

"Make way, in the name of the king!" Came the echoing challenge.

"Which king do you serve?" Aldrain called out in answer.

"The true and rightful King of Carathon, Aldrain Draegondor! Stand down and identify yourselves!"

"Then come forward and pledge your allegiance. Lower your weapons and come." Aldrain then whispered to Kalon over his shoulder, "Be prepared to strike if they deceive us."

Kalon acknowledged and stepped before Aldrain.

They could hear shuffling as some muted whispers reached their ears, though none were comprehensible.

"Your Majesty?" questioned the voice.

"You have been ordered to come forward. To whom do I speak?"

"Captain Boltun, Sire." There was a brief pause. "I'm coming to you."

The sound of the man's footsteps preceded his arrival. A middle-aged man in plate and mail armour stepped forward. His face was angular and lean and his head close-shaved. Once the captain recognized that his king truly stood before him, he immediately knelt and offered a salute. "King Aldrain—Truth be praised—we thought you dead!"

"Pacek spared no attempts to bring that about, but I live. Stand Captain, and tell me: how is it that you are here? How many are with you?"

"When I heard that Kalon had returned to the city and was attempting to secure a way into the palace, I assumed that meant there was some hope." He nodded to Kalon, who returned the gesture. "I began immediately to round up all the men I could. It was difficult, seeing as Pacek disbanded many of the units and broke up the greycloaks. Still, they did not forget who they are, or to whom they owe allegiance."

"Well done Captain. You will be rewarded for your honour and foresight. What of your numbers, then?"

"We have several hundred regulars inside the city proper who are ready to throw off the yoke of Pacek's puppet king, and a score of greycloaks are lying in wait in the upper levels of the palace. I have nearly two dozen men with me. Lieutenant Aldar is mustering more out in the countryside. I should think you'll have several thousand in a few days' time."

Aldrain paused, apparently pondering the report. When his eyes lifted once more, the small glimmer had flared to a fierce light. "We'd best tell them to polish their ceremonial armour, because they'll be too late to help us retake the palace. Captain, have your regulars alerted to await my signal and gather your greycloaks at once."

"If I might ask, King Aldrain," Llaw interjected, "do you think it wise to confront Pacek in his power base under your…present circumstances?

Wouldn't it be wiser to gather your forces, then attack in strength after you have a better understanding of your own condition?

"Master Llaw, while I do appreciate your opinion, I am not prepared to let Pacek reinforce himself. With two hundred soldiers and nearly fifty greycloaks, I can retake my throne now." He glanced down at his *metanduil* limbs. "I feel fine—better with each passing moment. Strong, even."

"But—"

"It is decided, *Valir* Llaw." Aldrain fixed him with a hard stare. "I will understand if you do not wish to participate. If that is the case, I would suggest you escort Jaren and Iselle to a safe place until the fighting is done. I'll have one of my men see to it."

"I want to help," Iselle blurted, stepping before the king. "I wasn't able to before, so I'm not going to miss out on this chance."

"I don't think that's a very good idea, young lady," Aldrain frowned.

"I'll help *Valir* Llaw protect her," Jaren vowed. "She'll be safe. Besides, you don't seem to have much in the way of magical aid besides us."

The king pondered the idea for a moment. "I suppose you are right. I do need as much of an advantage as I can get. You may help if you wish." Aldrain turned to Llaw and Kalon. "I charge the two of you with the safety of our young friends. Do what you can to shield them from peril, or you will answer to me." Aldrain nodded to both in turn.

"*Valir* Llaw, I have one further task for you. We will head back through the door to the palace basement. I need you to seal it off. I want to take no chances that Pacek will escape me again."

"But, Your Majesty," Llaw objected, "that will prevent us from fleeing as well, should the need arise."

"We have the upper hand," Aldrain said. "We'll not be stopped."

The king wheeled to address his men and cried out, "Now then, lads— let's win the day!"

◆ ◆ ◆

The few remnants of Pacek's men combing the basement were quickly dispatched by the king's bolstered group. They took care to secure the upper exit, ensuring that news of their activity did not find a way out of the lower levels. Aldrain then led them up into the palace proper, once Ensin Llaw had sealed off the escape tunnel.

The king's plan was to catch Pacek, Machim and several other key nobles in the throne room and keep them there until the main force of regulars arrived. That way, they could get no orders or warning out to the barracks and city watch. Aldrain received word that a number of greycloaks had already answered the covert directive, taking up positions at the rear entrance to the throne room and several other strategic posts.

"I'll leave both of you here," Aldrain said to Jaren and Iselle, "with Master Llaw, Kalon, and the soldiers guarding the doors. You will be safe enough outside the room, out of direct conflict."

The king turned to the two guardians. "Keep them secure. *Valir* Llaw, I may need your summoning, depending on the turn of battle." He nodded to them once again, the intensity of his eyes obvious. "Please ensure that your charges are close at all times."

"Rest assured, Your Majesty, they won't leave my sight," Kalon vowed.

Uncomfortable at being deemed in need of protection, Jaren lowered his eyes. He could sense the greycloak's intense gaze on him. He wondered if the man was still upset, although whatever had angered him was still a mystery. Jaren did not hazard a glance to check.

Aldrain wheeled to face the broad entry, which yet stood closed. Drawing steel, he gave the order to breach the throne room.

A knot of heavily armoured soldiers launched themselves at the stout portals, which splintered inward on impact. Aldrain followed them inside the high-ceilinged chamber, trailed by another squad of soldiers.

Cries of alarm rose up. Jaren peered through the mass of metal-clad warriors pouring through the sundered entryway. He could just make out the forms of several men gathered around a raised throne at the far end of the room. As the commotion rose, guards from beside the throne's dais rushed to intercept the newcomers, though the defenders were hopelessly outnumbered.

As the first of Aldrain's forces met the royal guards, one of the men in Jaren's line of sight—a balding, portly fellow with a flushed complexion— seized the lapel of his countryman on the throne and shoved him toward the fray. For a brief instant, the first man paused at the now-empty throne and reached down. A section of the far wall disappeared, revealing a flight of stairs, and the stout fellow wasted no time in fleeing through the exit.

Even over the clash of weapons and shouts of battle, Jaren heard Aldrain shriek in rage. The king broke from his ranks, charged past the remaining few hostile guards, and bolted up the stairs in pursuit of the man Jaren assumed was Count Pacek. Aldrain barked a few orders to his soldiers before he vanished from sight. Only two greycloaks followed their king. The others stood fast, securing the doorway.

Howls of rage and challenge from behind caused Jaren and the others to turn their attention. A large contingent of soldiers, obviously not loyal to the rightful king or his cause, bore down on them.

"Quickly, get into the throne room and stay behind me," Kalon ordered the youths before calling his fellows to brace for the coming assault.

· 12 ·

Matters of Death and Honour

"Y OU WILL NOT ESCAPE ME AGAIN!" Aldrain roared after Pacek. He could hear the footfalls of the traitorous noble just above him on the stairs. Aldrain gained on his quarry, but not fast enough for his liking. The last time they faced one another in battle, Pacek had strength of numbers to protect him against Aldrain's wrath. Not now. The king spurred himself onward, surprised at the vigour he felt returning. Since Jaren had freed him, the sensation of strength built, as had the king's hunger for justice.

He pushed himself harder, to his very limits. Aldrain could see the trailing edges of Pacek's clothing and the blur of his heels. The sound of the noble's laboured, heaving breaths only encouraged the king in his pursuit.

Just as Aldrain reached for Pacek's shirt, the stairway ended abruptly at a narrow door. Unable to stop, the men ran full-force into the slim portal. It barely withstood Pacek first and Aldrain's added mass was too much. It blew inward, spilling the two onto the rough flagstones of the tower floor.

"Secure the stairwell!" Aldrain yelled over his shoulder as he clawed toward Pacek, who was scrambling backward, crab-like, away from the king.

The count's eyes went wide as he observed, for the first time, Aldrain's altered condition. First at the silver-hued limbs, then into the king's eyes he stared in bewildered disbelief.

"What—" he rasped as Aldrain seized hold of an ankle and held him in place. The count groped feverishly behind himself, but found only the immovable stone of the tower wall.

"Do you approve of your handiwork, Pacek?" Aldrain sneered as he rose to his knees, still clutching the other's leg and bringing his sword point to bear.

"Get away from me, demon!" Pacek howled. His other hand struck out at Aldrain's grip, a dagger clutched white-knuckled in the pudgy fist. It glanced harmlessly off of Aldrain's forearm.

The panic-stricken noble hurled the weapon at Aldrain. His aim was wide. The king did not flinch.

Aldrain stood, releasing his hold on the man's ankle, sword pointed at Pacek's chest.

"Your treachery is ended, cur."

"Y-y-you must try me. I must be allowed to speak in my defense." His whining voice was high-pitched and desperate. The count pressed backward against the wall in futility. Aldrain matched his movement.

"Your actions have spoken for you. The trial is all but concluded."

"You cannot do this!"

"Of treason, Count Rondul Pacek, you are declared guilty—"

"I…I demand justice!"

Aldrain nodded, "—and by the authority of House Draegondor, rightful seat of Carathon—"

"Please, you must stop him—h-he's mad!" Pacek pleaded to the soldiers guarding the darkened stairwell behind Aldrain.

"—I decree the sentence of death."

"You cannot—" Pacek's words transformed to a sharp scream, cut short as Aldrain's sword point pierced his racing heart. The count gave one last convulsion and then lay still.

The king stared at the wall, gazing beyond, past the stone and mortar. His voice was hollow, devoid now of emotion, though he still breathed heavily. "I have won redemption for House Draegondor, Father. I have taken back the throne."

◆ ◆ ◆

You fool! Aras berated himself while lithely sidestepping a rushed stab. He spun and struck down the soldier immediately behind the man who had charged him, then reversed the stroke and dispatched the initial assailant. *You should be long gone, with the young whelp bound and draped across the back of your saddle!*

The assassin stole a quick glance backward, assuring himself that Jaren remained untouched. The boy was standing ahead of Iselle, his quarterstaff raised in a defensive posture. So far, though, Aras hadn't let anyone get close enough for him to use the weapon.

He willed himself to stay calm. How had he been so careless as to put himself in danger? The boy had acted to save Aras's life. Though the assassin was certain he would have reacted in time to avoid a mortal wound, the bolt that Jaren blocked would have struck him all the same. *The boy would have done that for anyone. He wasn't doing it for you.* He didn't even know Aras's true identity. What had happened was irrelevant. He had a job to do.

So, why are you angry?

You've spent too much time here. You need to go, at once. Aras parried another clumsy attack and dropped his opponent with two horizontal slashes across the man's midsection and back.

There remained few among the enemy who dared approach Aras, warned away by the growing number of corpses cooling at his feet. Instead, those who still had the will to fight assailed Aldrain's men rather than take on the skilled greycloak officer.

A blue flash erupted, signalling another of Llaw's attacks on the enemy *Valir*. Aras knew that at least one was dead, and he'd seen only two others, though they were loathe to reveal themselves to the senior *Valir* who opposed them. The assassin growled in frustration. It was too much to hope that the elder *Valir* would be slain by the remaining pair. This sad bunch couldn't even do him that small a favour. Aras himself would have to misdirect Llaw, or otherwise deal with him.

It was not personal; the *Valir* had simply come between him and the boy, a situation that needed to be remedied. Such was the business of killing for money and Aras had become accustomed to the more distasteful elements of the career some time ago.

Have you, now?

It then begged the question as to why he'd remained so long. Why take chances with the discovery and failure of the mission just to find out more about the mysterious young man? *No matter,* he vowed to himself once again. *It is settled. You will seize him, with or without his companion, and leave the city as soon as this is over. If the Valir proves too much a hindrance....*

Shouts rang out behind them, and Aras spared another glance to the rear. A battered form lay crumpled at the foot of the stairwell. Bloody smears that disappeared up and out of sight suggested that whoever it was had rolled down the steps.

It took scant minutes for the remainder of their foes to surrender as they realized the true leader of the new regime was dead. The defeated were herded into small groups and escorted under guard to the dungeons. Those loyal to the rightful king showered them with jeers and occasional blows.

Aras sighed. *Now to it*, he told himself, catching a view of Jaren out of the corner of his eye. *Time to honour your clan.* Movement further on drew his attention. Aldrain approached the youths.

Aras silently cursed his bad fortune and stomped over to join them.

◆ ◆ ◆

"I see you are alive and well. It seems the True One has kept his benevolent gaze on you two." Although Aldrain was smiling, the expression did not touch his eyes. "For the rest of us, we make our own destiny. You would do well to depend more on yourselves," the king continued, "before that watchful eye shifts and you are left at the mercy of others."

Jaren shifted uneasily under the weight of Aldrain's attention. Iselle looked away in discomfort.

"Ah, but enough of this dreadful subject—we have won a great victory today!" Nodding, he lifted his eyes to scan the room. "For Carathon!" Aldrain bellowed.

Instantly, answering cries went up from all corners of the chamber. "For Carathon! For House Draegondor! Long live the king!"

Jaren, relieved that Aldrain's focus was elsewhere, sighed and looked to Iselle. She merely shrugged.

Kalon drew up, still appearing sombre.

Aldrain noticed the officer's arrival. "I was hoping to find you sooner than later. I have a task for you—"

"Congratulations, Your Majesty," *Valir* Llaw said as he neared the group. "It was a bold move, but effective nonetheless."

The king nodded. "I may not have spent as much time studying the affairs of state as I ought to have, but the lessons I attended were not lost on me. It is not rash to move when you hold the advantage, even if it appears too soon."

"Not in the least, Your Majesty," Llaw acknowledged, "and clearly, victory favours the man who understands himself before his enemy."

Aldrain pondered the *Valir's* words momentarily, face pensive. He then continued. "What will you do now, Master Llaw?"

The *Valir* glanced at Jaren and Iselle. "I suppose that would be up to our two young friends."

"I would like to visit Dal Farrow," Jaren stated. "It's been a long while since I've seen my parents. I'd like to know if they are all right."

Aldrain frowned and paused, his gaze growing distant. Jaren had the feeling that his words alone were not the cause. "Going back is not possible, my young friend. Sometimes the past is better left behind us." The king shook himself from whatever reverie had befallen him. He fixed Jaren with a sombre, measuring gaze. "But the choice is yours. If you wish to return home, I will send you with horses and an escort—the lands about are far from a lawful state."

"And you wish for me to accompany them, Your Majesty?" Kalon inquired.

"No, Kalon. I need your skills in another matter. Come, and I will give you the details."

Jaren couldn't be certain, but he thought the barest of shadows clouded Kalon's features. "Very well, Your Majesty."

The king and his officer withdrew, leaving Jaren, Iselle and Llaw alone, an island in a sea of milling bodies and commotion. A crowd of servants and soldiers were busy returning the room to its use as an audience chamber, and they'd already been joined by several junior administrators. Apparently, word of Aldrain's victory was spreading quickly.

"Jaren, do you think it wise to return home?" Llaw began.

"*Valir* Llaw? *Valir* Ensin Llaw?" A tall, thin youth at the doorway called out above the din.

"Over here lad," Llaw replied, his eyebrows curling in curiosity.

The young man took a moment to zero in on the responding voice, then acknowledged and hurried toward them through the mob of activity.

"I was sent to find you as soon as possible, Master Llaw," he huffed, clearly exerted by his duties. "I am to give this to you, and you alone." His lank brown hair was dark with perspiration and his chest heaved. He wiped his brow with a dark green sleeve. The rest of his robe, the same emerald colour, bore a patch on his left breast that identified him as a runner from the *Valir* Guild.

"Thank you, young man. Yes…well, you may go now. Here is a reward for your haste." Llaw pressed several coppers into the messenger's palm. The other smiled, then disappeared back into the blur of motion that surrounded them. More servants and a few additional officials had arrived.

Llaw broke the seal on the folded parchment and read the document. His eyes narrowed and his brow creased as he read through the message. He drew in a long breath as he finished reading and after a moment his eyes found Jaren and Iselle.

"Now, then," he began. "Where were we?"

"You were just asking Jaren if it was a good idea to go back to Dal Farrow," Iselle said. "Why would that be a problem?"

The *Valir* hesitated before answering. "For several reasons, actually. First, the *Valir* Council is not likely the only group looking for Jaren. Where else to keep an eye out for him than at his former home?"

"Former home?" Jaren and Iselle asked in unison.

"You don't actually think you can just return to the way things were and settle back down in Dal Farrow, do you? From what I remember, that was a life you weren't particularly fond of in the first place." A hint of a knowing smile pulled at the corners of Llaw's mouth.

"That's different than saying I don't belong there any more, or that I can never go back."

"No. No, that's not quite what I meant. But you do need to adjust your thinking a bit. The second reason: even if no one is currently keeping watch over the village, by going back at this point, you will almost assuredly draw attention to your parents. I don't think that is something you want for them."

"No," Jaren admitted. "I don't want to put them in danger. But what are we going to do then? Go to the council in Neval Ketarra?"

"I think not," Llaw answered quickly with a glance at the letter in his hand. "You are not yet ready to return. We need to further explore your...talents."

"I thought you were supposed to bring him back," Iselle said.

"I am supposed to keep him from getting into trouble," Llaw replied. "We can go to the council eventually, but not until he is ready."

"When will that be?" Jaren wondered aloud.

"When you have a better understanding of your circumstances and your abilities," Llaw said.

"And where do you propose he find that?" Iselle asked.

Llaw shrugged.

"You're not going to start imitating Ver, are you?" Iselle groaned. "He was the best protector we could have hoped for, but you know very well he never told us anything or answered our questions."

The *Valir* chuckled. "He was a guardian sent by the True One, not a herald. I think you're being hard on him."

"He's a grown man. He can handle it," Iselle said. "Or, he could when he was around." She gave Jaren an apologetic look.

Jaren shrugged but didn't respond right away. "What about the journal?" Jaren asked then. "Ravien Alluminara was from the islands to the south. Perhaps some information still exists there."

"Perhaps," Llaw considered, though he took on a concerned look. "However, as I said when you first told us, you must be wary of any gift that comes from the Witch. She gave you that journal for a reason. I have very little belief in the notion that her *kindness* was for the benefit of anyone else. Better to just discard it altogether."

Jaren frowned.

"What other choice is there?" Iselle demanded.

"I did not say going south was out of the question," Llaw said. "Just that we must be cautious if we act based on anything to do with the Witch. Besides, the passage south from Vetalas is a dear one. There are many sailors who claim the waters are haunted and that the sea itself comes alive to drag ships to the depths. The islands are no better. Primeval, steamy jungles with all sorts of unnatural creatures running around they are, or so I've heard."

"You believe in tales of ghosts and monsters?" Iselle cocked her head.

"I believe that discretion is warranted. I didn't live to my age by rushing headlong into the unknown."

"Probably a wise choice. At your age you need to be careful." Iselle began to giggle.

"We've already carried you on a litter, thanks!" Jaren joined in.

Llaw couldn't keep up his feigned expression of indignation. He soon began to laugh along with them.

· 13 ·

Forged in Hearts of Stone

MALHAENA CRINGED AT ANOTHER BURST of the insectoid screeching. The high-pitched squeal threatened to blast her eardrums. She leaned away from the column behind which she had taken refuge, searching the cavernous chamber for Sithas and Galda.

For all their differences, the two worked very well together in combat. Galda normally engaged a foe head-on, while Sithas crept around behind and delivered stealth attacks. Only, these foes were different.

The four stone statues came to life as soon as her party reached the midpoint of the chamber. The massive beasts, at least a full head and torso taller than Galda, scuttled on six legs like beetles. Their stony skin turned away all but the sharpest of blades and they attacked with a pair of huge, menacing pincer-talons capable of cutting clear through a body armoured in heavy mail. Malhaena need only look at the several corpses sprawled on the floor for proof of that. The creatures—like the insects she'd seen fighting one-on-one in the betting dens of Vetia and Parcea—held their pincers poised before them, as if praying, and moved with lightning speed to either stab or grasp their target—sometimes both. Cold, stone eyes with a vertical, metal-filled slit glared dully at Malhaena's party from above snapping mandibles.

These were creatures of nightmare. But this was certainly no dream and she needed to achieve her objective before her group was overcome.

As she watched, Galda landed a crushing blow against one creature's pincer-arm. The impact would have reduced a normal man to paste, but on these monstrosities, only a thin crack appeared as the hit dislodged splinters of rock. Galda barely managed to dodge the return attack. The warrior behind Galda was not so fortunate. The claw seized his upper thigh and he was dragged into the air. The man's death shriek was cut short as his ruined body was cast to either side in separate pieces.

Meanwhile, Sithas had managed to sneak up behind the same creature and leaped onto its back, straddling the thing. The assassin plunged his long knives into breaks in its armour over and over again, sending sparks and silver liquid up in gouts.

Malhaena glanced at the other scenes of combat. At each, a knot of armoured soldiers fought savagely to fend off the remaining pair of creatures with pole-arms and spears. Two men died horribly during the brief moment she observed.

Time was definitely at a premium and that price could not be paid for long.

She detached herself from the column and raced to Galda's side, her curved knives, joined by a silvery chain, flashed into her hands.

"We must get to the door," Malhaena called out to the huge combatant. "We need to see the lower level to fulfill the contract!"

"To the Deceiver with the contract," Galda bellowed, avoiding another claw strike, "we need to get out of here!"

With the force of the creature's attack, one of its pincer-talons embedded itself into the stone floor and the beast struggled to free it. As it worked the appendage, Malhaena noticed that the crack from Galda's strike opened with the stress of its efforts.

She acted quickly, flinging one blade out to wrap the chain loosely about the pincer. Both hands on the other blade, Malhaena whipped the metal line as hard as she could. The chain cinched tightly about the claw with a sharp snap—at the point where it had been damaged—and the appendage ruptured at the break, sending chunks of rock and liquid metal flying.

The creature screamed in pain and fury, stumbling to one side, one of its supporting limbs now shattered. With a roar, Galda launched himself atop the beast and Sithas attacked with renewed intensity from his perch. Several others crowded forward about the downed monster, stabbing at it with their spears and pole-arms.

An instant later, the beast gave a shudder and lay still.

Galda moved to join one of the other ongoing struggles but Malhaena motioned him to a stop.

"Stay here and watch the doors. Don't let any of them down. I'll be back up as soon as I see what's there."

"But—" Galda began, gesturing toward the embattled soldiers.

"We don't need them to survive," Malhaena cut in, coldly. "We just need them to hold out a bit longer. You are only to lend aid if they look about to fall."

Galda frowned, but did not say anything. Sithas nodded and turned to view the fighting, face expressionless. He could just as easily have been watching miniature versions of the insect-things in the betting dens. *Watching without coin on the line, to boot.* Malhaena smiled inwardly at the man's lack of concern.

Malhaena wheeled and broke for the doorway at the chamber's end, the screams of the hired warriors following close behind. She reached the portal and fished out a set of lock picks, forcing the sounds of the battle to the back of her mind. Her fingers nimbly worked the tools and after several attempts, Malhaena heard the welcome sound of the latch releasing. Pulling the door open, she cautiously slipped into the blackness as hot wind blew past her and through the gaping doorway.

The rush of air smelled of bitter ash, like that of a brickworks, and of sulphur, with traces of other unpleasant scents Malhaena could not identify. Her eyes teared with the heat and fumes, but at least she could still breathe.

After a few lengths, a set of stairs began. She probed her way forward cautiously, hands outstretched, following the stone passage down. Malhaena could make out a reddish glow below her. As she descended the rough-hewn stairs it grew steadily less dark. With the increase in light came an increase in heat. By the time Malhaena reached the landing, the tunnel was ruddily lit, as if by many torches. Ahead was an opening. Walking toward it was much the same as nearing a roaring fire, though the place held none of the comfort of a welcoming hearth.

Malhaena stepped from the passage and onto a short expanse of stone. The scene before her threatened to squeeze the remaining air from her lungs. The ground on which she stood fell sharply away a dozen paces or so before her, leading to a drop of hundreds of lengths to a river of molten rock. High above, the ceiling of the massive cavern peeked out occasionally from an obscuring cloud of ash and fumes. Malhaena caught only the briefest glimpse of a dark opening and assumed it must be the volcano's funnel. To either side, the natural, jagged stone walls of the vast chamber retreated. Unearthly breezes stirred the surroundings, carrying glowing embers and soot that pranced and raced about as fairy spirits in a summer glade at dusk. The entire sight was bathed in a sinister, orange glow. Countless shadows danced all about her, as though keeping time with the infernal rumbling of the mountain's heart.

The only feature that appeared human-made was a massive orb suspended over the flowing magma. It was held in place by four gargantuan lengths of chain connecting the sphere to the walls—north, south, east, and west—each link tall as a man and just as thick. Malhaena squinted as she studied the sight. The orb appeared made of glass and within it roiled a viscous, black liquid streaked with ribbons of a silver, metallic sheen.

A sharp peal of thunder rang out and a blinding flash issued from the sphere. Her ears felt as though they might explode with the echoing boom. An arc of lightning shot from the orb and sliced down into the flowing lava. As if in answer, the river of stone spewed gouts of molten rock that reflected silver light. Hundreds of metallic slivers settled on the molten course, some sinking, others floating along, only to be lost from sight as the flows exited the chamber and continued their underground passage.

Malhaena felt an otherworldly presence although she could not identify the source. Her unease grew. It felt to her as though the very mountain vibrated, its uncanny thrum running through her body to the core of her being.

She peered more intensely at the lava flowing below as she thought she saw some disturbance on its surface. A stirring beneath caused it to roil and churn violently. Sweat ran freely from Malhaena's pores to evaporate just as rapidly in the dry, driving wind and heat. She swallowed, her throat parched. Eyes burning from the arid and hot blasting gusts, she abandoned her observation and turned to ascend the rough stairs, anxious to escape the place and its unnatural sensations.

Her task fulfilled, all Malhaena needed to do was return to the *Valir*. It didn't matter that many of her company would not make the trip. That was life in her business. Or death. Regardless, it only need concern her if it was her own.

As she climbed, her sense of unease lifted and Malhaena began to smile.

◆ ◆ ◆

"They should have aided you," the image of Sonja said. *"Instead, they did nothing. Can you afford to leave their intentions to chance?"*

Aldrain ran a hand through his already ruffled hair. She was dead. Sonja Redsteele had been slain months ago by one of the Deceiver's blacktongues. She had sacrificed herself so that he and his companions might escape to Ensin Llaw's tower. Aldrain recalled seeing her corpse, animated in death by the foul being who murdered her. He closed his eyes, struggling to dismiss the dreaded vision. So how was she here, speaking to him? The king had hoped his release from captivity would mean an end to these visitations. Still, if he ignored them, they would go away.

Won't they?

"*I know you doubt what you see, Your Majesty,*" Sonja added, as if reading his thoughts. "*Yes, I am dead, but I've been sent to warn you. Just as your parents came to you throughout your ordeal.*"

Could that be true? Perhaps the True One hadn't totally abandoned Aldrain and his people. No, his inner voice lashed out, *we were left on our own. I was—we were—abandoned.* He shifted in the throne, pointedly avoiding Sonja.

"*Your judgement does you a disservice, although you are not wrong to doubt what only your eyes tell you.*" Sonja's form moved within his field of vision once more. "*But ask yourself, what do you feel?*"

"I feel I am losing my mind!" Aldrain stood and shouted, his voice echoing about the empty chamber. He heaved a great sigh and sank once again to his seat. He averted his eyes anew.

"*Does an insane man know he is mad? Would he really ponder the shape of his thoughts?*"

Aldrain huffed. "Very well," he trained his glare on the woman's form. "If I am not mad, then what am I to make of these visits? Tell me that."

"*When one is connected to another, death cannot keep them apart. Not when the bond is so great—and so crucial. I do not know exactly how it is possible that I can be here. But that does not matter. Not nearly so much as what happens to you. And to Carathon. Your parents have told you the same, I am certain.*"

The king breathed deeply and gave a barely perceptible nod. *So they had.* "And what then would you add?"

"*You have regained what was lost—lost by no fault of your own—and you must ensure that the rule of Carathon remains in the hands of those to whom it belongs. Before you set out to deal with the Valir, you must make certain your lands are safe.*"

"By invading Ergothan?"

"*By determining whether or not they are truly to be trusted. An embassy can help to fathom their intentions. Should they refuse to openly and publicly declare their support for you and your kingdom, we must send the message that interfering in Carathon's affairs will not be tolerated.*"

"An embassy," Aldrain echoed.

"*Negotiation is all that should be needed, Truth willing. You can deal with the situation as you see fit, in the unlikely event that Ergothan proves less than committed to support you.*"

The ephemeral form of Sonja Redsteele wavered and began to dissipate. As it did, her final words echoed within the chamber, "*You are destined to lead, Aldrain. You will return Carathon to greatness.*"

The king rested his head on clasped hands and pondered the message. He did not notice the slight flickers of movement in the corner of the room, in a corner that would have appeared darker than the others, had there been anyone nearby to investigate. In fact, the room's light seemed to avoid that one place—to retreat from it, even. Aldrain sat, consumed by his thoughts, oblivious to this and all else.

· 14 ·

Signs and Readings

SMOKE CURLED UP FROM THE BOWL of Ensin Llaw's pipe, one hand holding it absently in his lap as he studied Jaren. The boy was half-way through his staff form on the flat below the *Valir's* perch, a rocky outcropping common to the landscape of northern Ergothan. Beads of sweat flew from Jaren's limbs and soaked hair with each sudden shift, swing or thrust. The white fabric of his shirt, soaked with perspiration and streaked with dust, clung to his torso. As Jaren swept the long weapon back and forth and stepped through the pattern, the elder *Valir* gazed on, both watching the youth's movements and apparently holding a mumbled conversation with himself. Every now and then, Llaw's forehead would crease, his lips would purse, or he'd unwittingly produce some other indication of deep, intense thought.

Iselle wasn't convinced of which was more entertaining, the old man's facial expressions and mutterings, or Jaren's fumbling at one specific, intricate series of movements that repeatedly sent the staff tumbling to the ground. Iselle sat a few yards from Llaw on the same rock formation, watching Jaren work through the form that Kalon had taught him and, though his skills were improving noticeably, that same section foiled him every time.

She had to stifle a giggle at Jaren's expense.

"I see you are quite entertained at the moment," Llaw's matter-of-fact tone cut into her amusement. He had not turned his face toward her.

"What's not to enjoy?" she asked.

The *Valir* nodded, chuckling to himself. "I wasn't sure if you were smiling at Jaren's attempts or pining over him."

"Pining? Hardly."

Jaren cursed, and the words were immediately followed by the sound of the wooden staff as it bounced to a stop in the dirt.

"Admiring his *skill* is more like it," she grinned.

Now, Llaw did look her way. "Have you given any thought to what will become of him?"

"What do you mean?"

"You know he's special. His talent is unique. It is both a blessing and a curse, depending on how one looks at it."

"I'm still not exactly sure what you're saying."

"I am saying that Jaren's road is a long and dangerous one. He may not be willing to share such a path with anyone else."

"Are you suggesting he'd just leave?"

"I'm suggesting you should let him know how you feel before it's too late. It may impact a decision like that, if he feels the need to make one."

"How I feel?" She shook her head to emphasize the fact that she didn't know what he was talking about. *Old fool.*

Llaw ignored her implied denial. "With the uncertainty surrounding his sister, you may be the most important person in his life right now. He needs to know your true feelings. Not to tell him could be dangerous, especially if others notice and think to use it to their advantage in dealing with him."

"We're friends. That's all."

The *Valir* gazed intently at Iselle. "If you say so, my dear girl." Then, he turned his attention back to Jaren. "But fate can turn in an instant and regret may prove a long-suffered, bitter companion in the absence of others. We've still some time before we reach Vetalas. Use it wisely."

A great clap of thunder sounded and the two of them were showered with pebbles and rock chips as a sphere of light hammered into the stone just yards beneath them. Iselle and Llaw tumbled forward, sliding down the decline toward Jaren atop a rolling mass of loosened rock.

Jaren stood transfixed, eyes locked on the staff before him.

As if called, Dagger burst through some nearby scrub and bounded up to Iselle, nuzzling her hand and wagging his tail.

"Well, then," Llaw began, "that was rather…unexpected." He stood up and glanced about while brushing dust and splinters of stone from his robes. "Iselle, can you see where my pipe ended up?"

"To the Deceiver with your pipe," Iselle said. "What was that, Jaren?" She trained her eyes his way as she demanded an explanation, absently scratching behind Dagger's ears at the same time.

"I…I'm not sure," Jaren stammered. "I was just concentrating on finishing the form. I got to the part that I usually mess up, but this time I got it. Sort of."

Llaw crossed his arms and focused on Jaren, nodding. "Hmmm. That would be interesting. Very interesting, indeed."

"What?" Jaren asked.

"You appear to have summoned while not explicitly intending to," the *Valir* said. He crossed his arms, one hand raised to support his chin. "I can assume that you were very intensely focused?"

"Yes," Jaren said, "I didn't want to drop my staff again."

"But it's so fun to watch," Iselle quipped.

Jaren frowned at her.

"What you've done, my boy, seems to be something like the Jamnite Warwitches used to do, if I recall the histories. They were able to summon while fighting. It was said they could even use their weapons to direct the magic."

"But, didn't they use *metanduil* as well?" Jaren asked.

"Yes."

"Then it's not really the same," Jaren said.

"Well, it is and it isn't."

Jaren sighed. He wiped at his forehead.

He was still breathing hard. *Funny,* Iselle thought, *I don't remember his chest being that full.* She abruptly threw her gaze to the ground before her, then eyed Llaw as if he'd just pinched her. *Old fool!*

Llaw did the unthinkable. He winked.

Iselle's eyes flew wide. "I'm going for a walk," she announced in a voice that sounded all too loud to her own ears. "Come on, Dagger." She wheeled around and began to stomp off, the great dog following obediently.

"Hang on a minute and I'll come with you," Jaren called.

"No!" She nearly yelled over her shoulder.

Jaren recoiled, blinking in surprise. "Uh, okay then. See you later." He looked at Llaw helplessly, as if to ask what he'd done wrong.

His un-worded plea was lost on the *Valir,* who had apparently drifted into his habitual, silent contemplation.

Something else came to Jaren's mind. "Valir Llaw?"

The elder man shook himself from his thoughts. "Yes, Jaren?"

"I didn't want to ask while Iselle was around, but do you think Aldrain is going to be okay?"

"What exactly do you mean?"

"Well, he just didn't seem right. He's been acting differently than before. I thought I'd ask you without Iselle here, because I don't want her to feel any worse about what he went through."

"But she didn't have anything to do with what happened. It was completely out of her hands."

"I know, but she still feels partly responsible. That bothers her. And then she bothers me," he added with a helpless sigh.

"Yes, well, women can be like that at times, my young friend. At any age." Llaw chortled to himself, then his gaze was attracted to the ground nearby. "Ah, my pipe!" He quickly moved to retrieve the object, tapping it on a stone to empty it of any dirt or debris.

"But, do you think he was...all right?"

"Hmmm? Oh, yes. Aldrain." The *Valir* finished stashing the pipe in the inner front folds of his robe. "I don't think you need to worry about the king."

"But there was something about him. A feeling I got when I was near."

"A sensation of some kind, you mean?"

"Something like that, but I'm not sure how to describe it. It just felt off, somehow."

"Perhaps something to do with your healing?" Llaw raised an eyebrow, then muttered quietly to himself.

Jaren was going to add that he didn't think so. He first felt it on entering the dungeon chamber where Aldrain had been kept. He had the same experience each time he was near the king after that. But Jaren held his tongue and considered the suggestion that it could have been his imagination. It was, after all, a very chaotic and stressful event. Still, it was hard to believe his mind had made it all up.

Llaw must have seen the doubt reflected in Jaren's eyes, because he offered another encouraging word. "Jaren, the king went through a great deal in the days before you met him. He probably had no chance to deal with his feelings—or even acknowledge them—until he was captured. Then he had nothing but time to go over those events in his mind, to relive the great losses he'd experienced. He had little hope to avail him. In Aldrain's mind, not only had he lost his family and legacy, but for all he knew, you and your companions had been overcome, too." Llaw's face grew pensive as he frowned. "I would be more apt to worry if the king did not show some outward signs that he was finally coming to face this emotional turmoil. Now he has the time to properly sort through his feelings; a period tempered with the determination and hope that follows when one has recovered something once feared lost. I think that's why he was so insistent at first that we accept his offer of an escort."

"I got the feeling he wanted to keep an eye on us."

"I suppose he did—he doesn't want his friends to suffer further misfortune."

"No, I don't think that was it. It was like he didn't really trust us anymore."

"Jaren, you just saved him and helped return his kingdom. Of course he trusts you."

Jaren shrugged. "Well, Iselle does say that I tend to focus on the negative at times."

"Does she, now?"

"Yeah *your cup is half empty* and that sort of thing—say, I'm sorry about the ledge. I didn't mean to—"

Llaw waved his hands in deference. "No need to apologize, my boy. In fact, it was a grand discovery! Now, let's examine what happened and see if we can't make it happen again, shall we?"

Jaren looked longingly in the direction Iselle had gone, then drew a deep breath. "Sure, let's see if we can't."

◆ ◆ ◆

The Valir have been gracious enough, though my instruction has been basic, to this point. They seem intent on discovering from me what they can of the little magic that still exists to us. I see no harm in that, as I stand to gain much greater knowledge of what we have lost in exchange. It is strange to me that theirs is based on the use of the material they call metanduil. *Of all the elements, it is the least life-like and most removed from the essence of Vraellon's spirit as can be found in Evarlund. Even the rock from which it is taken would serve better, to my mind, as it is more natural than the extracted ore. I must not forget to discuss this with Saer Cryllaen when I return.*

Tomorrow, I am to see the High Valir. Hopefully, he will allow me access to higher forms of their magic and other tutors. I have much to learn.

Jaren yawned and rubbed his eyes with a thumb and forefinger. He had a headache from squinting to read by the dim firelight. He stretched his back, which was stiff from being propped against the stump of an old oak.

"Anything exciting yet?" Iselle asked.

He thought she had been asleep. "Not yet. I don't think this is one of those adventure stories the bards sing about. It's just a journal."

"The journal of the last *An'Valir* in a thousand years," Iselle said. "There should be something worth reading in there."

"I'll let you know when I get to a good part."

"Please do." Iselle turned onto her side and looked at him, head propped on one hand. Dagger, who was snoring loudly beside her, gave a twitch and shifted until he was snuggled against her again. She rolled her eyes at the dog and shook her head before focusing on Jaren again. Minutes passed. "Where do you think she is right now?"

Assuming *she* meant Morgaine, Jaren shrugged. "I wish she would come back to us."

"She will, when she's ready."

"What if it's too late by then?"

"What do you mean?"

"Well," Jaren said, "we can assume that, since they're looking for me, the *Valir* are also looking for Morgaine. And not only them, but the Witch and Joselle, too."

"She may be hard-nosed and a little on the pushy side," Iselle said, "but she can take care of herself. Especially now."

"But you saw what she looked like—what the Witch did to her. What if she's gone back to not remembering? She needs our help. All I'm doing is running away again."

"You didn't run from the Witch. You fought her."

"That was different. And I didn't intend to fight her. I went to—well, you know." Jaren's voice had grown shallow and distant.

"Still, this is important, too. Learning how to develop your power is as important as anything else. In that way, you're actually helping everyone at the same time."

Jaren shrugged again. "I suppose you're right."

Iselle said nothing and stared at him.

"I'm not saying it."

"Fine, I'll take your silence as agreement," she announced with a matter-of-fact nod. "Just keep doing what you think is right, and things will work out. We all just have to accept that's the way things happen."

"You sound like Llaw."

"Nah. I couldn't stand having that long, scratchy beard. I'd be more of a crazy old hag like Mother Haddie."

Jaren was silent for a minute. The old woman had died horribly at the hands of a blacktongue. "I hope no one else is hurt because of me. Especially not Morgaine. Or—" he glanced quickly at Iselle, then looked down, hiding the colour that rose in his cheeks. Hopefully, the light of the fire was too low to reveal his embarrassment.

"I know," Iselle said, patting the slumbering dog. "I don't want anything to happen to Dagger, either. Now go to sleep. You have to be up early to make me breakfast before Llaw marches us out."

Iselle rolled over and pulled her bedroll up around her ears. Dagger shifted back against her immediately and Jaren heard an exasperated sigh.

Jaren shook his head and grinned to himself, then opened the journal once more.

• 15 •

On the Road to Ansalar

THE SQUAD HAD STOPPED TO WATER THE HORSES at a clearing where one of the Marthuin River's many tributary streams wound its way through the rolling hills. The area was ringed with leafless trees. They did little to hinder the crisp autumn wind that carried the murmuring of the narrow waterway in its flight.

They were still less than halfway to Ansalar, despite pushing their mounts to the brink of exhaustion. Every mile weighed on Aras like a millstone about his neck. He was more than angry with himself over the way he had allowed events to overtake him. *You and your foolish commitment to honour*, he chided himself. *You should be back at Neval Ketarra with the boy by now.* He grunted an all-too-audible *humph*, bringing more than one curious face swivelling his way. Aras ignored the others and their unspoken wonderings, all but scowling in return. That alone was a testament to his current state of mind. He never drew unnecessary attention to himself on a job; right now he was attached to an armed troop on assignment to deliver the king's ultimatum.

No doubt, his reputation with the Talons was irreparably damaged at this point, no matter the final outcome of his real mission. Malhaena and the others were willing to extend to Aras the courtesy of indulging his quest for true challenges, but only as long as it did not jeopardize the group's interests. Or anger its clients. On both accounts, he had long since crossed the line.

Aras's blood boiled. He could no longer endure the game. If he continued on the present course, he would only get further from his target and any chance at redemption with the Jades.

He willed his cloak to cease its disguising magic and slid from his horse, approaching the knot of soldiers at the brook, most of whom talked loosely while filling water skins or between sips of the cool, refreshing water. Though several of the men were at his rear, still mounted and gazing out from their position for signs of threat, he paid them no heed. All of his attention focused on the warriors before him.

One of the soldiers turned, his eyes popping wide as he called to the others, his gaping mouth spewing water. "To arms, brothers! An intruder!"

Aras had dispensed with the guise and stalked forward so abruptly it appeared a stranger had simply strolled from the wood into their small clearing.

Aras stopped, feet planted, hands on the hilts of his sabres.

In answer, a dozen blades slid free of their scabbards as steely eyes measured him.

He could have simply turned and driven his horse from them at speed. They may have followed for a distance, but he could have outrun them. Instead, Aras decided to take the more challenging, most extreme course of action. He was, after all, in a very bad mood. Some exercise might help to lighten it.

"State your business," one of the soldiers demanded. It was the sergeant, a grizzled veteran with close-cropped, salt-and-pepper hair and a large scar that ran horizontally across his left cheek.

"I'm going to kill all of you," Aras replied flatly. "Then, I'm going to go back and fulfill my contract. As I should have done long before now."

Blank or puzzled looks were his only response.

"I don't expect you to understand," Aras said with a shrug, "it's complicated, after all."

The sergeant looked unimpressed and only a few of the men chuckled nervously at Aras's words. Something about the stranger suggested that he would back up his claim—that he wanted to, even. The soldiers cast anxious glances back and forth and their sergeant frowned. "Enough of this," he bellowed. "Either move along or we'll arrest you for interfering with the king's affairs."

Aras willed the disguise to return, for an instant only, then let the image of Kalon disappear. A quick glance over his shoulder indicated that, though they observed, the mounted soldiers had not moved in.

"Arrest him. If he resists, kill him," the sergeant ordered in a flat tone. He was apparently trying to avoid a fight.

That's wise of you, but I'm not going away.

A group of them, while not looking overly confident, obediently started forward, swords in hand.

Aras waited until they were nearly within striking distance before brandishing his own blades, which, to the dismay of his startled opponents, seemed to appear on their own. The approaching men halted. After shared, furtive glances, they began to encircle the assassin.

At least they'll provide some sport, then, Aras thought, a dark smile forming.

Once in position, the soldiers attacked in unison, sword points and spear tips trained on Aras. He became a vortex of liquid, deadly movement. He spun from attack to defence and back again effortlessly, faster than his opponents could track. They hoped to overwhelm their adversary through sheer numbers, but each attack met either empty space or glanced harmlessly away, deflected by the assassin's dual, blurring counters.

The clearing rang with the clash of steel and the whistle of blades slicing the air. Shrieks of bewilderment and howls of pain erupted. Echoes of the clamour bounced off of the rough bark and bare limbs of the surrounding wood, adding to the chaos of battle.

The encircling soldiers drew back from their initial assault, now several men fewer for their efforts. These fallen comrades lay still, dark streaks spreading beneath them, soaking into the earth. Those still standing looked to the sergeant for answers, but he would have none of their hesitation. Striding forward, he took one of the downed warriors' positions in the encircling formation.

"You're soldiers of Carathon," he roared. "Act like it! Or can one lone man best all of you?"

With that, the circle of blades and spears drew inward once more. This time Aras was first to the offensive. He darted forward at a gap between two soldiers, engaging them with a flurry of strikes and feints. They fell back immediately, one due to grievous wounds and the other out of a desire to spare himself the same. Aras pushed on, past the encircling line, headed toward the edge of the clearing. He dashed to the fringe of the trees, then turned, putting his back to a particularly broad old ironwood.

The sergeant kicked at several of his nearest charges, sending them forward against their impossibly nimble foe. One attempted a high strike aimed at Aras's neck. The intended blow met no resistance; Aras spun away. Instead, it slashed into the shoulder of the soldier's nearest comrade. As they looked at each other in confusion, Aras dispatched them with several lightning-fast strokes.

The sergeant, with only a handful of his command remaining, bellowed at the riders for assistance. He growled and rushed forward, sword high over his head. "For Carathon!" he roared. His downward sweep proved just as fruitless as the attacks of his men, however. He found himself attempting to pull several inches of metal from the trunk of the tree behind his target as Aras ducked. The assassin used his pommel to stun the sergeant in mid-tug, then cut down the two soldiers who'd taken up his flanks. Of the three soldiers left standing, not one dared approach, though they did not flee. Aras heard the telltale twang of bowstrings and wove his blades in a defensive pattern before him, intercepting the arrows and scattering the broken shafts about the clearing.

The sergeant stirred on the ground before him. Aras moved to finish him off. Instead of finding the sergeant's heart, his blade deflected and was snapped forcefully from his hand as a figure stepped before him. The stranger's straight, strong blade stopped the assassin's counter strike and threw it sideways, sending that weapon clattering away as well. Aras followed the line of the blade to its wielder, eyes narrowed to take full measure of this unexpected visitor.

The figure's dark, ash-hued cloak swept back, allowing Aras the chance to size up the stranger. Before him stood a man of average height and build, clad in tunic and pants that matched the cloak. He was poised for further combat, though he did not appear tense like the soldiers had. Both the man's expression and posture projected an aura of focused strength. Aras's study halted at the man's eyes. They were grim and sharp.

Slowly, Aras knelt and picked up a sword dropped by one of the dead. He kept his gaze locked on the other, who spoke over his shoulder to the soldiers.

"Sergeant, you may collect your men and continue with your mission. I will see that you are no longer hindered."

"Th—thank you, good sir," the sergeant stammered in awe, as if amazed he was still alive. He swallowed hard. "You do a great service for King Aldrain."

The stranger nodded curtly, eyes not straying from Aras. "You should be off, then."

The sergeant nodded, picking himself up and hustling back to his mount, shoving his remaining men ahead in the rush to be somewhere else. Soon, the sound of their hoof beats faded, leaving the two combatants to face one another in the silent clearing.

"You're not from a rival guild," Aras said finally. "You carry no markings, at any rate."

"I am no killer for hire."

"But you are skilled, otherwise you'd have joined the dead by now."

"I am what I am."

"Do you have a name, at least? So I might know who it is that I fight?"

"There is no need to fight. You are summoned to a higher calling, though you have done your best to ignore it so far."

"A higher calling, eh?" Aras chuckled. "If you're recruiting for politics, I'm not interested."

"No, I am not much for the laws of humankind, either."

Aras squinted. "Surely you're not a holy man or True One's priest?"

"What I am is of little importance. This is: you have many doubts. You yearn to fight for honour and a purpose, but you have found little of either in your dealings lately. For longer than you care to admit."

Aras's eyes narrowed again. "You claim much familiarity with me, for a stranger. What did you say your name was, again?"

"My name is Verithael. I am to remind you of your own conscience. Of your true calling."

"My conscience. Well, that's rich," Aras scoffed. "I'm quite good at what I do."

Verithael sighed. "You have been observed for some time. I was told to be here when you assaulted the king's men. The Deceiver is trying to influence your decision—to complete your fall. I was sent to give you one more chance at redemption."

"You knew I was going to attack them." Aras blinked. "So...you are an agent of...of the Truth? Is that it?"

"Something like that, yes."

"Aren't you interfering in the scheme of things by doing this? It's been a while since I attended the weekly Readings, but don't we get to act according to our own free will?"

"Which question do you wish me to answer?"

"Both."

Verithael nodded. "The Deceiver has many paths of influence. Once you started down the darker road all those years ago on the streets of Vetalas, fighting and clawing to exist, it became gradually easier for his minions and his foul essence to lead you. What began as choices that you made to survive became ingrained behaviour. Your innermost character, however, truly wishes for a more meaningful life. I am here simply to remind you that your heart desires to go elsewhere."

"You're right," Aras conceded, his eyes darkening at the recollection of his desperate, younger days. "I do wish to be elsewhere—"

Before the last words were spoken, Aras lashed out with the sword. As they talked he had focused his energies on the attack. All of his considerable skill and determination went into the strike. It would surely land and the confrontation would be ended.

Aras's sword struck. The conflict ended. His blade met Verithael's and a shower of sparks erupted as the assassin's weapon splintered into fragments. Bright shards of metal flew into his face and his world went dark.

At last, Aras had met his match. *Who could have guessed it would be some crazy, religious zealot?* The assassin fell to his knees, awaiting the killing strike.

The darkness of his thoughts shattered into flashes of illumination as a heavy blow descended. Aras's head swam, and he felt as if he were floating, submerged in black water.

As he lay there, drifting into the ebony depths, Verithael spoke softly to him, "Tell Jaren a friend says hello."

• 16 •

The Swelling Tide

JOSELLE HAD TO KEEP FROM SPRINTING the final, short distance to her enclave, a secret warren in the sandstone hills near to Rhianain's camp. They had found him and brought him to her. She smiled wolfishly at the thought. If she could not somehow catch Morgaine or her brother unawares, perhaps she could get at them some other way. It was for this reason she sent her followers out to find the young thief, Turan. The prospect of her plan for him pulled her leer even wider.

At the entrance to her secure hideaway, the sentinels finally showed themselves, though they knew not to hinder her progress in the least. She was very good at making examples and they were not interested in experiencing another. They melted back into their places of concealment in all haste—anxious to avoid Joselle. She had rounded up her band of hirelings from amongst Rhianain's greater host several months ago. Since that time, her followers had learned the value of obeying and keeping busy; both kept them as safe as possible from the ever present threat of Joselle's short temper.

Her eyes adjusted to the lack of illumination almost immediately: a welcome side effect of her transformation. Others, like the bone-rending pain that occasionally gripped Joselle, were not so desirable. Still, she had power now: power to match her exalted status. Such strength was bound to exact a price and the gift was well worth its few costs. Compared to the Mother, Joselle had hardly to suffer at all due to the change.

Down the rough passage she stalked, looking forward to reacquainting herself with Turan. She had little to do with him when they first met at the fortress of the Warwitch months ago. Turan had been ordered to carry out whatever ruse was necessary to gain the trust of Jaren's little friend, Iselle, and to capture her if possible. In that, the thief had done well. After the confrontation, however, he had slipped away. That would not do. They were not finished with him. At least Joselle was not.

The thought brought an involuntary shudder. The Mother had no idea of Joselle's secret plans. Rhianain would likely have agreed but Joselle desired to do this thing on her own. She would use it to show the Mother that she could be trusted to plan and execute schemes of her own. That would surely overshadow any misgivings over her secrecy. Her true value would shine through, value that came from Joselle herself and not simply from inheriting the gift. She rationalized that it was like giving Rhianain a gift in return.

Joselle stopped at the crudely fashioned door barring entrance to the thief's temporary cell. She scowled darkly at the guard, who on catching sight of the younger mistress, scurried frantically to release the lock. After a few shaky attempts, he succeeded, then yanked the door open and bowed his head as she stomped through.

"I apologize for the lack of better accommodations," Joselle offered in a tone barely masked of its sarcasm, "but we set up rather quickly and had little choice in the location." Her smile remained cold.

"I've had worse." Turan offered a wan smile in reply. He sat up on the makeshift cot and stretched. "Though I must admit, I usually know why I've been jailed."

"Again, my apologies," she responded, though her body language expressed no regret. "I shall have the men who captured you flogged for failing to properly inform you of my invitation." At that, the icy smile broadened.

"Well, as we're on the subject of your *invitation*...." Turan was careful not to place too much sarcastic emphasis on the final word.

Joselle simply nodded. "I have need of your services once more. Though I cannot remember her actually dismissing you the last time, I wasn't present during your conversations with the Mother, so I am willing to excuse your departure as a lack of understanding on your part."

Turan nodded and pursed his lips slightly. He said nothing.

"Very well," Joselle continued, "I want you to find the girl again. This time it's easy. You don't need to fool her. Just take her and bring her to me. To me alone."

Almost imperceptibly, Turan's eyebrows raised. "I see," he said. "And the compensation for this venture? Seeing as it's a new directive, it would fall outside of the original agreement." It was Turan's opportunity to offer a wry grin. He added a wink. "Or, I could renegotiate with your Mother instead...."

Joselle sniffed. "That will not be necessary. I'll pay double your previous fee." She raised her head, looking down her nose at the thief through narrowed eyes. "That should guarantee prompt delivery. And...discretion."

The grin tugged more strongly on one corner of Turan's mouth and he leaned forward. "Of course, my lady. Have you any information on the current whereabouts of…the girl?"

"That's what *you're* being paid for," Joselle said. "I can tell you she's somewhere south, probably near Eidara, if our fool agents have it right." She tossed her head dismissively. "I have one or two additional preparations to make for you. In the meantime, I will let the guards know that you are free to come and go, and not to be hindered. If you so desire, take one or two with you. Though if you plan to make any sort of haste or travel in secrecy, they may not be up to the task. I had little choice in recruiting them. Do not stray too long from the caves, or go near the Mother's army. Is that understood?"

"Of course, my lady. I prefer to find my own help, anyway."

Joselle offered a disinterested shrug before proceeding to exit.

"My lady—" Turan interjected.

"Yes," she exhaled wearily, half-turning.

"Once you are done with…Iselle, what are your plans for her?"

Other than a dismissive wave, Joselle's only answer was dark laughter. As far as she was concerned, Turan could marry the troublesome wretch. Though when Joselle was through with the thief, the girl would be farthest from his mind. What little of it remained.

◆ ◆ ◆

"They have declined to sign the peace accord."

"*That can mean only one thing, Aldrain,*" Sonja spoke in hushed but urgent tones.

"Why did they not just sign it? Perhaps we might—"

"*Hesitation may cost much, Your Majesty,*" Sonja continued. "*You have already lost more than most could bear. Your family's legacy must not continue to suffer.*"

Aldrain closed his eyes. "I…I will *not allow* further insult to the Draegondor name. Ergothan must be dealt with. I will order the precautions taken as we discussed earlier."

"*Excellent,*" Sonja agreed, "*and you must also begin to marshal your forces. We can allow no doubt to exist in the minds of the Ergothani that our borders will be respected during your army's march north. It cannot be left to chance.*"

"That will not be difficult," said Aldrain. "We have mobilized many and reinstated most of the officers that Pacek decommissioned." He nearly spat the name. "We can then conscript what extra numbers we may need from the Ergothani to further encourage their loyalty."

"*Make haste, Your Majesty,*" Sonja cautioned. "*We must move soon. First to Ergothan and then to Neval Ketarra to deal with the serpents in their lair.*"

Aldrain's eyes widened initially, but he finally nodded in agreement. "Yes, we need to show them we are not afraid to march against any threat. There can be no danger to Carathon while the army is engaged elsewhere."

"*You are absolutely right, Your Majesty.*" Sonja smiled warmly, placing her hand on Aldrain's cheek. "*I knew you had much of your father's spirit in you. Soon, people in other nations will come to know your strength of resolve as your humble subjects do.*"

Aldrain clasped her hand tightly in his own. "I will avenge everyone. All those wronged by the deceitful *Valir* and their treacherous council. They will not escape my justice. The True One shall smile upon Carathon once again, after I have righted these grievous wrongs."

"*And if the True One will not aid us,*" Sonja added in a quiet, but firm tone, "*we shall help ourselves.*"

The coils of the spectralkin, its invisible connections to the king, continued to project the image of Sonja Redsteele into his troubled mind. The tentacle that pressed against his face feasted on Aldrain's volatile emotions, gaining strength and a tighter grasp on his ailing spirit.

◆ ◆ ◆

Morgaine lay prostrate, spent and sobbing amid the rubble of her destructive outburst. Her voice was a hoarse croak, though none of her muttering was coherent. Dust and ash thrown up during her onslaught floated on the slight breeze, then came to rest on bent iron and shattered stone alike. Morgaine had returned to her place of self-imposed exile, still hurt and enraged after her encounter with Joselle. Broad tracts of grass, dirt still clinging to the roots, lay upturned here and there, as if ripped up by some mad, giant gardener. Dark hulks of splintered trees criss-crossed the scene or jutted at severe angles from jagged trunks; the same violent hand had snapped them, too.

Morgaine's silhouette shuddered, Sholara's rays bathing her in the early morning light and casting her shadow across a crumbling section of ancient wall as she cried in anguish.

She was just another broken relic, a cast-off ruin haunting the debris of her present home. Her parents were gone. Murdered. She herself had tried to kill Jaren under the sway of the Witch's magic. Now she was completely alone. Mother Haddie—the kind, old healer they had first sought out and with whom Morgaine had felt a sort of kinship—was dead too, another result of her cursed existence. Even before the change, she brought death and misfortune. Before the gift. Everything and everyone she cared for, it seemed, suffered from the effects of her blight.

All she had wanted was a chance to be something on her own. Not separation from everyone, but to be her own person among them. The magic had once promised that. Now it promised only torment and death.

Birds took up their chorus in the trees about the clearing and its ruins, at ease once more, now that the screaming and explosions had stopped. Their songs seemed to mock Morgaine in her misery. Swiping a hand across her grimy face, she looked about, taking in the scene of her black tantrum. The ancient ruins had stood abandoned for centuries as nature gradually ground down and reclaimed them. Morgaine had caused as much destruction in just a few moments. All that stood now was one main tower foundation, mostly intact to its second floor, and a section of adjoining wall. The remainder, reduced to jumbled piles, continued settling to a permanent rest on top of the uneven carpet of grass or the few exposed, cracked and weathered flagstones.

Still on her hands and knees, Morgaine looked down at her arms. Pale and cold, they were. Beneath the skin, she could see the darker veins, matching in hue the ichor they carried. *Metanduil.* Dark, liquid magic. That was her essence now. She threw her head back and howled, as an animal would, a woeful and hollow bay. It was all she could do in her state. Formal language had left her. Primal rage remained.

Through the red haze, Morgaine recalled a vision of Jaren. It was back at the Witch's stronghold, where she had forced Morgaine and Joselle to aid her assault against him. Morgaine didn't understand it while the events unfolded, but time had allowed ample opportunity to knit the fragmented episodes into a somewhat recognizable scrap of memory. Jaren entered the courtyard from the far gate, and seeing the Witch, strode toward her with an unmistakable look of determination etched in his features. Morgaine knew him well enough to read that no hope reflected from that grim expression. He had come to destroy the Witch and fully expected not to survive the ordeal. He more than possessed the power. Morgaine had witnessed that truth. But Jaren stopped before taking on the Mother. He stopped because he had seen Morgaine. He risked his own death rather than continue, rather than placing her in jeopardy. Morgaine repaid that compassion by attempting to kill him.

Morgaine had stolen a small taste of the magic's destructive power in her maddened demolition of the ruins. *But you started to turn long before the gift, didn't you? You deceived yourself for too long, pretending that you stood for the Truth, all the while embracing the lie.* Another memory surfaced, this one of the clearing near Llaw's tower where she had destroyed the blacktongue. Even then some small part of her had enjoyed it. Yes, she could do it. She wielded the same energy, though perhaps not with Jaren's raw strength. Still, it would be enough. She'd had enough. Enough of her cursed existence, of failing so many and harming the rest. Morgaine saw behind the intent of Jaren's actions the truth of what she needed to do. She could not be redeemed—her crimes went too far for her to be worthy of the True One's grace—but she could do the next best thing. She could take up Jaren's struggle where he had left off. Where *she* had forced him to leave it.

⋅ 17 ⋅

Finding the Way

THE SWAYING OF THE HORSE BENEATH HIM made reading somewhat of a chore, but Jaren persisted. He was more than half way through the journal now and had yet to find anything in Ravien's writing that offered more insight into the magic or his own connection to it. He absently pressed his fingertips to the throbbing in his temples—a product of trying to read through the jostling—as he continued. His eyes narrowed and he gripped the slight book more tightly as he read the next passages.

I cannot form a proper bond with the metal. Although they have instructed me in various exercises to establish a link to the magic through this conduit, the metanduil, my attempts have proven unsuccessful. I continue to sense the magic; I know it is there, but it remains beyond my reach. My situation has attracted the attention of several high Valir. Perhaps they will be able to guide me through the process. Despite my failures, the Valir have continued to be hospitable and accommodating, if still presenting an air of distance. Perhaps my incompetence is partly to blame. If I were to prove a better student, they may choose to become more open. For the sake of my people, I shall increase my efforts to make this happen. We need to learn more about them to better understand their ways.

"Did you get to a scary part?" Iselle asked in amusement, observing his tension.

"What?" Jaren said, looking up at her with blank eyes.

"In your book. Have you come to a frightening spot?"

"Oh—no, it's just…she seems to be affected by the metal the same way I am. Like our paths are similar, or something."

"Does it have any maps?"

His blank look returned.

"If it does, maybe she can show you where to go."

Jaren still regarded her wordlessly.

She laughed. "That's a joke, Jaren. You know, since you're on similar paths, and the map—oh, never mind." Her head shook in mock condescension. "You know, reading is supposed to make you *more* intelligent."

"Sorry, but I'm just trying to figure out what her writing has to do with me."

"Maybe it doesn't."

"According to the Witch, it does."

"And *she's* been trustworthy so far."

"I know what you're thinking," he said matter-of-factly. "But it's not just what the Witch *said*. It's what Ravien *wrote*. I can feel some sort of connection with her thoughts. Almost like they're mine, in a way."

"Well, the Witch could have given it to you as a distraction. Not that there haven't been enough shiny things around us at times to do the same thing, but she probably didn't give you the book to make you less of a dim-witted farm boy."

Jaren was about to respond, but Llaw spoke first, "Regardless of the Witch's intentions—and my own initial misgivings—I believe the journal may offer valuable information. Though, Jaren will have to be mindful of the bearer's possible motives." He had been riding in quiet contemplation behind the two youths and these were his first words since they purchased the horses at a farmstead in northern Ergothan and started south along the route to Vetalas.

Both Jaren and Iselle glanced back at the *Valir*.

"Think of it as a game of pieces. A person moves the stones in a fashion that will get the other player to move his or hers in reaction. The objective is to manipulate the opponent into going where you wish. But if one steps back and looks at the whole of the other's moves, it is possible to determine the motive behind them." He peered at them through his spectacles, which were perched at the end of his nose. Apparently satisfied, he continued, "The tokens themselves do not reveal much more than what they are: their movement and attack allocations. This journal, however, may afford more of an insight into Jaren's circumstances than the Witch intended. My boy, you must use this to your advantage, all the while being conscious not to play into the Witch's plans."

"I'd be okay with that," Iselle said dryly, "if Jaren wasn't such a terrible pieces player."

"I've beaten you once or twice, Iselle."

"Those were mercy victories," Iselle said in a haughty tone. "I only let you win so you'll still play."

◆ ◆ ◆

Aras sat up. The blackness was complete. What sort of night was this? No stars or moon disturbed this nightfall's total darkness. But, it wasn't night, was it? He could feel the caress of Sholara on his skin and the noises about him were the sounds of daytime activity. A hawk cried out high above and other, anonymous birds chirped or cackled in the trees.

Then it came to him. Aras recalled his attack on the king's men and the subsequent confrontation with Verithael, warrior of the Truth. Their brief encounter had left him blind.

A shuffling to his left drew Aras to scramble into a crouch. He groped about for some form of concealment. A soft whinny followed and he relaxed. Aras rose and took a few furtive steps toward the sounds of the animal. His hands stretched forth of their own accord and he felt his way along. Fortunately, his searching fingers came across a cold, metallic object—one of his sabres. The other was lying right beside it. They must have been set nearby for him to discover, he supposed. Otherwise, he might never have found them.

Still, what good did blades do when you couldn't see to use them?

Aras heard the swishing of the horse's tail and then its steady breath. He stumbled on a loose stone, dropping low to regain balance. His careful steps led him to a hard, vertical surface. It was rough and warm. The trunk of a tree. Aras's hands moved up and down its length, stopping on a thin, horizontal band that wound around it. It was smooth and tightly wrapped about the trunk. A tether? Feeling along the strip, he found a lead that branched from it. A light tug brought confirmation: the slack taken up, there was resistance on the other end. Not immobile, but something with substantial weight. In response, his mount whinnied once more, then drew the tether taut as it continued to forage in the underbrush.

"I'm sorry to cut your breakfast short, but I have need of your eyes," Aras announced in a soothing tone. He followed the reins to the horse's side and gave a few gentle pats.

"Are you lost?"

Aras wheeled, a hand instinctively dropping to one of his sabre hilts. The voice sounded young, which annoyed him. How could a child have snuck up on him so easily? He was sightless, yes, but his other senses were still highly tuned.

"Who are you?" The assassin challenged.

"I'm Matt. What's your name?" His voice was light and cheerful.

"What do you want?"

"That's not very polite. 'Answer someone when they ask you a question.' That's what my dad says." The boy's tone hadn't changed.

"Fine. My name is Aras," he said. "Are you alone?"

"Yes, I'm by myself." There was a pause. "Actually no, I'm not."

"Look, boy, I'm not about to play games with you. Are you alone or not?"

"Call me Matt."

"Okay, Matt," Aras grumbled. "Are you by yourself?"

"No, I'm here with you now, silly!" Matt laughed.

Aras exhaled slowly. "Are you expecting anyone else to come by—Matt?"

"No. So, what are you doing here?"

"Look, boy—Matt—I don't have time to waste. Why don't you just move along?"

"You don't look like you're in a hurry. You were moving pretty slowly."

Aras untied the tether, which seemed to take an agonizingly long time. He felt his way alongside the mount again and swung himself into the saddle.

"It was nice to meet you, Matt," Aras said through gritted teeth. "But I have to go now."

"Okay. See you later. Where are you going?"

Aras was about to snap back at the youth, but realized he truly didn't know. He'd intended to go after Jaren and drag him back to Neval Ketarra. That plan had obviously been interrupted. "I have to go find my friends," Aras finally said. Something that a child could relate to.

"Okay. Bye then."

He heeled the mount's sides lightly, easing it into a saunter. Since it was morning, Sholara was low in the east, so he put his back to her warmth. Other than that, he let the horse do the navigating. It would find a path to follow. Right now, he just wanted to put some distance between himself and the annoying child. Then he could focus on what had just happened to him.

◆ ◆ ◆

It seemed to Aras that the horse plodded steadily upward; his sense of the short journey suggested it wasn't essentially a lateral progression, a balanced ascending and descending of rolling hills. It appeared to be a gradual, yet unmistakable climb. But that didn't make sense. He was a hundred leagues from the foothills of the Forge mountains.

His ears picked up the faint murmur of running water. It grew in short time, until he felt the horse stop and crane its neck downward. *Good idea,* Aras thought, *I could use a sip myself.*

He slowly dismounted, careful to test the footing beneath him. It was a mixture of hard-packed dirt and rocks. It was dry, offering a sound footing. *Funny,* he mused as he knelt by the brook, *what you take for granted when you can see.*

"This is one of my favourite places to stop and have a drink," said a familiar, young voice.

Aras jumped to a guarded stance, instantly unsheathing his sabres while orienting to face the intruder. Then, his reasoning mind caught up to the instinctual reflex. It was the boy from earlier in the day. *But that's impossible!*

"Wow, you're really quick!" the boy exclaimed excitedly. "I'm glad I wasn't standing right next to you."

"You cannot be here," Aras replied flatly. "You should be a dozen leagues behind me by now."

"I'm where I'm supposed to be," the boy said.

"Where you're *supposed* to be?"

"With you," the boy continued. His tone and inflection suggested he was smiling.

"And *why* are you *supposed* to be with me?" Aras growled, sheathing his swords.

"I don't know," came the answer. "I just am."

Aras took a calming breath. "Listen, boy." He stopped himself. "Listen— Matt. I am not accustomed to travelling with others; children and strangers included. No strange children, especially. So, you can just forget about whatever little game you've got going here, and move on." *How did he catch up to me?* Aras strained his ears, but could pick up no sounds of others. If he'd followed, or if someone else had brought him, they would have needed to use horses, wouldn't they?

"But then how will you get to where you're going?"

"And *you* know where I'm going, do you?"

"I know where you're meant to go. Where you've always wanted to go."

"Where's that?" demanded Aras, his tone dry.

"Don't you know," Matt chided, "that you need to get your sight back?"

Aras started. His eyes narrowed. "So, let me get this straight. You are coming with me somewhere, to somehow get my sight back."

"Yes, sort of."

"Okay. Can you tell me where that is?"

"It's up to you," Matt responded, and Aras sensed that he was still smiling. "It's your journey, after all. You know," the boy added, emphasizing the word *know*, "you ask a lot of silly questions for an adult."

"If you'll excuse me for a moment," Aras said, "I think I need that drink now."

"Okay."

Aras knelt again, cupping his hands beneath the water. He brought the cool water to his lips and sipped. It was instantly exhilarating, sending a tingling sensation through his whole body. It radiated from his throat and stomach, spreading to his core and then outward to his limbs. Despite the refreshing drink, his world remained dark. He wondered if a tavern was out of the question along the way, though that sort of drink wasn't likely to help. Then again, the boy wouldn't be allowed at the bar, so Aras would have some peace and time to think things over. He took another invigorating sip from the stream.

He threw a vain glance in Matt's direction, a thin smile lifting the corners of his mouth. He had no idea why he felt suddenly more at ease. Aras the assassin had never been so vulnerable.

"Are you ready to go?" Matt asked.

"It depends."

"On what?"

"Do you still plan on coming with me?" the assassin questioned.

"Yes."

"Then not quite yet," Aras replied.

・ 18 ・

Of Tightening Grasps

ALDRAIN'S EYES HELD A STEELY CAST. "How long until they arrive?"

The sergeant scowled. "Likely not more than a few hours, Your Majesty. We left only shortly before they intended to. And by King Haelric's reaction, they would not dare waste a grain of sand in the hourglass."

"Nonetheless, Haelric will come to see reason." Aldrain sighed wearily. Though he had regained a measure of his former weight after his release from captivity, his face was still gaunt and the shadows cast by the ruddy lamplight carved his features as a skull. "I did not want it to come to this, but we need to show the Ergothani that our words do not carry on empty breath."

"They have several companies of elites with them, along with the few hundred regulars, Your Majesty. There were a over a dozen *Valir* in attendance as well. Likely, Haelric summoned the additions from the surrounding counties when word of your demands—ah…your proposal—reached him. That and news of our greycloaks' activity surrounding the capital."

"Haelric gathers the *Valir* for counsel as well as added strength," Aldrain muttered. "Just as Sonja advised he would."

The sergeant shifted slightly at the mention of the late *Valir's* name, glancing sidelong to several of his men nearby.

"You needn't worry, Sergeant," the king said. "I have made arrangements. We will try to reason with the Ergothani cohort." Aldrain nodded to one corner of his command tent, where a bundle of leather satchels, containing what appeared to be rolled parchments, lay. "Letters from their loved ones will suffice, with the promise of more to come, as added incentive to keep the peace." He gestured to several nearby clerks. "Sergeant, please inform these officials of the Ergothani officers' names and counties, as best you can recall. We will present a more meaningful collection of letters that way."

"Yes, Your Majesty," the sergeant saluted and moved to join the clerks.

"Dastrin, please have the sergeant and his men help you remove the letters to your quarters. Then have Captain Boltun sent in. I'll need to go over our battle plans with him in case the Ergothani think our message a bluff. Have him wait for me outside."

"Yes, Your Majesty," the clerk said stiffly, motioning for his fellows and the soldiers to begin moving the bags. "I will send you the list of names as soon as it is compiled." Dastrin bowed deeply and ushered the attendants out, their arms laden with the satchels.

Not long after, Sonja's form materialized in the gloom. *"You are doing everything well, Your Majesty. Your father would be so proud of you."*

"I do not wish to engage the Ergothani," he replied in a hollow voice.

"Surely they will see reason. It should not come to fighting," Sonja replied. *"But, on the chance it does, you are wise to take the necessary precautions."* She moved to place a hand on Aldrain's shoulder. *"As you have seen recently, few can be trusted in these dark times."*

"I do not understand how Kalon's impostor could have fooled me so completely. He was before me for long enough. I should have seen it!" Aldrain pounded a fist on the table before him, upending a number of small metal icons from their places across the sprawled map.

"Do not burden yourself with such thoughts, Aldrain. He is obviously a cunning agent of the Deceiver." She opened her mouth to continue, but stopped herself.

"You have more to add?"

"I do not wish to speak ill of those you hold in esteem."

"For the good of Carathon, you must tell me."

"Talented as this rogue must have been, it is impossible that he succeeded as he did without help."

Aldrain frowned deeply, his forehead drawing canyons of shadow. "But who would have helped him? Surely not—"

"Forgive me, Your Majesty, but I should not have spoken of this. It is too dear a subject." She pulled away.

The king grasped her retreating hand. "Sonja, you must tell me. I have no one else to trust in this. I am…alone."

"Very well," she consented after a moment's hesitation. *"I would ask you, who accompanied this man into Eidara? Who has taken leave of you, refusing your generous offer of protection?"*

"You aren't suggesting—"

"I am only pointing out the most logical explanation, Your Majesty. I do not propose to accuse anyone."

"Surely the young ones would never engage in such deceit? And Ensin Llaw is your own former mentor and friend—yet you suggest they conspire against me?"

"As I have told you, Your Majesty," Sonja bowed her head, "I merely offer a reasonable account of the situation, as much as it pains me to do so."

"Leave me," Aldrain said, his voice thickening. "I must consider this on my own."

The spectralkin's summoned illusion wavered and dissipated. The ethereal beast dug into the mind of its host ever more deeply, revelling in the chaotic thoughts and raw emotions it found.

◆ ◆ ◆

Horses impatiently tamped the short, brown grass and snorted plumes of steaming breath. The golden dragon standard of Carathon snapped in the crisp autumn wind, the serpentine creature thrashing about with angry movements. Aldrain's cohort of mounted cavalrymen sat erect in their saddles behind the king, grim-faced and sombre, an exact mirror of the liege lord at the head of their formation.

The king of Carathon was impatient too, much like his and the company's mounts. It was well and good that Haelric's men had not come to fight as Aldrain initially thought, but they arrived with maddening delay. Now visible in the distance, upon the road his own host travelled, the smaller Ergothani contingent plodded toward them.

"A mire slug moves faster," Aldrain muttered under his breath. The officers nearby stiffened almost imperceptibly, their discomfort unnoticed by the king. He had taken to mumbling often these days, and any comprehensible bits were generally unsettling to those who happened to overhear, especially the snippets of conversation. More often than not, King Aldrain was alone when these reached the ears of his men.

An insufferable amount of time passed, to Aldrain's mind, before the leader of Haelric's force presented himself.

"Well met, King Aldrain. I am Yaltein, high captain and leader of this company, Haelric's Hammer."

Aldrain tried to hide his irritation, but his scoff at the introduction did little to aid the attempt. He nodded curtly, which also belied his true mood.

"Perhaps a lighter hammer would swing faster," Aldrain quipped, "or the wielder needs more skill."

Yaltein blinked. He opened his mouth, then closed it. He blinked again. "Ah…my apologies if we took overlong to arrive, Your Majesty…but King Haelric desired a company large enough to…to suit the station of our most esteemed guest." He bowed in deference, but his expression became a tight mask.

Aldrain's frown did not deepen, nor did it disappear. "An escort, then. Very well, High Captain Yaltein. Just take care that our horses do not find your men underfoot for the remainder of the journey."

"Your Majesty," Yaltein bowed again, his face reddening, "I will do my best to keep them from tarrying."

"Then lead on, High Captain. My business with Haelric cannot wait."

Yaltein's party wheeled their mounts and trotted back to the main body of Ergothani.

As soon as they rejoined the larger force, Aldrain nudged his horse forward.

Hesitantly, his lieutenants signalled their charges to follow.

• 19 •

Matters of the Heart; Business of Kings

FINDING JAREN WAS EASY ENOUGH, once Morgaine knew how to look for him. It was simply a matter of what she now referred to as *sensing* for her brother. She sent streams of energy out in the four cardinal directions, and sooner or later, one of them would indicate his presence through attraction to the formidable power he held. Once Morgaine ascertained the general direction, she would send out more to pinpoint his location.

The difficult part, she feared, was deciding what she might say to him. They had not seen one another since the battle at the Mother's hold. Morgaine was afraid. Not of what Jaren would do, but of what he would say. How could he do anything but condemn Morgaine for her actions? She had joined the attempt to kill him. Then, after the conflict ended with the Mother's disappearance, Morgaine ran. She could not face him then, not after taking part in the attack.

Can you face him now?

Like most of her advancements in the magic, the means to locate her brother came through a combination of trial and error and intuition. Morgaine wondered if the same held for Jaren. It would be an awkward question to ask, though, since many of their past arguments centered on the magic and their different experiences with it. Would he even trust her enough to discuss his abilities with her? It was reasonable to think that Jaren would not, after the events of the battle. He might believe that she was unstable or still in league with the Mother. If he could not be sure she would remember him or was not allied with the Witch, there was little hope in getting him to talk.

On several occasions, Morgaine had attempted to make contact but never carried through. She had gotten as close as a few leagues once, but then retreated.

This, the first glimpse of Jaren in several months, after all of the chaos involved in their final encounter, was emotionally overwhelming. Tears streamed down her face and Morgaine trembled uncontrollably. She struggled to steady herself but her lungs resisted with sharp, catching breaths.

Morgaine willed her focus to the scene below, absently brushing a strand of stray chestnut hair from her forehead.

Jaren sat reading a book, his back to an aged, leaf-bare tree. Iselle lounged nearby, throwing a stick that Dagger enthusiastically fetched and carried back to her. Ensin Llaw was visible at the far edge of the clearing, resting on a fallen log. Circular puffs of pipe smoke wafted in the calm air above him, undisturbed in their slow ascent. He gazed toward the youths, but it was impossible to tell whether he was actually watching them or was absorbed in his own musings, as was so often the case with the older *Valir*.

There existed an unmistakable pull toward the group, though Morgaine could not explain it. This close to her brother, could it be her mind's preoccupation with their related magics—different, yet akin to one another? Or was it her heart, yearning to reconnect? *You still love him, don't you?* Her feelings were sometimes confusing and often conflicted since the *metanduil* became part of her.

Was she thinking it or feeling it?

Morgaine closed her eyes and drew a calming, deep breath. She no longer trembled. She willed her feet to begin moving. To her surprise, they obeyed, and she headed down the small incline toward the only family and friends that remained to her.

She prayed to the True One for a happy reunion.

◆ ◆ ◆

They stared at each other, unmoving, neither breaking the frigid silence. One powder-faced Ergothani noble, the proximity of his seat indicating high status in Haelric's court, appeared paler than the white makeup he wore. Beads of sweat flowed from beneath his extravagant wig and down his face, creating trails in the powder that ended in tiny clumps of white goop. He glanced nervously from one ruler to the other. He was not alone. Officials, clerks, soldiers—and even aged *Valir* accustomed to politics and perilous negotiations—observed with apprehension the tense exchange between Aldrain and Haelric.

At last, the low, rough voice of The King of Ergothan shattered the quiet. "And I am to simply accept this new arrangement, then? Ergothan becomes subservient to the whims of Carathon's king under threats of blackmail?"

Haelric cursed in a strained voice, his eyes raking over the open parchment he clutched before him. He jumped from the throne and threw the parchment back at Aldrain. "Has house Draegondor stooped so low?" Haelric nearly spluttered with rage, his reddened face standing in stark contrast to his close-cropped, white hair.

Aldrain remained standing, motionless, hands clasped before him. If not for the steady rise and fall of his shoulders with each breath, he might have been a statue. His attention diverted momentarily to the discarded document at his feet. Once returned to Haelric, Aldrain's eyes held their dark, steely glint, his drawn cowl transforming them into twin silver stars peering from a midnight sky. They appeared all the sharper framed by his gaunt features, each angle and recess more pronounced by the shadowing effects of the hood.

"Have you no answer for your deplorable actions?" Haelric charged. "Perhaps we should consult with Aldradein—or even Sonja Redsteele?"

Aldrain's head rose slightly, but otherwise there was no reaction.

Haelric waved a dismissive hand, his exasperated gaze scouring the chamber of his personal court. The balcony of the room was lined with his subjects, but other than the seats surrounding the throne area the main floor was populated mostly by men of Carathon. The sight caused a deep scowl to twist his features. The veins in his temples and neck stood out sharply. "Your father would be ashamed to learn of your actions, Your Majesty. I would know. I spent more time at court with him than you."

"Nevertheless," Aldrain finally responded, his low and composed tone a stark contrast to the highly charged environment within the chamber, "I am here now and I am king, not Aldradein. That fact is exactly the reason I have come to you. The old ways are inadequate to deal with the current threat. You need only visit my family's estate to see this truth."

"As I first expressed, King Aldrain, I am deeply sorry for your loss and the tragedy that has befallen Carathon, but that does not give you the right to conduct yourself in whatever manner you see fit. There are still conventions to which we must adhere, examples we must set for our subjects. Otherwise, we descend into anarchy." Haelric's voice took on a tone of urgency. "Surely, you must see that your course of action is madness."

"Madness, now?" Aldrain offered a wry smile. "I can talk to you of madness. In the blink of an eye, your entire rule could end. Not by my hand, but by the whim of the *Valir* and their infernal council. *That* is madness."

A rustle of dismay issued from Haelric's subjects, especially his summoners.

Haelric's eyes widened, but Aldrain continued before the Ergothani king could object. "Do you honestly believe that this Witch could have single-handedly orchestrated the events that have befallen Carathon? The same events that now test the will of Evarlund's leaders? She clearly does not act alone. The *Valir* can no longer be trusted—former allies…even friends…are now suspect. Much has changed. New methods are required."

One of the Ergothani *Valir*, seated to Haelric's left, erupted from her seat. She strode the several paces to her king's side in a flourish of raven hair and blue and silver robes. She kept a white-knuckled grip on the ornate *metanduil*-inlaid staff she bore.

"Your Majesty," she hardly bent a knee to Aldrain. "Your claim is a bold one, if poorly advised. I see you have several *Valir* with you, yet we cannot be trusted?"

"These few have proven themselves worthy of my trust through a new testing. You are Myrillain Davena, are you not?"

The *Valir* nodded, eyes narrowed, lips pressed to a thin line.

Aldrain glanced rearward to one of his clerks holding the satchels of parchment, then back to Myrillain. "I trust only Sonja, and a handful of other *Valir* now."

"I hear," Myrillain said, "that Sonja is…*indisposed.*"

"Rumours should not be trusted," Aldrain countered, "nor should human institutions." He addressed his counterpart. "Haelric. I need your answer. I have no more time to spend on this…negotiation."

"This has been no negotiation." Haelric drew a deep breath and looked aside to his *Valir*. "Myrillain—give King Aldrain our response, if you would."

The enchantress drew to full height, bowing her head and planting her staff on the floor with a tight, two-handed grip.

For the first time, Aldrain noticed the small globe fixed atop the *Valir's* instrument. It was a clear glass globe, filled with *metanduil*. The liquid metal began to roil within the tiny sphere and pale blue illumination poured forth. A gasp went up from the Ergothani, and many scrambled from their seats or places of observation, eager to escape the coming conflict.

Movements above, at several points in his periphery, drew Aldrain's eyes to the balconies. In contrast to the milling citizens seeking exit, at least half a dozen *Valir* had stepped to the edge of the low retaining wall. They sported a variety of *metanduil* items: circlets adorning heads and arms, vambraces and breastplates, and others. The summoners focused, heads lowered as Myrillain's, facing toward the latter's staff.

Light streamed from the *Valir* and coalesced about the glass globe, brightening and deepening to a twilight blue.

Myrillain's head rose, her eyes meeting Aldrain's. "It is not lightly that we do this, Your Majesty, but you leave us no alternative."

The glowing nexus surrounding the glass sphere drew larger, as if a living creature drawing a great breath, then abruptly constricted. A beam of intense, white light shot toward Aldrain.

Aldrain calmly lifted his arm, his palm intercepting the blast. Snakes of electric energy emerged from the ray and enveloped the king of Carathon, striking wildly about.

Myrillain grinned in disdain, knowing that the king's gesture was futile. No one could withstand their joined energies.

Impossibly, Aldrain kept standing.

Myrillain's grin faded as she focused on the king. He stepped toward her. Her eyes, moving to focus on the king's upraised arm, flew wide in realization.

The blinding ray remained centered in the palm of Aldrain's metallic hand. The serpentine ribbons of electricity snapped and flailed. They did not stop the king, though his face tightened and he bared his teeth as he strained to endure the assault.

He closed on Myrillain.

Each step grew more difficult, took more strength. Aldrain felt as though he were wading through dense mud that clutched at his legs with each step. He pushed himself harder, his expression twisting into a hybrid mask of determination and pain. Brow furrowed, lips baring more of his gritted teeth, Aldrain kept going. The lancing pain travelled along his arm and continued inward, boring into his core. He had endured such agony before, at the hands of the late Count Pacek. He endured and overcame it, just as he would this time. *Justice!* His lips formed the word around a jaw too tightly clamped to comply. *Vengeance!* The words screamed in his mind, his anger and suffering channelled through them, fuelling his determination. Feeding his strength of will.

The sleeve of his tunic and surrounding edges of his cloak burst into flame. Aldrain thrust the pain to the back of his mind along with all other sensations. As with the energy bolt, it was nothing compared to the countless hours of anguish and despair he faced after losing his parents, the men under his command, his freedom. His hope.

Sonja.

At the thought of her, his mind cleared. There was but one objective now. *The sphere.*

Aldrain reached Myrillain. In desperation, she uttered a prayer and raised the staff from the floor. As she brought the rod swiftly down to strike at him, Aldrain caught hold of it with his unoccupied hand. Myrillain shrieked in dismay, trying to pull the staff from him. She could not.

Aldrain reached for the globe, struggling against the stream of magic. He bellowed in rage and determination, drawing deeply within himself, using the last of his physical and mental strength—still bolstered with raw emotion—and felt his fingers close about the heart-sized sphere.

Aldrain managed a final, primal scream as white-hot agony enveloped him. He clenched his fist with all his might.

A thunderclap rocked the chamber, knocking all but Aldrain from their feet as streaks of energy burst forth. Boiling *metanduil* sprayed from the small globe as it shattered. Several drops landed on him, insignificant pricks of a pin compared to the anguish he had already suffered. The searing pain of the magic disappeared, as had the ethereal glow.

He gazed about shakily, taking several staggering steps. His vision was blurred and his mind buzzed. Myrillain lay nearby, unmoving, blood flowing from her ears and nose. Haelric moaned and stirred weakly. Above, none could be seen along the balcony's edge. Six scorched patches outlined blasted gaps in the balcony wall. Behind Aldrain, his men picked themselves up, though they peered about warily, still dazed.

Aldrain looked into his hand. Several fragments of glass remained, a steaming glob of *metanduil* attached to one larger piece. It matched perfectly the colour of his own transformed skin, indistinguishable from the metalized flesh of his arm. He turned his palm downward, dropping the ruined shards.

"Captain Boltun, secure the palace and keep everyone under guard. I will have Haelric sign and proclaim our new agreement as soon as he recovers his wits." His tongue felt thick. Already though, his vision and his head were clearing. There remained much to do.

◆ ◆ ◆

Morgaine stood for a few moments just inside the clearing. Being there, even with the others unaware of her presence, it felt good to be with them. The mild breeze shifted directions and Dagger's head snapped up, his nose catching her scent. He turned and barked, dispelling Morgaine's nostalgic thoughts.

The other three stared for a moment, apparently unsure what it was they were seeing.

Jaren was the first to react. He cast the journal aside and ran to his sister, arms flung wide. Morgaine accepted the firm embrace and returned it. She wished for that instant to last forever, knowing that when it ended, the awkward conversation must begin. For now, Morgaine allowed the strength of Jaren's embrace to overcome her anxiety.

Too soon the moment passed. Jaren pulled back to arms length, though his hands clasped about hers tightly. His questions came in rapid succession: what had happened to her? Where had she gone? Why hadn't she come to find Jaren sooner?

"Are you all right?" he asked when she did not answer, the concern in his eyes plain.

"Jaren..." she managed as tears streamed down her cheeks. "I'm sorry. I'm so terribly sorry—" Her voice came in a whisper, husky with emotion. The breath caught in her chest, her shoulders shuddering as sorrow took hold.

"It's okay," Jaren soothed, holding her again. Iselle joined them, adding her embrace to the mix. Dagger loped over, nuzzling and licking whichever hand he found. Llaw stood nearby, a thick-sounding *ahem* escaping his throat. He turned and busied himself cleaning a spot from his wire-rimmed spectacles.

The greeting took some time, as Jaren and Iselle comforted and welcomed Morgaine. The three of them simply sat where they were and began talking. They conversed freely and without pause at the outset, then Morgaine became more pensive and guarded as the subject turned to their current business.

"So, you think this island might hold answers for you?" Morgaine asked.

"I hope so," Jaren replied. "She seemed to be going through something similar."

"How did you come by the book?"

Iselle's eyebrows rose. She pointedly looked away, reaching over to Dagger and scratching behind his ears.

"It's from…from Rhianain."

Morgaine said nothing, but her expression betrayed her misgivings. "You simply accepted it? And began to read the thing?" She threw an accusatory glare at Ensin Llaw. "How could you allow this?"

Llaw shook himself from his ponderings. "*Allow* it? My dear girl, I do not *give* or *deny* permission to your brother. Nor did I with you. It is not my way of mentoring." He appeared visibly put off.

"That's not what I meant. But you know that what *she* gives is destruction. And pain."

"Nevertheless," Llaw gave a pointed nod, "to understand an enemy's motives, it is sometimes necessary to play along."

"But what if she's cursed it? Enchanted it to trap him?"

"Morgaine," Jaren said. He waited for her to look at him. "I defeated her once. I'll have to do it again. If I can't overcome whatever she plans, then anything I do is really pointless, isn't it?"

His sister inhaled sharply, but no reply followed. She simply frowned. "She cannot be trusted. Not in the least. Be cautious beyond a doubt, Jaren."

"You're talking to the boy who's afraid of forest animals, remember?" Iselle added jovially. "I doubt he's ever been anything but."

To her great joy, Morgaine did remember. Months ago, at the outset of their adventure, Jaren had started at a noise outside the cave where they sheltered for the night. He declared it was a fear of wolves, but she and Iselle had teased him, reminding him of the time he'd been scared by a raccoon. For the first time in countless days, Morgaine smiled.

"Now I know you're okay," Jaren grumbled. "If you're laughing at me, things are back to normal."

"All is right in the world," Iselle echoed, laughing to herself. She stopped abruptly. "Except that no one has made me breakfast yet." She looked pointedly at Jaren.

He shrugged. "I think Morgaine's missed her share of the cooking and cleaning for a while." He grinned slyly at his sister. "I'm looking forward to sleeping in for a change."

Morgaine's smile faded. "I'm not going with you," she said.

"What?" Jaren asked, his look of concern returning.

"You mean not right away," Iselle added.

"No, I mean I'm not going with you. Period."

"What are you going to do, then?" the younger girl asked.

Llaw's face turned their way.

Morgaine's expression hardened. "What I should have done on the island."

"You can't go after her. Not alone," Jaren said.

"For once, I agree with your brother," Iselle said. "Listen to him. This time, anyway."

Jaren cast a brief, irritated look at his friend. "Morgaine, promise me you won't."

She stood, brushing at the front of her tunic. "Don't worry, Jaren. I'm not rushing into anything. Besides, whatever happens, I've learned a thing or two since she gave me the *gift*."

"Then come with us," Jaren pleaded as he rose and reached for her hand. "Once I've learned whatever secrets the island holds we can face her together, whenever the time is right. Just don't leave again!"

"They are right, you know," Llaw cut in. "You have a much better chance of success working as one, whether you go after her or wait for her to move against you."

"I am better off on my own. I can't go with you and I can't go home. Not now. Not after—" Morgaine stopped abruptly, a dark shadow crossing her face. She stepped back, separating from the group. "I've caused too much pain and suffering already. Jaren, Iselle, I love you both. *Valir* Llaw, please take care of them." Her eyes welled with tears once more.

"No, Morgaine, don't—" Jaren began, moving toward her.

"Don't be stupid!" Iselle said, rising to her feet.

Llaw frowned and Dagger whined.

Morgaine's form dissipated, then scattered with the breeze like tiny wisps of smoke. Jaren reached futilely for her, his hands finding nothing but empty air.

· 20 ·

Lost and Found

ARAS HAD NOT GOTTEN HIS DRINK and his mood had not improved.

"I love the fall colours. What's your favourite season?"

Aras was beginning to wonder if the boy—Matt—stopped talking even in his sleep. The assassin had not spoken to one person so much in his life. Though he tried to keep his responses limited to gruff, single words, it was little help.

"Winter," he growled.

"Why?"

"Things are quieter in winter." He looked sharply at Matt.

"I like summer. It's so warm and there's lots of animals around. What's your favourite animal? Mine's a wolf. Have you ever seen a wolf before?"

Aras shook his head. "Silver Falcons. Yes, I've seen many."

"Wow. I've never seen a Silver Falcon. How come you've seen so many?"

"I was talking about wolves."

"What? You just said you liked falcons."

"Look, Matt," Aras tried to smile, but it turned out more like a grimace. "If you want someone to answer your questions, try asking one at a time."

"Oh. Okay." He sat silent for one blessed minute. "Where do Silver Falcons come from?" He clamped his mouth shut deliberately, but before five heartbeats had passed, he blurted another. "How big are they?"

Aras sighed, shaking his head. "The Forge Mountains. About the size of an eagle."

"Sorry. I guess I need to work on that. I just like to talk to people. Do you? Hey, do you have any brothers and sisters?" Matt paused. "Oh. Sorry."

Aras chuckled dryly. "No, and no." He frowned. "Actually, I don't know."

"You don't know if you like talking or if you have brothers and sisters?"

"Matt."

"Sorry." He looked away, into the distance. "Hey, there it is!"

Finally. Aras took a deep breath. He wasn't sure how much more of this grilling he could take. He'd endured tortures that were less arduous. "There *what is?* Where are we going?" he demanded, his tone a mix of exasperation and impatience.

"That's two questions!" Matt exclaimed, overjoyed in catching him.

Aras was certain he could sense the boy's finger pointing at him accusingly. "Could you be a bit more *specific?*"

"It's the path, silly!" Matt tried his best to mimic Aras's tone, but to the assassin, he still sounded too annoyingly young and cute.

"Aren't we on *the path?*"

"Yes. But now, we have to walk."

Great. Aras huffed. Now he couldn't rely on the horse's guidance. "How much farther is it?" he grouched.

Matt laughed.

"What's so funny?"

"I used to be scolded for asking that question!"

"Only that one?" Aras chided.

Matt looked at him blankly, then stuck out his tongue and laughed again. "What now?"

"Oh, nothing." Matt skipped on ahead.

◆ ◆ ◆

"It doesn't sound very stable," Aras said as they stopped before the bridge.

"It's fine," Matt said. "Just don't look down." He caught himself. "Oh, sorry. I forgot."

"Let's just get going, shall we?"

According to Matt, they stood at the edge of a deep canyon. The bridge was the only way across. After that, he announced, it was a long walk to the top.

"What's up there? And where exactly are we?"

The boy placed his hands on his hips, and tried his best to imitate Aras once more, "You have to play by the same rules as me. One question at a time."

Aras fought down a string of curses and nodded compliantly, though it still felt a bit stiff. "Fine. What *place* are we going to?" It was hard to keep his jaw from clenching.

"It's hard to explain, really."

"Try me."

"Look. It's just where you have to go—where I've been told to take you. I can't say more than that. It's not far. You'll be fine."

Aras had to chuckle at the absurdity of it all. Blindly—literally—he followed this strange boy along an unknown path to somewhere he could not explain. Then, the reality of the boy's last statements occurred to him. "Someone told you to take me here?"

There was no answer, only the sound of the wind. It whistled briskly, driven across the rocky lip of the expanse.

"Matt, this isn't funny. I need to know who told you to bring me here."

Aras waited. Still, there was no response.

"Matt?"

The assassin groped for the bridge supports. Finding one, he drew himself alongside. "Truth judge you, you little—" he stopped himself, instead raising his face and shouting to the skies he could no longer see. "WHY AM I HERE?" By the measure of his remaining senses, he was alone. He could either go on, or go back.

What is happening?

He sank to the ground, leaning his back against one of the bridge's supports. *Have I gone mad?* He fished though his tunic and found a strip of dried meat. Chewing it absently, he pondered his circumstances. *Do people going mad worry over their sanity?*

◆ ◆ ◆

Aras's eyes fluttered open. He couldn't tell exactly what time it was, but the sun had apparently set, as it was much cooler and the sounds of night reached his ears.

How long had he slept?

"Matt?" he ventured. As expected, only the keen of the wind through the nearby defile answered.

Abruptly he stood, his course decided. He would continue on. After all, what choice did he have? He didn't know where he was, or what his next move would be anyway. Better to finish this madness—or whatever it was—and be done. If it ended in his death, then so be it. He was useless as an assassin now; or for anything else, he reasoned. He could easily be dispatched by anyone.

A cruel boy with an accurate sling stone could be his end. Or, it might be a chance fall off a cliff—

Perhaps not a chance fall. A bitter laugh escaped his parched throat. He rubbed at his temples, trying to clear his mind. Aras, survivor of the cruel streets of Vetalas, the most feared assassin in the six realms, would not consider such an end.

He started forward, hands guiding him along the bridge's rope railing. His ears had not deceived him. The creaking of planks and heavy twine he'd heard on arriving indicated it was a rope and wood bridge, as he'd feared. *Excellent.*

"Thanks for your *guidance*, Matt. See you around, I guess." He gave another bitter chuckle at his own frustration.

The swaying didn't reach an uncomfortable level until some distance into the crossing. Still, he was not unaccustomed to heights, even though he could only imagine his predicament. He kept on, sure feet testing every rung for strength. Several times, Aras had to take hold of both ropes to keep from being torn from his perch by the screeching gusts. He hoped they did not rend the bridge to pieces. Putting his head down and carefully placing one foot before the other, he continued.

The bridge had to be incredibly long, as it took an eternity to cross. Gradually, the swaying and the wailing gusts subsided and Aras sensed he was nearing the opposite edge of the chasm.

Aras stepped from the bridge onto solid footing. He heaved a sigh of relief and felt about. The rail supports ended, leaving him to wander forward without guidance other than to feel with the toes of his soft-soled boots. There appeared to be a path of laid stone before him. His prodding revealed hard blocks with narrow strips of grass growing between them. On either side, long, wild grasses stretched away for unknown distances. It was a flat and featureless place.

Curiously, there was no sound. After the wind died, it became utterly calm and quiet.

Again, endless time passed as he plodded along the pathway. His throat was no longer parched, nor was he hungry, which he thought strange. He'd been many hours on the journey before reaching the bridge, and other than the dried meat, had not eaten or taken a drink since then. The True One himself only knew how long ago that was. He frowned.

How long had it been since that name entered his thoughts?

A sound reached his ears. It took a number of steps to discern the source. Someone was singing. Aras felt an unearthly pull toward the beautiful music. It was the most incredible sound he had ever heard.

The path fell away to nothing. He stood at the edge of the drop—however far it was—straining to better hear the song.

◆ ◆ ◆

Once again Morgaine stood watching. This time, however, it was not a group of friends she observed. It was the Witch's army. She remained in ethereal form, not yet separating from the mists of the veil through which she now travelled so easily. Morgaine took in the vast body of Jhud'Haian soldiers, confident in her concealment as she chose her course of action.

In all truth, she'd already decided. It simply remained to carry out her plan. She perceived the outlines of several larger, more impressive structures in the middle of the sprawling camp, so Morgaine would make her way there and she was sure to find *her*. The Mother.

Morgaine had journeyed directly here from her meeting with Jaren and the others. She had wanted to stay, had yearned to remain where she was loved and welcomed. But she could not. And the longer she spent before coming to the Witch's encampment, the more difficult that urge would be to ignore. *No, better to get it over with. You've been a hindrance for far too long.* Soon, she would do something for the greater good. For once, Morgaine would make a positive difference rather than allow herself to thwart and harm those she loved.

Even if she found both of them together—the Mother and Joselle—Morgaine was confident she could defeat at least one of them before her end. That was difference enough, she reasoned, justification for what she was about to do.

"I'm sorry, Jaren," she repeated aloud. She'd told him in person, but he hadn't realized it was not only an apology for what had already transpired, but also for what was to come. He would truly be alone now. Except for Iselle and *Valir* Llaw. But she could do nothing about that. Just as she could do nothing about her parents' demise. Should she have told him? It was too painful. He would have to find out on his own. Sometimes, it was better to discover such things for yourself. Perhaps Jaren had an idea about the wider meaning of

Morgaine's final words. It would help prepare him for what he would find back in Dal Farrow.

Enough. Morgaine forced herself back into the present. *You've a job to do, farm girl.* She used the disparaging term purposefully, to rouse her anger with Joselle. *Very well.* Morgaine was quite possibly on her way to confront the other young woman. Strong emotions would lend strength to her magic.

Supposing they were both at hand, which would she focus on? The Mother was responsible for her current circumstances, certainly. She had forced the *gift* onto both Morgaine and Joselle; twisted them into creatures of metal and flesh, newer versions of the Mother. But was Morgaine's loathing of Joselle any less? The only daughter of a rich, noble family, Joselle had made constant sport of tormenting Morgaine and Jaren. In their final confrontation before leaving Dal Farrow, Joselle had come close to killing them both with the magic. Even now, Morgaine wasn't sure how they escaped that ordeal. She now suspected it was Jaren's magic all along, not hers, that delivered them. Later, after Morgaine came to her senses at the Mother's fortress, she and Joselle battled one another. Morgaine had come out on top. It had been a measure of sweet revenge, a taste that Morgaine was not certain she could overlook given a second opportunity.

Morgaine started forward, floating down the hillside toward the camp. She would let fate decide. Whomever it was she met first, she would deal with. If she met them in tandem, it would be the one who launched the opening strike.

Morgaine transitioned to the material world as she hit the periphery of the camp. That way, her presence would go unnoticed longer. Should she hold the ethereal form, her foes would surely be alerted to the presence of expended magic by the time she reached them. If they had not already sensed her, that was.

Cloaked and hooded, she hoped to be mistaken for Joselle. They were of similar build and height, though their hair colour and facial features differed enough for anyone who looked more closely to tell the difference. Morgaine strode through the rows of hide and canvas tents purposefully, making as straight a course as possible for the center of the encampment. It took a deal of effort not to gape, as the Jhud'Hai were a foreign people with vastly different appearances and a culture distinct from what she knew. Gawking about like a stranger was sure to give her away. Even so, she observed sidelong the groups of men, sitting cross-legged about their fires, conversing with their hands as much as with their voices. Women formed similar circles of their own, laughing and gesturing much like the men. The women, it seemed, spent a good amount of their time observing and subsequently mocking the men and their habits. Young girls and boys busied themselves attending to the needs of the adults, scurrying here and there. All were clad in dun-coloured skins, some lined with fur, and all among them appeared bronze-skinned and dark-haired.

She was surprised how far she got before the first shouts of alarm went up. One man from a knot of Jhud'Haian soldiers, the only one not standing casually about, had spied her and then took a much more thorough look. He called immediately to his fellows, who grabbed spears from where they leaned in a tented fashion against one another. The entire squad rushed toward her, shouting in their alien language.

As they neared striking distance, Morgaine unleashed a bludgeoning wall of energy. The magic sent them sprawling into a nearby tent where they thrashed and cried out in dismay. From that point on the entire camp began to swarm. Though not everyone moved to intercept her, many did.

Morgaine raised her hands, directing the magic up the path to her destination, not more than a few hundred yards distant now. Along either edge of her route, fire erupted from the ground, twin lines of flame leading to the largest of the tents before her. Behind, her walls of fire converged, protecting her back. The Jhud'Hai yelled in anger and confusion, none daring to attempt a crossing of the deadly firewalls.

Morgaine strode faster. Her heart pounded in anticipation, her breathing quickened. She wore a mask of sheer determination. With each step, her confidence built. She would succeed. Either the Mother or Joselle would fall this day. Dare she hope to overcome both? Perhaps, if the True One willed it. She offered a silent prayer and approached the great tent, certain it would hold at least one of her opponents.

Joselle stepped from within the tent into the afternoon light. "Greetings, Morgaine. I expected you earlier." Her tone was mocking, dripping with disdain.

Then the first of the Jhud'Hai broke through Morgaine's protective walls of flame.

2. Morgaine arrives to speak with Jaren, Iselle and Ensin Llaw, who are headed to Vetalas.

3. Aras Edndemol travels south on the road to Ansalar with the king's men.

• 21 •

Ill News and Setting Sail

JAREN WAS IN A TRULY SOUR MOOD THIS DAY. The sights and sounds of the bustling city were lost on him. Their clothing, dust–covered and rumpled from travelling, stood out for its dullness. Even Ensin Llaw's more extravagant robes, royal blue with silver hemming, lacked the fresh and vibrant hues that paraded before them in a constant stream of people. Far more varied than any city they had yet visited, the crowds of Vetalas became even more cosmopolitan as they wound their way through the afternoon throngs toward the docks.

Iselle gazed in awe at the city's architecture. Most of the buildings appeared constructed of off–white mud or plaster and were crowded together, creating narrow, snaking avenues. Squat, three-to-four-storey structures seemed the norm, most with external steps allowing access to the upper floors. Low walls edged the rooftops, as well as the stairways where they abutted an adjacent building. Interspersed at intervals were taller, grander structures with pointed, coloured domes. The most impressive of these sat some distance off, apparently in the wealthier districts on the west side of the city.

What is Morgaine planning? Jaren plodded with heavy steps behind Iselle, who had Dagger on a short lead. The great hound strained at the leash now and then, nearly tugging Iselle off the main route and into shadowed alleyways, apparently sources of many new, intriguing scents. Llaw strode purposefully in the lead, glancing back occasionally at them.

His sister's parting words were frustratingly opaque. Did she intend to confront the Witch on her own or not? Morgaine neither confirmed nor denied it. In his experience with females, mostly Morgaine and Iselle, that generally meant they were going to do whatever thing was in question. Either they thought the answer was obvious and that it was unnecessary to reply directly, or they meant for you to break down and ask. Either way, it was a frustrating habit, especially in this case. Even if he knew for sure what she planned, he didn't have the first clue where the Witch was and, by the time he found her, it would likely be too late. He shook his head and almost growled in his frustration.

Morgaine was right about one thing. They could not go home. At least, not yet. The Witch would never leave them alone—and he doubted Joselle would either. The two were probably working together somewhere, plotting against Jaren and Morgaine. *All the more reason for her to stay and face them with me. By the Truth, this is maddening!*

He looked down to the scuffed and dusty leather satchel hanging loosely at his side. It contained the journal. The book felt heavier now, though he had known all along the gift wasn't simply as it appeared.

He heaved a resigned breath. There was nothing to be done but stay the course and discover all he could about the magic. His magic. Afterward, he could track Morgaine down and help her, whether she wanted it or not. *Just let her try and keep me away, then. I'll—*

He walked straight into someone.

Staggering back, he looked up into the scowling, stubbled face of a grizzled soldier. The man sported a pointed steel cap, a swath of crimson fabric flowing from beneath to cover the sides and back of his head. His leather-lined, dusty mail hauberk hung to his knees. Well-worn, it was sleeved to the forearm and covered by a long tunic of the same crimson fabric as that attached to his helmet. An iron breastplate was fastened atop the long mail coat, while leather vambraces and greaves, also showing the results of long, hard wear, protected his limbs.

The soldier grumbled something unintelligible under his breath, still glaring at Jaren, then continued several dozen yards further to a tethered horse. There was a long line of them tied along the edge of the street, all awaiting the return of their masters. More of these arrived on the heels of the first, though they paid Jaren no mind. *Much like the first would have done,* Jaren scoffed at himself, *if you hadn't ploughed into him.*

Iselle quipped, "Thinking of taking another go at him?"

Jaren merely frowned at her.

"Want me to?" She grinned.

"Hardly."

"Well, then stop staring and let's get going," she said.

"Please, forgive the sergeant," came a low voice as another soldier stepped between them, attending to the nearest mount. "He's not much for words. Or patience." The man smiled, his youthful face dark, like most of the city's inhabitants. He was clean-shaven, and his smile was bright. The Vetian accent was thick on his tongue.

"It was my fault," Jaren said. "I wasn't watching where I was going."

The other nodded. "That's something you'll want to change. Many aren't as cheerful or forgiving as the sergeant, especially since word of the trouble has spread."

Jaren looked blankly at the soldier.

"You look as though you come from Ergothan. Or Carathon. Have you not heard?"

"I suppose not," Jaren admitted.

Ensin Llaw and Iselle had moved closer to hear the conversation. Dagger plunked himself down in the shade created by the group, tongue lolling rapidly.

"Very well, though it pains me to bear such ill news. Carathon has invaded Ergothan."

"What?" the three of them gasped in unison.

Llaw appeared dumbfounded. "What has Haelric done in answer?"

"News is still reaching us, but it appears as though King Aldrain has taken the Ergothani king prisoner, along with a great many others. He's using them to force Ergothan into a pact of non-aggression. Not that they were at odds before, mind you. We have been ordered to travel from Vetalas to our border with Ergothan in case Aldrain forces the Ergothani to move against us—"

A bark from the sergeant drew the soldier's attention. He received another few gruff words before the sergeant turned his focus elsewhere—after another hard glance at Jaren.

"Forgive me, but now I must go," the soldier bowed his head and made a curious, rolling gesture with one hand from his forehead to mid-torso. "Safe travels, my young friends, and to you, wise *Valir*," he nodded to Llaw. "Remember to keep your head up, young man," he smiled at Jaren, "and let people know you're from Ergothan, not Carathon. It might make things easier for you during your stay." With that, he swung into the saddle and, within a moment, his horse's clattering hoof-falls echoed down the street, joined with the retreating clamour of the rest of his company.

"What do you make of that, Master Llaw?" Jaren's face was dark with worry.

The *Valir* shrugged, his face grave. "I can only guess. Perhaps the king's state of mind is less stable than I thought. Though we cannot know for sure.

Perhaps he uncovered some plot among the Ergothani." The lines in his forehead deepened and his spectacles bobbed at the end of his longish nose as he scrunched his face in thought, shaking his head. "I doubt that, as I knew Haelric very well, once. I cannot believe he would do anything to invite a war. This is truly ill news for everyone involved."

"What about taking hostages? That doesn't sound like Aldrain," Jaren said.

"No, it does not. Again, we cannot judge with so few facts. What we *can* do, is make all haste to complete our journey and then return to find out for ourselves."

"Makes sense to me." Iselle nodded, tugging lightly on Dagger's leash.

"We must book passage and be on our way," Llaw turned and headed into the milling crowds once more.

"No daydreaming, now," Iselle called to Jaren over her shoulder. "We don't need any more delays."

Jaren thought about sending a few stinging nettles of magic into her retreating backside. Instead, he followed in brooding silence. The brief satisfaction would not be worth the endless reprisals if she ever found out it was him. Jaren had never been able to fool her for long.

◆ ◆ ◆

Flocks of sea birds circled above and a strong wind pushed at them from the waters of the harbour. Sholara had begun her descent to the west, casting long shadows throughout the city. The scent of brine was strong at first, but Jaren soon became used to it. He examined the ship moored just off the nearest dock as Ensin Llaw and its captain negotiated.

"Yes, I can take you out there," Captain Jenda announced indifferently. "But you may not find what you're after. And I don't offer refunds." He looked purposefully at the three of them, his forehead wrinkling as his eyebrows rose pointedly. The sun reflected off of his smooth, bald head and his colourful, open vest shifted in the breeze. His black breeches were tucked into the tops of his high, leather boots. Jaren had never seen so much gold before: the man must have worn a fortune in jewelry.

"Don't worry yourself over the details, captain, we just need passage to the islands."

"That's what I'm saying," he replied, glancing seaward. "There's no guarantee you'll even find the islands."

"How's that?" Iselle demanded. "They're not invisible, are they?"

"Invisible, no," the captain chuckled. "It's just that they can't always be found, is all. I hear tell of a captain who sets out to find them once. Find them, he does, but they are surrounded by jagged teeth of stone for miles around. He anchors off the coast of the largest, in the safest place he can find. He spies a few great clams in the crystal waters beneath the ship and sends a few of his best swimmers down in hopes of finding a giant pearl. Some others go ashore, the captain thinking to trade with the inhabitants. Only one of the swimmers comes back, due to the treacherous undertows. The others return from the island with not a few neat little trinkets and baubles that later fetch a good price. But a squall comes north toward them, and the captain, he has to pull anchor and run to deeper waters for fear of dashing on the rocks. The storm passes, but he can't seem to find his way back to the islands. Finally, out of supplies and with the men in low spirits, he returns to port. He never does find the islands again, despite trying many times."

Jenda looked at each in turn, his eyes settling on the *Valir*. "You may find the islands, or maybe not. It's almost certain you'll never find them again, if you do. I just wanted to tell you that right off. No guarantees...and no money back."

"No offense, Captain," Jaren said, "but we've come too far to give up without even trying. Anyway, I have a feeling we'll find what we're looking for."

"No offense taken, young master," Jenda smiled, holding his hand out to Ensin Llaw, gold bracelets clinking. "But the fee remains the same. I was just wanting to make sure you understood things, is all. Good honest business, it is."

Llaw pressed several gold coins into the captain's palm.

"Honestly," Iselle declared, "we could buy half of Dal Farrow for that much."

Jenda cocked his head and peered at her, amused. "You're free to find another ship to take you, miss, but I believe the price will be much the same. No one goes to the islands because there's no point. Even if you found someone to trade with, once, you'd not find them again. Little profit to be made in single chance encounters, there is." He crossed his arms. "I'm to hire a crew, outfit my vessel and come out with a few silvers for my trouble. That's the truth of it."

"Please, captain, don't pay her any mind," Jaren frowned at Iselle. "Long trips just put her in a bad mood."

Jenda nodded, "I cannot wait but to have a conversation with her afterward then, should we find the islands."

Llaw cleared his throat. "When would you prefer to leave, Captain?"

Wry grin fading, Jenda turned to the *Valir*. "Give me one day to make the preparations and gather some men. We'll leave the day after tomorrow." The grin returned as he looked at Iselle. "At dawn, barring it interferes with anyone's beauty sleep."

Iselle started, her face reddening.

"No Captain Jenda," Jaren replied, "that will do just fine." He began to usher Iselle from the dock. She was stiff-legged at first, but then went along, though she glared hotly at the captain for a moment.

· 22 ·

Songs of Sorrow and Acts of Remorse

THERE WERE NO WORDS IN THE SONG.
Weren't there?

At times, it was as if Aras could hear voices blending into the music, but he could not discern them or separate them from the overall tune. It was simply divine. The rhythm sounded completely natural, yet otherworldly. There were slow, gentle measures and rousing crescendos that touched every emotion at once.

Tears streamed down his cheeks, it was so beautiful. He didn't mind that he wept at the music. It felt right. He trembled.

The magic elicited memories. His entire life, it seemed, played out before him against the dark curtain of his blindness.

Starving, desperate, a young Aras stumbled through the streets of Vetalas. He was no more than four or five years old. With a rusty kitchen knife, he fought feral dogs and rats for food in the alleys. He stole clothing and other essentials because no one helped him. Time after time, he reached out to passersby for help but he was refused, even rebuked or struck. Just another orphaned child, he struggled for existence among the outcast and forgotten, fending off others like himself in order to survive.

There was a flash of white light. Instinctively, Aras threw up a hand to shield his eyes, a futile and meaningless reaction. The scene changed.

Several years passed and Aras remained alive. Many did not. He'd met a girl, Sirae, a year or two younger than he was. She didn't know for sure. She was slight, but had beautiful, bright eyes. He protected her and she stayed near him. Surely, she would have died without his help. She would have become another victim of the social war that raged daily on the streets. A war that was neither declared nor winnable. Not for them.

Sirae discovered a cache of food and various goods some other street children had abandoned. That, or they'd been casualties of the streets and never returned. They'd surely stolen all of it. He and Sirae shared the board. Then, Sirae found another young girl. Aras told her to give the girl some food and send her away, but she couldn't. He didn't trust her eyes. They were grey and cold.

Aras went out to trade the two coppers they'd found in the cache for new clothes. The first they'd ever had. He found a nice russet dress for Sirae. And a comb. For himself, he bought a tunic and long breeches.

The next thing he knew, he was standing over Sirae's dead body. She'd been stabbed. All of their treasures were gone. The alley was dark and quiet. There was no sign of the other girl. Aras knew in his heart that she had killed Sirae. He'd wept then. For the last time.

Another flash. This time, though he gave a start, Aras didn't try to cover his eyes. He stopped resisting, letting his emotions come and go freely.

Aras made a name for himself in the streets and found his way into the thieves guild of Vetalas. He was a star among them—fast, fluid, intelligent and unmatched with a sword or knife. Leading a small group of renegades, he was charged with securing a weekly due for the guild in his allocated section of streets.

Late one night, a wealthy merchant and his wife passed through his territory, their driver lost and desperately searching for a way out of the district. Aras and his band dropped onto the wagon from balconies above, dispatching the driver. They opened the door to the carriage and the merchant lashed out with a knife, seriously wounding one of Aras's group. He killed the man.

As usual, he pushed the sliver of guilt back down into the pit of his stomach with the others. They all fit, locked away and forgotten.

Over time, the slivers became smaller and smaller. Easier to banish.

The wife of the merchant, pulled from the carriage, screamed and hid something in her arms. It cried. A baby. Aras hesitated, the eyes of his band watching him. He snatched the infant from his mother and she screamed again, reaching for it. Begging him to release her child. Aras had the woman dragged deeper into the darkened alley, where her jewelry and clothing could be taken. The baby, he handed to a young woman in his charge. The thieves needed many recruits, after all.

This sliver of guilt was larger, more like a wedge. He forced it down with the others. He made himself cold and unfeeling.

He wondered if Sirae had screamed when she was stabbed, like this woman as she was robbed and her child stolen.

The wedge threatened to rise. Aras gathered his band, knowing the city watch would rush to the sounds of the screaming. He made himself focus on the escape plan. Their gains meant life. Survival. The wedge became a sliver and then was forgotten, shoved down.

The white light returned, shifting the scene once more.

Word of Aras's skills spread and the assassins, a sect within the thieves' guild, recruited him. He rose through their ranks quickly, winning more fame and greater fortune by taking only the most challenging and perilous jobs. These marks were usually the shadier, more corrupt figures in Vetalas; they were cunning and ruthless and assumed everyone else acted in similar fashion to them, so security measures surrounding them were the best. Aras desired to be the best, and so to gain honour.

But now another motive surfaced, one he had long since buried in the depths of his soul. Becoming an assassin was a quicker way to meet his end. A part of him always hated the killing and the taking and wanted it to be over. Surviving was not living. There was little inherent value in anything he did. He gave nothing back, could care about no one but himself. It reminded him constantly of where he came from, of what he'd always had to do to simply exist. It was no longer enough. Surely his choice of jobs meant he'd be killed sooner than later. Better than to go on with an empty, meaningless life.

But he had not died. He survived; he refused to give anything less than his best and no one had yet been his equal. Was it spite? His desire to seek vengeance from the city that had become his prison? His innermost being laid bare before him, Aras could see that each of the people he killed chipped away at his soul, becoming more slivers of guilt. To dispose of them, he kept deepening the well down which he'd cast his humanity. It remained a gaping wound that could not be filled. The most precious of treasures could not satisfy or complete him. As much as he'd tried to cover over this truth—to drown it in blood—it remained.

He was broken, incomplete, and had always been so. He hated the person he'd become and yet he hated more those who led him down that path. That was his existence: survival through skills forged by the strength of his contempt.

It was no longer enough.

His mind erupted in white light and he fell back, the hard impact of the stone blocks chasing away the last of the dream images, replacing them with a stinging shock. His breath came in ragged gasps and he wept openly. Aras's eyes wandered vainly, his vision still shrouded in darkness. Slowly, he regained his composure and sat up.

A breeze stirred, the first he felt since leaving the rope bridge. It was warm, comforting. He realized then that the song had stopped. No—not stopped, but changed somehow. The music now carried on the breeze, coming from behind him. It swept gently past him, into the unknown expanse beyond.

The breeze became a wind, driving more forcefully. The song's volume increased. It was a powerful tune, full of raw emotion, uplifting. Aras found he had to lean into the rushing air, its push had become so strong.

Even so, it built in force. He turned and lay prone, trying to expose less of his form to the ploughing gale. Aras dug his fingers into the soft grass between the stones of the path. He pulled himself forward, fighting against the buffeting gusts. He could just barely make headway. But the wind was so strong now that if he let go, it would carry him back over the drop.

The music roared past, but was not so loud it was painful. It conjured brief images of the memories he had just relived. Of Sirae, of the mother and infant. Of the people he killed and the feelings of emptiness each had added.

The strengthening gale ripped tears from his eyes as Aras strained to drag himself ahead. The edges of the stone blocks cut into his fingers. He forced his eyes closed and hauled himself forward one arm-length at a time. The voices on the wind sang louder and more aggressively, building in tone as the wind rose in intensity.

Small grains of sand assaulted his face and hands. Aras felt his eyelids open of their own accord, though he willed them shut. The sand continued to pelt him, scouring his eyes. It felt as though the sand was boring into his head through the sockets. He screamed in pain and tried to turn away but could not. The pain was unimaginable. His voice was drowned out by the others and their unceasing song.

The sand struck his face and coursed around the sides of his head, still driven by the brutal wind. The song it carried grew to a crescendo of urgent, forceful voices. The grains spilling from his eyes left searing tracks, as if heated to melting by some unnatural force. The burning sand continued to flow and, as it did, Aras could make out dim light.

The pain lessened and his mind complained in whispers now instead of consuming, silent screams. The music of the wind diminished too, withdrawing again to soft, melodic tones.

He ceased his struggling and lay still, letting the abrasive current wash over him as the light bloomed. He allowed himself to enjoy the relative peace and gathered his wits as the last traces of the searing pain ceased, replaced by tingling warmth.

He was aware then, that two choices faced him. He could keep fighting against what was happening and find his way back across the bridge. That meant continuing on his previous course, carrying on with the established pattern of his life. He would survive. The clawing, scratching, and fighting for existence would persist; the emptiness would continue to consume him. Aras the assassin would remain.

He could make out dim images now: his outstretched arms, the contrasting shades of the stone blocks and grass. He could keep going, return the way he had come and nothing would change. He would go on living for death. Somehow, he knew that.

Or, he could surrender to the wind—let the singing tempest take him where it would. He sensed it would be all right, yet he was afraid. It had been so long since he allowed himself to be vulnerable, since he had taken a chance on caring about something. He wanted to let go, to discover whatever was being offered to him. A second chance? It felt that way, though the reasoning behind that belief melted away like wax as he tried to understand it.

Why do I deserve a new beginning? Why me?

The past was comfortable, if not satisfying. He knew what to expect. There were no unknowns. This entire side journey had been nothing but surprises and it had not been pleasant. Was his old life so bad? He chuckled bitterly. Of course it had been. He was dead inside and had not even realized it. Still, he wondered at the reason for this chance at a new life.

Just as he knew the choice lay before him, he was somehow aware that regaining his sight was not conditional to his decision. He realized, though, that he had needed to become vulnerable to really understand the path his life had taken and to acknowledge the consequences it held for him. For Aras, the feared assassin. Since he would never have lowered his guard willingly, it had been lowered for him.

The final choice, however, remained his.

Taking one last, deep breath before committing, Aras chose.

◆ ◆ ◆

Whatever enchantment they had used to cross the barrier, Morgaine knew they could not withstand her.

She drew on the magic, feeling the exhilarating rush throughout her being as the *metanduil* in her blood channelled the energy.

Reaching out toward the few soldiers before the great tent, she blasted at them with bolts of white fire.

To her dismay, the fire simply washed over them and dissipated, though it scorched and burned through their leather armour in many places. They marched steadily toward her, closing within several dozen paces.

Morgaine lashed out again, this time with tendrils of electricity that erupted from her fingertips. They seared toward the soldiers, engulfing them in glowing arcs of sinuous energy. Still they came on, spears pointed toward her, apparently oblivious to the additional burns and smoking holes in their armour.

Her wall of flame disintegrated as her concentration broke. She perceived the others, hundreds—perhaps thousands—of them, standing nearby. So far, most remained where they were.

Eyes narrowed, she studied them, all the while fighting down a panic that threatened to seize her in its icy grip. What remained of their armour was similar to the others, mostly hardened leather, some with rings or scales of iron attached. Then Morgaine observed something different. Through the holes and gashes in the leather, under melted or blasted iron bands, she saw an all-too-familiar metallic glint. It came from finely woven shirts of mail. Morgaine struggled to keep the resulting, cold fear from spreading, from paralyzing her. The mail coats were made of *metanduil*.

Her magic was useless against them.

"Stop!" a familiar female voice shrieked from behind them. Immediately, the men halted their direct advance and moved to create a loose ring of spears about Morgaine. Their eyes were cold and their faces made all the more grim by the dark hair of peculiar, thin moustaches and beards.

"I was hoping you'd come here, Morgaine." Joselle pushed past the soldiers on the periphery and stalked toward her. "We didn't part on the best of terms," her lips formed a wicked smile. "Have you come to apologize, then? Thinking of asking for forgiveness? The Mother is willing to hear you. I, on the other hand, may need some time to think on it. You know—"

Joselle disappeared in a burst of white flame. It blasted her back into the front ranks of the gathered soldiers, who were bowled over or hurled aside by the force of Morgaine's attack.

"I did not come to talk, Joselle."

The other struggled to a sitting position, then pulled herself to her knees. A pair of soldiers moved to assist her, but she slapped them away. She brushed idly at a stray lock of scarlet hair, eyes fixed on Morgaine. "Time to answer to your betters, farm girl."

Joselle shielded herself against another blast from Morgaine and, remaining on one knee, placed a palm to the earth.

An instant later, the ground rippled with energy like waves on a great sea. The ribbons of magic pulsed outward, knocking Morgaine from her feet and stunning her. The encircling soldiers stumbled, struggling to remain on their feet amid the rolling tremors.

Joselle stood. She headed toward Morgaine once more, brushing dirt and clumps of grass from her fine, blood-red dress.

Morgaine moaned softly, willing her mind clear of the ringing numbness. It was taking too long.

Joselle stood over her, hands on her hips.

"You aren't worth the breath it takes to offer forgiveness. The Mother erred in keeping me from hunting you down and finishing what needed to be done. I'm not going to make that mistake again."

She raised her hands toward Morgaine and a brilliant, white glare enveloped them.

Desperate, Morgaine kicked out at Joselle, striking her knee.

Joselle had apparently not expected a physical attack. Her concentration wavered and the aura of offensive magic dispersed. She gave a startled shriek and cursed at Morgaine.

Aware that her instinctive reaction saved her, Morgaine willed herself to keep fighting. She rolled to her hands and knees and summoned. A shockwave burst from her arm as she flung it wide, toward her opponent. The swipe of energy slammed into Joselle, her concentration temporarily broken by the kick.

Morgaine staggered to her feet and advanced. She fought to control the rage that threatened to overwhelm her. She did not want to destroy Joselle out of hatred or a need for vengeance. Though she did intend to put an end to her once-sister in the magic, Morgaine wanted it to be for the right reason. The intent mattered.

She reached Joselle and stretched a hand toward her still form, clutching her in invisible folds of air, blocking her connection to the magic.

Joselle rose from the earth, the movement stirring her to consciousness. Her face registered shock, eyes widening in dismay.

"Tell them to stay back," Morgaine ordered. "Tell them not to move."

Joselle gave a sharp cry as the energy holding her fast constricted for an instant. "Stay where you are," she shouted at the soldiers surrounding them. "Don't come any closer!"

Morgaine nodded, her face grim. "I want you to know, Joselle, that I didn't want to do this. But you left me with no other choice. You killed my parents and threatened to hurt the only people I have left. I have to stop you."

"No, please," Joselle begged. "I'll leave—I'll leave and never bother you again. I swear it!"

"If only you'd made that promise back in Dal Farrow. I might have believed it then." Morgaine closed her fingers the tiniest bit, causing Joselle to shriek in pain. "I am not glad to do this, Joselle. I will pray that the True One forgives you."

Joselle's hands clawed instinctively at the band of magic constricting her throat, her eyes widening further. Her face paled at the lack of air. "Please don't," she wheezed.

A blinding flash of white engulfed her and Morgaine found herself lying on the ground, her head spinning.

A blurred, dark form hovered over her. The image cleared enough for Morgaine to make out a scarlet hood and robe. And a grinning face that was half flesh, half metanduil.

Rhianain!

"Now, daughter," Morgaine felt the icy tones cut through her jumbled, whirling thoughts, "this is how you return to us?"

· 23 ·

Alien Shores

ISPY CLOUDS RACED ACROSS THE OTHERWISE CLEAR blue sky, driven by a healthy wind out of the northeast. Gulls circled overhead, fighting against the strong breeze in hopes of picking an early morning meal from the ship or surrounding waters. The scene had replayed itself over and again every day for the week they had been at sea. Today, the swells were especially grand, tossing the ship about like a bit of cork.

The captain praised the weather and at the same time cursed their fortune, for a safe passage into the southern islands eluded them. Every time land had appeared in the distance, it turned out to be another course of treacherous, tooth-like rocks or sandbars that emerged from the surrounding shoals. They were beginning to look the same: frustratingly familiar and too dangerous to approach.

"It's a big ship," Iselle lamented, "shouldn't that mean a smoother ride?" Her face reflected a green hue only several shades lighter than her cloak, which was bundled beneath her head at the moment. "The last boat I was on didn't have this rocking problem."

"It was probably the tons of ballast your escorts added," Jaren shrugged. "The Witch's iron men surely helped to steady the boat."

"Never mind that," she pouted, "come here and make me feel better. Can't you use your magic?"

"Iselle!" Jaren scolded. "I can't use it for just anything." He sat next to her.

Iselle, without lifting her head, felt about for him. When her hand found his upper leg, she immediately balled her hand into a fist and punched it. Hard.

"Ow!" Jaren protested. "What was that for?"

"I'm not *just anything*," she advised. "And, if I'm in pain, then it's only fair that you should be, since we're on this blasted ship because of you." She reached about for his hand and, pulling him closer, placed it on her head. "Comfort me."

Her head cradled in his lap, Jaren stroked her chestnut hair and glanced at Dagger, lying some distance away. He appeared to be quite at home although he did little more than doze, which was normal for him. The great dog raised his grizzled head, cocked it sideways as if considering something, then wagged his tail several times before returning to a quiet slumber.

"Promise me something," Iselle said, rousing Jaren from his thoughts.

"Sure, I guess."

"Promise you won't leave me behind, wherever your magic leads you."

Jaren fumbled for a reply.

"Don't tell me you haven't figured out my feelings for you."

"Well, I...I wasn't sure."

"Why do you think I followed you from Dal Farrow? Why did I resent leaving you to go with king Aldrain? And why would I still be here?"

"I never really thought about it."

"No kidding. A girl won't stick around if she's not interested. You're such a...such a *boy* sometimes."

"You say that like it's a bad thing," Jaren smiled wryly.

"It can be, when there's not a girl around to keep you out of trouble and make you use your sharp-as-a-plough mind."

Jaren pursed his lips. "So, what sort of feelings are they?"

"You know very well, Jaren Haldannon."

"I don't know. It might take the words of a girl to clear things up."

Iselle sat up, her look a mix of exasperation and amusement. "Now, don't you let this go to your head—" she lurched to her feet suddenly and leaned over the ship's railing.

Jaren rose, rubbing her back while attempting to avert his eyes. The sounds she made were less than pleasant, as was the language that escaped in between bouts of retching. Jaren felt only a little guilty that he wasn't sea sick.

Iselle finished, sinking back to sit on the deck, wiping her face. Once more, she pulled Jaren close. He let her guide him, dropping to the deck beside his slumped friend.

He tried to meet her azure eyes, while at the same time attempting to avoid her breath.

"As I was saying," she started again.

Jaren cringed, pulling back.

"Don't worry, I'm not going to kiss you with my breath smelling of sick-up. But you still haven't promised."

◆ ◆ ◆

Llaw found them sometime later, leaning on each other, Iselle's head resting on Jaren's shoulder.

Jaren's eyes fluttered open and he raised an arm to fend off the bright, stabbing sunlight.

"I'm jealous," the *Valir* acknowledged, "I haven't found a minute's rest since we boarded this infernal rat trap."

"There's been no sighting of land, I take it," Jaren said, already quite certain of the answer.

"Don't let it bother you," Llaw said. "We'll find the island soon enough."

"Are we to sail aimlessly about until luck shines on us, then?"

"If it is meant to be, it will happen."

Jaren scoffed, then offered an apologetic smile. "Maybe we're meant to do something to help with the voyage."

"Have you any ideas?" Llaw's eyebrows peaked.

"None," Jaren admitted, "but that hasn't stopped me before."

"Sea travel has never been a favourite of mine," Llaw admitted. "There are no set paths to guide one's way, other than blindly following charts others have laid out before you." His eyes took on a sudden glint of awareness. "Hmm," the *Valir's* lips formed a pensive line.

"Have you thought of something, then?"

"Well, it is not so much an idea as something I recall only vaguely."

"A chart?" Jaren pressed.

"No, a guide. Or, more specifically, a Guiding."

"What's that?"

"It is something that I'd forgotten. In the few scattered accounts describing Ravien's abilities, one seemed to be that she could discern a path where none was to be found."

"How did she do it?" Anxious, Jaren shifted forward and Iselle stirred as her headrest moved.

"Well, that's the trick, isn't it? No one knows."

Jaren sighed wearily. "Why does everything have to be such a blasted struggle? And a struggle wrapped in a veil of secrecy, no less!"

Iselle's head rose. "Can you two discuss things somewhere else, please? I'm trying to get a wink of sleep, here."

"Sorry," Jaren stood, fluffed Iselle's cloak and gestured for her to lay her head down.

"Too late for that now. I'm already awake." She glared daggers at them both. "What's so blighted important, anyway?"

✦ ✦ ✦

"What exactly am I meant to try?" Jaren asked. He stood, none too steadily, on the prow of the ship. "And why do I have to be up here?"

"That's where Ravien positioned herself, according to the annals. From there, she discerned the route."

"It's not very instructive," Jaren scowled.

"As you said earlier," Llaw replied, "not having an idea hasn't stopped you before."

"Good thing," Iselle added, "or you'd still be in Dal Farrow, yelling at spoons and forks."

"You're not helping, Iselle," Jaren said, recalling his earliest failures with the magic. He frowned. "This is a bit different than experimenting with Morgaine's talisman."

"Just you never mind, Jaren Haldannon. Hurry up and find the way so we can be done with this sea-silliness."

Ensin Llaw cracked a thin smile, unable to completely mask his amusement.

Dagger yawned and lay down at Iselle's feet. Unfortunately for him, her ire was not reserved for Jaren alone. "Lazy dog. Must you take everyone's share of the rest on this blasted boat?" Dagger's eyes opened briefly in response and his tail made several swishes along the deck, but Iselle was having none of it. She crossed her arms and switched her glare to Jaren once more.

Oblivious to this and everything else, Jaren attempted to focus on the magic. He had no idea what else to do beyond that.

Think of finding the island, he prompted himself. *See it in your mind, appearing on the horizon.* He did just that, though the concentration was difficult. It seemed not to bother him before, but now every small dip and sway of the ship felt magnified a hundredfold. He flailed his arms several times, the sensation of falling nearly causing Jaren to pitch over and into the undulating swells of greenish-blue water.

After several moments of trying, he finally achieved an inner calm. He closed his eyes and his focus allowed him to remain steady on the prow. In his magically rendered sight, the rolling waves took on a silver hue. The sky appeared white, the clouds dark grey. For some moments nothing happened, but Jaren continued to feed his strength of will into the exercise, to maintain the relaxation. He no longer felt apart from the ship, a passenger, but now as much a piece of the whole as the mast or the prow on which he stood. Movement was inconsequential, as was time. He wandered on the waves, a length of driftwood on a sea of eternity.

Dimly at first, then growing more intense, a single ribbon of blue light stretched forth from the vessel. From Jaren. It snaked away into the distance.

"To port!" a far-away voice called out. In a small corner of his mind, Jaren knew it to be his own. His words, become the voice of the wind on the waves.

"To port—you heard the young master," Llaw called up to Captain Jenda at the helm.

The latter, a less-than-convinced expression belying his true feelings, shrugged and nodded to the sailor at the wheel.

"Now straight on," Jaren's voice boomed, the magic adding volume and intensity.

Llaw merely glanced at the captain, who nodded and again conveyed the directions.

Iselle put her hand on the *Valir's* elbow, smiling as his eyes met hers. Llaw nodded, beaming. Jaren could have been his own son, just succeeding in a rite of manhood, for the breadth of the grin.

For several hours Jaren guided the ship, occasionally calling out the tracking, the captain resigned to acknowledge the headings without Llaw's further encouragement. Jenda himself had taken the helm, his previous misgivings now forgotten with the ship's rapid progress.

Not only did they follow a true course, but the wind had come fair and steady from the stern, allowing the ship to run with great speed. It seemed they were flying just above the waves. The clouds above paralleled their route, streaming in long swaths high above.

Iselle sat, snoozing against the railing with Dagger's great, black bulk curled up beside her. Llaw had seated himself on a sizeable crate, gazing forward, his flowing grey hair and beard whipped about by the winds, gusts snapping his grey robes.

An excited cry loosed from the crow's nest above; an island rose in the distance.

• 24 •

New Beginnings, Old Regrets

ARAS OPENED HIS EYES. For the first time in days, this simple action brought elation as daylight flooded his vision. He was no longer blind. He peered about. Bare trees ringed the oval-shaped, flat expanse. At one end trickled a brook. His horse stood at the other, tethered quietly, tail swishing at flies that buzzed in bright trails, illuminated in the morning sunlight. A packed-dirt highway stretched off into the distance to the north and south. Aras knew this place.

It was the clearing where he assaulted the king's men. The clearing where he faced Verithael.

The colours were more vibrant, the light more brilliant. No longer dreary and dull, the trunks and leafless branches of the trees held the promise of new life. The brown carpet of leaves, no longer a shroud of death, had transformed into a temporary veil waiting to be lifted free.

A glint of sunlight near the brook caught his eye. Squinting, he could make out the forms of two swords standing vertically, side by side, planted into a fallen log. These too were familiar, the peculiar curve of the Drisian blades unmistakable. They were his sabres.

Aras observed the boot prints in the dust and the imprint of horses' shod hooves. At the sight of the numerous dark-stained patches—the blood of the soldiers, blood that he had spilled—he felt sharp pangs of regret.

He glanced about uneasily though he sensed no danger. Waking in a glade many leagues from where he had lost consciousness to find his blades merely set out for him to retrieve should have been unsettling.

Instead, he felt at peace. He was no longer an assassin. He knew that. Something deep within him had awakened. Some part of him that had been asleep for many years was now fully aware. The knowledge of his new purpose had yet to fully reveal itself. It was not yet completely formed. He did know, however, that his blades were a necessary complement to his new life. Only now, he would employ them differently. No longer were they to be his central focus. He would not simply take lives. Dealing death was a final resort and only justified if necessary for the protection of others.

Aras strode to the brook. He paused beside his standing blades to take a deep, refreshing draught. It was cool and sweet like no water before. Still kneeling by the stream, he glanced sideways at his blades. They too, looked renewed. Freshly oiled and free of mark or nick, they had the appearance of newly forged steel. The leather bindings on the hilts were oiled and dark in colour, no longer carrying the signs of time and use.

One new feature, though, stood out among the others. Familiar as they were, each blade bore new, curious markings. He studied them briefly. How Aras knew to decipher them was unknown, but he could read the inscriptions. The first consisted of a symbol of fire, seared into the steel through intense heat. Hints of yellow, orange and red tinges flashed as the rays of Sholara's brilliance played upon it. The symbol etched into the second blade was the rune for wind. Shades of colouring, dazzling white, azure and lustrous silver, shone under the sunlight.

On further inspection, an identical etching accompanied each of these symbols. It took a moment to properly read these, as they proved obscure, even with his new command of this apparently forgotten language. They indicated a name. His name—except it was altered.

In the common tongue, it read as *Varas*. In the old writing, it translated into *The true Aras*.

Musing over his discovery, he withdrew the blades from the wood. Well balanced before, they now felt weightless. He weaved the weapons into a short pattern, the blades virtually singing through the air. It felt good to hold them again.

It felt better to hold them for a nobler purpose.

Varas sheathed the blades, then retrieved his mount from the edge of the dell where it was tethered, picking gently at clumps of grass.

He had a fair distance to travel and he sensed time was running short.

◆ ◆ ◆

"I knew you would return to me, daughter Morgaine," the Witch said. "No matter that you do not yet understand why. It will soon be made clear."

Morgaine did not respond. Bound, she strained against the unyielding, hard-backed chair, her limbs strapped to the armrests and chair legs. The interior of the tent was dark, though thin bands of sunlight shone through a few seams. Morgaine struggled to maintain calm. It was too familiar, too close to the manner in which *the gift* was first imparted months ago. Then too, she'd been restrained in a seat, forced to endure the process of the giving. *Metanduil*, hot and searing, was injected into her veins…she could not go through such agony again. *Not again.* Jaw clenched, she pulled against the straps.

Joselle grabbed Morgaine by the throat. "You will answer, traitor!"

"Joselle," Rhianain cautioned, "restrain yourself."

The young woman's eyes narrowed to slits but she released her grip. "Yes, Mother."

"You must forgive Joselle's impatience, daughter. She simply cannot understand your reluctance to embrace the magic as she has done. I, on the other hand," she added a gentle smile, "know all about your reservations. You see, I had them myself after the change. It is a lot to take in, daughter. But you will see that your path truly lies with us. With your new family."

"You murdered my true family," Morgaine hissed, eyes condemning first Joselle, then settling on the Witch. "Except for Jaren. You cannot touch him. He is beyond you."

"Silence, farm hand! You address our Mother!"

Morgaine replied through gritted teeth. "She is not our mother! She is evil and her gift is death—" she glared at them both in turn. "Jaren will stop you even if I cannot."

Rhianain, eyes grown wide in fury, drew nearer as Morgaine spoke. The Witch slapped her across the face, hard, then lowered her hand and inhaled deeply, closing her eyes. "He is talented, yes. But he is a fool to think he can best us—*the three of us*—together." Her composure regained, she patted Morgaine's hand. "You will see, daughter. You cannot run from the truth. Not from destiny."

"I will die before I aid you against Jaren again. I promise you!"

"In a manner of speaking, daughter, you will do just that." The Witch's smile was no longer gentle. "Joselle, please fetch the equipment."

"As you wish, Mother," she replied, tearing her burning glare from Morgaine.

"I do apologize for what is about to happen, daughter," Rhianain said, though the concern she expressed still did not register fully on her face. "I feel I should take the blame for your…incomplete transition…the first time around. But with your sister's help, I believe I've worked out the problem. Once we are finished, you will be in your right mind."

Morgaine felt the icy panic return, seizing her.

"You will likely experience some unpleasant effects afterward." The Witch shrugged. "That cannot be helped."

Morgaine's heart pounded against the inner wall of her chest. *She had to get out! She had to escape!*

· 25 ·

Greetings and Bad Company

THE SUNLIGHT REFLECTED BY THE PEARL-WHITE SANDS caused Jaren to squint against the glare. If he had not already become used to the light thrown back off of the waves like thousands of brilliant, tiny diamonds, he would probably be blinded. Still, he was able to make out the figures on the beach clearly enough.

They appeared of average height and thin build, but not gangly. Their hair—light brown or blonde—was long and flowing, both on the men and the women. They were bronze-skinned, like the inhabitants of the warmer, southern regions of Evarlund, the Vetians and Parceans. They stood gracefully, postures reflecting a sense of purpose. The garments they wore were coloured after the jungle foliage behind them. All manner of green and brown hues wove together upon their tunics and robes. Jaren imagined that they could very easily disappear from view if they stepped back into the cover of the vegetation.

The thought was unsettling. If others were nearby, the newcomers would likely have no forewarning. Even so, Jaren did not perceive any hint of danger. The entire island appeared calm and tranquil. He peered toward his friend and found her still propped heavily against the ship's railing, ready to lean overboard if need be. Hopefully, the landing would improve her mood. And her breath. He smiled to himself.

She caught sight of the grin and her eyes narrowed to slits. "If you're smiling at my expense, Jaren Haldannon—" Whether by design or due to her illness, she let the threat hang open.

He wiped the smirk from his face and looked back to the beach.

"Are you ready to learn more of your abilities?" Ensin Llaw asked from beside him.

"I just hope we haven't come all this way for nothing," Jaren said.

"Well, for one thing, we learned—ah, you learned—how to use the magic for seeking. Who knows what other uses such a skill might have?"

"I suppose you're right, Master Llaw."

"Of course I am, my dear boy." Llaw chuckled lightly then cleared his throat. "Now. If I might offer some advice, we know next to nothing about these people. We can presume they know equally little about us. If you don't mind, seeing as I used to be somewhat of a diplomat, I'll take the lead. It wouldn't do to go insulting anyone. Who knows what sensibilities these people may have."

Jaren nodded. "That sounds just fine." He hesitated. "But, maybe you should tell that to Iselle, too. She can be...assertive at times. It can be awkward."

"Hmmm. Yes. Yes, I do believe you have a point, young man." Llaw scratched at his long, iron-streaked, white beard.

The ship lurched to a stop; the anchor had been dropped. The sailors scrambled about making the final adjustments in mooring the vessel and readying the lifeboats to disembark.

"That's my cue," Llaw grinned wolfishly, "I must attend to the captain and brief him about our stay." He threw an amused, pointed glance at Iselle before settling his eyes on Jaren. "While you're cautioning Iselle about her tongue, please ask her to rinse her mouth with some mint leaves. Her breath is horrible." With that, he turned and moved back toward the helm.

"Wait—" Jaren began, but the *Valir* was already out of talking range. He huffed, then put on as genuine a look of caring empathy as he could before going to Iselle. If he wasn't careful, he'd be swimming to shore. At least the water looked quite warm.

♦ ♦ ♦

As the small boats approached the beach, each member of the welcoming party bowed formally. They remained in that position until the tiny craft landed.

The sailors at the bows hopped into the shin-deep water and pulled the lifeboats partway onto the sand. Jaren and his companions disembarked, moving into a group before the welcoming party. They were a stark contrast to the finely garbed islanders. The soldiers sported worn and mismatched clothing and looked in dire need of a shave and bath. Jaren and Iselle also appeared dishevelled, their garments lightly soiled and wrinkled. Only Llaw's seemed fresh, as did the man's face, leaving Jaren to wonder how he managed to look respectable when the rest of them could have been inmates after a week's stay in debtor's prison.

They—or, rather, Ensin Llaw—had chosen to leave Dagger aboard the ship, much to the great dog's apparent dismay. The *Valir* announced in no uncertain terms that it would be improper to have the hound leaping about or even bowling over their hosts. Iselle had protested but in her condition lacked the energy to sustain a prolonged argument. Looking forlorn and not a little put-off, Dagger was left in the care of a sailor who had apparently taken a keen liking to him. Jaren hoped Dagger felt that way too, for the poor man's well being.

Smiling warmly, a tall woman with golden chains woven through her long, flaxen hair stepped out from the group. Her fine robes trailed in the sand. They were trimmed and accented in gold and bore an eagle upon the breast, embroidered with fine golden thread. Other valuable-looking jewelry decorated her neck, arms, ankles, and feet. The others' adornments were similar, if not so exquisite or plentiful. Their garments were embroidered with images of other animals, including tigers, bears, wolves and hawks.

Jaren wondered if that meant such creatures roamed the island. He looked up and scanned the edges of the jungle. Out of the corner of his eye, he caught Iselle peering at him. She'd regained some of her colour and, apparently, her sense of humour. She flashed a quick smirk. She must have observed his reaction to the sight of the embroidered animals. He frowned and straightened.

The woman from the welcoming delegation waited until all exiting the vessels had gathered before addressing them.

"Welcome travellers, I am Selhanna Adairn, speaker prime of the Sylvarii. We have been expecting you for some time now."

Jaren started at the announcement. Selhanna's gaze fell on him.

"You, most of all, young *Ves'Talein*, are most welcome. We have much to discuss."

Jaren looked sidelong at Ensin Llaw.

"We are privileged to meet you, Your Elegance," Llaw bowed. The others in the landing party followed suit. "I am Ensin Llaw, *Valir*, former ambassador and counsel in the court of King Haelric of Ergothan." He gestured to Jaren, then Iselle. "These are my companions, Jaren Haldannon and Iselle Breit. It is regarding Jaren that we have come to seek your wisdom. With us are members of the crew who wish to trade with your people, if you will allow it."

"We have foreseen that young Jaren—as you name him—would arrive," she nodded to the youth, then her eyes sought Llaw's again. "And we welcome you all. Your crew may trade with our artisans and craftspeople, or any others they wish. As you may well appreciate, we do not often receive visitors. You may stay for however long you desire."

She bowed again, in the same fashion as before, the others in her group mirroring the action.

Her expression darkened. "Please, do not be alarmed. It was decided, however unwisely, that you must have an escort during your stay. Although several of us argued strongly against it, there are those who remain wary of strangers. Even strangers in the company of *Ves'Talein*. Please, accept my apology for the inconvenience."

A member of her group, an exceptionally lean, scowling man, turned and gestured toward the jungle. Instantly, armed soldiers materialized from the foliage. Two columns marched hastily forward and formed lines to either side of the newcomers. Their armour was peculiarly fashioned, imitating the curves and angles of foliage, and coloured in a manner similar to the robes of the welcoming committee. Armour plates were leaf- or petal-shaped, coats of mail appeared as the bark of trees and all surfaces bore etchings of leaves, vines and other organic features. The faces of the men—and women—were stoic, much the same as any soldier Jaren had seen. He was surprised that females formed a part of the Sylvarii army. He couldn't wait to hear what Iselle thought about it.

The scowling man stepped up beside Selhanna.

"Please, do not attempt to visit any areas of the island without a proper escort. There are dangers here with which you land-bound are unfamiliar. It would be a shame to lose anyone to the perils of the jungle. I am Nestroel. Feel free to inquire of me what you will during your stay." He pointedly did not smile.

Selhanna's face tightened. She looked down at the sand.

The man glanced at Jaren and he felt a sudden chill despite the heat and humidity.

◆ ◆ ◆

Varas watched as Sithas disappeared into the tavern, a shadow drifting in from the darkened street. Moments before, the massive Galda had dipped his head to enter through the very same doors. After waiting to see if any additional Talons arrived, Varas detached himself from the shadows of the nearby alleyway, glancing up and down the street. Satisfied no others approached, he strode toward the Dancing Leopard Inn.

He had no doubt Malhaena was inside.

It was time to check in. And out.

The door swung closed behind him, sealing in the commotion and artificial light. Several lanky-haired musicians played lively music on the flute and lyre near a roaring fire that filled the massive stone hearth. The great room surrounded this colossal feature. To his left was the bar, manned by an overweight man and woman Varas assumed were the proprietors. They kept a wary eye on the place, their beady orbs peering out from within puffed, ruddy faces. Their aprons, apparently white at one time, were soiled with grime. Across from them and hidden from their hawkish glares by the bulk of the massive fireplace, stood two burly, crook-nosed doormen. They were well-placed, able to keep an eye on the innkeepers' blind spot and still within shouting distance if needed.

At the back of the grand common room, two staircases rose to a second floor, only the outermost edges visible to either side of the hearth. Similarly, all except the very periphery of this level was hidden by the stone-block chimney which climbed to the peaked ceiling high above. The more elevated the feature of the establishment, the more it was obscured by the clouds of bluish leaf smoke rising from numerous patrons and swirling about the occasional, hanging oil-lamp.

Varas caught the expected movement out of the corner of his eye. A Talon initiate, clothed in dark green, hurried toward the left-hand stairway, shouldering his way through those gathered about as quickly as he could. It wasn't necessarily the outfit that gave the man away so much as the fact that his eyes kept sweeping back to find Varas.

He looked as though he'd seen a ghost.

Varas picked an empty corner table to his left, put his back to the adjoining walls and waited.

Soon enough, a serving maid wandered by.

"Anything for you, love?" The petite, blonde-haired woman asked in a voice that was surprisingly soft for her line of work. A career of talking over crowds in smoky places tended to coarsen the vocal chords.

"The travelers on the second floor," Varas replied, "the impatient woman, quiet giant and sly foreigner. You've seen them?" He noticed her look of recognition.

"Ah...y-yes. Yes, love, I did. Shella's the one what's serving them, though." She rubbed at an apparent itch beside her nose, shifting her stance anxiously as she looked down and then quickly back at Varas.

He gave her his order, adding, "They'll pick up the tab. Thanks." Varas leaned forward, pressing several gold coins into her palm. As she peered down, her eyes widened, wonder replacing the puzzled look.

"Something for you. They don't tip well. And a little extra for any mess we may leave behind."

She gave him a curious glance, then turned and disappeared into the crowd, expertly balancing her tray of mugs.

Deeper into the tavern a familiar figure loomed, coming closer, head and shoulders above the tallest of the nearby patrons.

"Greetings Galda." Varas offered a chair as the other neared. "It's been a while."

"Too long, Aras." He eyed the smaller man while engulfing the chair. "You know Malhaena is not pleased," his deep voice rumbled.

"It's Varas now. And Malhaena is rarely pleased about anything."

The big fellow scrunched his face. That was his expression when thinking, which apparently took a great amount of effort. "Oh...okay, then. Ar—Varas. You shouldn't have come here."

Varas searched the immediate vicinity for Galda's usual partner. He spotted Sithas, hood lowered, lurking in the shadows of a recessed wall nearby. The resulting glint of white, Varas took to be a smile. Had he known less of Sithas, Varas might have mistaken it as one of greeting.

"She coming down?" He asked Galda.

"In a moment," Galda nodded. "She wanted things checked out first."

That fit Malhaena's paranoid tendencies. Her rise to power produced many enemies, outside the Talons and even within their ranks. Varas knew the reality all too well: if you weren't cautious, you soon just *weren't*, period.

The serving maid returned, setting down Varas's drink. "Gralla nearly couldn't find any, you know. It's a rare vintage, he says. Does your friend…." She trailed off as Galda frowned at her and crossed his arms.

Varas took a sip and watched her flee to the next table. It wasn't as refreshing as he recalled.

Galda cleared his throat. "Did you at least bring the boy?" he asked. He sat forward, elbows coming to rest on his knees, which were nearly as high as the table. He fidgeted with his hands.

"Nothing to worry about, Galda. Malhaena and I are simply going to have a chat. That's all."

"I don't know, Aras." He blinked. "Varas. You know how she gets."

"I do."

"So why don't you just leave? I mean, before she gets here?"

"Galda, I've always liked you." Varas smiled. "I never really understood why you stayed with the Talons. You're not a bad person."

Galda half-smirked, shrugging his doorway-wide shoulders and sighing. "Probably same as you, I guess. I just never really knew what I'd do anywhere else. And someone has to watch Sithas's back—he's wily, but he can't sneak past all of them."

Varas nodded. He'd heard of the story of Sithas and Galda, but never cared enough to ask them about it. He doubted Sithas would have told him, at any rate. Varas pursed his lips. He also doubted that the cunning assassin would show the same level of loyalty to Galda. Varas suspected ulterior motives in Sithas's reputed saving of the huge warrior. Motives like having the eternal gratitude of a three-hundred-plus-pound giant who could crush a man's skull with one bare hand. Varas opened his mouth to speak again, but was interrupted.

"I expected you to have some company, Aras."

Galda's brow furrowed and he looked down at his feet. "Excuse me, Varas." He got up and moved several paces away, stopping to lean against one of the broad columns that stretched to the ceiling. Varas marvelled that it didn't snap like a twig.

Malhaena scowled, hands planted on her hips. Though the table obscured his view, Varas knew her foot was tapping furiously against the wooden planking of the floor.

"I am sorry, Malhaena. I just came to bid you and the Talons farewell."

Her eyes bugged, but her response was swift. "You can't be serious, Aras."

"Please, it's Varas, now."

Her head cocked to one side and her eyes narrowed. "Found a new career and a new name, have we? What's *hers?*"

"Pardon me?" Varas questioned, looking amused.

"The only reason a man does that sort of thing is because of a woman. A woman who's probably entertaining someone else at this very moment." She drew Galda's empty chair to her and sat, leaning forward with her elbows on the table. "So, why don't you stop this nonsense and just tell me why you decided to put the entire contract in jeopardy."

"There is no woman. There is no contract. Not for me. Not any longer."

Malhaena drew back a little, her head angled upward as she took a hard, measuring look. After several moments of silence she said, "I'm losing patience, *Varas.* I was simply going to give you a verbal thrashing for letting arrogance and this petty quest for *honour* cloud your perspective. Now, I'm becoming angry. You should start making sense."

Varas took another drink, then pushed the mug to the side. He no longer felt thirsty. He sniffed. "Do you ever question yourself, Malhaena?"

She said nothing, simply staring at him flatly.

"The kind of questioning that makes you really take a look at things?" Seeing that her expression hadn't changed, he sighed. "No, I thought not. Self-examination isn't for a person like you."

"People like *me.*" Malhaena's eyebrows tented. "That's rich, *Varas.* You and I are the same."

"Perhaps we were similar at one point." Varas shrugged. " Looking deeper, perhaps not. It really makes no difference now."

"No, it really does not—*Varas.*"

"You can spew out my name with as much venom as you like," Varas stated coolly. "It doesn't change a thing."

Malhaena's hand whipped forward in a blur.

Impossibly, Varas was faster.

The throwing knife that he intercepted between a finger and thumb, only inches from his throat, disappeared beneath the folds of his cloak with equal speed.

People about them continued laughing, drinking and carrying on. Casual glances passed over the pair—eyes locked with one another—and then continued on. Most of these fell on Malhaena, as they had since she entered the tavern, on her athletic curves unobstructed by snug leathers, or her high cheekbones and pert nose, but the looks did not tarry for long. Her beauty was great: her danger clearly greater.

No one, save perhaps Galda and Sithas, had registered anything of the quicksilver exchange.

Out of the corner of his eye, Varas noticed Sithas sidle closer. He was within several bounding paces. Apparently, the man leaned nonchalantly against the wall, but Varas knew differently. The assassin was tensed, ready to spring. Galda had not moved and his expression grew troubled. Varas had no delusions that Sithas would aid Malhaena. He was not completely convinced about Galda's intervention. Still, he had to be prepared. Some previous lessons, he supposed, were not to be discarded offhand.

Malhaena's eyes narrowed to slits, her right hand inching closer to the throwing knife Aras knew was concealed in the vambrace that protected her left forearm.

"I told you," Varas stated, "I came merely to say my goodbyes. And to tell you to forget you ever knew Aras Endemol. He is dead and only disappointment lies in pursuing his memory." He looked down at the mug, rising from his seat. "I'm finished with this. I no longer have a taste for it. Fortune can be a curious thing," he said, gathering the cloak about his shoulders, then nodding to Sithas and Galda in turn. "It's wise to listen when your name is spoken on the winds."

Malhaena's hand gripped the knife.

The doors burst open and a squad of soldiers bustled inside. Lightning flashed behind them; their armour was sodden, rainwater dripped from them to pool on the floor. They glanced around and, after one in the group pointed it out, moved to an empty table next to Varas and Malhaena.

When Malhaena turned her heated glare back to Varas, she found only an empty chair. Cursing under her breath, she grabbed his drink and guzzled the contents. She stood, slamming the mug back onto the table hard enough to draw several curious glances from the soldiers, then turned and stalked toward the stairs, not stopping as she jostled several other patrons aside.

None protested and any who dared even meet Malhaena's burning eyes quickly looked away.

Sithas and Galda followed swiftly after her.

• 26 •

Matters of Truth and Loyalty

JAREN MARVELLED AT EVERY NEW SIGHT within the Sylvarii city. It was a part of the jungle itself, a living, breathing community and a testament to the relationship between the people and their island home.

The walls were a towering barricade dozens of yards thick, formed of massive, intertwined trunks topped by broad-leafed canopies. At intervals he caught sight of the wall's defenders—when they allowed themselves to be seen—in breaks between leaves or natural crenellations formed by the growth and arrangement of the trees. As they passed through the great, arched entrance, Jaren noticed a multitude of roots and vines lining the interior of the organic gateway. They quivered at the group's passage. He imagined the roots and vines reaching outward, entwining, trapping and finally crushing the life out of any who might trespass. It would be a difficult fate to avoid, even attempting it at speed.

Their armed escorts led them through twisting, winding avenues. The place was truly a maze. Jaren quickly grew disoriented and had no recollection of which way or how far they'd come. Llaw, just ahead, was lost in his own thoughts as usual. Iselle walked beside him, her face a mask of astonishment. Jaren's attention returned to the sights of the city.

The Sylvarii people's homes, too, were a natural phenomenon. Either composed in a manner similar to the outer city wall or of a single, hollow and broad tree, they were living spaces in the truest sense of the term.

The people themselves formed a stark contrast to the inhabitants of Evarlund's cities, especially the more metropolitan south. Nearly to a person, the shades and manner of clothing were similar to those worn by the delegation that greeted them on the beach, if perhaps less ornate and formal. Even in rural communities like Dal Farrow a small range of colours and garment styles could be observed. The true spectrum of diversity existed in Vetia and Parcea, though, with their great ports, marketplaces and the constant flow of people in and out. There, all colours of the rainbow—and many in between—made their way into clothing and adornments, worn by people of similarly varied hair and skin tones. The Sylvarii, by contrast, though not identically dressed, reflected a more uniform likeness.

As the trio marched on, their escorts halted at apparent dead ends. Each time, the tree-wall before them drew open, trunks bending and shifting to allow passage. Once the group had exited the space, the living barrier reformed, sealing off the way back.

Jaren stared back at one of these closing barricades and bumped into Iselle by accident.

"If you want to touch me, Jaren, just reach for my hand."

He did, offering a half-amused, half-amazed smile as their fingers interlaced.

"This place is amazing," he said.

"Have you wondered what we'd do if they wanted to keep us here?"

"Why would they do that?"

She shot him a patronizing look. "People don't always do as they say, Jaren. You should realize that by now."

"I do, Iselle." He stared back. "But I have a sense of these people. This place. I don't feel any hostility. There is curiosity and expectation. And maybe wariness, but that's all."

"It's all the plants," she said. "They're probably dulling your senses— something you can't afford." She waved at a fly that began to buzz about her head.

Jaren smiled. "And the magic," he said, his grin widening. "It's like I can reach out and touch it with ease. I barely need to concentrate."

"Don't get too attached too soon," she advised, her smile pressing to a thin line. "Strange things can happen." She slapped at her neck. "Ouch. Stupid bugs."

Jaren's smile grew wider, though he tried to stifle it. "Yes, they're biting today."

Iselle's eyes darkened. "Funny, they don't seem to be biting you."

"Maybe they don't like how I taste."

"They have some intelligence, then." She slapped at another. "Ow."

She looked more closely at his face.

He pointedly avoided her eyes and concentrated on the wall of vegetation ahead, still trying to straighten his grin. They stopped at another barrier while the warriors leading their party conversed with a group that guarded the portal.

The sentinels stood aside to allow them passage and the barrier parted, the trees groaning and creaking as they separated. Iselle lost all interest in scrutinizing Jaren. Both stared in awe at the sight revealed before them.

It was the largest living thing either had ever seen.

At first, Jaren had believed it to be an enormous tree growing atop a steep-walled, low mountain of some sort at the centre of the city that was heavily overgrown with trees and brush. But the truth of it was even more astounding.

As they passed through the parted barrier, Jaren realized the gargantuan structure was a collection of living things and in perfect keeping with Sylvarii tradition. Massive trees, roots, vines, and all manner of other vegetation grew and fused together as one to create a monolithic multi-organism in the image of a single tree that rose to dizzying heights.

They were directed inside the entity through another of the mysterious tree-wall openings and guided up twisting, labyrinthine and spiralling stairways formed of thousands of living roots to a broad chamber. The great room was a circular, hollow space with smooth walls, floor and ceiling. Most of the far wall lay open, revealing a breathtaking vista of the city and surrounding forest that stretched out below in a great swath, bordered in the distance by seemingly endless, turquoise waters.

At a massive table of the now familiar organic composition, Jaren, Iselle and Ensin Llaw seated themselves across from Selhanna and several attendants.

"Once more, I apologize for the escort," Selhanna offered." There are many who have distanced themselves from our original teachings. They are paranoid and have lost faith."

"Faith?" Ensin Llaw asked.

"In the hope of *Ves'Talein*." Once again, she gazed at Jaren with affection.

Llaw nodded. "You named him that before. What does it mean?"

"It means *the child returned*. Specifically, it refers to one of our own—a young woman—who left long ago to study with your *Valir*."

"Ravien," Jaren whispered.

"Yes." Selhanna smiled warmly in reply.

"I received this journal of hers some time ago." Jaren retrieved the small book, placing it on the table. "I've been reading it. Much of it seemed... familiar."

"So it should," Selhanna beamed. "We believe you are kin to her in magic."

Ensin Llaw placed an encouraging hand on Jaren's shoulder. "You can teach him? About his abilities and how to best use them?"

Selhanna shrugged. "I suspect that—Jaren—has learned a good deal on his own. But, yes, I…we…can perhaps lend some insight. We do not so much instruct our own as facilitate their development."

Llaw frowned, "I'm afraid I haven't been much help to him. I wish I knew more. His abilities are beyond mine, or any other *Valir's*."

Selhanna sighed, shaking her head. "It is such a disappointment."

"It wasn't for lack of trying," Iselle spoke up in defense of the elder *Valir*. "Surely you can't judge him for that?"

"You misunderstand, bold one," Selhanna spoke gently. Her smile remained kind. "It is not—"

A doorway formed in the nearby wall, and a beautiful, golden-haired young woman stepped into the room. She was very similar to Selhanna in both face and overall appearance, though—perhaps because of her younger age or minor station, Jaren supposed—she wore less jewelry. She offered what the trio had come to know as the traditional Sylvarii greeting, the same formal bow as they had received on arriving. She moved gracefully to a spot behind Selhanna, peering down at the floor, but not before she braved a quick look at Jaren.

He straightened.

Iselle frowned.

Selhanna continued. "This is my daughter, Arynelle. I have asked her to assist Jaren with whatever he might need during his stay as I must attend to other business and cannot always remain near at hand."

Arynelle offered another bow, smiling but still eyeing the floor.

Jaren smiled as well.

Iselle crossed her arms, giving a sniff.

"Now, as I was saying. The disappointment does not lie with you, Master Llaw. It resides in the manner of the magic. The same magic that your people share with mine. And yet we are, all of us, divided from it."

Llaw leaned forward. "What exactly are you saying?"

"Though the magic is one and the same, the means we use to wield it is not. Jaren, like us, has no need of *metanduil*," Selhanna stated.

"None of you need *metanduil*?" Llaw asked, receiving an affirming nod from Selhanna. "I thought that perhaps Jaren and a few others shared this talent—like Ravien many centuries ago. But you are talking about an entire people?"

"Yes," Selhanna declared. "The metal-magic—the *metanduil*—is a lie. It is a deception begun a thousand years ago and perpetrated by the *Valir* ever since, even though most, like you, never knew of it."

◆　◆　◆

"I do not presume to dictate your affairs, Mother," Joselle conjured as respectful a tone as she could and tried to lessen the intensity of her gaze. "But we do not need her. We cannot *trust* her. She has already betrayed you once."

"For some, the past holds much sway," Rhianain said. "Do not worry yourself. It will no longer be an issue."

"Very well," Joselle bowed her head, though the fire in her eyes did not diminish.

"What do you think of the new squad, daughter?"

Joselle nodded, but her cheeks flushed slightly. "They are impressive. And they will be useful in the coming struggle."

"Yes, I thought so, too." Rhianain's eyes sparkled. "The Jhud'Hai seem unbothered by the thought of facing the magic, now that Morgaine saw fit to test their new equipment."

"Yes, Mother."

"And how is your little effort going?"

"Excuse me, Mother?" Joselle's heart skipped a beat.

"The thief," Rhianain answered bluntly. "Has he sent any news?"

Joselle's skin broke out in a cold sweat. "I…I…Mother, forgive me…I did not want to trouble you with trifling matters. I—"

"Silence, child. I can appreciate initiative. Your efforts may aid us."

Joselle breathed a sigh of relief. "Of course, Mother. I wished only to prove myself worthy in your eyes. I am honoured by your approval."

"Yes, daughter. Just remember to give me regular updates, however trivial. It would not do to miss an important piece of information."

"I would not think of it, Mother." *Does she know what I've done to him?* Joselle wondered in silence. She forced herself to breathe evenly.

"That is good. We will need to be vigilant in the coming days. The *Valir* in Neval Ketarra are no doubt aware of our pending arrival."

"They will be no match for us, Mother."

"I do not intend to strike at them first, child."

"The Carathonai, then?"

"Nor at King Aldrain's forces. We will be better served to wait while they resolve their own conflict. We'll deal with whomever emerges the victor. We can expect the boy to show at some point and take him, too." Rhianain gave a slight nod. "Which, of course, is the reason I am not displeased with your actions. Specific news of when and where he might turn up would be most useful. I assume you've sent Turan after the boy's little friend?"

"Yes I have, Mother." *She must not know, then.* Joselle strained, concentrating to keep her pulse from racing as the Witch took her hand. "I will serve you well in this."

Rhianain patted it. "As you shall, child. As you shall." The Witch turned her gaze to a corner of the tent, where a lone figure stood, motionless. A mask of *metanduil* obscured the figure's face. The visage was quite plain; it formed a woman's features with lips set in a frown and a single, molded tear frozen on one cheek beneath the etched eyes. No holes existed to allow for the wearer's vision.

"Morgaine, dear, would you care to join us?" Rhianain asked. She nodded to Joselle, who motioned toward the figure.

Morgaine obediently walked toward them. Once she drew near, Joselle motioned again. "That's enough, *sister.*"

Morgaine stopped.

"I am honoured, Mother, that you have entrusted control of my sister to me."

"It is a reward of sorts," Rhianain said. "And also a reminder," she looked into Joselle's eyes, "of the important and privileged place you hold. I am confident that *you* will not err in your duties as your sister has. Perhaps, some day," the Witch lamented, "she will follow of her own accord."

Joselle's eyes broke from Morgaine's mask, seeking Rhianain. She fought to keep her voice steady." I will serve, Mother. I will not disappoint you."

• 27 •

The Truth Revealed

"So, THE WARWITCH WAS TELLING THE TRUTH—" Jaren hesitated as Ensin Llaw and Iselle shot him incredulous looks. "I mean, to a point, anyway."

"What did this…Warwitch…tell you, exactly?" Selhanna asked.

"She said I'd been lied to," he searched his memory, "that I'd been… misguided. I didn't realize she was being truthful."

"Yes, she was very forthcoming. Then *she tried to kill you*," Iselle scoffed, arms still crossed. She pointedly did not look in Arynelle's direction.

Jaren regarded her, puzzled.

"Peace, my dear girl," Llaw soothed.

"I have not heard of her," Selhanna said. "We do not come by news of the mainland often. However, by your reactions, I would advise you to be wary of this person. One can use the truth as a weapon if only certain parts are revealed. Partial and half-truths can be as devastating as deception."

Llaw sought Selhanna's eyes once more. He stroked his beard absently. "So, you are telling us what? That there is no need for *metanduil*?"

"No. It was created by the first *Valir*. It is artificial. And unnatural."

"But then why does everyone on the mainland other than Jaren need to use it?"

"I do not have the answer to that."

Llaw frowned. "It is a difficult truth to believe."

Selhanna raised an eyebrow. "Tell me, Master Llaw, have you attempted to summon since arriving?"

"No."

"Then try to create something simple with the magic."

"I don't see what point—"

"Please, indulge me," Selhanna said with a knowing look.

"Very well." He raised a hand, gazing nonchalantly at the others. Nothing happened. He shifted in his seat, sitting straight. He gestured again. Still, nothing happened.

"What is it you wish to summon?" Selhanna asked.

The *Valir* cleared his throat. "I must be more fatigued from the voyage than I thought…just a small globe of light." His brow furrowed in concentration. Again, his gesture proved fruitless. He gave a huff, then rummaged through his belt purse.

"Haven't I seen this somewhere before?" Iselle observed lightly. "Jaren, maybe you should conjure up a spider or two?"

Jaren had to restrain himself from laughing out loud. That was one of the experiments Llaw himself had tried when first attempting to aid Jaren in coaxing his magic forth. The *Valir* had thought emotional reactions, like fear or panic, focused Jaren's abilities and allowed him to summon.

Llaw threw a frustrated glare at Iselle, but said nothing. He withdrew two exquisitely forged, fingerless *metanduil* gauntlets. Shoving his hands into them, Llaw took a deep breath and closed his eyes. He opened them.

Before him was a pale, blue sphere of light, not bright enough to add much illumination to the day-lit room.

"See," Iselle said to Selhanna. "It still works."

"Master Llaw?" Selhanna deferred to the *Valir* for a response.

Wiping at the perspiration forming on his forehead, Ensin Llaw looked at Iselle. "My dear girl, this proves her point. I used as much of the magic as I could summon just now. And the result was a light that would barely let you find a chamber pot in the dark."

"But," Jaren broke in, "it did work."

Selhanna nodded. "The further you travel from Evarlund, the less effect the *metanduil* will have. It is only useful within a certain range. Out here, leagues from the mainland, it is already weakened beyond utility."

"So, what happens?" Jaren pressed.

"And," Llaw added, "why can only Jaren wield magic without the metal? What has caused him to be unique?"

"We have spent a long time studying the process," Selhanna said. "Because we do not travel to the mainland, it has been difficult to obtain *metanduil*, though not impossible. Tell me, Jaren. Do you know how the magic itself works?"

"I have given him some rough information," Llaw replied. "However, thinking I was dealing with an unknown talent, I did not give him a full accounting. Please," he nodded in respect, "if you would?"

Selhanna responded in a gracious tone. "The magic, as far as we can understand the All-Father's design, operates by manipulating the ether. This intangible substance is much like the air we breathe. We believe it exists within the air, in all things, both living and nonliving. It brings life and structure. It is the life-giving breath of the All-Father himself."

"Do you mean the True One?" Jaren interrupted.

"Yes, though you name him differently, I believe he is one and the same. The use of magic is simply calling on the ether to behave in certain ways. For example, if I want to create fire, I force the ether to separate into small bits and then crush them together. The energy created ignites the air. To continue the process, I keep dividing the ether and feeding energy into the flames."

Jaren nodded. "And to create cold, or ice, you would slow the ether's natural movement." His voice carried obvious excitement.

"Yes, Jaren. And if electrical energy is desired, the ether is shaped into sheets which are drawn across one another. When this is done properly, lightning forms and travels along the seams."

"If I want to move something, I harden the ether and use it to push or pull."

"Exactly, Jaren. You already have a great foundation that will surely serve you well."

Llaw smiled, despite his earlier struggles.

Arynelle also studied Jaren through approving eyes.

Iselle leaned forward, planting an elbow on the table and plopping her jaw onto her hand. She yawned.

"So then, how does the shielding work? And the bolts of energy?" Jaren's questions followed in rapid succession, his excitement building.

"The shielding works similarly to the creation of electric energy. It's simply formed into a closed path." She grinned widely. "Would you like to know how to keep a summoned effect in existence without further concentration?"

Jaren's eyes widened, as did Llaw's. The *Valir's* face grew sombre once more. "This still does not explain Jaren's abilities when others cannot do as he does without *metanduil*."

Selhanna pursed her lips. "An absolute answer, I cannot give you," she said. "But, I have my suspicions that the True One's own hand has been active in the circumstances—whether in reaction to events on the mainland or according to design, I can only venture a guess. Of course, it could be merely a chance turn of events, however unlikely that seems."

"The True One has indeed taken interest in our young friend," Llaw acknowledged. "An avatar befriended him shortly after he began his journey."

"An avatar, you say. Then at least some evidence suggests the intervention of a higher power. "

"After witnessing events alongside him, or on hearing of those I was not present for, it becomes more and more difficult not to believe," the *Valir* agreed.

Selhanna regarded Jaren. "I will have Arynelle assist you in learning more about our ways. Perhaps in this fashion you may learn more about yourself and your destiny. Jaren—*Ves'Talein*—" she rose and took his hand in hers. "It has truly been a privilege and a pleasure to speak with you. And with your companions." She met the others' gazes in turn. "I must now meet with the elders. They require an account of our conversation."

"Before you take your leave," Llaw said, "might I make one further inquiry?"

"What would you ask of me?"

"Why could we not sense Jaren's potential? Why did we believe he had none?"

"That is interesting," Selhanna mused partly to herself. "Perhaps, the *metanduil* was a barrier to your sensitivity. On studying the magic-metal, we found it hinders our abilities, even here at a distance, during times when ill-favoured winds descend from the north. It is something we might examine together." She acknowledged them once more and turned, nodding to Arynelle, then exited through the newly-formed doorway.

"I am anxious to work with you...Jaren Haldannon," Arynelle said, voice cheerful and bright. Her green eyes shone. "Please, if you will all follow me now."

They filed after the young woman, who started off through a different portal than had Selhanna.

Last in the line, Iselle grumbled something to herself.

"What was that?" Jaren paused.

"Nothing," she said. "Now turn around. *And don't lose your way.*"

He hesitated for another instant, wearing a puzzled look, then simply shrugged and kept going, too worked up to give her peculiar tone further thought.

With a huff, Iselle stomped after him.

· 28 ·

Of Foundations and Relationships

OVER THE COURSE OF THE NEXT WEEK, Arynelle met regularly with Jaren to explore his grasp of the magic. Each time, they gathered in the same location, a wide, green space near the base of the mammoth tree. There were many of these secluded parks within the Sylvarii city. This one in particular, with its high vantage, afforded the best view of the sprawling city and the scenery beyond. The two practitioners had just finished a short break from their exercises, the time spent gazing out over the sweeping vista below.

Iselle sat nearby, as always, a book spread before her. The pages had barely advanced in the time she spent in their company. More often than not, her eyes glared past the pages to Jaren and Arynelle. They rolled, or narrowed to slits as her forehead creased and her eyebrows knitted into a sharp *v*.

"Your focus and control have improved, *Ves'Talein*," Arynelle said in familiar tones. "And you have shown much talent and insight. Mother has suggested we try something different."

"All right," Jaren replied. "I'm ready."

Iselle's eyes rolled and her fingertips turned white, pressed tightly against the book's cover.

Arynelle sent several bolts of white fire streaking toward Jaren.

He immediately formed a barrier, the magical missiles bursting harmlessly against the shield.

"I thought you wanted to do something different this time."

Arynelle smiled wryly. She inverted her hand, palm up, and raised it.

The earth beneath Jaren began to shift upward at an angle, roots beneath the surface extending and poking through it. He found himself sliding down the incline.

Arynelle sent another three bolts tearing toward him.

Still fighting against gravity, Jaren sidestepped to avoid falling. His magical globe flickered, wavering with his divided focus. One of the bolts shattered against the shield, but the other two found their way home.

"Ouch!" Jaren cried, losing his balance and rolling down the remainder of the incline. He came to a stop after a few dozen paces, rubbing his shoulder and abdomen. "Those sting!"

Iselle's eyes brightened. "Yes!" she uttered in a hushed voice, but not as quietly as she'd hoped.

Jaren eyed her. "What did you say?"

"Nothing," she lied. "I just found a very entertaining bit here. Good writing." She ignored his return scowl.

"I expected as much," Arynelle interrupted with a laugh.

"You cheated," Jaren said. "If you hadn't moved the ground, I'd have stopped them."

"That was the point, Jaren. You cannot always assume a solid, immobile stance. You need to be able to move and remain focused. If you can't you'll be defeated sooner than later."

"Okay then," he said. "Show me how to do it."

"Take up your stance."

"I already know how to do that."

"Just do it," Arynelle ordered, sounding more amused than impatient.

Jaren complied, concentrating, letting his body, mind and spirit meld into one entity. He could see the ripples of ether more clearly now, knowing from Arynelle's guidance what they were and how to notice them. They surrounded him, Arynelle, and even Iselle. Each movement, even the most subtle, caused the ether to stir and ripples to form. A gentle breeze swept across the clearing, leaving translucent waves of ether in its wake. This was the essence of the magic. *Val'Tial.* It existed through, with and in everyone and everything. It was the eternal breath of life, created by the True One.

He wove his arms in a circular pattern, watching the ether swirl around the limbs, fluid, alive. Stopping the movement in the familiar warding pose, his shield sprang into being.

"Now, walk forward, keeping your barrier up."

Jaren inhaled deeply, letting the energy fill him. He knotted his face in concentration and took a shallow, faltering step. The barrier held. Several more steps, longer this time, and steadier. The blue screen of protection remained intact.

"Very good," Arynelle said. "Now, faster."

Jaren frowned. Beads of sweat formed on his forehead and torso as he clenched his muscles tighter. He managed several quick, staccato steps before an exposed root snagged his foot. Stumbling, he caught himself, but the shield dissipated.

"Was that root yours?" he asked Arynelle.

She nodded in reply.

"But how? How can your magic affect me while I'm shielded?"

"It was the root, encouraged to grow more quickly by magic, but still just a normal root."

"So, you can affect something with the magic but that object can still be used to defeat a barrier?"

"Yes. It's using the magic while not using it."

"I think I understand," Jaren nodded. "Do you think the same thing would explain how a normal object like an arrow or a bolt—or even one that's enchanted with *metanduil*—could get past a shield?"

"As for the arrow and bolt, yes. Unless you've attuned your barrier to natural items, they could pass through. As for the *metanduil*, I don't know."

"Well—" a small rock glanced off the side of Jaren's head as he spoke.

"Barrier's down," Iselle called, grinning from ear to ear.

"Iselle," Jaren growled. "Read your book!"

Arynelle chuckled. "You must be ready, Jaren. Still, not bad for a beginning. Now, try to hit me."

"But—" Jaren began.

"Just do it," she mock-scolded once more, then sprinted away.

Jaren took up his posture, calling on the magic.

Arynelle had gone several dozen paces, then turned to face Jaren. Her barrier appeared and at the same moment, she began to pace back and forth, eyes on Jaren.

He sent a thin trailer of lightning after her.

She cartwheeled away, shield still in place. The lightning reached the empty space she'd just vaulted from, then curved toward her once more. She ducked under it, moving back in the opposite direction. Each of her movements, though graceful, sent waves of ether spinning and rippling outward.

Jaren focused harder, firing several bolts of energy while continuing to chase after her with the lightning. He'd gotten better at summoning several different elemental energies at once—another product of his recent training.

She continued to evade the snaking tendril of electric energy and the white bolts shattered against her barrier without effect.

Iselle clapped her hands, the book lying open on her lap, forgotten.

"Whose side are you on?" Jaren demanded.

"Sorry—want me to see if your barrier is still working?" Iselle reached for another small stone.

Jaren rounded on her. "Now that I know to expect it, go ahead," he challenged, arms crossed.

"Okay, that's enough practice for now," Arynelle laughed. "Come, Jaren, sit with me." Her back to the Dal Farrow youths, the Sylvarii sat and gazed out over the cityscape.

Jaren joined her, after shaking his head at Iselle.

Iselle mimicked Arynelle silently in a gross exaggeration, crossing her own arms in disgust. She retrieved the book, hiding all but her glaring eyes from the other two.

"I think I already did something like this on the mainland," Jaren announced, gazing across the island himself. "Just one time, and by accident. But it had the same feel."

"That's interesting," Arynelle smiled. "Maybe you'd have found out how to do it on your own, eventually."

"That's sort of what I've been doing to this point," Jaren admitted. "Seems to be the hard way to learn, though."

"I expect you've done just fine without proper instruction—taking nothing away from Master Llaw—but he doesn't understand the manner in which we use the magic."

"He's made some good observations in his time with me."

"Yes, he's to be commended for his efforts."

After a short time spent in silence, Arynelle leaned toward Jaren, "Now what are you thinking?"

Jaren shook himself from his thoughts. "My sister, I guess. I'm worried about her."

"Would you…like to see her?"

Jaren peered at her with a questioning look.

"I wasn't supposed to begin this lesson until later, but I can see you're troubled." She bit her lip, considering something. "It might help you focus better, not being worried. That would actually move things along more quickly."

Jaren wasn't sure if she was explaining her reasoning to him or doing it to convince herself.

Arynelle shrugged, apparently decided. "You've told me how you communicated with the Warwitch."

"Yes," Jaren said.

"Well, seeing at a distance isn't so different. Instead of projecting your voice, you just send your…eyes." She gazed into his.

"Oh, well, if that's all there is to it," Jaren chuckled lightly.

Iselle leaned forward, angling her head to better hear their conversation. Her train of sight fell on the tiny rock. Frowning, she cleared her throat.

The other two glanced at her.

"Excuse me," she apologized too quickly.

"Okay," Arynelle instructed Jaren, "think of your sister. Recall her features, her movements, her being. Then, just *lean* into the image, without actually leaning."

"Lean without moving?"

"Yes, that's how you move while focused, too. You think it first. Will yourself to move, then your body will react, aided and further empowered by the magic. It's the same with *Tel Vrista*." She read his confusion with her unfamiliar language. "Sorry. It's the same with *long sight*."

"Okay," Jaren said, still digesting the information. He closed his eyes, picturing Morgaine and her mannerisms, observing her through his memory.

His surroundings materialized before him in the ghostly hues of magic-enhanced vision. The flows of ether appeared more like wisps of mist than translucent ripples in this state, but he could see them nonetheless. There was a tugging sensation, a feeling that he was being pulled forward. He focused more tightly, trying to shut out all outside interference. Jaren thought about leaning, of giving in to the invisible drawing force. He could feel himself begin to float, transported on the ethereal mists.

His stomach lurched and he recoiled, his vision snapping back violently. He gasped, eyes flung wide.

"Well," Arynelle asked, "what happened?"

"I don't know," he said. "I started floating up and off, then…then it was like I just fell." He wiped a sleeve across his perspiring brow. "I don't feel so good."

"Need someone to rub your back?" Iselle asked glibly.

"It's as good a start as any," Arynelle smiled, ignoring the interruption. "We'll try again later. For now though, it's back to basics."

Jaren suppressed the churning in his stomach and rose to his feet unsteadily. Arynelle clasped his hand. "Are you all right to continue?"

"Just give me a moment and I'll be ready." He smiled back at her.

There was a smack as another tiny rock bounced off the back of Jaren's head.

"Shield's still down," Iselle called in a too-cheerful, melodic voice.

Jaren turned to glare at her, rubbing his scalp. He couldn't see her expression through the book she held before her face, but her eyes said she wasn't really smiling.

◆ ◆ ◆

Jaren cast yet another anxious glance back over his shoulder.

"I don't think your friend would hide in the bushes, Jaren."

"That just shows how little you know her." Jaren gave Arynelle a meaningful look. "Just when you don't expect it—"

"She can't be that bad."

"She's not *bad*, she's just…Iselle. Actually, her skills come in handy at times." He gave their surroundings another pass. "At others, they are not so helpful."

"I can only imagine. Anyway, is it safe to continue?"

"Yes. I don't think she followed us."

"I meant you, Jaren. If you are not focused, your magic can be a little… unpredictable. Especially if you are focused on her."

"What? Oh—yes. Let's get started." He paused. "What do you mean, *if I'm focused on her?* You meant if I'm not focused on the magic, right?"

"All right, Jaren. If you say so."

"I mean, how would you know if I was focused on her or something else?"

"A girl can tell, Jaren. It's pretty obvious, actually. I think a blind beggar would likely notice the way you two carry on."

"What? Carry on?" He tried to sound as indignant as he could.

"It's almost enough to discourage someone else if they were inclined to pursue you. Almost." She grinned at him wolfishly and brushed a stray strand of golden hair from her forehead, tucking it behind her ear. Her eyes sparkled like emeralds at the bottom of a deep, clear pool.

Jaren swallowed and looked away. "I...I'd like to try the long sight again."

"If you feel like gazing elsewhere, go ahead. I'll wait."

He cleared his throat and closed his eyes. He felt hot. *That's all you need, for Iselle to see you blushing at her. She'll pick up a boulder, then.*

Jaren concentrated on his breathing, banishing the thoughts of Iselle, Arynelle and anything other than Morgaine. He focused once more on his sister, on her pale skin and drawn face. The tugging force came almost immediately this time. He relaxed further, exhaling. Again, the sensation of rising up on currents of air enveloped him. All too soon, though, he dashed back to the earth, thrown from the experience and his concentration.

Twice more Jaren attempted the feat and both ended in failure. He plunked himself on the ground with a huff after the last.

"Tell me," Arynelle asked, "how do you picture your sister?"

"Exactly as she was the last time I saw her. I thought the more recent the image, the better."

"Describe her to me."

"It's difficult. She's been...changed...by the Warwitch. She's different now. She looks sad—like she's lost something dear to her. And her appearance has changed. She's pale, almost ill-looking."

"When you think of your sister, is that how you think of her?"

"No, not really. I still think of her as the old, bossy Morgaine. The one who's barely been sick a day in her life and is always advising what's best for me."

"Try picturing her that way the next time you reach out with the long sight. Picture the Morgaine of the past, the person you believe her to be. The way you really remember her."

"Okay. I guess it can't turn out any worse."

"That's the spirit," Arynelle laughed, leaning closer to Jaren. "So, what would your sister's advice be right now?"

Jaren blinked. He could smell the sweet scent of her perfume. The shine of her eyes was dazzling. Almost hypnotic. "She'd...she would tell me to get back to practicing. Stop messing around. You know, the usual."

Arynelle's hand reached for his. Jaren froze, unsure how to deal with the attention. Arynelle smiled, amused, as her hand caressed his forearm. "I'm sure I *don't* know," she offered softly, "so maybe it's good that she's not here to...interrupt."

Jaren swallowed hard. If he'd taken another opportunity to scan the surroundings, he might have noticed as Iselle crept from her vantage point in the brush at the edge of the park and hurried away, one trembling hand muffling the retreating sound of her sobs.

• 29 •

Musings and Dire News

ENSIN LLAW SAT, ARMS CROSSED, pipe hanging forgotten from his thinly pressed lips as he stared vacantly out the opening in the wall. It would normally have been a window, but the organic buildings populated by the Sylvarii had no such things, just as the doorways were different. *So many differences,* Llaw thought. Soon, however, the inhabitants of the mainland would know the most fundamental of these. Everything would change, then.

Of course, some of them already knew the secret. Knew it and continued to feed the lies. How would they react, those who perpetuated this façade?

Outside, twilight gave way to full night, stars winking into view across the darkening canopy of sky. At the same time, points of light sprang up all across the cityscape like a myriad of firelings—the tiny, glowing insects that inhabited the steaming jungles of these southern islands.

It wasn't really a valid question. They would react as they always had, Llaw assumed. They would move to eliminate the source of the knowledge and limit the damage done. Clearly, the events surrounding Ravien Alluminara's fate had been carefully recorded to reflect what the *Valir* wanted everyone to believe.

Had there been others before Jaren, he wondered? Others since Ravien who'd been eliminated, all traces of them extinguished? It gave the elder *Valir* pause. Jaren had been right to suspect them, and Llaw himself had been a fool. How could he have believed they wanted anything but complete control? He drew deeply from his pipe. They had purposefully downplayed his role in bringing Jaren to heel for them. They had stressed *mentorship* and *guidance* in his role. They would have seized Jaren the moment the opportunity arose. Would he have helped them, unwittingly? Llaw exhaled, the faint breeze stirring the smoke as it rose. Would he have delivered Jaren to his doom?

And how many on the council were implicated in this deceit? It most surely could not be all of them. Many were likely as blind to their ambitions as Llaw had been. A shadow council, then? A smaller, hidden group within the main council body that secretly maintained their unnatural grasp on the use of magic? It seemed the logical explanation.

The idea also presented numerous difficulties. Who could be trusted? It would not be easy to determine, especially at a distance. Anyone could be an agent of this shadow guild, ready to betray them at the slightest hint that Llaw knew the truth. What could be done? If no one could be relied upon, the task of revealing their lies became even more difficult and dangerous. Only a handful of others, including Morgaine and King Aldrain, would be safe to approach. The former was nowhere to be found and the latter, despite Llaw's assurances to the contrary, was not overly dependable at present. Though he'd told Jaren otherwise, Llaw did not believe that the king was in any position to help them, let alone himself. In fact, rumour suggested the opposite: that Aldrain Draegondor was delusional at best and, at worst, completely mad.

And would Jaren continue to trust that he, Ensin Llaw, was loyal? That Llaw had been ignorant of their schemes and acted with Jaren's best interests at heart? It was a delicate matter.

Perhaps the Sylvarii could help. They had suffered the most with the advent of the six realms. Their lands and way of life had been taken from them. They had first been marginalized and then exiled to these islands as the fledgling nations of Evarlund expanded and prospered.

Even if they could help, would they?

How likely would they be to assist the very people who had shunned and banished them? Not very, Llaw suspected. Though as options went, there weren't so very many to choose from. The Sylvarii were the best place to start if only because he was among them to raise the issue.

The *Valir* turned his attention once more to the piles of parchment and stacks of leather-bound books covering the table. Pulling his spectacles out of a pocket, Llaw put them on and took up his research once more. He needed a firm grasp of historical fact when he finally broached the subject with their hosts.

◆ ◆ ◆

"I truly hope you have enjoyed your time among us so far," Selhanna said. "If there is anything more we can do, please do not hesitate to ask."

Iselle sank lower into her chair, arms folded, but issued no sound.

"Actually," Llaw began, "I would like to speak with you and any others among the leadership who would be willing to listen."

Selhanna's face darkened. "Has there been some problem, *Valir* Llaw?"

"No, no. Nothing of the sort," Llaw said. "But I would very much appreciate the opportunity to discuss…matters of state…so to speak."

Selhanna nodded. "I will see to it that as many as possible can be contacted. When would you wish to meet?"

"It's not urgent," the *Valir* admitted, "but the sooner the better, as the saying goes. I'm sure I don't have to tell you that things on the mainland will be greatly affected by the knowledge we've gained. Not everyone will be happy to hear what I have to say."

"I understand, *Valir* Llaw. As soon as we've finished here, I will begin notifying the others. Now, was there anything else—"

The wall-opening burst wide, admitting Jaren, clearly agitated and breathing hard, as though he'd run all the way.

"I have to leave!" he announced in a raspy voice.

"What has happened?" Selhanna asked.

"The Witch has her again—Morgaine has been captured!"

"How do you know this?" Selhanna questioned.

"Are you certain?" Llaw asked.

Jaren glanced at both of them. "Yes—I've been practicing the long sight. I finally did it. And I saw her—she's in the Witch's tent, held prisoner. The Warwitch has done something to her again, but I can't tell what. She's fighting it, but I don't know how long she can hold out. I'm sorry, Mistress Selhanna, but I have to go. Now."

"Even if you could go this instant, lad, there's no guarantee you'd get there in time to help."

"I agree with *Valir* Llaw," Selhanna said. "The voyage will take many days—weeks even, if the weather is not favourable. And, you've just begun to discover your true abilities."

"I'm not planning to sail there," Jaren's face showed a steely determination. "And, forgive me for being forward, but I wasn't asking your leave. I'm going."

It took a moment for his words to register, but the light of realization shone first in Selhanna's eyes, then Llaw's.

"You mean to spirit walk," Selhanna said.

Llaw sighed heavily, his shoulders slouching.

Iselle sat up finally, hands planted on the table. "That's insane, Jaren, and you know it."

"It's not insane, and I've learned how to spirit walk well enough since arriving. What good is the knowledge if it's not used when needed?"

"No one has used the walk to travel to the mainland," Selhanna declared. "Ever."

"That doesn't mean it cannot be done."

"The metanduil hinders our abilities. We could not get close enough. If we tried, the results could be—"

"My summoning isn't affected by the metanduil like yours. I can do it."

"You've just acquired these new skills and have yet to attempt them on the mainland. How do you know they will work there, even for you?" Llaw questioned.

"It has to be tried sometime."

"At some point, yes," Selhanna reasoned in an urgent tone, "but with more practice, and under different circumstances. You are hardly composed at the moment. Using a new skill with compromised focus—especially attempting to go where it's never been used—is only tempting fate."

The sound of running footsteps preceded Arynelle's entrance. She halted beside Jaren in a flurry of white and tan robes, huffing in deep breaths, her face flush with exertion and worry.

"I'm sorry, Mother," she gasped, "he would not listen to reason."

"At least we can agree on that," Iselle grumbled.

"Jaren," Arynelle pleaded, "don't rush into this." She reached for his hand but he recoiled. "You've only walked short distances—a few dozen paces," she paused for breath. "This is beyond anything you've tried before. And we don't know what might happen once you reach the coast."

"Jaren," Llaw added, trying to hold the youth's anxious gaze. "Think of what happened the last time you rushed to action."

"I won," Jaren said, flatly.

"Yes, but it was most assuredly not guaranteed. You yourself told me it was only by the will of the Truth that you prevailed."

"Whether I go now or later," Jaren met the others' eyes in turn, "it will still depend on the favour of the Truth."

"But would you run recklessly toward an encounter, demanding that the All-Father grant your victory?" Selhanna asked. "Or would you prepare for it and, therefore, earn such grace and the right to prevail?"

"Morgaine chose the riskier path," Llaw said. "She waited for neither the right time nor the aid that could have prevented this."

"Enough!" Jaren shouted, shocking even himself. Still, he gathered his thoughts and went on, "I understand your fears, and your cautions are well-placed. But I don't have the time for this. I know Morgaine was wrong in rushing off to face the Witch." He shook his head, looking down, "But if I only help others when it's safe for me, I'm not truly acting for the good of those people. I'm acting in my own self interest. I have decided. I am leaving. Now."

"And I'm going with you," Arynelle stated. Absolute silence reigned for several heartbeats.

Everyone then spoke at once.

"No, you're not!" Jaren exclaimed.

"Arynelle, I forbid this!" Selhanna declared.

Llaw spluttered, "You'd be risking her life, too!"

Only Iselle remained quiet, though her eyes narrowed to intense slashes of blue.

Arynelle eyed each in turn. "Mother, you cannot forbid me. I am of age to make these decisions for myself, according to custom. *Valir* Llaw, no one risks my life but me. It is my choice, and mine alone." She saved the most severe look for Jaren, her emerald eyes cool. "Jaren, I will do what I wish. If you are committed to this decision, then I will follow, whether by your leave or not."

"How do you know you'll be of any help?" Jaren asked. "For all you know, you cannot summon on the mainland."

"Then I'll stand by you to make sure no one sticks a dagger in your back," she said. "I am no stranger to fighting."

"Don't make me choose between you and my sister, please," Jaren begged.

"Your choice is yours. Mine is out of your control."

"This is—" Llaw cut short as Selhanna made a halting gesture toward him.

"Daughter, you are within your rights," she said. "But know this: we cannot help you. You will be alone with the *Ves'Talein*, far from our reach. It would be better for you to continue to speak against this madness. Better for us all."

"I am sorry, Mother, but if he leaves, I go with him. I'll not let the time spent exploring his talents be in vain. Not when I can do something to protect against it. We knew he would bring change. Conflict. Who is to say we are allowed to choose the what or the when of it all?"

All eyes fixed on Jaren.

He could not bring himself to meet anyone's gaze. "We'll leave tomorrow morning at first light." He wheeled and left the room. The others continued to watch, even as the doorway shifted closed behind him.

• 30 •

Going Back

JAREN HATED TO LIE, BUT HE FELT there was no other alternative. He could not live with the idea of others putting themselves at risk because of his decisions. He would not wait until the first light of dawn.

It was the reason he now sat cross-legged in the middle of the darkened clearing that he and Arynelle used for training. He had already used the travelling to get here. He knew that his Sylvarii companion would be observing the room he occupied. Just as he knew Iselle would be planted somewhere nearby, hidden in the shadows, watching for him to try and sneak past her.

What neither of them knew was that he had trained with the spirit walking every free moment he possessed since learning it. Every night he experimented. Jaren knew that the Witch, Joselle, and Morgaine all knew how to do it. As long as he was in the dark about the knowledge, he was at a disadvantage. He considered it the most important of the skills he was shown, even before seeing Morgaine in her distress.

Now that it offered the means to go to her and to evade anyone foolish enough to try and tag along, it would prove its worth.

He hoped his deceit would not count against him too dearly. Enough lies and falsehoods existed in the world without Jaren needing to invent another. This one, though, was sincerely done in the hopes of keeping others safe. Jaren believed that should count for something.

He breathed slowly, controlling the air as it entered and exited his chest, just as the focusing exercises demanded. He reached outward, not only hearing, but moving along with the sweeping breeze as it brushed the tops of the surrounding trees. He felt the solidity of the earth beneath him, envisioned the roots as dwelling there.

Connection.

That was the key to the spirit walk. In order to travel outside the barriers of the physical realm, one needed complete awareness of it. Once that awareness was achieved, it was a matter of passing through the barriers between worlds. Jaren likened it to walking through a screen of hanging threads, like the ones he'd seen often enough in doorways in the city of Vetalas. Though it was a very simplistic image, the visualization was an important component. Even so, it was more difficult than merely parting the threads of a hanging screen with your hand. It was more than simply reaching out. He had learned that the hard way several times, caught with his arm outstretched, groping forward in the empty air as Arynelle giggled.

Jaren forced the thoughts of her from his mind. He needed absolute focus. Once more, he concentrated on breathing. Spirit walking was like moving and summoning. The mind needed to will the action initially. But that was where the similarity ended. The reaching part happened in the mind. If you were not properly focused—and connected—the veil would simply dissipate.

He could feel himself spreading outward, sensing the energy all about. The sway of the treetops, the cackle of the night birds and even the pinpoint lights of the firelings; they were all one, all part of the True One's creation. And Jaren was at one with them.

Slowly, gently, he probed forward with his mind. The ether before him stretched outward at his touch, like a translucent sheet of gossamer silk. He continued to push with his thoughts, moving his conscious self into the expanding space. The shimmering material of the veil became a spherical cavity as Jaren proceeded. It began to constrict behind him, closing in around the point through which he'd entered. It did not shut entirely; he could still see the clearing through the opening. All about, however, past the faint glimmer of his enshrouding globe, he saw the heavens. They were above and below, to his left and right. The only connection he sensed with the physical world was through that remaining, narrow portal.

He had not thought to seal it entirely before. Small trips of a dozen paces did not appear to require it. Now, it seemed the only way to manage a journey of the distance that lay before him. It vaguely occurred that he should have asked one simple question of Selhanna or Arynelle: whether it was disastrous to sever the link completely or not. Yet he had not been thinking clearly and none of them were in the frame of mind to assist him in this mission.

The sphere about him rippled, its glow fading, and Jaren thrust all distracting thoughts aside. He could not waver in his focus now. It was past time for that. He had either to go on or abandon his plans and he had no intention of doing such a thing. Not now. Not when Morgaine needed him. The globe stabilized, the pale blue illumination steady.

She had been in such anguish! Blinded, somehow, the Warwitch had her locked in a form of sightless paralysis. She could not move of her own volition, only when commanded. It remained a matter of time before the Witch owned her thoughts as well.

His wavering focus resulted in another shudder that shook the sphere. *Relax*, he soothed himself. *Breathe.* Slowly, the globe's integrity renewed itself. In a corner of his mind's eye, Jaren regarded the opening. He sensed, as much as felt or saw, the slight breeze and the buzzing firelings. The portal had to be sealed, he knew. Again, he was not sure how the awareness came—it seemed to come in the same way as judging the distance one could leap from a standing jump—but Jaren knew that the farthest he could travel with the connection open was, perhaps, to the edge of the Sylvarii city. At most, he might be able to reach the coast.

He needed more. He needed to reach the mainland. From there, he hoped it was only one or, at most, two more walks to the camp of the Warwitch, once he'd pinned down the exact location. He sensed it was north of the Forge, somewhere in northern Carathon or southeastern Jamnar. Once he got closer, he would be able to find it easily. He would sense the Witch's presence.

Jaren hesitated. He knew the danger that lay in closing the gateway. He could be lost behind the veil. Forever, possibly. He did not know for sure. He just knew that once the connection was severed, he would have to use his memories to find the way back. He needed knowledge of a real place to properly guide his return to the physical realm. The knowledge would have to be first-hand, in the form of an accurate image in order to work—to get him to where he could view the surroundings and guide himself from that point.

At least, that was the idea that came to him. It was becoming a habit, acting in accordance with this mysterious insight. For all Jaren knew, it could be his subconscious mind simply guessing. Perhaps Master Llaw and his logical assumptions were rubbing off on him. Except he could come up with no reason to doubt his intuition; it had proven accurate every time he needed to rely on it. Still, it was not the most iron-clad of certainties.

Jaren had already picked an initial landing spot in Vetalas. From there, one or two more travels should suffice to reach a point as close to the Witch as possible. As for where that final place was, he had not yet decided. Jaren considered the options. One kept recurring, one scene that he would not easily forget. Granted, he needed to envision the place without the others who were present at the formation of the memory and still the emotions that it stirred, but the image was burned clearly into his mind.

If the strength remained to him, Jaren could travel from that location by observing the ground below and picking his point of emergence. He was far from certain, though; it depended on the difficulty of the journey leading up to that time.

He calmed his thoughts, willing himself to relax. After one last, steadying breath, Jaren sealed himself inside the portal.

◆ ◆ ◆

"I honestly thought you would try to sneak away—" Arynelle began, her eyes sweeping Jaren's bedchamber. They landed on Iselle. She was seated on the side of the bed. Arynelle stiffened perceptibly.

"He did," Iselle replied hollowly. Her sapphire eyes glistened. "Only the True One knows how he managed to outwit both of us. At the same time." She wiped absently at her cheek, then pushed a lock of dark hair behind her ear.

"How long has he been gone?"

"Since sometime early this morning—though I know he came back to the room. I was watching."

"As was I."

Iselle glanced up at the other's admission, though the fire kindled in her eyes died soon enough. "Either way," she shrugged.

Arynelle's lip curled into a smirk.

"Something amuses you?"

"He used spirit walking to get past us," Arynelle said. She brought clenched hands to her hips. "I should have expected as much."

"You couldn't tell he was using the magic?"

Arynelle sniffed. "It's not that easy. If I were camped outside his room," she threw an accusatory look at Iselle, "I would be aware that he used magic. For what purpose, though, would be very hard to tell. That he used spirit walking complicates matters. Once Jaren went behind the veil that separates our world from the other realms…well, there would be no way to track him. Not even for someone good at tracking."

"I wasn't camped by his room," Iselle replied. "I was outside, in back. I thought he'd try to sneak out that way." She frowned. "He would have had to, if you hadn't shown him otherwise."

It was Arynelle's turn to glare through narrowed eyelids, her green eyes stormy. "There are many things I haven't shared with Jaren. Yet."

Iselle's voice hardened. "If you intend to steal him from me, your words had better be true."

Arynelle scowled back. "And what words were those, exactly?"

"That you know how to fight." Iselle stomped past the Sylvarii, brushing her slightly with a shoulder. She paused as the entry widened. Glaring back at Arynelle, Iselle said, "I haven't travelled across Evarlund and back with him just to give way to some pampered island princess. I may not have magic, but magic isn't the only thing that Jaren cares about."

◆ ◆ ◆

"I'm afraid the captain won't hear of it," Llaw said. "He's intent on getting the goods he's traded for back to Vetalas. Even if he weren't set on this, he wouldn't sail north without first making preparations for a winter voyage; we're going to be arriving back with the first weeks of the new season."

The two of them glanced across the waves to the moored vessel. The crew worked feverishly to transfer the last of the cargo from the tiny lifeboats and to ready the ship for its return to the mainland. The voice of Captain Jenda carried over the water in angry snippets, most of it curses and vows.

Iselle grumbled, "That's at least two days' worth of delay. How long does it take to sail around the east coast?"

"That depends on the northeastern winds. If they're off to an early start, it could mean up to a week longer."

"But whatever is going to happen will be long over by the time we arrive."

"There's nothing for it, my dear girl; we don't have the ability to spirit walk like Jaren."

Iselle huffed, then fidgeted a moment with the sleeves of her blouse. "Do you think—now that we know a person doesn't need *metanduil* to do magic—" she stopped herself short. "Never mind."

Llaw placed a gentle hand on her shoulder. "Do not worry, my dear. Jaren will not forget about you."

"But what if the magic comes between us? I don't have that talent. What if he needs to be with someone who understands that part of him?"

"I think you understand him more than you give yourself credit for. In very important ways, you and he share kinship. He will not forget that."

"I just…it's just that…I don't know if I can bear to wait, especially now that Arynelle has gone after him."

The *Valir* nodded. "She is just doing what she feels is right for her. I'm sure it is nothing against you."

"It might be, if Jaren comes to love her instead."

"As unlikely as I know that to be, we need to remember that people are not objects. Just because we desire them, does not automatically grant us the right to claim their hearts. If the one we love chooses to be with someone else, that loss—although difficult—must be borne." Llaw's voice had grown soft and carried a tone of sadness.

"You speak as if you've experienced such loss before," Iselle said.

"A long time ago, young lady," the *Valir* sighed. "Too long ago to talk about now."

"*Valir* Llaw," the greeting drew his attention up the beach, toward the jungle.

Kenjon Samase, a stern-faced man who had been present during their landing some days ago, approached. His long hair was dark for a Sylvarii, save for streaks of white at the temples, and bore the two fine braids typical of men in high standing. They parted from the crown of his head and wrapped around his scalp to disappear from view. A golden circlet held the lengthy bangs from obscuring his age-lined, narrow face.

"I am sad to hear that you must leave us earlier than expected."

"My apologies, Kenjon, but matters on the mainland demand that we depart."

"Yes," Kenjon's hard features reflected his sombre tone. "The business with the *Ves'Talein*. Very disappointing. I hope that you encounter no further setbacks on your return." He held Llaw's eyes with his own steely gaze. "Yours is not an enviable position."

"Still," Llaw said, "the knowledge must be relayed. We've lived with this deceit for too long. The truth of it will be hard to hear, but necessary."

"I do wish, for your sake, that others are as reasonable and objective with the discovery. Otherwise, it could be…an unpleasant homecoming."

"What are you getting at?" Iselle asked.

Kenjon raised an eyebrow at her. "Forgive my cynical, old-man's words, young lady. There is most likely nothing to worry about."

"Then why say it?"

Kenjon laughed quietly. "Indeed. I know little of the ways of mainlanders. Sadly, if news of the same magnitude were disclosed here," his gaze shifted back to the *Valir*, "those with power and position to lose might be...less than welcoming. But I'm sure your ways are different from ours. Surely there is no cause to be wary."

"I appreciate your insight, Kenjon, and I will proceed with caution," Llaw said.

The other shrugged. "It will be as the All-Father wills. With little to prove that your magic-metal is an artificial creation, it may prove difficult to convince your mainland brothers and sisters of the true nature of things. I am certain a statesman of your influence will find the proper means to spread the word."

"Again, thank you for your thoughts."

"And, if ever you should need to return, please know that you are always welcome." Kenjon handed the *Valir* an intricately carved figurine. Palm-sized, it was the image of a tiger, fashioned out of brilliant, white marble, with bands of inlaid gold forming the animal's stripes. Glittering emeralds shaped the figurine's eyes.

"Oh my, this is exquisite," Llaw exclaimed. "What have I done to merit such a gift?"

"Please, take it," Kenjon bowed, "it is enchanted. Should you wish once more to seek out this island, the figurine will guide you." He stepped closer. "Know that you have friends among us, though you do not yet realize it. There are even those who would journey to the mainland to lend you aid. You have but to ask."

"I...I am grateful," the *Valir* said, pausing to find the right words. "I don't know what kind of reception your people might receive, however, especially if you arrive at my side bearing this news."

Kenjon smiled. "I would not worry over details like that. The scale of our assistance would be...considerable. My friends and I believe strongly that the boy's arrival heralds change. We are prepared."

Again Llaw was at a loss. "Ah...I'm not exactly sure what you are proposing, Master Samase."

The Sylvarii cocked his head as if hearing something. He nodded, stepping back. "Rest assured, *Valir* Llaw, the time will come to discuss this matter further."

Llaw glanced down at the figurine in his hand. "I would offer you something in return, but I neglected to bring any of my own artifacts along. In fact, most of them no longer...survive."

"His tower was destroyed," Iselle said flatly.

The *Valir* shot her an annoyed look. Kenjon simply smiled once more.

"Master Llaw, Iselle," a fair voice called. "I hoped I'd get here before you left. And...Kenjon. I wasn't expecting to find you here."

"Greetings, Selhanna," he said stiffly. "If you would excuse me, *Valir* Llaw." He nodded to Iselle. "Good journey, young lady." He soon disappeared down the jungle path.

"I trust Kenjon wasn't making a nuisance of himself," Selhanna said as she watched after him. Her expression steeled.

"No. He simply offered some of his thoughts." The *Valir* smiled. "Is something troubling you?"

"No, Master Llaw. Nothing out of the ordinary. Just the same old men with the same tired arguments. Nothing to fret about."

"I am glad to hear it."

"And you, Iselle, how do you fare today?"

"I'll be glad to step off the ship once more," she grimaced. "I did not enjoy the trip here. I hope the return voyage is better."

"Perhaps I can do something to help with that." Selhanna reached into her forest green robes and produced a small vial. The liquid it held was a pale brown and some sort of granules floated within. She handed it to Iselle, who grimaced all the more on closer examination of the contents.

"It looks like a concoction of partly strained pipe-leaf. What's it for?" Iselle asked.

"If you feel the ocean illness come upon you, take a drink. Not too much or you will sleep the whole of the way home. Perhaps longer. And you'll awake with a nasty ache in your head." Selhanna crossed her arms. "It's the least I can do, seeing as your journey here was so unpleasant, and that you're leaving under less than ideal circumstances."

A shrill whistle from the ship interrupted them.

"I suppose we had better get on board, or we'll be here until the captain manages to find his way back," Llaw announced.

"Farewell," Selhanna bid them, "until we cross paths again." She shifted uncomfortably. "And, if I could ask a small favour, please do what you can to see that Arynelle is returned safely."

"We shall do what we can," the *Valir* vowed.

"I'd like nothing more than to send her back home as soon and directly as possible," Iselle added.

Selhanna nodded at the two of them. She peered at Iselle with a partly amused and partly knowing smirk, then waved as the two rowed out to the larger vessel, their small craft tossing on the waves as it drew away.

4. Jaren, Iselle and Ensin Llaw reach the southern islands and the city of the Sylvarii.

• 31 •

Struggles of the Mind

MORGAINE BURROWED MORE DEEPLY WITHIN her own mind. It was the only way she had of fighting back. Any other attempts had simply exposed her to the skull-splitting pain that threatened to tear the conscious thoughts from her head, to rip from her the memories and the fabric of her identity. Burying herself, walling herself away from all contact with the external world, was her only hope.

Time ceased to have meaning; Morgaine did not know whether it had been days or months since exiling herself to the very core of her being. She had considered giving up, but the hopelessness and grief had not yet overtaken her rage. Morgaine could not guess how much longer that might take. On the other hand, removed from contact with the physical world, denied sensory experience, she was losing her human self anyway. She might just become a product of her anger and regret, a dark vestige of her black thoughts. It was hard to say which end might be worse, surrender or annihilation.

That she had bested Joselle one-on-one gave her some satisfaction and fuelled her resolve. Had the Mother not appeared to interfere, Morgaine would have succeeded. Now, though, captured and harnessed, she would have to free herself before she could even attempt to fight. Or to flee, drained as she was by the ordeal.

If only—

Her thoughts became fuzzy as an obscuring fog descended. Where was she? Who was she? Morgaine could remember being angry. Enraged. She remembered travelling somewhere. But where was it? And why?

Burning pain shattered her thoughts and Morgaine screamed. She could not tell whether it was out loud or in her mind, but it was a scream of defiance, of hatred. Ironically, it also brought lucidity. She had been slipping away from herself but the shock of the Witch's intrusive magic brought her back.

She was Morgaine. Morgaine Haldannon. She had come to face the Witch—the *Mother*. And her daughter-servant, Joselle. Morgaine had failed.

Another stab of searing, red agony struck and Morgaine withdrew again, retreating inward from the mental attack of the Warwitch, descending to her innermost self. Here, she felt nothing. She simply *was*. There was no heat, no cold. Neither was there hunger or thirst.

Even if the Witch failed to break through, how long could she remain isolated from her humanity and stay sane? Morgaine was being squeezed in a vice, crushed either between the eventuality of surrender or of oblivion.

If the Witch figured out that her own attacks were defeating her attempts to erase and control Morgaine's mind, she would change her tactics. She would start to use more subtle magic. That might prove the end of Morgaine's resistance. Still, the Mother had not put it together.

Yet.

Morgaine had to come up with some way to escape the mask and flee the Witch's encampment. Time, however it continued to work, was surely against her. How to even begin her plans, she lacked the slightest idea.

◆　◆　◆

Jaren managed to peel his eyes open. He felt he could sleep the entire day, he was so exhausted. It took some time before he could even prop himself onto an elbow. Every muscle cried out in protest, stiff from exertion. He crawled to a nearby tree and leaned back against it, waiting for the mist clouding his mind to clear.

As Jaren listened to the sounds of midday about him, a hand shielding his eyes—for Sholara was almost directly overhead and too bright for his aching head—he tried to recall the journey that had brought him to this small hillock and its sheltering copse of trees.

The spirit walk succeeded. But at what cost? He prayed to the True One that he sustained no serious, permanent damage during the inter-planar voyages. He had realized, as he passed briefly back to the material realm in Vetalas, that it was going to take a great deal of magic—not to mention an intense mental and physical toll—to continue further into Evarlund. That realization had dawned as he approached the mainland. Though beginning smoothly enough, the comfort of his passage deteriorated the closer he got. The placid, dark pools through which he travelled, home to innumerable glittering stars, became roiling, turbulent stretches that battered his mind and body. He jounced and rolled, buffeted relentlessly, slammed by storms of energy that exploded all around him in violent, blinding flashes.

He knew it had to be the essence of the *metanduil* that hindered his use of the magical gateway. That was the only explanation for the completely different experiences between the start and the end of his traveling. It did not matter. Morgaine needed him and that meant he could not stop.

His next waypoint was strongly imprinted in his memory. He landed at the clearing where Ver had battled the second blacktongue after he and the others escaped the doom of Llaw's besieged tower.

Getting to the clearing was not easy. In fact, it proved to be another of the battering journeys, made all the worse due to his growing fatigue and, apparently, his decreasing distance to the mountains. Jaren literally flew out of the gateway and crashed headlong into the wooden boathouse that marked the glade. Already, Jaren could feel his muscles and his mind rebelling against the thought of spirit walking a third time. But his sister needed him.

He took one last chance and passed behind the veil again, finding himself instantly beset by the hammering energies as he made his way to Aendaras. He flew past the city and headed west, retracing the first few leagues of the route Llaw had taken him and his sister toward the Forge Mountains. Consciously slowing his progress, Jaren ventured north. Peering down through the portal opening—he found that it appeared as soon as he thought about leaving the planar pathway—he sought a suitable place to exit.

As he feared, this proved the worst part of the journey. Trying to keep his travel-weary eyes focused on the blur of the landscape below, or above, as the fancy of his spiralling, jolting globe dictated, had made the last stretch nearly insufferable. The resistance thrusting outward from the center of the Forge, from the source of the magic-metal, sapped his strength and continued to hinder his progress. Finally, nearly blacking out from vertigo after clearing the spine of mountains that marked the border of Carathon and Jamnar, he simply bailed from the voyage at the first suitable patch of woods he spotted.

He had awakened to find himself here.

Jaren was glad for Sholara's heat, at least, as winter's icy grasp had seized the land. Now that his eyes were not so light sensitive, he gazed about. Though no snow blanketed the ground, the trees were completely bare of leaves, their brown, red and yellow coats scattered in a moving carpet across the land. The wind, gusting at times, sailed down from the northeast. From the direction of the Witch's former stronghold. *So fitting, that is.* Jaren chuckled dryly.

He could sense the Witch, faintly, as well as several others. Two, he believed to be Joselle and Morgaine. A third, he guessed, was Aldrain: his newly-acquired *metanduil* limbs marking his presence for those who were sensitive to the magic.

All were relatively the same distance from him at present. Which should he go to, he wondered? He originally thought to go straight against the Witch, but now, thoughts of Aldrain gave him pause. Would the king help him? He might not if he was focused on getting at the *Valir*. Still, with Jaren and Morgaine at his side, Jaren reasoned, Aldrain would have two additional, powerful allies in the coming conflict—if it came to that. Jaren did not fancy being the one to inform the king's followers of the truth about the magic, but he would do so if it meant saving lives. Perhaps most of Aldrain's *Valir* were unaware of the situation. He had talked with Ensin Llaw about it. It was entirely possible that a good number were ignorant of the deceit, as Llaw himself—a powerful and influential member of the guild—had been.

With his newfound abilities, Aldrain could prove to be a great help. He had shown an ability to defend from and attack with the magic, two talents that would definitely aid in a confrontation with the Witch.

Jaren inhaled deeply, then let out a long, steady breath. It turned to vapour on contact with the bitter-cold wind. Using the tree for support, he eased himself to his feet. Unfortunately, all the short rest had provided was a chill that settled into his muscles. They responded in protest, screaming all the more loudly now. He shuffled forward a few steps, then stopped, remaining still. He sensed outward for the nearby presences. Eliminating the strongest, which he knew to be the Witch, Jaren then ignored the two that were closest. That left the third.

Aldrain.

"You look in need of rest, my young friend."

The voice caused Jaren to jump. He whirled to face the speaker, embracing the magic as he spun.

The other, a man, held his hands out peacefully. "Please, do not be alarmed. I have not come here to harm you."

Oddly, the stranger's presence did not trigger Jaren's sense of danger, though his appearance clearly identified him as a dangerous master of stealth, not to mention the fact that he had approached completely undetected. Jaren felt unexpectedly calm after the initial scare.

Jaren eyed the newcomer closely. He was of average height and athletic build and wore a light suit of dark leather armour. Beneath this were a black tunic and dark leather breeches. As Jaren watched, the man shifted, moving to lean casually against a thick tree trunk. His high leather boots made no whisper of noise. Jaren could make out his weathered face clearly enough as the cowl of the stranger's cloak, though drawn forward, did not obscure his features.

"Perhaps, if you announced yourself earlier, you wouldn't have to make assurances like that," Jaren said.

"My apologies for the abrupt appearance," the stranger nodded, smiling. "But it's sort of a habit with me. My name is Varas. Varas Endemol."

Jaren hesitated.

"And you are Jaren Haldannon from the village of Dal Farrow."

"How do you know of me?"

"You're beginning to create quite a name for yourself in some circles. I don't mean to suggest that you're famous, or infamous as others claim, but you are no longer a mere farm boy."

Jaren maintained his hold on the magic. The feeling of calm remained, though he could not have explained why. Even the sight of the man's two curved sabres, sheathed on either hip, failed to cause Jaren distress. "I'll assume that you're not just here by chance. What do you wish of me?"

Varas smiled warmly, nodding. "A fair question. It is a rather long story. I'm not sure I understand the whole thing myself." He shrugged. "But I'd like to accompany you, if you would have me."

Unlikely and absurd as the request should have been, Jaren had half-expected it. Even so, he was not about to simply grant this stranger's wish. He needed more information. "Where are you from—and why join me?" His mind still burned with urgent thoughts of Morgaine, so his questions carried a note of impatience.

"Again, fair questions. I gathered that you were determined to go somewhere, and rather quickly. Your tone confirms it. Do you wish the long or the short of it?"

"Make it the short version." Jaren said curtly.

"I saw your reaction to my appearance," Varas said, gesturing to himself. "I am dressed as one who makes a career of stealth. However, I've recently—how to describe it—changed allegiances, if you will." Seeing that Jaren still listened, Varas continued. "You see, I used to be an assassin. One of the best in the six realms, actually."

Jaren blinked. "And now?"

"Now I'm…something else."

Jaren looked a question at him.

"As I mentioned, it's still not totally clear even to me. Though this much is true: I've been led to find and help you." He shrugged. "I realize it's a bit much to take in immediately and I don't begrudge your suspicions. But that is the shortest version I can relate."

Inhaling deeply, Jaren studied the man. His instincts and his mind were in agreement about the stranger. That was the most troubling part. His gut should have recoiled at the very thought of trusting someone, a former assassin, no less, on their first meeting. Jaren's inner voice should have been screaming in alarm against even remaining to talk. Nonetheless, he was. And against common sense, he was seriously considering the fellow's request.

"I'd be a fool to let you accompany me with nothing but your word of assurance. Whether you've given up the ways of an assassin or not, you *do* look like one. Even if you used to be a sheep herder, I'd be crazy to blindly take you at your word. People may become more than they were, but I think there's something, some small part of them, that doesn't change."

"You don't realize how truthfully you speak," Varas smiled. "Yet if I were still killing for hire, I could easily have taken you already. You wouldn't even have seen it coming."

"Maybe." Jaren pursed his lips. "But I'm not just a farm boy any longer either, as you said yourself."

"And so we're at an impasse," the former assassin said.

"And I have somewhere I need to be. If you truly mean to help, you'll let me go my own way. For now at least."

"I'll just wait here, then. We can talk when you return."

Jaren nodded. He concentrated on forming the portal, making sure to keep the newcomer in view. It seemed more difficult than usual, no doubt due to his preoccupation with the stranger. Jaren tried to ignore the feeling that the other watched, even measured him. His thoughts wandered to the king and how

Jaren might ask him for help. He huffed in frustration, creating another plume of steamy breath. Despite these distractions, the portal stubbornly yielded to his will, finally widening enough for entry. He grimaced as he stepped stiffly inside.

Forget about asking Aldrain for aid, Jaren laughed to himself. If he felt as bad on arriving as he did now, the first thing he would want to inquire about would be a hot meal and a warm bed.

• 32 •

Before the Plunge

OF THE TWO OFFICERS AT ALDRAIN'S SIDE, one had previously marshalled the Carathonai army on this very plain. More than a decade ago, his father's forces had engaged the Jamnites in a pitched battle here that proved to be the final confrontation in the prolonged border war. Aldrain studied the elder soldier on his right with a sidelong glance. He was of average height and sturdy frame, built more for ground fighting than mounted combat. Still, he was no stranger to the saddle. Hard eyes stared from beneath shaggy brows that nearly rivalled his moustache. The man's beard, peppered with grey as was the rest of his hair, grew long and thick. The officer was Rhodal Seva, a grim-faced, decorated general who had served Aldrain's father during the Jamnite conflict.

On the king's left was a commander from Aldrain's grey watch, chosen for leadership because of a sharp mind and the respect he earned from the men under his command. In his short lifetime, he had managed to create quite a name for himself, though not through fighting of the sort that Seva had witnessed. Yet the clean-shaven, youthful-looking officer's skills could not be underestimated. Many raiding parties and outlaw bands had learned this lesson the hard way. In direct contrast to Seva's, Cordan Arantar's long, dark hair trailed in the wind. His pale blue eyes glittered with a hardness not yet reflected by his youthful features.

Aldrain and the officers trotted their horses lightly across the brown, short grass of the field toward the leaders of the *Valir* forces. The mounts' hooves produced a hollow sounding clop with each step as they contacted the cold-hardened earth. Snow had yet to fall here, but the ground had already taken on its winter rigidity as temperatures dipped and the frigid northeastern winds gusted. Behind the *Valir* contingent, the distant spine of mountains retreated to the north and east on its course to the sea. Scattered stands of evergreen trees dotted the landscape as it approached the line of peaks beyond in a gradual, rolling ascent.

Above it all, a slate-grey sky showed the promise of the snows to come. Aldrain grinned. His men were no stranger to winter warfare. He wondered if the *Valir* Guild's mercenary corps would be up to the challenge.

The king studied his counterparts as his party of three drew near. Their group was composed of a senior veteran warrior and two *Valir*. Three obvious mercenaries—assassins, by the look of them, outfitted lightly in dark leather armour—sat atop their mounts a few dozen paces back. One was a cold-eyed female, the other two were a mismatch; a gigantic fighter and a shifty-looking, smaller rogue.

The veteran, clearly a career soldier for hire with many battles behind him, examined Aldrain as he himself was scrutinized. The man had a curious scar at the side of his upper lip that resulted in a permanent, lopsided sneer. His broad face was decorated with greying stubble. The square set to his chin and wide jaw line, together with the flat-topped cut of his short hair, gave the man a rather block-headed look. Aldrain hoped his appearance reflected his ability to command.

As with the others, and similarly with his own trio, all in their company sported fur-lined cloaks to lessen the impact of the frigid temperatures.

The *Valir* wore dark blue vestments beneath their cold-weather dress. They regarded him with disdainful, though wary expressions, the same way a man might observe a poisonous serpent. They believed themselves superior, but still saw him as a threat.

However they see me, he vowed silently, *the* Valir *will be heeled.* The thought echoed in his mind, at home with the many warnings delivered by Sonja and his father against the *Valir*. Aldrain reined in his mount, still a hundred spans from the *Valir* command. Rhodal and Cordan followed suit at his side, remaining one stride back from the king's lead position.

The elder warrior sat in silence, a smirk spreading across his grizzled features.

Cordan, puzzled, turned to his king. In a subdued voice he said, "Your Majesty, is there something amiss?"

"No, Cordan."

The youthful officer pondered for a moment longer. "Would you like me to go ahead and announce you?"

Aldrain and Rhodal shared a chuckle.

"No, Cordan," Aldrain smiled. "You should know I don't require formalities like that." He paused, waiting to see if the young man registered his intent.

"Perhaps he's not as sharp witted as you'd hoped, your Majesty," Rhodal said in his bass rumble.

Cordan eyed his elder peer, then nodded. "You mean to make them come to us, then." He continued to hold Rhodal's gaze as a wolfish grin formed. "Perhaps we shouldn't wait too long, Your Majesty. I don't know how much time Rhodal can waste before the grave calls him."

At that, all three laughed.

Aldrain could see the faces of the other party clearly. Their expressions belied a variety of reactions, from bewilderment to frustration. Except for the mercenary officer. His features alone remained stoic, though Aldrain thought he perceived the faintest hint of a bitter grin. A seasoned soldier *should* be used to such mind games before a meeting with the enemy, Aldrain thought.

Apparently, the *Valir* had no such military experience, as they nudged their mounts forward, much to the obvious chagrin of the mercenary. His face sprouted an obvious scowl, but he too put spurs to his mount and followed them.

"Well met, King Aldrain."

The *Valir* both nodded. The one who spoke did not appear much older than the other, as both had a middle-aged look. Each stole repeated glances at Aldrain's *metanduil* limbs.

Aldrain nodded, but said nothing. He barely registered their curiosity at his peculiarity of his appearance. His own soldiers still acted strangely and he had grown accustomed to the looks.

The speaker held his breath, apparently waiting for a verbal reply. Finally, the enchanter let out his breath and continued. "I fear we've come together through a misunderstanding, but we might yet make an agreement to our mutual advantage," he said. "We have reports that the army of Rhianain Othka is camped not far to the west. I beseech you, King Aldrain, to join us in the struggle against her, whatever your claims against the council. Afterward, we may sit and draw up an agreement as allies, rather than unwilling adversaries." The man's eyes wandered again to Aldrain's arms.

Aldrain did not speak. The *Valir* squirmed in their saddles, finally sharing a brief, uncertain glance.

Only then did Aldrain reply. "And what would an arrangement with you advantage me?" He glared at them intensely. "At best, incompetence—for the Witch has seized her power under your council's very watch—and at worse, betrayal. No few *Valir* were among the conspirators who murdered my family and nearly brought about the destruction of my realm. So tell me, what benefit does a continued *alliance* with your council afford me?"

The *Valir* stared at the king as if knocked senseless with a club. Finally, the speaker regained some of his wits. He began to speak while looking down, avoiding Aldrain's intense glare. "Your Majesty, it is with the greatest of regrets that the council acknowledges the harms you and your people have suffered. However," he managed to meet the king's eyes, "we were not implicit in the Witch's plans. Nor were we able to counteract them in time."

Aldrain sneered, spitting to one side.

The summoner swallowed, then continued, "I have been authorized to offer our official apology, and after the business with Rhianain is settled, we may forge an alliance that will undoubtedly raise Carathon above the other realms."

The king laughed in contempt. "What need do I have of your guild to accomplish that? I have already taken measures to strengthen my position among the kingdoms of Evarlund. I see no need for you or your pathetic kind. You cannot police your own, so how do you propose to assist me in securing my place?"

The *Valir* was at a total loss. He hesitated, mouth opening to attempt a reply, but no sound escaped his lips. Turning to his comrade in the magic, his eyes pleaded for assistance.

Aldrain seized upon the advantage. "I see that your High *Valir* is not in attendance. Perhaps he foresaw the outcome of our negotiations and chose to be elsewhere? Or, perhaps it was the outcome of the coming conflict he guessed at?"

"Your Majesty," the mercenary offered as his mount stepped up beside the dumbstruck *Valir*. "I assume you have demands of us?"

"Finally," Aldrain sighed, "a man who knows how to parley." The king nodded. "I will accept your men's surrender. They may go free, unmolested. All that I ask is that all *Valir* are handed over to me. Immediately."

The two summoners shifted uncomfortably in their saddles.

The mercenary raised an eyebrow, glancing at the mages appraisingly.

Behind him, the three assassins tensed in their saddles.

"General Szendil," the *Valir* spokesman managed after nervously clearing his throat, "need I recall the costs to you of breaching our contracted arrangement?" The desperate tone of the man's voice did not bolster his intended warning.

The old warrior shook his head in disgust, then turned back to Aldrain. "It's a tempting offer, Your Majesty, but unless you're willing to offer me and my men lifetime employment, I'll have to decline. If news spread that my men and I turned our backs on an employer...well, I'm sure you understand."

Aldrain acknowledged with a shake of his head. "So be it. Should you change your mind, you have until daybreak to send word. After that, anyone approaching from your camp will be treated as hostile."

The king tugged abruptly on his reins, wheeling his mount. He and his two officers were soon lost from view in the distance.

"I hope you've brought enough of your fellows," the general said none too delicately. "Because our scouts say he's got ten thousand swords. And more than just a handful of your former *brothers* and *sisters*." He cocked his head. "And what under the light of the Truth happened to his arms?"

◆ ◆ ◆

"Your Majesty." The soldier from Aldrain's personal guard saluted. "You have a visitor. He approached our sentries and requested an audience with you. We searched him and, other than a quarterstaff, he carried no weapons. Should we fetch him, Your Majesty?"

Aldrain nodded, guessing the person's identity. "I expect he's a young man, no more than a boy, really? Dark haired and harmless looking?"

"Yes, Your Majesty. Were you...expecting him? Forgive me, as I had no idea—"

"You were right," Aldrain muttered to no one in particular, then shook his head as he peered intently off to a darkened, apparently empty corner of the tent.

"Your Majesty?"

Aldrain turned once more to the man, frowning as if he'd forgotten about the other's presence. "I expected him at some point, though I wasn't sure when. Bring him to me."

"At once, Your Majesty." The soldier hurried off, looking as though he was glad to be going anywhere else at the moment.

"The estranged son of Ergothan has arrived at last, as you predicted." The words were not directed at the retreating form of the attendant, but again to the shadowed corner.

· 33 ·

No Rest. No Help

"IF YOU'VE ABOUT FINISHED YOUR MOPING, young lady, we've reached Vetalas. It's time to disembark." Ensin Llaw studied Iselle's brooding face. It was not nearly as greenish in hue as on the previous voyage to the islands and yet her expression was far from an easy one.

"How soon can we be off after them?"

"Captain Jenda requires time and resources to outfit the vessel again. I won't have to visit the lenders to finance the expedition since he swears he'll give us a deal because of the profits they'll make from trading their island goods, so that will save part of a day. Still, we won't be leaving before the day after tomorrow."

Iselle scoffed. "I could be there by horseback before then."

"Not likely, young lady, unless it was a winged breed."

"Fine," she said begrudgingly. "Let's get to the inn then."

"My thoughts exactly."

"Come on, boy." Iselle clapped a hand against her thigh and the huge canine bounded over from his makeshift bed of spare canvas, tail wagging. "At least you're happy to stay with me, aren't you?"

He nuzzled Iselle's leg and licked her hand in response.

She allowed a wan laugh as she stumbled back from Dagger's enthusiastic nosing.

"Easy now, boy. You'll push me overboard. I need a bath, but not that soon." She reached out to scrub behind his ears.

With a wave to the captain, the two passengers descended the narrow catwalk to the dock, the great dog loping easily behind. They planned to return to the inn where they had previously stayed and wasted no time heading through the milling crowds toward the adjacent city quarter where the Harbour's Haven was located.

Once there, Llaw handed several silver coins to the innkeeper—it would have been coppers, except that Iselle once more refused to keep Dagger outside in the stables. The owner was a frail-looking scarecrow of a man with a bald pate and dark circles beneath his eyes. He pointedly avoided looking at Iselle after a quick glance over his shoulder at his wife, a portly, rosy-cheeked woman cradling a heavy rolling pin beneath one thick arm. She nodded at Llaw and Iselle curtly, barely taking her intense gaze from her husband's narrow back.

Iselle stifled the grin that threatened to form; she remembered the man. Olauf, she thought his name was. The man had snuck many a glimpse of her during their earlier stay. Apparently she had not been the only woman to notice the attention.

Iselle immediately threw herself onto one of the beds on entering the modest room. Dagger leaped on also, curling into a mountain of hair at her feet.

"Are you hungry, my dear?" Llaw asked.

Iselle did not lift her head from the folds of her down pillow. She mumbled something that sounded as though she did not want to eat.

"Very well," he added after stowing his possessions in a small trunk at the foot of the other bed. "I'll just be downstairs having supper if you need anything or change your mind."

His offer was met with another muffled grunt.

Shaking his head, Llaw exited and closed the door lightly behind him.

◆ ◆ ◆

"King Aldrain, it's good to see you again!" Jaren exclaimed as his eyes fell on the other. Jaren stepped free of the tent's entry flaps and walked further inside the structure.

Aldrain did not answer. He sat completely still in his gilded chair in the centre of the tent. His eyes appraised the younger man, his face impassive.

Jaren blinked but continued closer. "I hate to ask anything of you so soon after returning, but I need your help. Morgaine needs your help." As he neared, Jaren's scalp prickled. The feeling of unease returned and it was not wholly due to Aldrain's reaction.

The king's posture was slightly forward, one elbow perched on the chair's arm. His eyes narrowed only the tiniest bit and his chin remained propped on the knuckles of one cold, metallic fist. Still he gave no response.

Jaren paused. He was at a loss. Why would Aldrain not answer? Had he done something to insult the king, or come at an inconvenient time? Knowing

Aldrain as he did, neither of those possibilities seemed a likely explanation. His sense of disquiet grew. Jaren felt as though he was being watched. He forced himself to ignore it. "If I have disturbed you or done something to anger you, please tell me, King Aldrain. If not, then in the name of the True One, I beg you to answer me—Morgaine is in danger!"

The king's chin fell to his chest and he sat back in his seat. His hands rubbed back and forth along the arms of the chair as his expression darkened. "Your timing is curious, Jaren Haldannon."

His look of confusion deepening, the youth gazed back at Aldrain.

"You leave my side, heading off on unknown business and then return begging my assistance, just when I am about to strike the first blow against the deceitful *Valir* council."

"I'm sorry King Aldrain, I don't understand what you mean."

"What I mean is this: what have you been doing? You and Ensin Llaw. And your sister, no doubt. I know you haven't been furthering the cause of my struggle against the *Valir*. I'd have learned about it." Aldrain rose from his seat, crossing his arms before him, gaze still levelled at Jaren. "So, if I have been kept in the dark about your activities and I know you have not been acting on my behalf, there remains only one logical explanation."

Jaren breathed in sharply. His forehead creased and he shook his head. "You believe we've been working *against* you, Your Majesty?" He couldn't believe what was happening.

The reply was flat. "Convince me otherwise."

"I…I needed to know more about my own magic, how it works, why I'm different from everyone else. It was important to find out—not just for me, but to know how I could truly be of help. So that I knew what I could and couldn't do."

The king remained unmoved, his question more a cursory response. "I see. And what did you find, then?"

"Your Majesty speaks the truth about the council, though I doubt you know how deep their lies have run."

This appeared to pique Aldrain's interest.

"The magic—the *metanduil*—is not what it seems. The *Valir* created the magic-metal a thousand years ago to seize control of the power and limit its use to people of their choosing. They have maintained their strength and positions by continuing that lie to this day."

Aldrain did not offer an immediate reply. Instead, he half-turned his head, as if listening to something or to someone else. Jaren's sense of unease changed, transformed into the perception of a malign presence, a presence other than the king and himself. It left Jaren with a feeling of cold apprehension.

"Tell me, Jaren, how did you know where to find this information?"

"I was given—" Jaren stopped himself.

Aldrain inclined his head, eyes narrowing.

"I was given word of islands to the south, where the original inhabitants of Evarlund now live. They were forced into exile after the creation of the *metanduil*, as it weakened their own magic. They—the Sylvarii—told me of the council's actions. I learned about one of their own, someone like me, who sought knowledge from them in hopes of liberating her people from the effects of the metalmagic."

"Yes, Jaren. That makes sense. But you did not answer my question: how did you know where to look?"

"I was given a journal. The journal of Ravien Alluminara."

"By whom?" Aldrain raised his voice, demanding and impatient now. Several of his men hurriedly gathered at the entrance to the tent, drawn by the king's outburst. Aldrain waved them off.

Jaren's eyes went to the entryway, then turned back to the king. "By Rhianain."

"By the Witch." Aldrain sneered. "You would take the word of our enemies and go behind my back? I suspected as much when you refused my escort from Eidara."

"Aldrain—King Aldrain," Jaren reasoned, "that's not what I was doing!"

"No, you are right, Jaren." Aldrain walked toward him, eyes blazing. "What you were doing was worse. You betrayed me. And you continue to do wrong by me. You come into my camp, seeking an audience against the Witch? No, you mean to deceive me. You would lead me into her clutches."

"That's…King Aldrain, that's not true! Morgaine needs our help!"

"Whether she is a prisoner or not makes no difference, though I doubt even that story. I believe she's turned as well. All of you have turned against me!"

The king was mere paces from Jaren. He was enraged, his face contorted wildly like some savage beast. Jaren drew in the magic, fully wary now. This was not the man he knew. Something was desperately wrong with the king, with this man he'd thought of as a friend.

"Please, Aldrain, stop this! What you are doing—what you are saying— is insane." Jaren braced himself within the magic. "Please, listen to reason!"

Aldrain laughed bitterly. "You know nothing of insanity—and I am finished talking!"

Once again, the shouting attracted a knot of soldiers. This time, Aldrain gave them the signal to stand fast rather than depart.

With a roar, the king launched himself at Jaren.

His fist slammed against the magical barrier Jaren cast, tiny arcs of electricity and sparks bursting outward on contact. Maddened beyond reason and infuriated that he could not reach the traitor before him, Aldrain continued to rain blows upon the shield, the crackling of electricity and bursts of light exploding alternately as both fists pounded. He snarled in a bestial frenzy, spittle drooling past bared and gritted teeth.

The hammering punches were powerful—enhanced as they were by Aldrain's magic—but Jaren held his center, blocking out the noise and light and maintaining his balance. Still, he knew it could not go on forever. Either the king must tire soon, or Jaren would have to flee, though he did not know if he could summon a doorway quickly enough to escape. He never had to do it in haste, nor had he practiced transitioning so quickly between shielding himself and travelling. The growing doubt caused his focus to waver and in turn his barrier gave slightly, buffeting him with shockwaves. Jaren fought to renew his focus.

At least the soldiers at the entry had not moved.

Aldrain ceased his assault. He wiped his mouth with the back of one hand and turned away abruptly, raking the barrier with the clawed fingers of the other as he spun.

Jaren quickly considered his options. He could try to form a portal, or he could attack the king. *You can't harm Aldrain—it's not really him! There's something wrong!* He made up his mind to stun the madman with a blast of energy. Hopefully that would give him time to escape.

Focusing just above and between Aldrain's heaving shoulders, Jaren thrust outward with the magic. He sent a bludgeoning wave, strong enough to knock the king down and disorient him, but not enough to do serious harm.

Aldrain wheeled about, impossibly fast, and redirected the energy.

Jaren barely had time to throw his barrier up once more. Though he succeeded, he was driven back by the blast.

The king looked down at his hands, considering something. He stepped forward and pressed his palms against the barrier. Once more, tendrils of electric light danced at the points of contact. He began to push. The electric arcs responded by snapping outward erratically, their blue glows intensifying.

Aldrain pushed harder, a guttural roar building in the depths of his throat. He continued to press forward, straining with increasing might against the barrier.

Jaren found himself forced to push back, drawing deeply from the magic to hold his ground and maintain his balance.

Slowly, incredibly, the king's palms sank into the barrier. He roared louder, his veins rising and eyes bulging.

Jaren responded by delving deeper into the power, drawing more energy and focusing all of his intent on keeping the king at bay. He became oblivious to everything else.

Aldrain's arms penetrated the sphere nearly to his elbows. In reaction, cascading, blinding blue light poured outward, strands of electricity searing and snapping at the king in protest. He continued to vent his animal rage, roaring all the louder.

Jaren drew the magic back for the barest of instants, then thrust forward with all of the strength he could summon. Like a person pushing against a force that is suddenly removed, Aldrain pitched forward, imbalanced by the instant-long void, then was violently hurled back.

Jaren was also blasted from his feet by the impact. His center dissipated and he lay dazed on the thickly carpeted floor of the tent. His vision blurred and his ears rang. He knew he was finished; the king's men would rush him soon enough. The cold realization was insufficient to jar him back to his senses. He floundered in a sea of murky, muffled sensation.

There was a lightening of the fog that obscured his vision. Perhaps it had come from the wall of the tent behind him, though the vertigo that gripped him made it impossible to be certain. The light joined into the greater mix of vague sights and sounds spinning in his mind.

Jaren felt pressure on his arm. His upper body rose. His head bobbed unsteadily about as he tried to catch some hint of the sensations' origin. He felt a touch against his forehead and his vision began to clear, several layers of the curtaining blur drawn back.

"Are you all right, Jaren?"

The voice echoed hollowly at first and Jaren blinked when he realized someone was speaking to him. He groped blindly about and discovered that someone was holding him in a sitting position. He was not yet coherent enough to answer.

"Can you hear me?"

Jaren tried to nod. He had no idea whether or not his head obeyed.

"Okay. Listen to me."

His pupils began once more to focus and he saw a face. Someone was leaning over him. There was an edge of worry in the voice. Genuine concern. He made the connection. It was the stranger from the clearing, the man he met before coming to the king.

"What—how did you—"

"Jaren, there's no time for that. Can you stand?"

This time, Jaren found he could nod.

"Good. The others are still stunned, though the king is about to recover. We need to leave. Now."

"Okay, I'll see if I...can stand." Jaren struggled awkwardly and would not have succeeded without the strong support of the other. He could not remember the man's name. He must have been staring with a lost expression, as the man answered his unspoken question.

"Yes, it's me, Varas. Now, let's get out of here. Unless you'd like to try reasoning with him some more?"

The man led Jaren through a rip in the tent's side—the opening had been the source of the white light—and he shivered with the cold of the late afternoon breeze. The brightness of the sky forced him to squint and brought tears to his eyes. Though, after being so completely shaken up and disoriented by magic, it was good to feel natural sensations again, however uncomfortable.

Jaren stumbled along with Varas supporting him. He moved surely and smoothly, or at least he would have, had Jaren not been at his side slowing him up. They moved in a cautious crouch past innumerable canvas tents, each one indistinguishable from the last. Jaren's legs wanted to fold completely.

Varas navigated with sure-footed certainty. They made a more or less straight line toward the southern edge of the camp. As they stole forward, peeking out from behind corners and dashing through the avenues between the makeshift structures, Jaren gradually regained his strength and wits.

At one point before he had come completely back to his own mind and his body once more obeyed his wishes, they stopped suddenly along the side of a tent that sat on one of the main concourses. Jaren found himself lying on the ground, Varas tossing several sacks and spare sheets of canvas on top of him. He warned Jaren to be quiet with an emphatic *shushing* gesture and then stepped casually out into the thoroughfare.

Jaren observed the approach of several soldiers through a tiny gap in his coverings. They conversed briefly with Varas, the tone of the soldiers curious, carrying an edge of urgency. After several exchanges, Varas gestured back the way he and Jaren had come and the others headed off in that direction.

"What…how did you get them to leave like that?" Jaren mumbled, struggling to emerge from his coverings.

"My cloak. It has some…useful magic. It's woven partly with *metanduil* threads. I'll show you how it works sometime. Sometime later. Now, we have to be off before they realize I've sent them the wrong way."

Jaren, now largely stable save for the occasional lurch, followed after the rogue. While his mind was mostly his own once more, he couldn't keep his thoughts from straying. He knew he should be focused on escaping, but his inner voice kept fighting back, forcing itself to be heard.

What happened to Aldrain?

• 34 •

A Glimpse of Darkness and A New Arrival

THEY DID NOT LEAVE THE FOLLOWING DAY, or the day after that. Iselle grew increasingly agitated. Llaw stepped out frequently, to think, he said. She knew better and did not blame him. Iselle could hardly stand herself, she was so restless and impatient. Dagger even padded softly around her. She was a complete and total bear.

She decided to go for a walk herself, hopefully to relieve some of her pent-up frustration. Her pace was swift and she darted like a silverfish through the vibrantly-coloured masses filling the streets. Dagger loped easily beside her, equally happy to be out getting some exercise. He seemed to be grinning. She laughed, an unfamiliar sound the past few days—weeks even—and patted him on the head as they stopped under the shade of an overhanging canopy and she decided where to go next.

As the sun began its gradual descent, the shadows of the sunny afternoon lengthened. They had a thinning effect on the crowds, signalling an end to the day's jostling and trading. Fewer and fewer people came and went.

A flicker of movement at the far end of a side alley drew her eyes. There, for an instant she saw him. She blinked and he was gone.

Turan.

Iselle blinked again. *It couldn't be. Could it?*

She felt rage boiling up from her gut once more, dying embers rekindled to intense heat, the benefit of her hour's worth of walking ruined by that single, fleeting image of the hated young man.

Before Iselle knew what she was doing, she found herself halfway down the alley. At the intersection, she peered in the other three directions. There was no sign of him. Shady, darkened niches and discarded bits of refuse inhabited the laneways, but nothing else. Nothing moved.

Again she laughed. This time, though, it was bitter and hollow. Iselle reached over and scratched behind Dagger's ear. "I guess I'm so riled up I've started seeing things, hey boy? It couldn't have been him. What are the chances? Besides, I think he knows exactly what would happen to him if I ever was to find the lying little thief again."

Another flitting movement danced in the periphery of her vision. She whipped her head around and again the figure appeared in the distance. This time he was further away, but she'd had a good enough glimpse of his face the first time. She was certain.

"Hey!" Iselle yelled, starting toward the silhouetted figure at a trot.

He turned and headed in the opposite direction, down another darkened alley. Soon enough, he rounded a corner and disappeared.

Iselle bolted ahead, determined not to let him escape. Not after what he'd done—what he'd said. She was breathing in heavier gulps now, her body reacting to the increased exertion and her rising emotions. Iselle realised she held her fists clenched, so she flexed and extended her fingers, trying to work out the tension.

She followed the figure down the darkened alley and around the bend only to discover another, empty intersection. She had travelled into the dock district and found herself among the lesser-used avenues of the quarter, surrounded by the high walls of warehouses and the rear accesses of workshops. About her, all was quiet.

Iselle spied the vague form she sought. He rounded a corner several lane lengths away, disappearing from view. With a curse, she darted after him.

The cat-and-mouse chase went on for the better part of an hour, ending with Iselle confused, sweaty and most of all, frustrated. The Turan-figure remained out of her grasp.

She leaned against the back wall of a slat-sided warehouse. She kicked the wall hard, then retreated to the rear wall of another quiet building, sliding down to sit on an upended ale cask. Iselle crossed her arms and raised her face to the darkening sky. In the gathering stillness, she could hear her thundering heartbeat and little else.

"I'd hoped you wouldn't give up too soon."

Iselle was so tense that she leaped to her feet at the sound of the voice. It was most definitely Turan's. But at the same time, it wasn't. There was a familiarity to it. A feeling of disquiet stole over her. The early evening breeze stirred and she felt goose bumps rise across her skin.

"I have missed you."

Iselle's eyes narrowed as she took him in. Again, much like the voice, the person standing a few dozen paces away was surely Turan. And yet there was something off about him. Iselle could not place it.

"Aren't you going to say hello?"

"Hello, you treacherous little—"

"My, my, Iselle. Aren't we past that? It's been some time, you know."

"I have an idea that might help me feel better about everything. Just wait and I'll show you." She started forward. It was only then that she noticed Dagger had not advanced alongside her. Throwing a quick glance back, she jolted when she saw the dog. *He's backing away.* His haunches were raised, ears lowered. *And he's whining.* She had heard him whine on only a handful of occasions. Only when—

"Don't worry about your dog. I'm sure he'll get along without you just fine."

Iselle suddenly felt as though she was walking through gelatine. Her head swivelled back to Turan, eyes widening with horror-stricken realization. Now she knew what was different. The voice of the other was lower, cold and callous, his appearance pale and sickly.

"Oh, come now, Iselle. Don't tell me you've changed your mind already? No longer happy to see me?" The Turan-thing licked its ruddy lips with a blackened, pointed tongue that slid all too readily between yellowed, jagged teeth.

Iselle nearly dropped her long knife.

Somehow, Turan was a blacktongue.

◆ ◆ ◆

Jaren set his palm on the skull-sized rock in the shallow pit. He summoned enough energy to heat it to glowing once more, its pale, amber light obscured by the earth surrounding it. It was the only source of light and warmth he and Varas dared so close to the armed encampments, especially since they could number none of them as allies. Even with the heating source for their tiny encampment renewed, Jaren felt the chill of the evening settling into his bones.

"I don't know what's gotten into him, but that's not the Aldrain I knew."

"I sensed something as well. Though, most of this is even newer for me than for you. I couldn't tell you what it was, beyond the fact that there was a malevolent aura about the king."

Jaren nodded. "Yes, that's what I felt, too. It's not the first time, but this is the worst it's been. It's almost overwhelming."

"Perhaps it has something to do with his…change in temperament."

"I hadn't thought of that. But I suppose it makes sense," Jaren admitted. "What could do that?"

"I have no answers for you," Varas replied.

Jaren huffed sarcastically. "That's encouraging. I've heard something like that before."

"Oh?" Varas smiled knowingly.

"Yes. Shortly after our flight from Dal Farrow, we met up with…someone who was very helpful…but not very informative."

"I'll wager I can guess his name."

Jaren laughed in disbelief. "Go ahead and try."

Varas smiled. "It was Verithael. He said to tell you *hello*." His smile broadened as Jaren's jaw gaped.

"How could you—that's not possible, unless—" his eyes widened further. "You're…an avatar? Like him?"

"Somehow, no, I don't think we're exactly the same. But I think we're on the same side."

Jaren sat upright. "When did you see him? Where is he now—is he coming to help?"

"Hold on, now," Varas raised his hands in mock warding. "I can only answer one question at a time, and only questions I have the answers to." He cocked his head to the side. "I think you'll be able to help me understand a few things as well. Deal?"

Jaren returned his genuine smile. "Deal."

"All right, then. First of all, I don't know where Verithael is. I don't think he's coming to help—I believe that's what I'm here for. I met him on the road…. In short, it was a very curious meeting. In the end, some truths were shown to me. Things I hadn't thought about for a long time. Mostly, they were things I'd forgotten about myself, even though they turned out to be very important." He sighed and there was a long pause as he gazed out from their dimly lit refuge, studying the silent landscape and the dark, evening skies above. A great many stars twinkled brightly across the chill nightscape, the tiny, bright pinpoints cold and distant. "In the end, I came to know a couple of things. The most crucial was that I needed to find you and help in whatever way I could. Verithael must have known it, because he gave me the message to send his greeting." Varas looked back at Jaren. "Your turn. What exactly did he—as an avatar–do?"

"Mostly he was a guardian. He showed up the first time we encountered a blacktongue—a spirit-creature that takes over another's body—and saved us. And that wasn't the only time. Still," Jaren shook his head, "he was frustratingly short on details and information. We were meant to find our own way, he said, and he was just along to make sure we were allowed the chance to do so." Jaren looked into Varas's eyes. "I've never seen anyone handle a sword as well as Ver. I think he might have been invincible."

Varas chuckled. "I think you might be right."

"So, now tell me—" Jaren stopped abruptly with a startled jerk of his head. He scanned about, eyes narrowed.

Varas was on his feet, sabres in hand almost before Jaren started peering around. "What is it? What do you sense?"

"Magic…someone's summoning. But it's strange. It's growing stronger, like they're coming closer." Jaren scrambled to his feet and turned in circles, his eyes searching the surrounding darkness.

"I don't see anyone. Or hear anything." Varas had moved to the edge of the little clearing and skirted the perimeter. "There's nothing moving out there. Are you sure?"

"Yes," Jaren said. "It's here."

"That's impossible. We'd be able to see it by—"

A glowing blue orb materialized several paces from their small rock pit. Jaren drew in the magic, preparing himself to meet whatever threat emerged from the widening portal.

Varas crouched, his curved sabres at the ready.

A young woman stepped from the magical gateway. Despite her obvious fatigue and frazzled appearance, she was beautiful and exotic-looking. Her long, straw-coloured hair, though tousled, framed an exquisite, tanned face. Her sky-blue eyes found Jaren and she called to him in a wavering voice.

"Arynelle?" Jaren's voice was incredulous.

"Ah. Company, then." Varas's voice had lost its edge and he straightened, sheathing his weapons. "Should I expect more guests?"

"I wasn't expecting her," Jaren said dryly.

Arynelle managed an embarrassed smile, colour rising in her cheeks. Then she stumbled and collapsed.

· 35 ·

Into Corners and Dangers Unknown

"I WAS BEGINNING TO THINK YOU'D STAY in your room forever. Then I'd have had to come in after you." Turan's crooked leer sent a shiver down Iselle's spine.

"What do you want?"

"You first," the other taunted. "*You* followed *me* here, Iselle. What were you after?" The foul being winked.

Her hatred of that simple gesture pushed Iselle over the top, rage momentarily overcoming her revulsion and fear. She lunged at Turan with the long hunting knife. It sank into his midsection with a sickly *tchuck*.

He merely looked down and gave an apathetic *tisk*. "Now, does that make you feel any better?"

Iselle drew back and yanked the weapon out, then brandished the short blade like a talisman. Strings of oily, black blood trailed from it back to the wound that seemed not to bother Turan in the least. "Why are you here?" Iselle demanded, her voice rising an octave.

"For you of course." The leering grin spread across his pallid face from ear to ear. "We have some unfinished business, you and I." He gave a brief shout. In answer, several silhouetted figures appeared down the alley behind Turan. From the scuffling sound of boots at her back, a couple of them had taken up positions blocking that direction as well. She heard Dagger's low, feral growl. The blacktongue might have cowed him, but not flesh-and-blood foes. Not when his mistress was in jeopardy.

Turan lunged for Iselle but she sidestepped him and ran past. Knowing that the alley was blocked at both ends, she dove into the darkened doorway from which the blacktongue had appeared. She quickly shoved the door closed, latched it and then turned to flee down the dim corridor. It was a warehouse, with a high ceiling and discarded crates and casks scattered the length of the hallway. The going was agonizingly slow given her desire to escape but she needed to step with care along the debris-strewn passage. If she turned an ankle or crashed into a wall, she would quickly be overcome.

What Iselle needed was another exit or window of some sort. Several doorways opened off the passage to the left and right as she struggled on with as much speed as she dared. All the while, she fought for breath against the talons of clutching fear that threatened to seize and hold her fast. Back down the corridor she heard crashing and muttered curses. Furious barking mixed with panicked shouts, then a cry of pain: a human shriek of agony. *Good boy, Dagger, keep them busy for just a few moments!* Iselle smiled briefly before her footing shifted and she was forced to concentrate fully on keeping upright.

None of the side rooms offered the exit point she so desperately wished for. There were no windows or other doors that she could make out, only stacks of crates and shadows. Iselle had to fight off the urge to head inside one of these and hunker down in a crouch behind the stacks. Her only chance was to get out.

Iselle rounded the corner—the only direction she could go—and kept running. Another cry of pain rose up behind her, then she heard Dagger's own sharp yelp. She staggered to a halt, chest heaving. Her lungs burned with the stale, dry air. She was torn between her need to escape and her longing to help the dog. At the same time, her eyes fixed on a shaft of light extending from a doorway at the far end of the passage. Another cry of pain and several angry barks followed. *He'll be okay*, she reasoned, *you can't help him anyway! Once you get out, they'll have no reason to harm him—and it's only because you're in here that he's staying to fight anyway.*

Her course chosen, Iselle bounded down the remaining stretch of corridor, slowing up only enough to enter the storeroom. It was much like the others, with crates and other miscellaneous containers piled nearly to the height of the building, except for the narrow window set into the midpoint of the wall, just a few hand spans shy of the ceiling. It would take some climbing, but she could definitely reach the opening.

Feverishly, Iselle scampered forward and began her ascent. Some of the containers were heavier than others, so she took care once again, lest a lighter crate tumble away beneath her. Everything was coated with a thick layer of dust that stirred on contact, catching in her throat and nose. But most of the boxes were no bigger than waist-height and she was able to climb without too much difficulty.

Her knees and one elbow throbbed painfully from a few missteps, but she made it to within several arm-lengths of the window.

A chill voice reached her just as she spotted the heavy iron bars that fronted the opening. She was trapped.

"I don't think you'll be going that way, precious."

Iselle's mind jolted as an icy spasm of fear gripped her core. She spun and saw Turan stride calmly into the room. Near panic, her eyes raked the interior for some other exit point. There was none.

"If you come down, I'll be gentle, I promise." Turan laughed evilly. "And I might even have someone patch up your dog for you. He looked a bit worse for wear, last I saw."

Iselle nearly screamed in both anger and fear. *How could you have been so stupid?*

Turan advanced, his dead, black eyes locked on her.

◆ ◆ ◆

"You've a good deal more colour than when you arrived last evening," Varas commented on seeing that Arynelle had wakened. He knelt by the heating rock, which was still infused with some of the energy Jaren provided before he stepped away to wash up. He rubbed his hands together briskly, then held them toward the small pit.

"Thank you," Arynelle offered quietly as she sat upright in the bedroll. "Where's Jaren?"

"He's off making himself presentable—so he might be gone for a while."

Arynelle smiled. "You sound like his friend, Iselle."

"I suppose I do at that."

"Who are you?" she asked, smoothing away a lock of long, flaxen hair. She paused. "And how would you know what Iselle is like?"

"I'm…it's complicated," Varas sighed. "Suffice it to say that I'm a friend. I met Jaren and Iselle a short time ago. More than that, I can't offer at this point."

"You look like a thief…or worse."

"Now who sounds like Iselle?"

Arynelle laughed. "Yes, that was rather blunt, wasn't it?"

"Don't be troubled; it's preferable to false niceties. At least a person knows where they stand."

"Let me try again. You look like a person who's either able to get out of a situation or to handle himself when that proves too difficult. It's curious that you would come across the two of them, though."

"You could say I used to make a living at coming across people," Varas nodded.

"But not anymore?"

"Well, I still need those same skills on occasion. But—" he smiled and raised a finger to emphasize his point, "the motives for using them have definitely changed."

"I see you two have introduced yourselves." Jaren strode back into the encampment, face clean and hair wet.

"I thought farmers were supposed to be simple, polite folk." Varas feigned a grumble. "I decided not to wait for you to make the effort."

Arynelle smiled. "Varas was just telling me how you'd met before."

"Oh?" Jaren said.

"I was…in disguise at the time. I met you before as Kalon Eversmere." Varas hesitated, searching for the right words. He shrugged and exhaled deeply as he continued, "Back then, I was an assassin for the Jade Talon Clan. I was supposed to bring you back to Neval Ketarra."

Both Jaren and Arynelle gaped. Jaren reached for Arynelle's hand and moved between her and Varas. "You were sent to…to capture me?"

"I was," Varas admitted. "But as I explained, everything changed on the road to Ansalar. Everything happened as I've told you. Now I am meant to aid and protect you."

"Jaren, I wouldn't stay with him," Arynelle said. "How do you know he's telling the truth?"

"I don't, except that he met Ver—the avatar I told you about back at your home. Ver would not allow someone to trick me into believing a dangerous lie. And he couldn't know about Ver unless they actually did meet."

"Jaren, he's an assassin. Couldn't he have killed Ver after getting information about you?"

"Killing Ver would not be possible, I don't think. Not for a normal man. Even an assassin. And even if it could have happened, Ver would never give another information that could harm me." Jaren looked hard into Varas's eyes. "I will trust you for now. But only because of Ver—and I'll be keeping an eye on you."

Varas bowed. "I would do nothing less if I were you. Still, I have pledged my sword to your cause. I'll not betray your trust."

Jaren tore his eyes from the man, looked at Arynelle and took a deep breath before speaking. "How did you manage to get here? How did the magic work for you?"

"It was simple until I reached the mainland. Then, things got more... uncomfortable. Especially as I neared the mountains. But I managed to keep my focus up until I sensed you were near." Her forehead creased. "At least I was hoping it was you."

"You didn't know for sure? How could you take a risk like that? It's bad enough you came in the first place without knowing whether the magic would bring you safely."

"As bad as sneaking off in the middle of the night like a thief?" Arynelle glanced at Varas apprehensively.

He merely shrugged, a smirk curling the corners of his mouth.

"That was different," Jaren said.

"Why?"

"Because I was doing it to protect you. I knew you wouldn't listen to reason and agree to stay behind. So I left before you could commit to something dangerous."

"I don't need you to protect me, Jaren." She stood and straightened now, rounding on him. "I'm not a helpless girl."

"Wait—that's not what I meant—"

"It's what you said."

"I meant you shouldn't have come on your own without knowing the limits of your magic here on Evarlund. That's it."

By her look, Arynelle was about to give Jaren another blast when Varas interceded.

"Can we agree that you were both hasty in your decisions and move on?" He looked at one, then the other with a measuring stare. "After all, events continue while you two argue." He gestured to the northeast.

The pair turned their gazes to the near distance, shielding their eyes against Sholara's early morning glare. Vast clouds of brown dust rose in two separate columns in close proximity to each other. The occasional echo of beating drums and blaring horns found their ears. Armies were on the march.

Above the distant commotion, clouds of a different sort gathered: black, swirling swarms of carrion birds hungry for the anticipated feast.

"Time is running out," Jaren said, partly to himself.

"Have you found your sister?" asked Arynelle.

"I know where she is…more or less." He pointed to a spot on the horizon to the west of the moving armies. "She's somewhere over there with the Witch and her *daughter*, Joselle."

"You can sense her," Arynelle stated. "Just like I followed my senses to track you here."

"Do you think the Warwitch means to join the fight?" Jaren asked Varas in a bitter tone. "As an assassin, you must have been familiar with her sort of thinking."

Varas chuckled. "It doesn't sound like the sort of action she'd take unless she was assured of victory."

"I don't think she has any of the…of her weapons left—the ones she used to destroy the Draegondor palace, Caren Hold, or *Valir* Llaw's tower. She had to flee her stronghold after our struggle. Unless she's managed to make more." Jaren shook his head. "I doubt she has the weapons any longer if that's where she forged them. I think she'll try to sneak in and attack when an opportunity presents itself. That's how…her type…seems to do things," Jaren said with a pointed glare at Varas.

Varas scratched absently at the stubble on his cheeks as if ignoring the slight, then gave a nod. "The Jhud'Hai are used to hunting with stealth. It's a tactic that serves them well in The Barrens. I think you are right."

"Maybe we can use her scheming against her," Arynelle proposed.

"Sneak up on her while she's planning to sneak up on someone else? That could work." Varas nodded again.

"I thought you'd like that plan," Arynelle smiled at him uneasily.

"There's not going to be a *we*," Jaren said flatly. "At least not a *we* with *you* in it, Arynelle. You're staying here."

"I most certainly am not."

"You still don't know what else your magic can do here. Or whether it will continue to work at all."

"I got here well enough and I'm not staying behind. Say what you want, Jaren. I'm *not*." She planted her feet and set her fists on her hips.

"Fine." Jaren looked at Varas with a determined expression. "Arynelle, you stay with Varas—he will keep you safe; I may need to put all my focus into freeing Morgaine from whatever bonds keep her."

Varas nodded. "She will be protected."

"If anything should happen to her…" Jaren warned.

Arynelle's voice rose, "I do not need a nurse-maid, Jaren—we don't even know him—especially not an assassin!"

"Would you rather I tie you up?" Jaren asked.

"You wouldn't dare!"

"Please, you two—" Varas nodded to the northeast again. The stirring dust clouds drew ever closer together. "Can we make a decision?"

"Fine." Arynelle glared at Jaren. "But this isn't over. I didn't mentor you back on Sylvarii to have you suddenly think you know everything."

"I don't, Arynelle. And I don't like you putting yourself at risk again. Varas had to help me yesterday; I'm not above needing it myself. Besides, he's already proven himself trustworthy once."

She crossed her arms and mumbled something under her breath.

"I just wish we had Aldrain to help us. I still don't know what's gotten into him. He's not the same." Jaren sighed heavily. "He's unbalanced—he believes everyone has turned against him."

Arynelle's expression changed from frustration to a pensive frown. "Sometimes people change."

"Not like that—I've never known him to speak or act as he does now. Ever since we freed him from the prison…" Jaren trailed off, his face darkening.

"What is it, Jaren?"

"He was very weak—he'd been tortured, put through Truth knows what." He looked up, apprehension etched across his features. "I wonder if I harmed him in some way. The *metanduil* that was part of his torture—it became part of him."

"I confess, I have no knowledge of what the magic-metal might do to a person," Arynelle said, "but even if it is contributing to this shift, you did it to help him. Besides, from what I understand, it's really just a conduit for magical energy. If we encounter him, tell me right away and I'll see if I can sense anything else."

"Like what?"

"There are a few ways I know of that someone's character can be...altered... the way you describe. Perhaps I can help you identify the cause."

"All right, thank you." Jaren turned to Varas once more. "I have your word that you'll keep Arynelle from harm while I do what I can against the Witch?"

Varas raised an eyebrow, then added one last nod of confirmation. "You have my word."

· 36 ·

Darkening Skies

THE MERCENARIES FORMING THE *VALIR* ARMY had nothing to fight for other than money. Aldrain's true advantage lay in that reality. They were equally matched numerically, though the combined forces of the Carathonai and Ergothani boasted a larger number of cavalry units. The *Valir* host was almost entirely composed of infantry.

They were arrayed on the plain below the rise from which the king studied his foes. The *Valir* general was wise, Aldrain admitted silently–he'd placed several regiments of spear and pike bearers out front to discourage a cavalry charge. Behind these first lines were the *Valir* themselves, perhaps several dozen in total, flanked by lines of archers. The general's reinforcements waited behind, as did their smaller contingent of cavalry.

Sholara had crested the horizon little more than an hour before; both armies assembled in the pre-dawn hours and deployed as soon as it was light enough to see easily. The faint breeze that stirred hardly moved the plumes of dust rising from either army's movement. They towered overhead, ominous harbingers of dread that refused to be dismissed, while above them roiled black clouds of carrion birds, their cries echoing occasionally through the breaks in the armies' clamouring.

It was neither numerical superiority nor magic that would win this day, Aldrain believed. His own body of *Valir*—those who had survived the purge— numbered ten in all. He was unsure if he should count himself among them. Now that he was…changed…he could very easily be grouped with them, even if the extent of his abilities were not truly known. *This will prove a good test.* He gave a low, bitter laugh.

The Ergothani would ultimately deliver the victory. Aldrain deployed them at the head of his battle formation. They would be fighting for their kin, for their fathers, mothers, children, and whomever else the Carathonai had taken. This arrangement ensured not only loyalty, but total commitment. They all knew what would become of their loved ones should they fail to provide anything less than complete dedication. They would fight like their very homes were in danger. Again, Aldrain laughed darkly. Maybe not their homes, but certainly the loved ones who shared them.

Cordan and Rhodal shifted in their saddles, sharing wary, sidelong looks.

Aldrain was oblivious. His expression turned intense, a mask of contempt mixed with satisfaction. He would see a measure of justice delivered this day. The *Valir* council would see its army vanquished and with it, their hope of remaining a separate body. Their meddling and interference was done. They would become true servants of the six realms' leaders. They were complicit in the destruction of his home and loved ones, either directly or indirectly. It made no difference that their tenuous alliance had apparently failed—why else would the Witch be encamped separately rather than alongside them? It mattered little. He would overcome the *Valir* army and then turn his attention to the Witch.

She too would pay. Dearly.

Rhodal cleared his throat. Cordan patted his horse's mane, pointedly looking in the other direction as the king regarded them, stirred from his black reverie.

"Send them in," Aldrain commanded.

"Sire?"

"Everyone. We'll lead the charge."

Rhodal protested, "Shouldn't we leave units behind to reinforce—"

"No. We must overwhelm them completely. They will bend like rushes in the wind before us. They have no loyalty other than to gold. As soon as we press the men, they'll remember their lives are dearer to them than wages."

Rhodal's voice rose in opposition again, "But Your Majesty, the pikes. They have formed themselves—"

"It makes no difference!" Aldrain silenced the elder general, eyeing him hotly. "We drive straight for them. At fifty paces we'll angle our assault. That will lessen their defense against our charge."

The other two glanced at each other, then back at the king. They remained silent.

"Afraid of a fight? Then sit back here and sip some tea while the true heroes of Carathon bring justice to our enemies. But do not expect a place of honour at the celebration. That, I save for the bravest among us this day. Perhaps you'd rather see Ergothani warriors feasting by my side?"

Cordan turned his head and spat. "If you wish to be at the head of the attack, Sire, you'll need to beat me and my men there." The young officer nodded brusquely, wheeled his horse and trotted off to join his company.

Rhodal bristled, but saluted the king and nudged his mount down the line to his own command.

◆ ◆ ◆

Jaren eased a finger between the collar and his neck, trying to rid himself of the feeling of constriction. It did not work. He had not kept the *metanduil* collar with the intent of ever using it. The same went for the manacles that the Witch's agents had used to restrain him months ago. He looked up, risking a glance at Arynelle, whose wrists were shackled by the magic-metal bindings. She returned his look with an anxious frown. Apparently he wasn't the only one uncomfortable with their ruse.

They needed to hide their approach so that the Witch was not immediately aware of them. That meant spirit walking was out of the question. Rather than simply walk into the camp with her able to sense them, the *metanduil* restraints were the only logical choice.

Varas's magic cloak formed a large part of the overall scheme; without it their chances of reaching the Warwitch's tent undetected were slim. The guise had worked; few of the camp's inhabitants had done more than cast a casual glance toward the group. Those who took a closer look, roused by curiosity, had done just that and no more. So far.

The fact that neither he nor Arynelle could summon while wearing the bonds only added to Jaren's apprehension. If they were discovered, the two of them would have to rely on Varas to both defend and free them. As capable as he was, an army of hostile Jhud'Hai posed a considerable level of difficulty.

At least they were nearing the center of the camp. He could see the taller, sprawling tent of the Warwitch in the distance. He hoped Morgaine was still inside where he believed he had seen her through use of the magic. Right now he could not sense her at all: another annoying effect of the collar.

It crossed his mind—again—that Varas could be delivering them to the Witch. He might have saved Jaren from Aldrain's wrath simply to ensure another contract was fulfilled. The man had admitted he was formerly an assassin. Not only that, but he had been after Jaren. Who knew what level of deceit he was capable of? And once more Jaren rejected the notion. He had apparently been sent by Ver, whom Jaren trusted without pause. There were no holes in Varas's story, no pieces that did not fit. Perhaps the most compelling reason, Jaren mused, was that the man's presence elicited the same feelings of ordered calm that Ver had inspired. That was something he couldn't explain to Arynelle. But, he thought, she would go along with the plan.

He glanced at her and her eyes found his. She gave the slightest of nods, despite the apprehension he could see on her face.

Fortunately for Jaren's already rattled peace of mind, there were fewer encounters the closer they got to the Witch's quarters. The trio had observed most of the warriors mustering in the open areas on the camp's eastern perimeter. They spied the occasional lone soldier hurrying off, most likely to form up with the rest of his comrades, or small groups of guards patrolling the silent rows of mostly-emptied tents. These, they either steered clear of or passed with cautious steps and held breath. At least, that was Jaren's take on the experiences. He was more or less convinced that Varas remained calm and relaxed, albeit ready for any challenge they might face.

To Jaren's relief, the Jhud'Hai appeared to be sufficiently cowed by the Witch's authority that they received nothing more than intense glares shot from hard, slate-grey eyes. Had they been in charge of their own affairs, Jaren was certain things would have gone differently. The lines of distrust and wariness chiselled into the guards' faces was plain enough to see.

It helped that Varas knew enough of the Jhud'Haian language to greet the others and even to offer either a little conversation or brief explanation. Jaren did not know which he gave, but whatever the former assassin said seemed to deflate any building tensions that might have pushed the Jhud'Hai past their fear of the Witch and to fall back on their cautious ways.

After enduring an interminable amount of time and accompanying discomfort, they finally reached the tent. The only similarity it shared with the simpler, surrounding structures was the dun fabric that covered it. It dwarfed its neighbours in height and breadth, as grand and imposing in its appearance as the Witch herself.

Jaren examined his boots, trying to look as inconspicuous as possible while Varas conferred with the guards at the entryway. They appeared suspicious but did not dare to challenge someone claiming a personal mission from the Witch. Most likely, the Jhud'Hai were aware of her interest in Jaren, and seeing a young man of that description in Varas's company definitely added to his story's credibility. Giving the trio subdued nods, the guards bade them enter.

"Go to your sister," Varas directed in a low hiss after a brief scan of the interior. He hastily removed their bindings then gestured to a dark, hunched form on a chair to one side of the room. "I'll watch the entrance. Be quick about it!"

Jaren crossed the room quickly and knelt before Morgaine. Arynelle followed but kept a pace back from him, careful not to crowd the siblings.

"Gainey?" Jaren called softly to his sister. "Gainey, can you hear me?"

Morgaine was bound to the seat, likely to prevent a fall; she was slumped forward and would have tumbled off the chair without the restraints. She did not respond or even move.

"Morgaine, can you hear me? It's Jaren." His voice became husky with emotion.

Still, his sister did not respond.

"It's going to be okay, Gainey. I'm going to get you out of here." He moved forward and gently pushed Morgaine's limp torso against the chair's back. Her head lolled disturbingly. Jaren pawed ineffectively at the bonds with trembling fingers. Arynelle stepped close, placing a hand on his shoulder.

"She'll be okay, Jaren. You'll see."

He replied with a wan smile as she began to help.

From across the tent, Varas peered apprehensively in their direction, then returned his gaze to the entry.

"Can you hold her up?" Jaren asked as the last of the ropes slipped free. Then taking a deep, steadying breath, he grasped the sides of the mask covering his sister's face. It was the one he saw through the magic—a shaped, moulded face of metal set in a frown, with a single tear fashioned on one cheek. "Okay, Gainey, I'm going to take this off now. You'll be good as new, soon."

Jaren lowered his head and called forth the magic. As he had done some time ago with Aldrain, he let the soothing, freeing energy direct its own flow, going where it needed, willing it to examine and hopefully reassure his sister at the same time.

Morgaine gave a slight twitch as he sent the magic into her. She gave a low, barely audible moan.

Encouraged by this response, Jaren expanded the flow of the magic, now willing it to heal as well. Immediately, his hands received a shock from the mask. Though he was centered, it nearly caused him disruption enough to release his grip. He concentrated yet more deeply, searching for the divide between his sister and the hindering mask.

"I am impressed, Jaren. That is more reaction than I've gotten from her since I put the mask on."

Jaren instantly recognized the voice. Though he held firmly to his center and it reached him as though an echo from a faraway place, it was unmistakable: the chill, detached tone of the Warwitch.

· 37 ·

Discovered

WARMTH REACHED MORGAINE. WARMTH AND...comfort? It had been so long since she'd allowed herself to feel anything. The sensations were foreign and it was difficult to trust them. It had been necessary to switch herself off. Only by becoming completely isolated, removed from her physical self, had she succeeded in holding out against the intrusions of the Mother and of her sister in the magic.

Was this some new trick? A plan to fool her into lowering her defenses? Morgaine withdrew from it, sealing herself away once more. This was different from centering herself in the magic. Reaching outward, connecting, was required to summon. But this tactic, born of necessity, was the opposite. She did not calm herself to join with the magic now, but steeled herself in isolation; she pushed away the magic and, in the process, was separated from herself. Only the tiniest fragment of Morgaine's being remained in contact with her physical form, allowing her body to remain alive, carrying out vital functions. Other than that, Morgaine was locked away from reality, hidden away in the refuge of her mind.

Another sensation reached her, this time deflected by her strengthened resolve. In its passing, she thought she recognized it as an attempt to heal her, magic sent to ease her suffering. *Another ruse*, her conscious self warned. The Witch was probably trying to trick her into submitting. Again, Morgaine bolstered herself against the contact, welcome and soothing as it seemed. It was a struggle to deny herself the very things she so desperately craved, things she had been denied for so long. Morgaine recalled the promises of comfort and relief the Mother had made, if only she relented. She would not.

A fleeting thought then crossed the vast caverns of her mind. *What if Jaren comes and I don't recognize him again?* If she maintained her defensive posture, there would be no way to tell, no way for him to reach her. No, she would be able to tell.

Wouldn't you?

❖ ❖ ❖

Varas whirled about in time to see the Witch materialize at the center of the tent, but his attention snapped to the entry once again as several of her Jhud'Haian guards rushed inside. They began to fan out and Varas moved to engage them, driving the three warriors back together in a knot, making them unable to flank him or advance on the others. One of their number turned briefly and shouted a warning past the door flap.

"We're going to have company—soon! Whatever it is you're doing, do it quick!"

The Warwitch smiled broadly. "I'm afraid Morgaine is in no condition to travel." She shook her head in mock sympathy. "Your sister was behaving irrationally; she wouldn't listen to reason. I had to...protect her."

Jaren's anger got the better of him. He released all but a thin ribbon of the magic, enough to keep the connection intact. He rose and turned, stepping forward to place himself between the Witch and his sister and Arynelle. "If you harmed her—" Over his shoulder, he spoke in urgent and low tones. "If you can, Arynelle, remove the mask and rouse Morgaine."

"You've found a new girlfriend, then?" Rhianain's smile grew more wicked. "And I so liked the last one. Full of spirit, she was."

"Enough of your games, Witch," Jaren's jaw was set and he had to force the words. "I bested you before and I can do it again. But if you choose, I'll let you leave. Now."

The Warwitch drew a deep breath. "Very generous of you, *master* Haldannon. My, what difference a few months make. I'm afraid, though, I'll have to decline. I do have a counter proposal, if you are interested."

"You choose to stay?"

Rhianain went on, as if dismissing Jaren's warning out of hand. "If you surrender, I'll let your sister go free." She shrugged. "And I'll even let your new girlfriend and guardian go, too."

Jaren's response was immediate. Blue lightning exploded from his fingertips and sliced toward the Witch. She threw herself to the side, unable to bring her own magic up in defense against the sudden strike. Several tendrils of the lightning snaked after her, tearing into her side and sending out a shower of angry sparks where it contacted the patch of *metanduil* in her torso.

She shrieked in pain and anger, then reacted with a strike of her own.

Jaren's shield, already in place, deflected the tongues of fire she sent toward him. One washed over a nearby table laden with rolled parchments and several thick tomes, instantly turning the items to ash. Another rose to the tent's ceiling, searing a hole through the canvas and hide covering.

Jaren looked past the Witch briefly. Varas had dispatched two of the Jhud'Hai. One lay still on the ground, the other writhed in agony, clutching at his thigh. Crimson leaked between his fingertips, his face twisted with pain. The third guard, this one hefting a double-bladed spear, furiously struggled to keep Varas at a distance. Several deep, bloodied gashes to his limbs suggested it was only a matter of moments before he went down.

"Leave! Now!" Jaren ordered Rhianain once more, retraining his gaze on her scarlet-clad form. "I will still allow you to go. I do not want revenge. Leave, and do not meddle in the affairs of the *Valir* or King Aldrain of Carathon again. If you do this, I promise I will not come after you."

The Witch picked herself up and straightened. A tremor shook her for an instant, the only evidence that she was in pain. "Again, young Jaren, you are most gracious. But I cannot allow you to interfere with my plans, let alone dictate terms." She raised her arms above her head, more fire coursing from her hands. This gout of scorching flames, though, was not directed at Jaren. It reached the ceiling, washing outward in waves to envelop its entire surface, then licked hungrily down the walls.

The sight it revealed was telling. The Witch had not thought to defeat Jaren solely through the use of magic. He should have considered that she might plan a trap. Now he knew for certain. Jaren risked a glance over his shoulder to Arynelle. She shook her head. She'd had no luck with Morgaine.

Through tatters of falling, burning material, Jaren saw that the entire perimeter was ringed by a legion of Jhud'Haian soldiers, beginning in a circle not fifty paces out from the tent's now destroyed exterior. The front ranks bore weapons and armour that were either made from, or gilded with *metanduil*.

Joselle Banath stood among them, a cruel leer that matched her Mother's splitting her dark lips. With a nod from the Witch, she moved to join Rhianain.

Out of the corner of his eye, Jaren glimpsed the final moments of the third Jhud'Haian soldier. Varas spun, first one way then the other, working his way inside the spear's reach. With dual strikes, the assassin dispatched his opponent. He glanced around and then toward Jaren, merely shrugging as he wiped the blood from his blades.

The Warwitch offered an icy sneer. "Now, dearest Jaren. It's time for *you* to consider *my* terms."

· 38 ·

The Storm Breaks

ARYNELLE CURSED UNDER HER BREATH. *Concentrate!* She had found the ethereal tethers that bound the mask to Morgaine but could not manage to undo them. The physical ropes had come off easily enough, but it was not so with these. It did not help that things had turned so horribly against them. Facing two enemies now instead of one, Jaren was just holding his ground. And as skilled as Varas obviously was, even he couldn't hold off an entire army for long.

She swallowed hard and tried to dismiss her mistrust of the assassin. *Or former assassin. Whatever he is.* It was bad enough being here, surrounded by the Witch and her forces, without having to worry about the one who was supposed to be watching her back.

Varas had skirted around the Witch and her companion, a redheaded, vicious-looking young woman about Arynelle's age. They let him go as if completely uninterested in his activities, focused as they were on Jaren. Now the assassin pressed in behind her, urging Arynelle to pull the unresponsive Morgaine in as near as possible to Jaren. Varas warned him to remain in close proximity to his adversaries. With everyone knotted together, they were harder to pick off individually. As long as the soldiers did not simply overrun them—which was unlikely, as the Witch called on them to take the intruders alive—their small group had a chance.

It was nevertheless a dangerous situation and only a matter of time before fortune turned against them. Varas was literally forced to stand overtop of Arynelle and Morgaine in order to fend off the Jhud'Haian warriors who came at him. And while Jaren matched his opponents' power, he did not seem able to overcome them.

Again and again, he deflected their combined attacks—lightning, flames, bolts of energy—and with his countering magic managed to keep them from going fully on the offensive. Jaren even succeeded in redirecting a number of their strikes, sending them into the massed ranks of the Witch's soldiers. Sometimes these were deflected or absorbed by *metanduil*-enhanced weapons and armour, at others they dealt lethal damage where such no protections existed. It was not a precise manipulation, and Jaren appeared to have started using the technique out of desperation, but it had so far helped to keep the soldiers from rushing Varas in overwhelming numbers.

His twin blades flashed in a blur. The assassin twisted, coiling and uncoiling his body in perfect harmony with his deadly sabres. He was impossibly fast, darting from side to side, just evading a spear's jab here, a slicing cut there. Each time, his own blades struck back in response, felling or wounding one of his countless adversaries.

Whenever one fell, another sprang forward to take the man's place. The Jhud'Haians' eyes burned with intensity and their war cries rose above the scene of the struggle. They were an ancient people, Arynelle recalled, a people who'd shared Evarlund with the Sylvarii before their expulsion. They were a warrior people with a fighting spirit. They would not stop, no matter how many Varas defeated.

She took some reassurance in the fact that the assassin was fighting so fiercely against the Witch's soldiers. If he was in league with her, wouldn't he have shown his true colours by now? Even so, he might still secretly be working for the *Valir*. In that case, it was best not to let her guard down completely.

Again, she failed to remove the binding energies that fastened the mask to Jaren's sister. They might as well have been forged of steel. *Come on, Morgaine, help me!* she cried in silent anguish, absently gripping Morgaine's shoulder. Perhaps, in a corner of her mind, Jaren's sister sensed the unvoiced plea. Maybe it was simply chance. Either way, she felt one of the ethereal bands snap.

"That's it!" Arynelle gasped. It was loud enough to catch Varas's attention.

"Are you hurt? What happened?" He called out to her, though he dared not take his focus from the throng of Jhud'Hai thrusting and slashing at him from three sides.

"No, nothing. I'm okay—I'm all right!" Arynelle took Morgaine's hands in her own, clasping them tightly. *Help me, Morgaine. You do not know me, but I'm here to help. I'm here with Jaren. Help me.* Arynelle drew deeply of the magic, feeling the strength of the other flow into her. With it, she tore at the remaining bonds that held the mask in place. One by one they fell away, brushed away like spider silk.

"It's off, Jaren! Your sister is free!" Arynelle called out shrilly as the mask dropped to the ground. Her voice was lost in the overall din, but she knew

Jaren would hear her. She still embraced the magic and knew her message carried through more than just the air; it travelled through the ether. She hugged Morgaine to her breast, thankful for her aid, hopeful that she would wake soon.

A spear point finally managed to penetrate Varas's defenses, biting deeply into his flesh near his shoulder. He exhaled sharply, grunting in pain as he swung back a step to disengage with the weapon. He swatted the shaft aside, then sent the wielder spinning back after reversing the blow.

"Jaren, we've got to end this—now!" Varas called out, grimacing in pain. "There are too many!"

As if in answer, horn blasts pealed from behind the enemy's ranks. Clouds of dust rose nearer—reinforcements were coming.

Past the lines of the nearest enemies and beyond the perimeter of the encampment, the embattled companions could see the outline of cavalry charging toward them down the distant, sloping plain.

◆ ◆ ◆

No sooner had Turan the blacktongue reached the stacked crates than Iselle leaped overhead, landing behind him on the flagstoned floor. She was vaguely aware of heat blooming in her left ankle as she skidded to a stop on the dust-covered surface. Without pausing, she broke into a dead run toward the doorway on a diagonal path, one that would allow her to emerge into the hallway at some speed while avoiding a sharp right turn.

Iselle slammed into the far corridor wall at an angle, using her momentum to spin herself about and continue her flight toward the exit. Her ankle burned with each step but she pushed the pain to the back of her racing mind.

As she rounded the next corner, she heard Turan's unhurried footsteps and cackling laughter following behind.

She observed the sprawled bodies of Turan's henchmen scattered near the exit door. *Where's Dagger?* The question hit her like a slap, a hollow forming in the pit of her stomach. Nearing the door, she saw him. Her strength failed and she fell to her knees, scrambling the last few paces to the still dog's form.

"No!" Iselle cried, refusing to allow that the he was dead. Hot tears streamed down her face.

The great dog stirred in response to her voice.

"Oh, Dagger, good boy! I know you're hurt, but we have to get out of here!" Iselle leaned in to help the dog up.

He tried to comply, but his wounds prevented it. With a yelp, he settled back to the rough floor, licking at Iselle's distraught face.

"Come on, Dagger. You can do it," she pleaded with him. Though his eyes were bright and responsive and he wagged his tail, she failed to find a spot on his body that wasn't oozing blood or matted with it. Failing that, she caressed him anyway, burying her face in his gore-splattered coat.

"That's a loyal friend," came a mocking voice from down the corridor. "It would be a shame to lose such a committed companion. All you have to do is stop running and I can see that he's tended to."

Iselle rose and rounded on the blacktongue. "Get away from us!" She took a threatening step toward Turan. The hunting knife in her hand felt small and useless.

"Iselle, stop this. You're just postponing the inevitable. Quit struggling and there will be less suffering."

"Not for you, I promise."

"Those are bold words," he said darkly.

Iselle felt anything but. She stepped carefully backward toward the exit. Moving from Dagger's side tore at her heart, but she needed to know if the door was locked or barred. She gasped as her injured foot touched down but forced herself to reach back. She extended a hand, groping for the door as she backed away. All the while, she kept the knife levelled at Turan.

Turan's wicked grin widened but he remained where he was for the moment.

Iselle felt the solid wood of the door against her outstretched palm. She turned slightly, testing the door. It was somehow jammed, though there was no obvious lock or bar securing it.

"I don't think you'll find what you're after there," Turan called.

Iselle turned back to face him directly. "Then I'll just have to look elsewhere."

"Really, Iselle," Turan sighed heavily. "We need to be done with this." He started forward, stepping over several corpses.

Iselle settled into a crouch, her hunting knife before her. She moved to the center of the passageway to allow an equal space for escape to either side, though evading Turan at this point seemed unlikely.

Turan was several paces from her; Iselle's mind reeled with the decision she needed to make. Should she feign an attack and then dive to the side, or actually launch herself at him? She had more than enough pent-up anger and emotion to land at least one blow. After that, she could make a run for it.

She swallowed hard, her throat dry. Her ankle throbbed painfully.

Before she could make up her mind, Turan was jolted from behind.

She had not noticed Dagger lurch unsteadily to his feet and limp up behind Turan. The dog lunged forward, seizing the blacktongue's leg behind the knee, bearing down on it with all his weight.

Turan flung his arms out to keep balance as his leg was dragged down. His eyes grew wide with surprise, though his lips curled into a snarl rather than spreading to utter a cry of pain.

Iselle did not know whether the once-Turan creature felt pain any longer. She knew she should flee but she could not abandon Dagger. Or was it the fact that she longed to see Dagger do to the fiend what she could not?

Turan eyed her with disdain, followed her gaze down to the dog and then focused back on Iselle once more. A renewed leer split his lips, exposing yellowed, jagged teeth as he raised his hand, reaching toward Iselle.

The knife flew from her hand and into his waiting grasp.

Turan looked straight into her eyes and raised the blade.

"No!" Iselle screamed, releasing all of her anger and despair in a forward leap just as Turan drove the knife down toward the thrashing dog latched to his leg.

· 39 ·

Dire Straits and Questions of Honour

THE TEEMING MASSES PRESSED IN on Arynelle's barrier all the harder, their resolve to breach the shield and fall upon the few within bolstered as the blasts of the war horns sounded ever nearer. Several *metanduil*-clad warriors broke through at once, all of them rangy and ropy-muscled men. They pierced the veil of magical energy and rushed toward the defenders.

She had been quick to build on her discovery of linking to Morgaine, though she was still unresponsive. Arynelle had thrown out an encircling bubble of azure light that blocked the advance of the oncoming horde, driving them back a dozen paces. There they struggled against the barrier, mostly in vain, except in the rare instances when one or another succeeded in using their enchanted weapons to force open a temporary rent.

Varas moved to intercept the latest to accomplish the feat. Despite the deep wound in his shoulder and several other, more superficial gashes, the assassin still moved like quicksilver to cover the distance. Arynelle noticed that he had changed his tactics, using the blade on his uninjured side to engage the enemy while waiting for an opportunity to strike with the other when the time was right. That moment came almost immediately after he reached the first of his newest opponents. Varas spun and darted toward his next foe, dislodging the blade from the warrior's midriff even before the man folded to the ground. He cringed at the pain the move caused, but did not slow.

"Jaren," he called out, "we cannot hold much longer!"

Arynelle drew more energy through her link to Morgaine and tried to reinforce her shielding magic, at the same time trying to quiet the voice of doubt that rose whenever she glanced at Varas.

◆ ◆ ◆

The assassin's urgent words reached Jaren like the echoes of a voice carried down a deep well. *He has to be on our side!* Jaren kept repeating the words to himself.

Enshrouded in the magic, centered on his enemies despite his doubts about the assassin, Jaren withstood their joint attacks and retaliated with offensive energies of his own, but he could not break the impasse. Flashes of lightning and gouts of flame washed over his deflecting barrier and his assaults mirrored them in turn, one after the other breaking against the shields of the Witch and Joselle.

"You okay, Arynelle?" His focus did not stray from his opponents. Even his own voice sounded distant and muffled, as though his head was submerged in water.

"For now—but I'm not sure how much longer Morgaine's strength will last; and I don't know what this might do to her. We need to get moving!"

Moving. Jaren heard her and frowned at the thought it created. He had to try. There was no other option. Standing fast and trading magic back and forth had gotten him nowhere. He had practiced a good deal since Arynelle first tutored him in summoning on the move. But that was practice. There were no real stakes, other than saving face.

If he continued as he was, though, the stalemate would remain unbroken until Arynelle's link to Morgaine failed and the barrier fell. They would be finished anyway.

"Hold on just a little longer!" Jaren inhaled deeply, delving further into his consciousness, willing himself to move. It was an entirely different feeling from moving normally. It was as though he asked his limbs to operate at the mere thought of moving, rather than using his muscles to do it. The feeling was surreal, as if he were suspended by the ether itself.

He took a few tentative steps, slowly at first, then built a striding momentum as his barrier held and he found himself able to continue countering his enemies' attacks on the move.

Jaren focused on the faces of the Witch and Joselle; he watched them twist—first in disbelief, then anger and frustration. Their attacks came with less frequency as they tried to adjust to his new tactics. He circled to the side and succeeded in driving their barriers inward.

The peal of war horns sounded anew, much closer this time. The reinforcements had arrived.

The distraction proved too much for Arynelle. With a gasp, she released the magic and her barrier wavered. It flickered several times, then vanished completely. A number of the Jhud'Haian soldiers toppled to the ground, the resistance they struggled against suddenly gone. Others hooted, raising their faces and screaming their trilling cries.

Varas backed toward Arynelle in a guarded stance, stone-faced, unwavering *He is with us. He has to be!*

Arynelle stood, producing a curved short sword from beneath her robes. She stepped opposite Varas, beside Morgaine's still form, with her back toward the assassin.

The horns brayed again.

Innumerable warriors stalked forward, encircling them.

Then with sudden urgency, shouted orders rose from the ranks of the Jhud'Haian army. Their leaders yelled and gestured wildly. The rough, guttural commands echoed and were repeated up the lines of battle. Slowly, the host began to shift, to reorganize itself—to face the oncoming reinforcements. Row upon row of grim-faced warriors turned about and moved away from Jaren and his beleaguered company, pulling down and trampling tents in the effort to group themselves into units.

Then Jaren saw him atop his mount at the point of a wedge of cavalry, just entering the camp's perimeter. He barrelled toward their surrounded, hopelessly outnumbered company down the broad, main thoroughfare of the Witch's camp. Any disbelief in Jaren's mind was dispelled at the sight of King Aldrain's personal banner.

◆ ◆ ◆

"Stay with me," Malhaena growled. "Whatever the king is up to, I'd wager our lost comrade is in the midst of it."

"What do you plan, Malhaena?" Galda asked.

"To fulfill the contract."

Sithas grunted at the response, a predatory leer twisting the corners of his mouth upward. He adjusted the Carathonai riding cloak draped over his shoulders, ensuring the cowl remained low.

Their mounts trotted toward the enemy encampment, though with less speed than Aldrain's personal detachment and the main body of cavalry ahead of them.

Malhaena surveyed the encampment of the Witch as they drew nearer. The Jhud'Hai scrambled to form stable battle lines in preparation to meet the king and his cavalry charge. The Jade Talon leader gestured for them to veer off.

"Head to the south. We'll go around their lines. Once we're close enough, we can cast off these rags and go about our business while the rest try to kill each other," Malhaena said. "Just concentrate first on dealing with Aras—or whatever he calls himself now. Then we can take the boy."

Galda frowned. "Why do we need to bother with Aras at all? Surely he'll be busy enough fighting the Jhud'Hai that we can take the boy without him even knowing."

"Perhaps Sithas could manage it," Malhaena said with a doubtful frown, "but we're past the point of letting our estranged brother go in peace. What's more, I have another contract from the *Valir*. For him."

"I didn't agree to a new contract," Galda objected.

Malhaena glared at the massive fighter. "It's a matter of pride now—for the Jade Talons and for us as a group. Aras has spit on our traditions and our honour. He must be made to pay or others will believe they can do so as well."

The big man lowered his gaze. "Very well, but I still don't like it."

"You don't have to like it, Galda. You just have to do as you're told." Malhaena shot a dark glance at Sithas. The look was returned along with the slightest of nods.

Galda looked up, unaware of the unspoken messages. "I won't stop you, but I don't think I'll help you in this one. Not against one of our own. Not against someone who's saved my neck more than once."

"He ceased to be one of us when he abandoned his duty. When he forsook his oaths to the Talons. He no longer looks out for us. Remember that, as well as your place, Galda." There was no attempt to hide the threat.

"If we were acting with honour, we would have stayed to help the *Valir* army. That was our duty, was it not?"

"Galda—it is not your job to worry over business. Leave that to me. Our mission is to secure the boy for those same *Valir*. I see no possibility of succeeding in that without first taking care of Aras. You know as well as I, he'll not let us just slip past him and take the whelp."

"But what if we're wrong? What if we're on the wrong side? Aras is no fool."

"There is no right or wrong in any of this, Galda," Malhaena scorned. "There is loyalty to the group and the pride that comes with it. There is finishing a job and collecting your pay. Right and wrong are the stuff of wet-nurses' rhymes and fables."

Again, Galda dropped his gaze. And once more, unnoticed by the massive warrior, Malhaena and Sithas shared guarded looks.

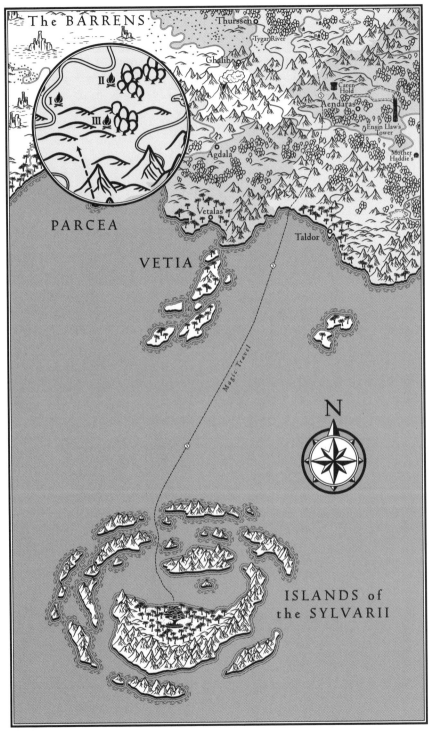

5. *Jaren uses the magic to find his sister in the camp of the Warwitch. He travels there and, along with Morgaine, Arynelle, and Varas, is trapped and surrounded by the Witch's forces.*

◆ 40 ◆

Acts of Desperation and Madness

A FEW OF THE JHUD'HAI REMAINED FACING VARAS, but most joined their brethren, bracing for the impact of Aldrain's thundering, iron-shod arrival. Those with spears drove the butts into the ground and braced themselves. Those without tried to assemble behind them. The handful who stalked toward Varas and Arynelle circled, trying to find an opening.

The assassin repositioned himself to thwart them and guided Arynelle with urgent, hushed directions over his shoulder.

Again, Jaren forced his mistrust to the back of his mind, banishing it from his current thoughts. There was too much going on to worry about Varas. He retrained his focus on the Witch. There was no telling what Aldrain's motives were, leaving him with little choice but to try and end the current fight before he was faced with another possible opponent. It was too much to wish that Aldrain had somehow miraculously come to his senses and was on his way to aid them; they had already received that supposed help in the form of Varas.

The thought triggered something. Jaren stepped closer to the Witch, considering his new idea.

Clearly, Rhianain had no illusions as to the king's intentions for her. She and Joselle finished a brief discussion about Aldrain's surprise appearance, if their worried glances in his direction were any indication. Joselle glowered at Jaren as she moved toward the spot where the king's attack was headed. Her dark eyes flashed disdain and then were gone with a toss of her red hair.

Immediately, the Witch sent a renewed torrent of lightning at Jaren, forcing him to raise his shield. Instead of fighting back, he concentrated on the flowing arcs of electricity as they scoured fruitlessly over the smooth, azure surface of his barrier.

Slowly, carefully, he reached out with the energy of the shield toward the lightning. At first, his probing was swept aside by the natural power of the elemental attack but eventually he was able to intercept the individual arcs, pulling the energy inward. He captured it.

The notion came as his thoughts turned to Varas. Initially, he sought to capture Jaren. Now, the assassin had joined them. Why not try something similar? Why not use the Witch's own magic against her? Jaren had been able to discover the Witch's weakness and use it to his advantage before, so this new tactic wasn't a completely new departure. It amounted to simply taking the next step. After all, there was nothing to lose by trying.

And it had worked.

Once he had the technique down, he allowed his shield to dissipate. At the same time, instead of merely absorbing the Witch's magic, he seized hold of her connection through the lightning's path.

The Witch gasped, staggering back as she tried to wrench her magic free. As hard as she struggled, Jaren held on. She attempted to release the energy, to cut off the flow, but Jaren fed new power into the vacuum, maintaining their ethereal ties. He had effectively seized the Witch's own grasp and control of the magic. He settled deeper into the connection, intent on maintaining his advantage.

He concentrated more deeply, letting the magic flow into him, into a vast, seemingly limitless reservoir. The experience was invigorating—euphoric, even. His considerable might coupled with the Witch's strength. He felt as if he were growing, expanding with each step.

Jaren reached the Witch at the same time as the point of Aldrain's cavalry wedge broke through the encircling Jhud'Hai. The king's company continued on, widening the breach, trampling many soldiers and beating others aside like reeds washed away by a cascading torrent of water. Aldrain reined his mount in sharply. His horse skidded to a stop, driving furrows of earth before its massive hooves. It reared with Aldrain's steady pull on the reins and he dismounted in one swift motion.

"Deal with the Jhud'Hai!" the king bellowed over his shoulder. "Leave these foes to me!"

Joselle stood firm a dozen paces before him. She struck at the king with bolts of sizzling, white-hot energy.

Aldrain merely batted them aside like annoying insects, directing the lancing energies into the ranks of swarming Jhud'Hai. The magic bore into them, burning through flesh and metal alike. Screams of rage and pain rose from the unlucky victims, adding to the overall chorus of death and destruction that already resounded.

Aldrain's company pulled up short as he had commanded and pushed outward, attempting to force the Jhud'Hai steadily back, away from their king. Horses reared, lashing out with forelegs before crashing down into the enemy ranks. More riders arrived, helping to reinforce the breach and drive the defenders apart. At close range, the king's men swung wicked, spiked morning stars, slashed with curved swords, or stabbed with long spears, raining death and destruction onto the heads of the shaken Jhud'Hai.

Jaren was wasting precious seconds. Ignoring the desire to remain as he was, to continue filling himself with the power, he compressed all of the collected magic into a ball of intense energy. He drew back, then shot his arms forward. An ear-splitting clap of thunder crashed as his sphere of concentrated magic hurtled into the Witch and detonated.

The blast flung the Warwitch into the air, far enough that she fell among the Jhud'Hai, landing several ranks deep into their encircling lines. The path of her flight trailed smoke and cinders. Jaren wasn't certain whether it was parts of her clothing or the Witch herself that had been consumed by the burning magic.

The resulting shockwave staggered everyone nearby. Those surrounding Jaren were battered all the more as the blast caught them unawares. All but Varas, Joselle and Aldrain were thrown violently from their feet. The nearest horses reared, throwing their riders. The soldiers fell into the knots of stunned Jhud'Hai.

Joselle screeched curses at Jaren, turning fully to face the target of her rage. She raised a hand to blast at him, but Aldrain reached her first and sent her flying with a backhand swipe. She landed down the Jhud'Haian line in a crumpled heap.

Varas helped Arynelle up, then moved between her and Aldrain.

"So there has been dissention among the conspirators," the king said. "Dark business brings darker fortunes, it seems."

Jaren's hope died. Aldrain had not come to his senses.

"There was no deal, Aldrain. We fight against the Warwitch and the *Valir* as you do, though you are blind to it."

"I did not come to argue, boy. I came to act." Aldrain's scowl widened. "Confess to your True One when you see him; perhaps he still favours you."

"Aldrain, listen to me—"

"No! That time has passed. Your allegiances are apparent, as is your betrayal."

"Jaren," Varas urged from behind him, "Let me handle the king. Get Arynelle and Morgaine to safety."

"I can't let you," Jaren refused. "I have to help him—I need to get through."

"He will not be reasoned with," Varas argued. "There is no point."

"I do not plan to use words, Varas. Please, just protect Arynelle and my sister. See that they are safe."

"Very well, if that is what you wish."

"You have my gratitude, Varas. If you can, get away with them—I'll catch up with you."

Aldrain had moved to within several paces of Jaren. He reached for his blade and drew the weapon while levelling a measured gaze at the youth.

"I will not enjoy this, Jaren. No more than a magistrate revels in a judgement of death. Still, it must be done. Your threat must end."

"You are the threat, Aldrain, to all those around you—to your entire kingdom!"

Jaren's words spurred Aldrain to action. He roared and swung the Draegondor ancestral blade at Jaren heavily, making no pretense at skill but swinging as he might have hewn a tree.

The arc of the sword stopped abruptly, jarred to a halt in mid-path as it slammed against Jaren's barrier. The force of the blow was such that it shattered the weapon into several pieces.

Both of them stared at the remains of the blade as they clattered to the ground. Jaren looked to Aldrain while the king peered in disbelief at the broken weapon in his hand.

The king roared anew, further enraged, and hurled the broken length of sword at Jaren. It too, bounced harmlessly away.

"These are your actions." Jaren nodded toward the ruined weapon. "And so your consequences, too."

Aldrain rushed forward and punched out at Jaren's face. Though Jaren fully expected it, he was hard-pressed to raise his own hand in time to intercept the blow. In his desire not to harm the king, he had allowed Aldrain to get too close; Jaren could no longer use a barrier. Had he not used his power instead to drive the block, to seek out the magical essence of Aldrain's limb, Jaren doubted he would have acted in time. Instinctively, he used the same method that had allowed him to seize control of the Witch's magic.

Thankfully, the tactic worked again.

Aldrain immediately tried to pull his arm free, but Jaren's was not merely a physical grip. Try as he might, the king could not free his fist.

Snarling, he balled the other fist and swung at the youth.

Jaren trapped it with his free hand.

Aldrain reared his head to scream, his face a contorted mask of rage and hatred, but the intended shout came to nothing as Jaren drove his magic into the king. Aldrain's eyes popped wide and he sank to his knees.

Jaren delved into the other's stricken form, searching for the source of the madness he was certain had overcome the king.

• 41 •

Old Acquaintance

VARAS DEFLECTED THE SPEAR-THRUST OF the Jhud'Haian warrior. He used its momentum to spin about and finished off his opponent with a rearward jab. As the other slid to the earth behind him, Varas resumed his guarded stance and peered about. No others approached.

The rest had apparently given up on the Witch's orders, instead heeding the shouted commands of their own leaders to turn and face the oncoming Carathonai host. Not long after the king's mounted company had smashed through, the forward lines of his infantry arrived and the Jhud'Hai massed into formation to hold against their push. The clamour of battle rose higher, horns and drums signalling the orders for their respective soldiers.

That left Varas and the others nearby relatively undisturbed—at least for the present.

He quickly scanned the area and saw that both the Witch and her young companion were down. Jaren was locked in combat with the king, the latter's fists seized in Jaren's grip. Varas felt obliged to aid Jaren, but the youth refused his assistance.

Varas went to Arynelle and knelt beside the young woman. She cradled Morgaine's head in her lap. Jaren's sister had awakened somewhat, but she still appeared pale and weak.

"Will she be all right?" he asked.

"She should be." The girl smiled. "I've tried to heal her, but without linking to her ability, my magic is very much limited here. The best thing will be to get her to a warm bed so she can rest and recover properly."

"I'm not sure how far off that might be," Varas said, craning his neck to complete another scan. " I'll do what I can to protect you until—"

He was yanked sideways, his words cut off. He looked down to see a thin, silvery chain wrapped about his forearm. He knew it all too well.

It belonged to Malhaena.

He twisted the arm about, disengaging himself, then drew his sabres and stepped further away from Arynelle, remaining between her and the newcomers. He flexed his wounded shoulder and winced at the resulting twinge of pain.

Malhaena raised her head haughtily as Varas turned to face her. A twisted leer curled one corner of her lips. With a flourish, she retracted the thin chain, spun it and caught the bladed end with her other hand.

"Greetings, Aras. Somehow I thought you might be at the center of all this."

"I am where I should be. Are you?" He glanced warily about for the others; she would not dare face him alone. Galda, he spotted immediately. He strode heavily toward them, approaching from the tents behind the reformed lines of the Jhud'Hai. Farther out Varas spied a glimpse of Sithas, just visible as a dark outline, snaking his way through the encampment.

"Whatever your quarrel with me, Malhaena, it does not involve these young ones."

"Oh, but it very much does, I'm afraid." Her feigned sympathetic tone turned flat. "They will all be taken to the council after you've been...tamed. Galda," Malhaena called sidelong to the huge man. "Head around him to the other side."

Galda looked about to carry out her command, but then his eyes met with Varas's.

Varas nodded, smiling genuinely. He knew Galda had no choice.

To Varas's surprise, the giant warrior continued to hesitate. He lowered his eyes, scowling and mumbling to himself, though he was too far away and the battle too loud for Varas to catch any of it. The giant was conflicted, that much was clear. Galda met Varas's eyes again. He remained where he was, arms crossed, frown replaced by a stony mask.

"Galda!" Malhaena shrieked.

"I will not," Galda said in his deep, bass voice. "This is wrong."

"You will suffer, Galda. *Remember your place.*"

The huge warrior hunched his shoulders, a dark look flashing behind his eyes. Then he advanced on Varas, great axe hefted.

Varas waited for them, unable to circle around without exposing Arynelle and Morgaine to danger. *How easy it was to have no cares in battle other than for victory.* He chuckled bitterly. *So be it,* he thought.

Galda came straight at him, as usual, while Malhaena approached on his left. That meant Sithas would soon appear on his right flank or behind.

Just as Galda's overhead chop came down, Malhaena sent her whip-chain at him again, intending to catch Varas occupied with the first attack.

Varas surged forward under the axe strike and smashed the hilt of a sabre into Galda's knee. As he moved, he felt the whip-chain's blade end sail past only inches behind his neck. He ducked under the curling line of steel as she snapped it back.

Galda roared in pain, staggering back to clutch at his injury. Varas spared an instant's attention to search for Sithas. There was no further sign.

Malhaena whipped the chain out again and again, each time thwarted by Varas's agility. Soon enough Galda rejoined the fight, though he favoured his leg. It took all of Varas's skill, concentration, and familiarity with his adversaries to withstand their joined efforts.

Arynelle's shout warned him of Sithas's arrival. He stole a second's glance in response, just in time to see the stealthy assassin lunge toward his exposed back, twin daggers in hand.

Varas dropped under the stabs, swept out an arm and spun, effectively vaulting Sithas over him and into Galda.

Immediately he felt the constricting grip of the chain as Malhaena succeeded in wrapping it around his torso, pinning his arms to his sides.

Sithas crashed into the big warrior, cursing and flailing. Galda tried to settle him down, but the assassin frothed with rage at being foiled. He kicked and shouted at his comrade.

Varas pursed his lips. He had an idea.

Malhaena gave another yank on the chain, an attempt to secure the weapon's binding hold. Varas let his sabres drop to the ground. He feigned being pulled from his feet and staggered to his knees, apparently defenseless.

Sithas forgot his rage and immediately started toward Varas, daggers brandished once again. A fiendish smile spread across his dark face.

Varas looked at Galda, who took an uncertain step ahead, raising his axe.

Again, Varas gave the giant a nod and smiled. *It's okay*, his look said.

Galda's eyes darted back and forth between Varas and Sithas. The giant fighter took another broad step forward, then reached out and seized Sithas by his collar.

"Not like that, Sithas. He was one of us."

"He's no longer fit to draw breath," Sithas hissed, his fury revived. "Release me, Galda!"

"Sithas." It was Malhaena.

The assassin ceased his struggling and looked at her.

"Perhaps our mountainous friend is right. Perhaps you need to reconsider." She levelled a black gaze directly into his eyes, inclining her head the slightest bit.

The assassin inhaled deeply. "Yes, Malhaena." He turned his head and smiled disarmingly at Galda, who dropped his hand in response. "Galda, I apologize. I was acting foolishly—" his next movement was so swift the mammoth warrior could only blink before Sithas drove his dagger home. It buried to the hilt in the center of Galda's chest. Sithas pulled closer to the giant man and spoke softly, "I should have done this sooner, my friend. You, too, are no longer fit for the clan."

Galda stared blankly at the knife-hilt protruding from his ribs. Then he grabbed the assassin in a crushing embrace. The move pushed the dagger fully into Galda's barrel chest, while popping and cracking noises issued from his struggling captive. Sithas opened his mouth to scream, but his cry emerged as a strangled breath. Galda fell forward, the hapless Sithas borne down, buried beneath the warrior's great bulk.

Malhaena blinked, unbelieving.

The exchange had taken just long enough for Varas to loosen the hold of her whip-chain. It dropped to the ground with a jingling of links.

"You killed them. Both of them died because of your blindness."

"I've not yet finished, Aras!"

She ran toward him at a sprint, then leaped into the air and spun overhead. Varas, still kneeling, quickly snatched up one of his sabres.

Malhaena landed directly at Varas's back, immediately grasping him about the neck with one arm. She pulled him close to whisper in his ear while the other hand pressed her dagger against his ribs.

"They don't matter. They are pawns. And now, you don't matter. The Jades will live on. I will lead them to greatness—" she exhaled sharply, a confused look blooming across her flushed face. "What—" she managed, stumbling backward. She clasped her hands around the hilt of Varas's sabre, then pulled the blade from her midsection with a subdued gasp. Malhaena let it fall from her hand and toppled forward, following it to the ground.

"They have gone where you led them." Varas retrieved his sabre and turned back to Jaren after a moment's silent survey of his three former companions.

• 42 •

Rude Awakening

JAREN DELVED DEEPLY WITH THE MAGIC, shoving aside the king's furious attempts to block him. The sensation of malice grew. Because he was centered it was no more than that, no more than an awareness of a black presence.

In a purely physical struggle, Aldrain held a clear advantage. Jaren, at fifteen, could not equal the king's size and strength. But this was not a wrestling match. With the magic, Jaren was more powerful and practised.

Their fight restored snatches of memory and Jaren thought back to his struggles against the Witch. He sensed that, like Rhianain, Aldrain's inner self suffered a disturbance. But their circumstances differed; the king's mind and body were not in discord. This was something else.

It occurred to Jaren that Aldrain was not alone in his body. There was something attached to his being, a separate entity. Something that most definitely did not want to be found.

Aldrain's mind railed against Jaren's prodding, but that was not what gave him pause. In the ethereal depths of Aldrain's psyche, Jaren found the source.

While he could not exactly *see* it, the image was quite clear and stark as perceived through the eye of his magic. A black, twisted and coiling mass of foul energy hunkered there, tendrils extended like the many limbs of some hideous sea creature, buried within the very fibres of Aldrain's mind and body.

No sooner had Jaren discovered the being than it began to attack him. Exposed, it could no longer hide. It lashed out in a primal rage and assailed him with a mind-numbing screech.

Jaren cringed but did not release the connection to Aldrain. He had no idea what to do. Pain and vertigo threatened to paralyze him as his concentration wavered. Jaren let out a growl of frustration and impatience. Would it always come down to finding a last-minute solution? Would it ever get easier?

Only one possible source occurred to him: Arynelle.

She said she might have some experience that could help. Perhaps she encountered one of these beings before. Or at the very least, maybe she had learned about it as part of her training.

"Arynelle." Jaren called through gritted teeth. The creature's attack was unceasing and he had to keep most of his focus trained on it. He waited for a moment, then called again, louder.

"Jaren?" came her reply.

"Yes."

"I can barely hear you over the fighting. What is it?"

"There's something here. Something has a hold on Aldrain's mind. It's...I don't know what it is. It's like some sort of dark presence. A ball of black energy."

The response came a moment later. "I think I know what it is. Does it look something like an octopus?"

"A what?"

Arynelle gave a heavy sigh. "It would have many arms that extend from a central body. Is that what it looks like?"

"I guess so. Yes."

"It's an *ichthyllogus*—your people call it a spectralkin—a dark world creature bred by the Deceiver."

"What do I do with it?" His tone grew even more urgent and impatient as he strained against the creature's assault.

"You have to separate it from Aldrain."

"It attacked me with...with a blast of sound. But I don't think anyone else can hear it."

"Yes, it attacks your mind with its sound-magic."

"How can I fight it?"

"I don't know. Jaren, I'm sorry. But I don't know."

A ball of orange and blue flames engulfed Jaren and Aldrain and exploded, hurtled from the Jhud'Haian ranks. The blast toppled everyone in the vicinity. Varas flew backward, landing awkwardly on his side. Arynelle and Morgaine, already on the ground, were pressed against the earth. The nearby Jhud'Haian soldiers and Carathonai cavalry alike were flattened.

Into this suddenly calm eye of the surrounding battle-storm strode the Warwitch. Still smouldering, her dress tattered and dark hair dishevelled, she stalked forward, eyes locked on Jaren.

◆ ◆ ◆

The air smelled of burned flesh and singed hair. Jaren's ears rang and his vision was blurred. He could not move. He could not remember where he was, for that matter. Or what he'd been doing. Searing pain stabbed his left side. Had he the proper use of his muscles, he would have writhed. He lay in wide-eyed agony but his vocal chords refused to utter the scream he desired of them. Instead, his mouth gaped silently.

He realized, with growing horror, that much of the burning smell wafted from him. His left flank felt as though it was on fire. What had happened?

A brief moment of lucidity descended and he noticed the other form lying still beside him.

Aldrain?

What was the king doing here? A flicker of memory stirred and Jaren remembered struggling against Aldrain, gripping tightly over the king's clenched fists as they fought. But why? Why would he be fighting Aldrain? They were on the same side, weren't they?

◆ ◆ ◆

Aldrain remembered dreaming of his parents. And of Sonja. Perhaps of her most of all. The dreams were far from comforting. In every one of them, he had failed to save the inhabitants of the reverie from a creeping danger he could neither see nor understand. Even so, it was ever present and threatened death to everyone he cared for. Time and time again, he arrived too late or hesitated at the crucial moment. Each nightmare ended with the same result. All of them perished.

And he was to blame.

The chance to deliver them from their fates was always his. Yet maddeningly, each time it slipped from his grasp and he was left alone, surrounded by the dead.

He drew a deep breath and choked on the smoke and ash in the air. For the first time, Aldrain discerned the smell of scorched hair and skin. Judging by the intense pain engulfing his side, Aldrain deduced that his body accounted for a good deal of the stench.

Still, he couldn't recall what had caused it. Nor could Aldrain remember what he was doing or where it was taking place. Everything was lost in a hazy fog that obscured his memory.

Then he noticed another's eyes locked on his own. It was a young man—really not much more than a boy. He had dark hair and eyes. Those eyes burned with intensity. There was a message for Aldrain, an urgent, pressing need reflected in them. Yet Aldrain had no idea what the message was.

The other was lying on the ground just as he was. Aldrain tried to push himself to a seated position, but a wave of nausea nearly overcame him and he stopped.

Again, he peered at the younger man. He had a vague sense that it was a familiar face. Then a name came to mind.

Jaren.

But why was Jaren here? Aldrain hadn't seen him since…when was it? Since they'd departed Aendaras? How long ago had that been?

Apparently, something of consequence had happened since then—and was very likely still happening, given his surroundings. Aldrain would have liked nothing more than to remember that missing time.

· 43 ·

The Killing Blow

VARAS'S HEAD SPUN BUT HE MANAGED TO SIT UP. He swayed uneasily, even though propped by his arms.

He sensed a presence. A malignant presence. Casting his gaze about, he took in his surroundings. The blast had come from Jaren and Aldrain. *No, the blast had hit Jaren and Aldrain. But it came from...there.* Varas saw the Warwitch purposefully making her way toward Jaren and the king along the path of the devastating fireball.

The Witch was not the origin of the presence, though. She was still too far away. This sensation was nearer. Much nearer.

A finger of cold caressed his ankle. Varas's attention went immediately toward the sensation. A tendril—smoky, half-transparent—groped at his lower leg. He kicked at it instinctively, attempting to dislodge the vile thing even without knowing exactly what it was. His boot passed cleanly through the writhing tentacle. *Word of Truth!* he gasped to himself.

He scrambled backward and thankfully the tendril fell away. He paused to take measure of the thing. It was a freakish sight: a formless, dark and roiling mass of what appeared to be vapour. Numerous tentacles—perhaps the creature's limbs—writhed, slithering across the short grass, disturbing nothing. It did not seem to have targeted him, rather it was just probing blindly with its many arms. Maybe it was as stunned from the fiery explosion as the rest of them.

But what was it? Where had such a creature come from? If it was struggling to regain its senses as he was, it stood to reason that it had been near the center of the blast. He wracked his mind, but failed to come up with a logical explanation.

A thought occurred to him.

"Arynelle." He called softly, not wanting to draw attention to himself or the girl.

"Varas? What happened?" She blinked, shaking her head. She reached weakly for Morgaine's hand.

"The Witch attacked Jaren while he fought the king—but do you know what this is?"

"What?"

"The creature beside me. The one with the tentacles."

"Varas, there's nothing—wait," her eyes grew large and she squinted as she peered about, her head barely raised off the ground. "Did you say tentacles?"

"Yes."

"That must be the *ichthyllogus*—the spectralkin. Somehow the Witch's blast dislodged it from Aldrain…"

"Very good. But what will it do now?" He had a sinking feeling he already knew the answer.

"Look for another host, I guess. I don't know, I haven't seen one except from a safe distance. And since my magic is so weak, I can't see this one." She instinctively dragged herself away from the direction Varas had indicated. She tried to do the same with Morgaine's limp form, tugging at her limbs in an effort to haul her farther from the creature's range.

"This thing, it's formed of magic?" Varas asked after avoiding another sweep of the thing's tentacle. Several more were beginning to creep his way. It was probably starting to come to its senses.

"Yes, dark magic from the Deceiver."

It made sense then that his kick had failed. They needed magic to fight magic. Varas looked about him, scanning the ground. Several dozen paces away, he spied what he was after. He took a deep breath, then mustered all of his strength and leaped to his feet.

The tentacles immediately stopped their quivering and pointed in his direction.

Varas sprinted the final few paces and dove, using both hands to grasp the broken shaft of a cast-off Jhud'Haian spear as he reached the ground. He continued his momentum, moving into a roll. He came to his feet, the shortened spear poised and ready.

A spear with a *metanduil*-bladed tip.

♦ ♦ ♦

So much has been wasted on the boy. So much time and energy. Rhianain sighed wearily. *It is of no consequence,* she mused. She had Morgaine once more. And by the presence she felt—though the traces were faint—the new girl possessed a hint of magic. Well enough, then. She would rebuild with not two daughters this time, but three.

She spared a glance back over her shoulder to the battle raging between her forces and the king's. Not much had changed. It appeared a stalemate would result. Even better. Rhianain did not relish the thought of having to recruit an entirely new army to assault the *Valir*. The cost in time and resources for the *metanduil* augmentations alone would have emptied all but the richest treasury. Not that she had paid for the ore she used to equip this force; still, its expense derived from the time and effort it took to forge enchanted implements on a scale suited to her needs.

Rhianain then glanced at the boy's other new companion. He was even more of a curiosity than the girl. Clearly some sort of rogue or assassin; it was a mystery how such a one would end up allied to the boy. What was more, he appeared to be genuinely invested, which ruled out the possibility that his services had been paid for. It was a pity that such talent was wasted in a lost cause. He was apparently preoccupied with something else and conversed with the young girl. As long as he remained so he would not interfere.

Besides, the task at hand wouldn't take much time.

The Witch smiled as she stopped and looked down again at the troublesome youth and the young king. Rhianain had decided some time ago that if it was not possible to bring Jaren to heel, she would destroy him. His was the most dangerous piece remaining on the board. While he remained a live threat, the Witch could not focus on her overall plans.

My time comes after all.

Rhianain began to summon, concentration locked on the stunned figures at her feet. Not only would she finally be free of the boy, but the rogue king was here for the taking as well. She grinned in self-assured satisfaction.

❖ ❖ ❖

Varas was aware that the Witch had nearly reached Jaren. Whatever he was going to do, he needed to do it quickly. The problem was the creature. It was determined to reach either Arynelle or Morgaine—he wasn't sure which. Most likely Morgaine, as she was the most vulnerable and, at least here, the more powerful of the two.

Why the thing would not just crawl off into some dark crevice was beyond him. Time after time, it sought to move past Varas and reach the girls. It had to be sentient, but it appeared to act more out of instinct. He slashed and chopped at it with the bladed spear and though the weapon seemed to damage the creature, he was no closer to defeating it. Any gash or slice he made in the body proper healed in short order, while any tendrils he lopped off simply grew back.

Precious seconds bled away each time Varas had to fend off the ethereal beast. The Witch had reached Jaren and was standing over him, reveling in her apparent triumph. Soon, she would move to end it.

"Can you remember any weakness? Anything at all?" he pleaded with Arynelle as he swung the spear, slicing through another of the thing's appendages. It dissipated like steam rising from hot water. Another took its place, growing outward, attempting to find a path around the determined assassin.

"I can't remember, Varas, I'm...wait—" More seconds dropped away, like sand through an hourglass. "—there's an organ deep within the body. Can you see anything inside it? It would be about the size of your head and sort of round."

Varas advanced and the twirling spear sliced through several impeding tendrils. He studied the being's core closely, looking for any sign of an irregularity within its greater bulk. As more precious time escaped he finally discerned a slightly denser area about the size Arynelle had described, a smaller shape floating within the creature's lower right side.

A burst of high-pitched noise blasted his thoughts to oblivion, the thrumming disruption causing his jaw to clench. Varas lunged back, severing the tentacle that had found his shoulder. The ghostly appendage dissolved on the breeze.

The Warwitch's hands moved—she was summoning.

· 44 ·

Of Death and Exile

THE KILLING BLASTS PULSED ALONG the lengths of Rhianain's arms. She ached to release the force building at her fingertips. Still, she hesitated. She did not desire Jaren's death. It was simply the only sure means of dealing with his frustrating refusal to submit.

To what she promised him was his destiny.

A part of her—a more primitive and savage facet—screamed to unleash the magic and be done with him. *That's why you gave him the journal*, it shouted. *You baited him!* Yes, she wanted him to discover the truth about the magic. She wanted him to act on that knowledge and had intended to be there when he did. So distracted, he would be an easier target.

And yet another side of the Witch desired to join with him, to mentor and guide him. The kinship, the unity the *Valir* had denied Rhianain was her true aim, she reasoned. Together they could have toppled the *Valir* council easily and forged a new age. It would have been an age of equality, where magic, not politics or deception reigned supreme. Certainly, Rhianain had considered it *her* age, but she would require a true heir to continue its proper governance. She could have allowed him some measure of self-direction in the process, once he had submitted to reason.

But Jaren had denied her the opportunity. He had scorned her gestures of good faith. He had nearly destroyed her.

The Warwitch closed her eyes and steeled herself, exhaling slowly, driving the last of the hesitation from her mind. Eyes opening, she released the magic.

◆ ◆ ◆

Varas acted out of desperation. Unsure if this last-ditch effort would succeed, he directed Arynelle to spirit herself and Morgaine away if it failed. Arynelle was to link with Morgaine one final time and use her strength to power their flight.

He would find them, he had promised. He truly intended to, but Varas supposed that eventuality now rested entirely in the hands of the True One. If Varas had been set on his new path for a reason, if there was any point to his transformation, then he simply had to trust in that belief and take another blind step.

Rather, a blind leap.

Varas did just that, spurred on by Arynelle's warning that the Witch had massed an incredible flow of energy and was simply holding it back, letting it build. She meant to utterly destroy Jaren.

He vaulted forward, spear raised. As he came down on the creature, Varas thrust out—all of his focus trained on the being's vital organ. He was jarred by the thrumming, piercing sonic wave as the spear tip descended and his hands entered the creature's body. Varas gritted his teeth against the numbing reverberations, fighting to remain conscious as he drove the spear down.

His thoughts shattered and he lost his grip on the shaft.

White bursts exploded behind his clenched eyelids as his head hit the ground. The rest of his body seemed to float to the earth. He opened his eyes. The spots cleared and his vision returned to normal.

He lay on the ground, looking at the spear's shaft, its point buried deeply into the earth. Around the weapon, the last of the creature's physical form dissipated into trailers of black mist and then scattered on the wind.

Varas took a single, brief instant to gather himself.

Clawing at the ground, he scrambled up and raced toward Malhaena's still form. He stooped to seize her whip-chain, hardly disturbing his stride. He gathered the chain and began to twirl it about overhead as he rushed toward the Witch.

The distance closed steadily but Varas feared he was too late.

At a distance of a dozen paces, he released the chain, launching the blade-end at the Warwitch.

◆ ◆ ◆

The exquisite sensation—the exhilarating release—never came. Instead of boring down in a ray of unstoppable energy, the concentrated power exploded in all directions as if thousands of fissures had opened at once in the ethereal vessel that contained her magic.

The Warwitch found herself lying prone. She opened her mouth to scream in rage, but coughed instead. Thick, coppery liquid filled her throat. Dumbfounded, she peered down, not comprehending at first what it was that she saw.

Several inches of polished steel jutted from the left side of her chest. Droplets of crimson coursed down its length as she stared, finally realizing what had happened.

The assassin. She had ignored him and it cost her dearly.

Rhianain's trembling hand fumbled within the folds of her dress. She managed to locate the object of her search quickly, then withdrew the tiny *metanduil* sphere. Already her sight dimmed, her life force ebbing. She pushed herself to a kneeling position, holding the orb aloft. It was the last of her weapons, the final device manufactured before her first confrontation with the Haldannon boy. Smaller than the previous versions, it was a miniature copy.

It would do.

The Warwitch laughed, coughing more blood with the effort, and tossed the dense, silver-hued ball toward Jaren, calling forth its magic. It absorbed rather than reflected the afternoon sunlight as it rolled toward Jaren and the king, the details of its arcane runes lost in the spinning motion.

Or perhaps it was her own lack of coherence that created the blurring effects.

Rhianain Othka toppled forward, her last thoughts those of regret—regret for what might have been.

◆ ◆ ◆

Arynelle saw Varas flung backward, buffeted by the explosion as the Witch's gathered energies burst outward with a blinding flash. He rolled to a stop and lay still, although still alive; she could see the slow rise and fall of his chest.

The Warwitch pitched forward limply. Whatever it was that she cast rolled toward Jaren. It was tiny and round, a small ball, but made of metal. *No, it is* metanduil, *she corrected herself.*

Immediately, a low-pitched vibration emanated from Jaren's direction. From the *metanduil* ball. The reverberations built as did the volume of the accompanying noise. The air hummed with a deep bass throbbing and a powerful wind gusted outward. Arynelle shielded her eyes from the dirt and debris thrown up by the strengthening airstream.

The throbbing noise shifted to higher pitches and the wind reversed its course, now drawing inward. As Arynelle watched, flickers of light burst into being, kindled to life by the abrasive air currents, then were sucked into a tiny black void at the center of the unnatural tempest. Bit by bit, the very ground and surrounding elements did likewise, all form and substance dissolving, drawn into the eye of nothingness.

A deafening clap of thunder rang out and stillness descended.

Jaren was gone. The king, too. The patch of ground on which they had lain was now a shallow, rounded hollow.

Arynelle could hear sobbing. She realized it was her own weeping.

She glanced up and noticed that the nearby Jhud'Hai no longer watched. They wandered away in small groups or individually, refusing any longer to look in her direction, or at anyone else who'd been involved in their tiny island of conflict.

The peal of horns and beat of drums had changed. Apparently, the shift signalled the armies' mutual withdrawal.

Morgaine stirred, moaning softly in her arms. Arynelle brushed the dark hair from her pale face and wondered how she could possibly explain Jaren's death to her.

Warmth spread in thin ribbons down Arynelle's cheeks; her eyes continued their mourning. A pit of despair opened within her core and she allowed the rest of herself to tumble down into the hopeless dark, wishing it led to the same place Jaren had gone.

• Epilogue •

Ensin Llaw had given up trying to keep each of the dirty street children in view at once. They appeared to move innately outside of his sightlines; falling back, drawing off to the side, or sneaking ahead. Despite constantly shifting his gaze to follow them, it was a lost cause. Their movements were doubtless a learned behaviour, probably a result of pursuit from the city guard, rival street clans, or even unscrupulous adults intent on somehow exploiting them. Their furtive body language, hyper-alertness and unwillingness to wander too close to Llaw all reinforced his suspicions.

The children scurried through the masses of Vetalas's market district while keeping within several dozen paces of Llaw. They dodged here and there, avoiding disapproving looks or the occasional swats of merchants and other disapproving adults.

To a one, they were filthy, stick-thin waifs with unkempt hair and ragged clothing. Several were so wild in appearance Llaw believed they might fit in with a pack of wolves just as well as humans. Even so, they seemed quite a tight-knit little family of sorts. The oldest boy, likely no more than twelve, kept a wary eye on the rest—a father figure of sorts. He was the boldest; probably a result of his age and status in the group. He had been the one to approach Llaw with the promise of information about Iselle.

The boy had not known her name, but Llaw was convinced they were both talking about his missing companion. After a full day of sending out messages and conferring with all sorts of dubious characters, Lessam had approached the *Valir* in the streets, asking Llaw how much he was willing to pay for information about his friend. His obvious desperation had surely cost him more than he might have otherwise negotiated, but the *Valir* was unwilling to waste any time following up on the only lead he had discovered.

The unlikely, loose procession continued down the main avenues for some time before Lessam directed them off and down a side street.

Llaw frowned but kept on. Because of his desire to find Iselle with all haste, he believed there was little choice other than to go along with Lessam's story. Llaw paid them everything he had already, so even if they were intent on leading him into an ambush, they'd get nothing out of robbing him. As uneasy as the back lanes of Vetalas's warehouse district made him, the *Valir* didn't think the children were deceiving him. There was something too genuine about their expressions and wary looks. Someone had truly frightened them.

He guessed it was the person responsible for Iselle's disappearance.

Their progress slowed as the group wound carefully through the back lanes of the district, the children in the lead scouting ahead for signs of hostile street dwellers or any number of other threats. At least that was what Lessam told Llaw when he inquired about the slackening of their pace.

The latter's hand went up and they stopped abruptly. The scouts ahead had halted and one of them, a lanky-limbed, blonde girl who was somewhere close to Lessam's age, raised her hand and made several sign-gestures.

"It's just down the next alley, to your right," Lessam announced. "Door's on the left, halfway down."

"Alright then, let's go," Llaw said.

"No."

"Pardon?" Llaw's eyes narrowed in suspicion and he tensed. Had he been wrong to trust them?

"We shouldn't be here in the first place. This is the Dock Rats' home. They'll kill us if they find us here. And you, too."

"I see," Llaw nodded. "So, we part ways then?"

"Yes."

"Thanks for bringing me, young man. Go in the True One's graces."

"The True One doesn't care about us. Otherwise, why would we have to live in the streets?" He spat to the side. "Doesn't matter, we don't need anyone but ourselves." Lessam looked around at the members of his little, adopted family, nodding to each in turn. One by one, they melted away, disappearing into the niches and shadows of the alley until only Llaw and the older boy remained.

"Good fortune," Lessam said, eyes intense. "You'll need it if what my friends said was right." He turned to go, then looked at Llaw once more. "Or your friend will, anyway."

In a flash of movement, Lessam was gone. From a distance, Llaw heard him call back, the voice echoing out of the gathering dark and stillness of the alley.

"If you need us again, post a note on the south message board in the square. We'll find you."

Llaw followed his directions, stopping before the warehouse door that Lessam had indicated.

He peered down at several dark patches in the dirt about the entrance. With the shadows lengthening, it was hard to make out any colour. Llaw decided it might be best not to know.

He listened at the door, pressing his ear to the rough wood. After a moment of hearing nothing, he tried the latch. The door swung open easily, though with a faint creak of the hinges.

It was even darker inside. Llaw summoned a pale, glowing orb and sent it ahead into the gloom.

Immediately, the dim illumination revealed several still shapes on the floor. Llaw's chest hitched—then he exhaled in relief.

They were all too large to be Iselle. And from what details he could make out, they were all male.

Then he saw another vague form a little further down. It was shorter than the rest.

He stepped forward, willing his suddenly leaden legs to move. This time, his breath caught and he gasped in shock. Llaw rushed forward and dropped to his knees.

He bowed his head wearily and buried his hands in the blood-matted fur of Dagger's still, cold body. Iselle was nowhere to be found; Dagger had obviously died trying to keep her safe. Many moments passed before the *Valir* could bring himself to pull Iselle's hunting knife free from his corpse.

◆ ◆ ◆

The dim, hazy light was disorienting. Jaren could make out none of his surroundings. Everything was obscured by a veil of white, clinging mist. He pulled himself to a sitting position and gasped at the pain the movement brought. His entire left side felt hot and irritated, flaring with pain as he shifted. He eased himself slowly to a stand, cringing at the hot stabs of pain that resulted. Finally, he was upright and the agony reduced to a dull ache.

The ground beneath him appeared to be some sort of smooth, hard-packed clay. Its dun colour was the only variation he could see, other than himself. Several paces from him, even the muted brown of the earth was enveloped by white fog.

There was a complete absence of sound. Along with the mists, the oppressive stillness weighed on him like a mountainous shroud. It was as if the place itself attempted to smother all trace of him.

Then Jaren did hear something. In this strange environment the noise was distorted and he could not make out its distance or direction. It was a hollow echo; one that could have originated at his shoulder or a hundred paces away.

It sounded like a moan, like the lament of a person waking from a restless sleep.

"Hello?" Jaren called. The distorting effect of the place tore the word from his mouth. Had he not spoken it, he wouldn't have known it came from him, so distant and drifting it sounded.

Only silence answered.

A small object nearby on the ground caught Jaren's eye. He hobbled forward and stooped gingerly to pick it up, the angry tightness of the skin on his side protesting. He retrieved a tiny ball of metal—*metanduil*—about double the size of a robin's egg. It was etched with curious symbols, with runes he could not read. He put it in a pocket and straightened with a wince, straining to hear any response to his call.

Again, he shouted out.

"Who's there?" Came the reply. The voice sounded weary and apprehensive. Then, "Jaren, is that you?"

"King Aldrain?" Jaren tensed as he thought better of replying. His body ached and he felt dizzy and weak. He knew another confrontation with Aldrain might be his end. He didn't know where the other voice originated. He swivelled his head, listening. At least the obscuring mists could prove helpful if he needed to slip away.

"Where are we?" The king questioned. "And why does my head feel like it was stuffed with cotton and used as a kick-ball by an entire village of children?"

Jaren paused. It didn't sound like the maddened, irrational Aldrain he had struggled against. A tiny spark of hope had kindled within him. *Could it be...?*

"Jaren, please answer me if you're here. Calling out makes my gullet want to rise." Aldrain groaned again and Jaren heard the faint echoes of shuffling.

"Yes, Your Majesty," Jaren said, hope building with each word. "Are you—are you yourself again?"

There was a pause. "If that's supposed to be some sort of riddle, I fear I'm in no state of mind to figure it out at the moment."

"If we keep talking, we should be able to find each other," Jaren answered.

"As long as it happens soon. I might pass out from the effort," Aldrain said.

It seemed to take an agonizing amount of time, but eventually they spotted each other. At first Aldrain appeared but a smoky outline amid the clinging mists. His form solidified as Jaren walked toward him.

"Ah, there now." Aldrain exhaled in relief, though he appeared pained with each limping step. "All that yelling did nothing for my headache. My side hurts something fierce, as well."

"I'm not feeling so good, myself, Your Majesty."

"Aldrain, please. Why the formality?"

"You don't remember, do you, King Aldrain?"

"Remember what? What are you talking about?"

"You were trying to kill me," Jaren informed him. "And you would probably have done away with Morgaine, too."

His brow peaked and the king eyed Jaren with a bemused expression. He burst out in laughter. It had been a long time since Jaren had heard the likes from Aldrain. It was hearty, genuine mirth. After a moment the king trailed off, one hand moving absently to his forehead. He saw that Jaren was not smiling in return.

"Ouch, that hurt," Aldrain said. He blinked, his brow creasing. He drew the hand away from his head and peered at it. "What under the eyes of the True One…"

"I have a lot to tell you, King Aldrain."

"So it would seem," he nodded, bringing the other arm up and examining both. His smooth *metanduil* limbs reflected the pale light with a dull lustre. Aldrain then ceased his study and his eyes met Jaren's. "Perhaps we should walk as you fill me in on the details. We might as well see if we can find something around here that might give us a clue as to where we are, or how we got here."

"I can tell you the last of that as well, though I haven't any further idea *where* it is we've come."

Aldrain nodded sombrely, then the pair struck off into the bleakness, labouring ahead shoulder to shoulder. Apparently, the king remembered virtually nothing after being taken to the gaols by Count Pacek several months before. Jaren began there, slowly recounting all that he'd seen and done since, as well as relating the things he'd heard of Aldrain's activities.

It took Jaren some time to go through all of it and afterward, Aldrain was quiet for a time. Then he spoke in a low, subdued voice.

"I am truly sorry, Jaren, for what I have done and for the many ways that I failed you." He shook his head. "And for the many ways that I failed my people. I have brought so much dishonour to my family's name."

"You weren't yourself, King Aldrain. You cannot be blamed."

"Perhaps not for all of it, Jaren. But, it was my sorrow and self-pity that left me open to the influences of that…that creature. In that, I did fail. I failed my family, my people and my friends—those of you who tried to do nothing more than help me. I—"

Jaren glanced at Aldrain, waiting for him to finish his though. Instead, the king hobbled ahead several more paces and looked down. He looked back at Jaren and beckoned him with a gesture.

"What do you make of this?"

As Jaren neared, the shape became discernible. It was a large, rectangular block of stone. It was mostly white, with a smattering of golden inclusions. They appeared as faults or veins of gold ore. "Is that a building block of some sort?"

"Yes. Yes, it is." Aldrain's voice had become distant. The king peered about, squinting his eyes to aid his searching. After a moment, he strode off purposefully, his gait improved but still showing a slight limp.

Jaren hurried after, jaw clenched against the resulting pain, afraid of losing him in the mists.

Not a dozen paces away, another of the blocks rested. Aldrain knelt before it, one hand brushing absently at its scarred corner. In his excitement at the discoveries, he seemed to ignore the discomfort that moving brought. As he gazed off into the distance, his fingers traced the jagged edges.

Since the fog was thick, Jaren had no idea what the king might be looking at. Then, whether it was a trick of his eyes or his imagination, a much larger outline materialized in the gloom several dozen paces away. But as quickly as the vision came, it melted back into the mists. Jaren wondered if he'd really seen something.

Aldrain harboured no such thoughts and was off instantly, rushing toward the space where the shape was revealed.

Jaren had no choice but to follow, increasing his pace and gritting his teeth all the more tightly against the stinging along his side.

This time, Jaren found Aldrain at the base of a jumbled mass of stone, a piled wreck composed of blocks identical to their previous findings.

"What is this?" Jaren wondered aloud.

"The remains of a tower."

"Are you sure?" Jaren asked.

"I would know this stone from any other, though I did not want to believe my eyes at first."

"What do you mean, Aldrain?"

"This stone is from my family's palace. The palace in Eidara."

"But wasn't it destroyed by the Witch?"

"That's what I'm going to find out." Without pause, Aldrain was off again.

Jaren had to run to keep up to him. He nearly fell over other blocks that lay scattered about, only seeing them just in time as they took shape out of the fog before him. Moving so quickly, and around obstacles no less, was almost too much for Jaren to bear. From the irregular, echoing footfalls ahead, Jaren supposed that Aldrain found the effort no less challenging. Perhaps his body had reminded him again of his injuries.

The king's echoing footfalls became heavier, more pronounced, as if Aldrain's booted feet impacted stone.

Indeed they had, Jaren found, as he came to the base of a wide set of steps. He gazed upward, and felt more than saw a mammoth bulk before him. The weight of the place seemed to dispel the disturbing vertigo of his surroundings. It was a solid form, a place of the natural world. But Jaren suspected they no longer inhabited the real world. Then where were they? Could this possibly be the Draegondor family palace? And if they were in some separate realm, how would they get back to their own proper world?

Jaren saw that Aldrain had reached the top of the stairs. He heaved against one of the massive, gold inlaid double doors and it swung inward silently on well-oiled hinges. The king disappeared inside.

From within, Jaren heard Aldrain shouting for his family. Again, the massively solid, earthy structure worked to give the proper depth and direction to the king's calls. Jaren felt yet more of his earlier disorientation dispelled.

He began to climb the steps himself, suffering each with a wince of pain, hoping that the two of them might find some answer to his questions—and a way to get back to those they had left behind.

• A Glossary of People and Places •

Andraste (Ahn-DRAS-tay): A *Valir* who visited the village of Dal Farrow in search of young candidates with talent in summoning. Revealed to be an agent of the Deceiver, she later cornered Jaren in the Forge Mountains but was defeated when he finally seized control of the magic.

Banath, Joselle (BANE-ath, JOH-zell): A seventeen-year-old from Dal Farrow, Joselle was abducted from her home and, through an artificial, unnatural process devised by the Warwitch, was transformed into a powerful wielder of magic.

Barrens, the: The inhospitable, westernmost reaches of the continent of Evarlund. Mostly unpopulated, except for the scattered tribes of the Jhud'Hai.

Blacktongue: A foul being who inhabits the bodies of others and uses them to carry out the wishes of the Deceiver. Blacktongues possess magical abilities and are fierce opponents.

Breit, Iselle (Bright, Iz-ELLE): A youth from the village of Dal Farrow and good friend to Jaren Haldannon. She is fifteen. Her father is a hunter and trapper.

Count Pacek, Rondul (PATCH-ehk, ron-DULL): A Carathonai noble who has always been a troublesome subject of the Draegondor ruling family. He conspired with followers of the Deceiver to aid in the destruction of the royal palace in Eidara and the overthrow of Draegondor rule.

Deceiver, the: In the faith culture of Evarlund, the Deceiver is a dark, spiritual overlord who seeks to undermine the law and order of the True One.

Draegondor, Aldrain (DRAY-gon-dore, All-DRAYN): Son of King Aldradein (ALL-drah-dayne) and Queen Sylviann (Sill-VEE-ahn) Draegondor, twenty-year-old Aldrain became the King of Carathon upon the death of his parents.

Endemol, Aras (EN-dim-ahl, AR-rass): A member of the Jade Talon Clan, a group of killers-for-hire, Aras is one of the most feared assassins in the Six Realms.

Haddie, Mother: An elderly healer, she lived alone in the hills not far from Dal Farrow. She was killed while trying to aid Jaren, Morgaine and Iselle in their escape from agents of the Warwitch.

Haldannon, Jaren (hal-DAN-ohn, Jair-ehn): A fifteen-year-old youth from the village of Dal Farrow, in northern Ergothan. His family are farmers. Jaren has developed the ability to use magic without the aid of the magic-metal. Because of this, the *Valir* and others want to find and capture him.

Haldannon, Morgaine (hal-DAN-ohn, More-gayne): She is the seventeen-year-old sister of Jaren Haldannon. She was captured by the Warwitch, who used an unnatural process to make Morgaine artificially into a powerful *Valir*.

Jhud'Hai (JUDE-high): A mysterious and reputedly nomadic people inhabiting the Barrens, the western region of Evarlund.

Kataine, Arynelle (KAT-ayne, AIR-in-ehl): The daughter of Selhanna Kataine, a leader among the Sylvarii people.

Kataine, Selhanna (KAT-ayne, SELL-ahn-ah): She is one of the leaders of the Sylvarii, a people who have settled on the islands to the south of Evarlund.

Llaw, Ensin (LAW, EHN-sihn): An elder *Valir*. He retired from his formal duties and has since become a mentor and teacher to Jaren Haldannon, although he has never encountered someone with the youth's unique abilities.

Metanduil (Met-AN-doo-ill): A valuable metal ore required for summoners, or *Valir*, to wield magic. Also known as magic-metal. It is often formed into trinkets or other items that the bearer wears or holds during the practice of magic. Apprentices are often given small, less-refined nuggets or even chunks of raw ore.

Ordren (ORD-Rehn): A Carathonai officer of the elite grey watch in the capital city of Eidara until his death at the hands of Count Pacek. Also friend and confidant of Aldrain Draegondor.

Othka, Rhianain (OTH-kah, REE-an-ayne): An ambitious *Valir* from Jamnar, known as the Witch or the Warwitch. She attempted to lure Jaren to her palace on the Isle of Ice, but the youth was able to beat her in a duel of magic. She remains committed to her goal of conquering the Six Realms and seeks to avenge her defeat at Jaren's hands.

Redsteele, Sonja (RED-Steel, SON-ya): A *Valir* who served house Draegondor in Carathon until her death at the hands of a blacktongue.

Six Realms: The six recognized kingdoms of Evarlund. In clockwise order on the continent they are, beginning in the north-west, **Drisia** (DREE-zhee-ah), **Jamnar** (ZHAM-nar), **Carathon** (CARE-ath-ohn), **Ergothan** (ER-go-than), **Vetia** (VEE-she-ah) and **Parcea** (PAR-say-ah).

Sylvarii (sil-VARR-ee): Inhabitants of the islands to the south of Evarlund. Little is known about them, as their island home is very difficult to find.

True One, the: The creator of the universe and recognized deity of Evarlund's six realms. Known by the Sylvarii as The All-Father.

Turan (TOUR-ahn): A young thief from the city of Aendaras (EHN-dar-ess) in south-west Carathon. Deceptive and cunning, he betrayed the friendship of Iselle and helped the Witch's forces overrun Caren Hold, where King Aldrain was defeated and taken prisoner.

Valir (Vall-eer): An individual with the ability to use magic. Other common names include: wizard, sorcerer, summoner, mage or enchanter. A special metal known as *metanduil* is required for these *Valir* to make use of magical energy. Also, *An'Valir* (Ahn Vall-eer): A person who is capable of wielding magic without the use of *metanduil*. Jaren Haldannon is the only known *An'Valir* in over a thousand years. See Haldannon, Jaren.

Val'Tial (VALL-tee-ahl): The essence of magic itself, which is summoned through the magic-metal, or *metanduil*. It is said to be composed of a balance of positive and negative energies.

Veenal, Malhaena (VEEN-ahl, mahl-HAYN-ah): A leader of the Jade Talon Clan, she is responsible for taking contracts and assigning jobs to the clan members. She is a very cunning and skilled assassin in her own right. Two of her most common associates are Sithas Kel, a very stealthy rogue, and Galda Baran, a gigantic warrior.

Verithael (VAIR-ith-ale): A stranger who befriended Jaren, Morgaine and Iselle on the first part of their journey after leaving Dal Farrow.

• About the Author •

DEREK DONAIS LIVES IN A SMALL TOWN on the east side of Calgary, Alberta, Canada with his wife and two children. Derek was a teacher in Alberta for most of the past decade. Before his career in education, he served for two years as a police officer in Saskatchewan. Aside from reading and writing, Derek's interests include martial arts, weight training and running. He holds a second-degree black belt in Shaolin Kenpo and won the WKA Western Canadian Full Contact Kickboxing Championship title in 1997.

Derek is an avid reader, especially of fantasy and science fiction, although anything compelling and well written is fair game. Derek traces his love of the former genres to his elementary school years, when an uncle's 1977 illustrated edition of *The Hobbit* first drew him into another world. Then, in grade four, his passion for epic fiction became permanent after reading *The Elfstones of Shannara*, by Terry Brooks.

Derek began writing the *MetalMagic* series in 2005. *Talisman*, (Book I of the trilogy) was first published in October 2010 by Wheatmark Books in the United States. *Talisman* was republished in a new edition in Canada in November 2011. *Revelation* is the second story in the trilogy. Derek hopes to have the third and final installment, *Liberation*, released by the spring of 2013.